POKÉMON ADVENTURES EMERALD™

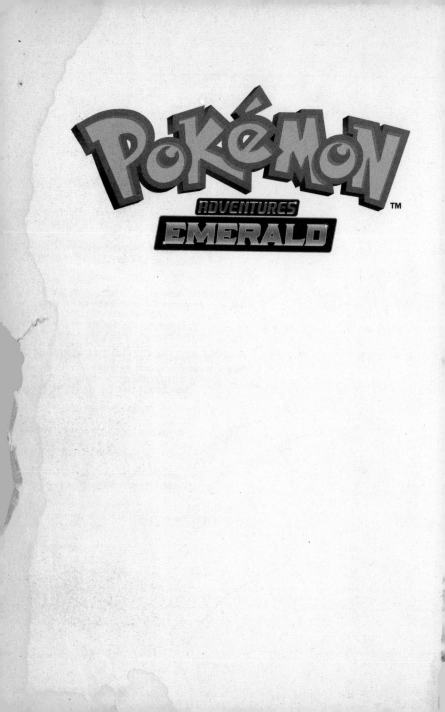

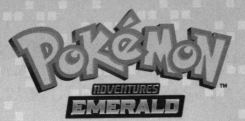

Pokémon ADVENTURES
Emerald
Volume 28
Perfect Square Edition

Story by **HIDENORI KUSAKA**
Art by **SATOSHI YAMAMOTO**

© 2015 Pokémon.
© 1995–2015 Nintendo/Creatures Inc./GAME FREAK inc.
TM, ®, and character names are trademarks of Nintendo.
POCKET MONSTERS SPECIAL Vol. 28
by Hidenori KUSAKA, Satoshi YAMAMOTO
© 1997 Hidenori KUSAKA, Satoshi YAMAMOTO
All rights reserved.
Original Japanese edition published by SHOGAKUKAN.
English translation rights in the United States of America,
Canada, the United Kingdom, Ireland, Australia and
New Zealand arranged with SHOGAKUKAN.

English Adaptation/Bryant Turnage
Translation/Tetsuichiro Miyaki
Touch-up & Lettering/Annaliese Christman
Design/Shawn Carrico
Editor/Annette Roman

Printed in the U.S.A.

Published by VIZ Media, LLC
P.O. Box 77010
San Francisco, CA 94107

10 9 8 7 6 5 4 3 2 1
First printing, May 2015

www.perfectsquare.com

www.viz.com

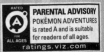

Story by

Hidenori Kusaka

Art by

Satoshi Yamamoto

POKéMON™ ADVENTURES EMERALD

VOLUME TWENT 28

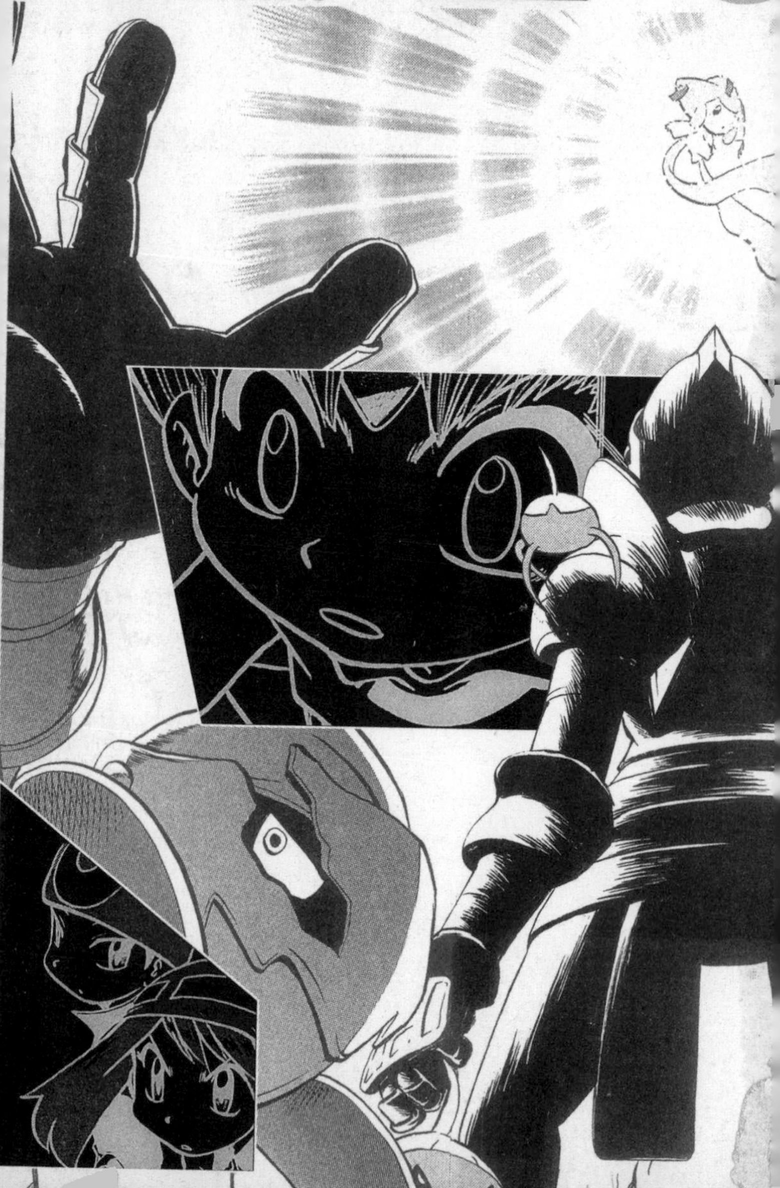

SPECIAL OBJECT

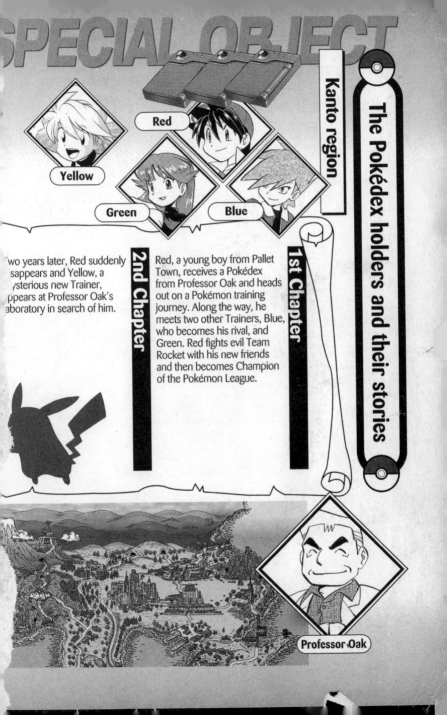

The Pokédex holders and their stories

Kanto region

Red

Yellow

Green

Blue

1st Chapter

Red, a young boy from Pallet Town, receives a Pokédex from Professor Oak and heads out on a Pokémon training journey. Along the way, he meets two other Trainers, Blue, who becomes his rival, and Green. Red fights evil Team Rocket with his new friends and then becomes Champion of the Pokémon League.

2nd Chapter

Two years later, Red suddenly disappears and Yellow, a mysterious new Trainer, appears at Professor Oak's laboratory in search of him.

Professor Oak

POKÉMON

Johto region

Standing i
Yellow's w
is the Kar
Elite Fou
led by Lan
In a major
at Cerise Is
Yellow mar
to stymie t
group's evi
ambitions.

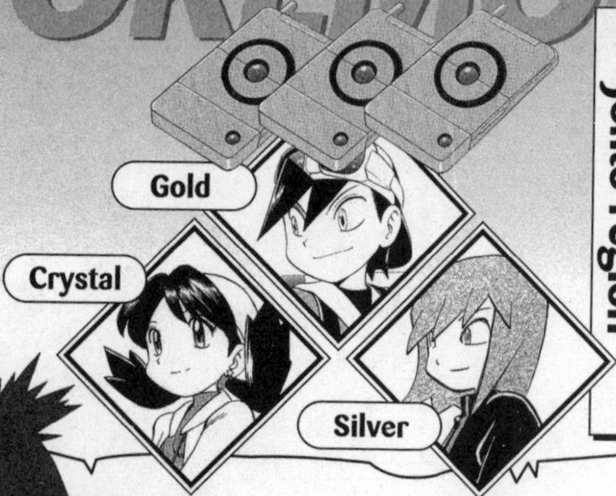

Gold
Crystal
Silver

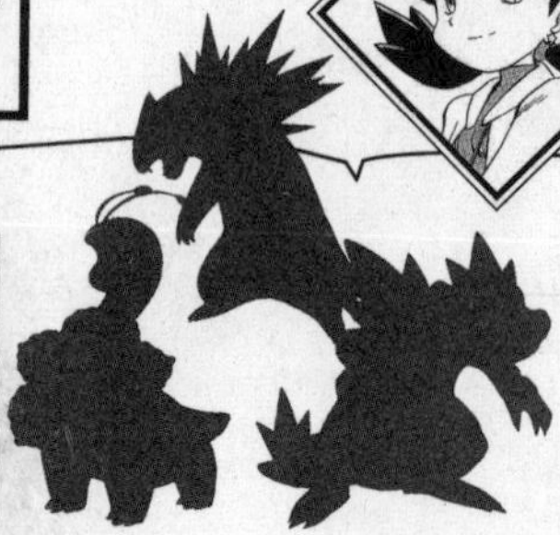

3rd Chapter

A year later, Gold, a boy living in New Bark Town in a house full of Pokémon, sets out on a journey in pursuit of Silver, a Trainer who stole a Totodile from Professor Elm's laboratory. The two don't get along at first, but eventually they become partners fighting side by side. During their journey, they meet Crystal, the trainer whom Professor Elm entrusts with the completion of his Pokédex. Together, the trio succeed to shatter the evil scheme of the Mask of Ice, a villain who leads what remains of Team Rocket.

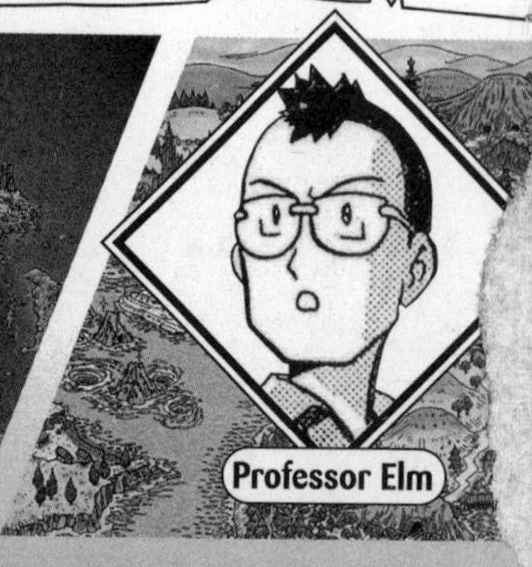

Professor Elm

Hoenn region

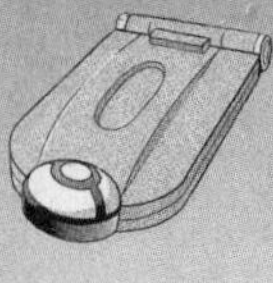

4th Chapter

Pokémon Trainer Ruby has a passion for Pokémon Contests. He runs away from home right after his family moves to Littleroot Town. He meets a wild girl named Sapphire and they pledge to compete with each other in an 80-day challenge to...

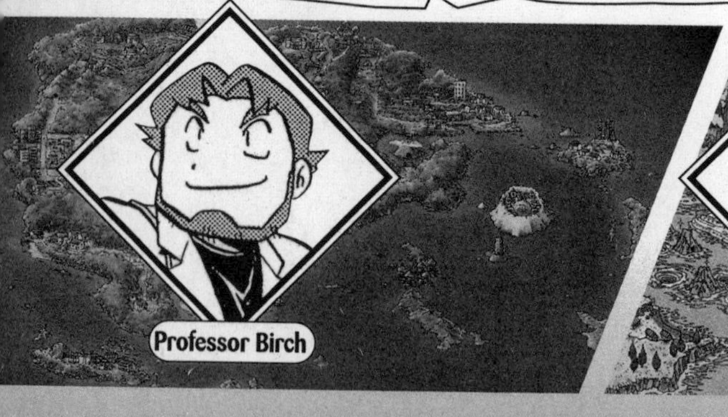

Professor Birch

SPECIAL OBJECT

Kanto region

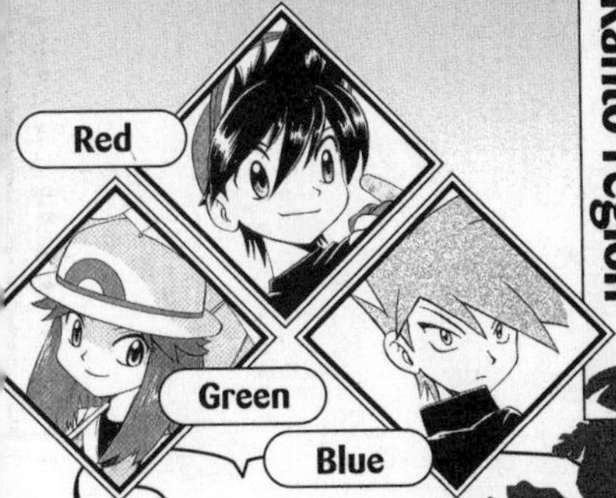
Red
Green
Blue

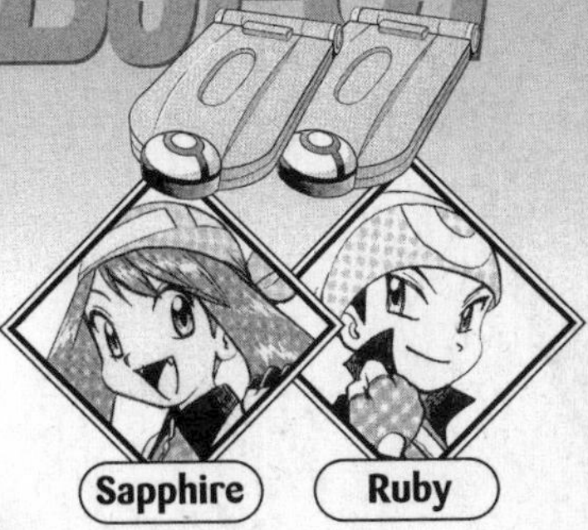
Sapphire
Ruby

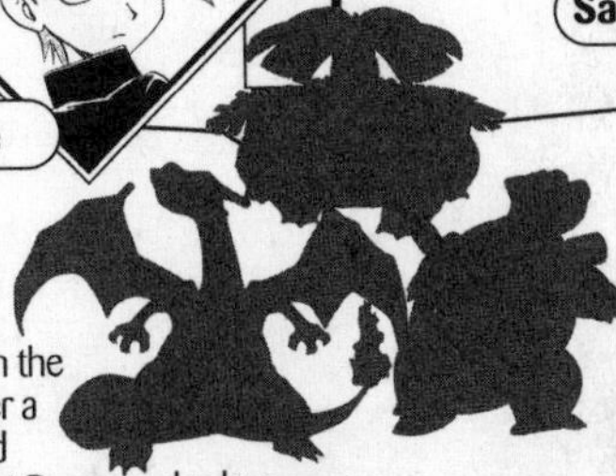

5th Chapter

Six months later, a new adventure unfolds for Red and his friends on the Sevii Islands. After a deadly battle, Red manages to defeat Deoxys, who has fallen into the hands of Giovanni. Silver, in search of his true identity, is faced with the shocking truth that Giovanni is his father. Red and his friends manage to safely land the Team Rocket airship, which was flying out of control thanks to Carr, one of the Three Beasts, who betrayed Team Rocket. But then another of the Three Beasts, Sird, appears, and in a mysterious flash of light the five Pokédex holders—Red, Blue, Green, Yellow and Silver—are petrified. Literally!

...win every Pokémon Contest and every Pokémon Gym Battle, respectively. Meanwhile, in the Hoenn region, Team Aqua and Team Magma set their evil plot in motion. As a result, Legendary Pokémon Groudon and Kyogre are awakened and inflict catastrophic climate changes on Hoenn. In the end, thanks to Ruby and Sapphire's heroic efforts, the two legendary Pokémon go back into hibernation.

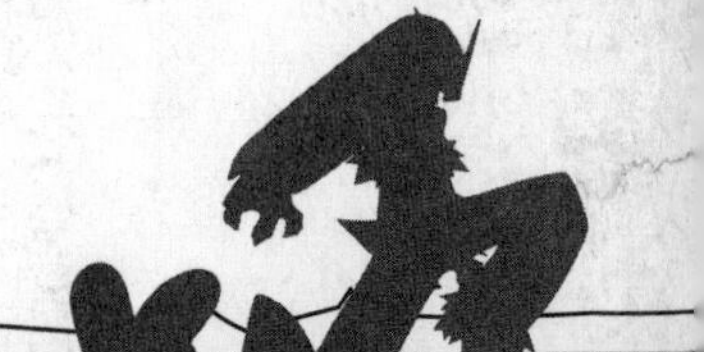

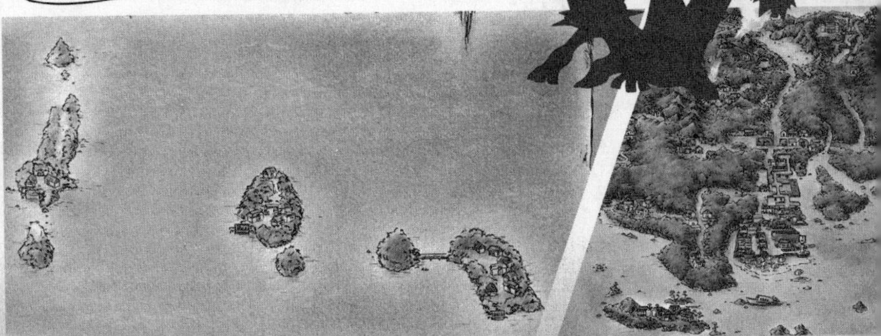

POKÉMON ADVENTURES EMERALD

VOLUME TWENTY-EIGHT 28

CONTENTS

POKÉMON

Hoenn region

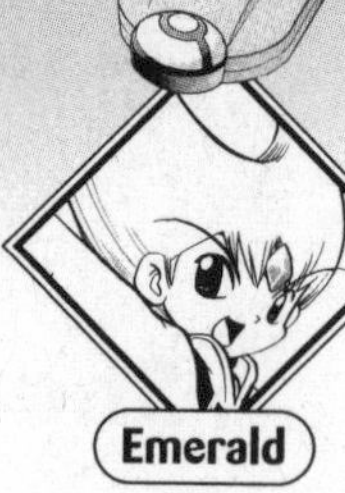
Emerald

6th Chapter

A few months later, construction is completed on a thrilling new Pokémon Battle facility, the Battle Frontier, located in the Hoenn region. A young Trainer named Emerald crashes the press opening for the media to challenge the facility's Frontier Brains. Now he has just seven days to defeat them all!

Thus far, Emerald has won his battles against Factory Head Noland, Lucy and Brandon. His other mission is to capture and protect Jirachi, the Wish Pokémon, who awakens every thousand years for seven days and can grant any wish. Now the battle to prevent mysterious armor-clad Guile from getting his hands on Jirachi first continues...!

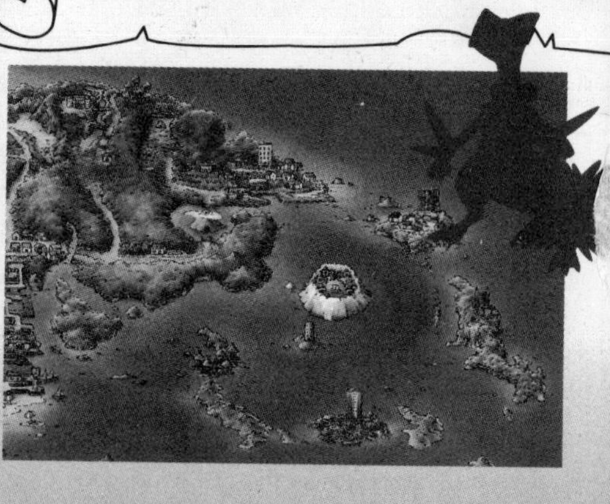

Sneaky Like Shedinja
II

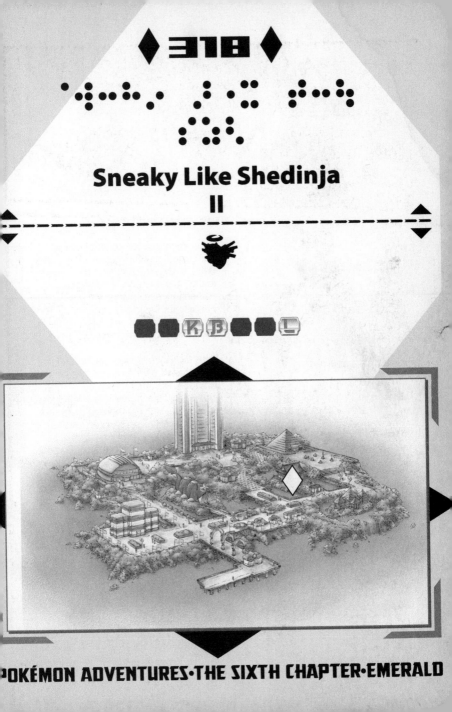

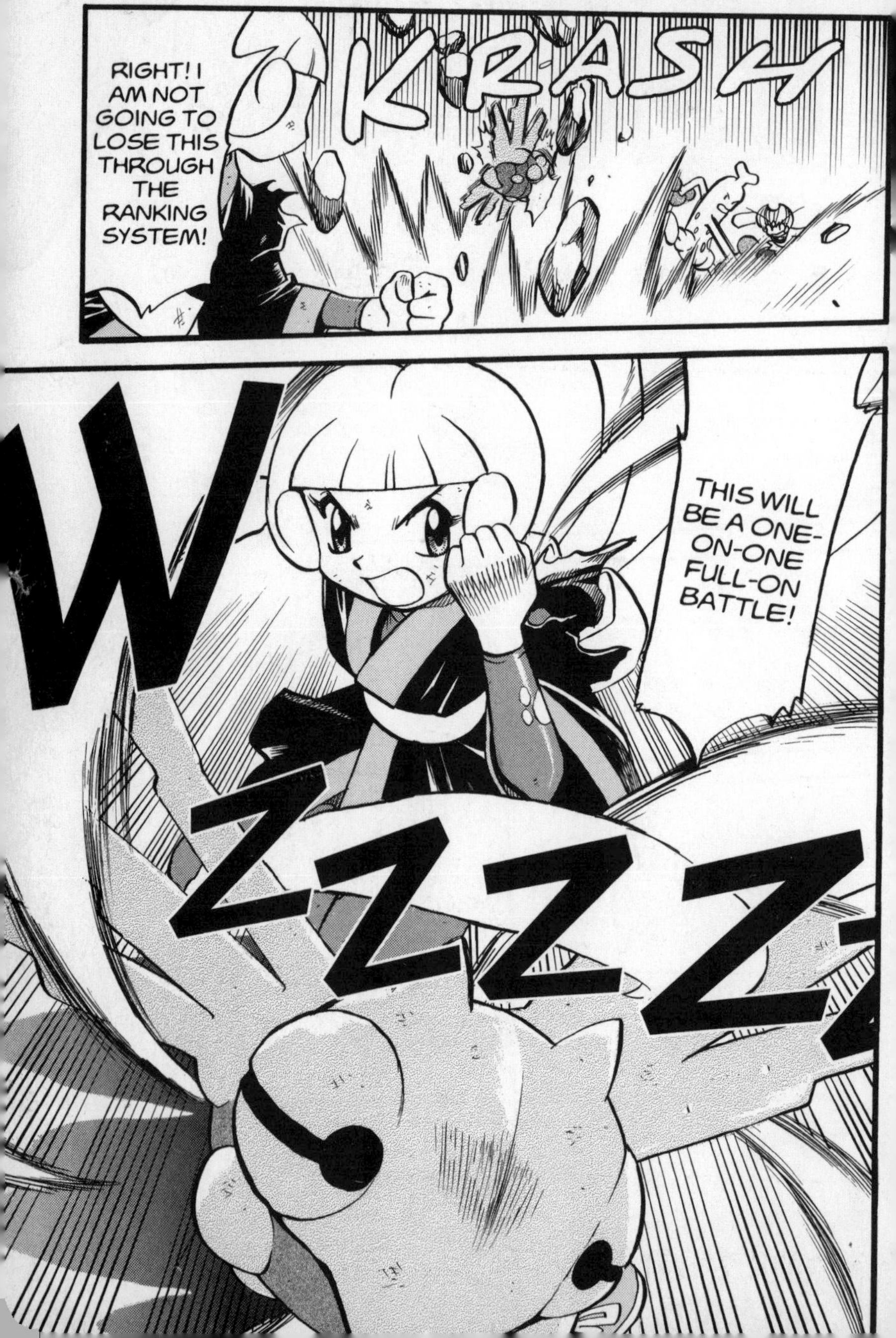
KRASH
RIGHT! I AM NOT GOING TO LOSE THIS THROUGH THE RANKING SYSTEM!
THIS WILL BE A ONE-ON-ONE FULL-ON BATTLE!
WZZZZ

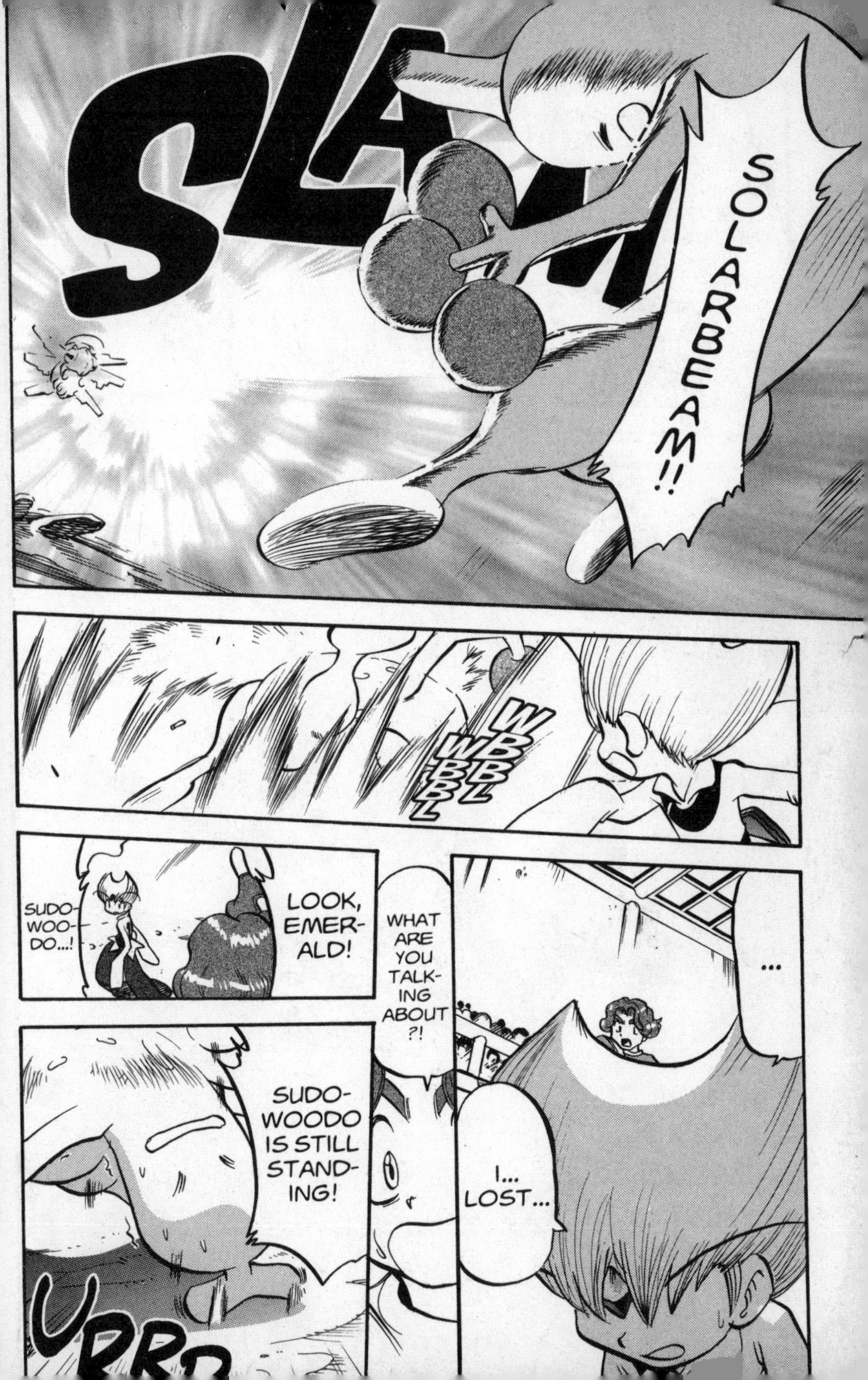
SOLARBEAM!!
SLAM
WBBL
WBBL
...
WHAT ARE YOU TALK-ING ABOUT?!
I... LOST...
LOOK, EMER-ALD!
SUDO-WOO-DO...!
SUDO-WOODO IS STILL STAND-ING!
URRR

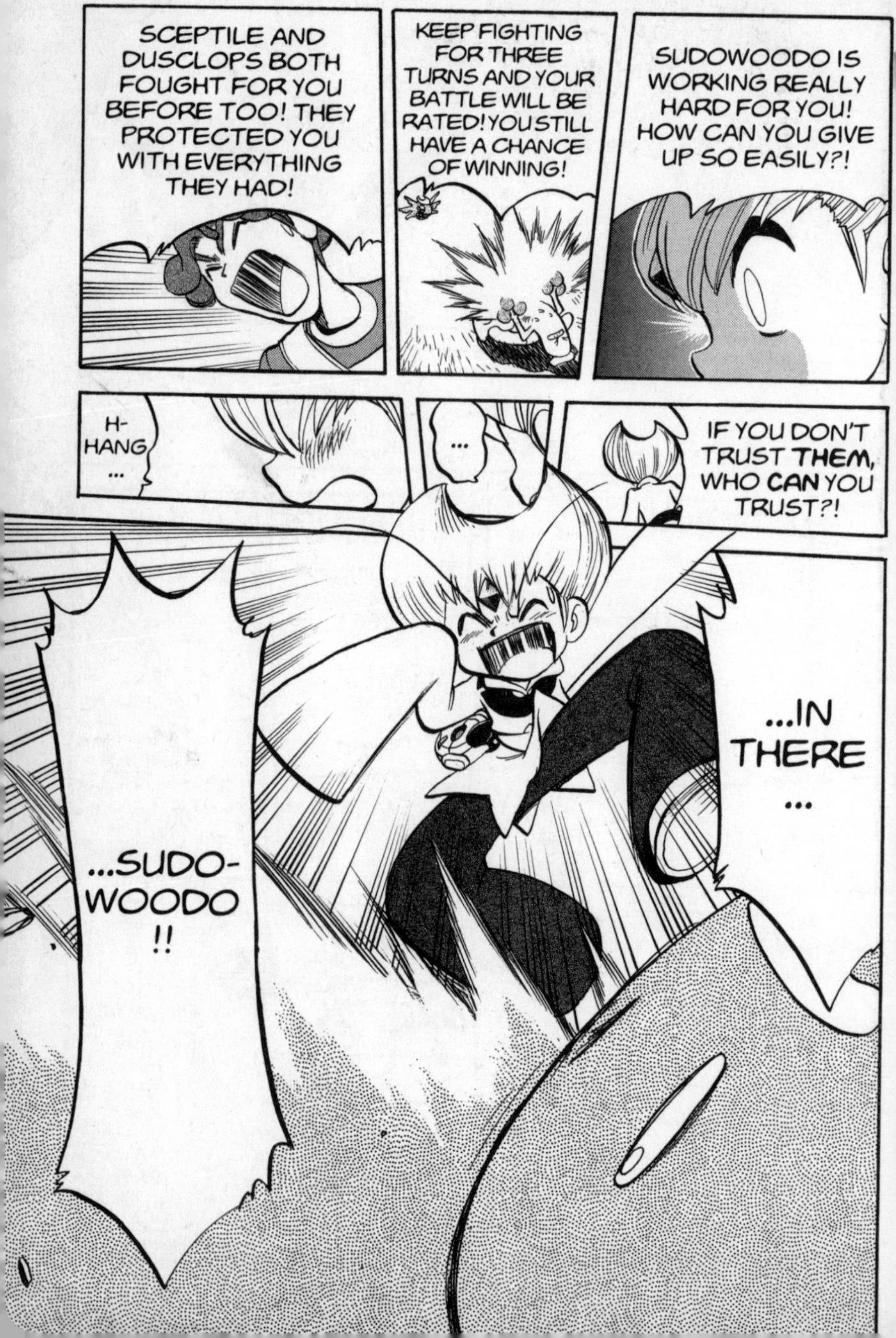
SUDOWOODO IS WORKING REALLY HARD FOR YOU! HOW CAN YOU GIVE UP SO EASILY?!
KEEP FIGHTING FOR THREE TURNS AND YOUR BATTLE WILL BE RATED! YOU STILL HAVE A CHANCE OF WINNING!
SCEPTILE AND DUSCLOPS BOTH FOUGHT FOR YOU BEFORE TOO! THEY PROTECTED YOU WITH EVERYTHING THEY HAD!
IF YOU DON'T TRUST **THEM**, WHO **CAN** YOU TRUST?!
...
H-HANG...
...IN THERE...
...SUDO-WOODO!!

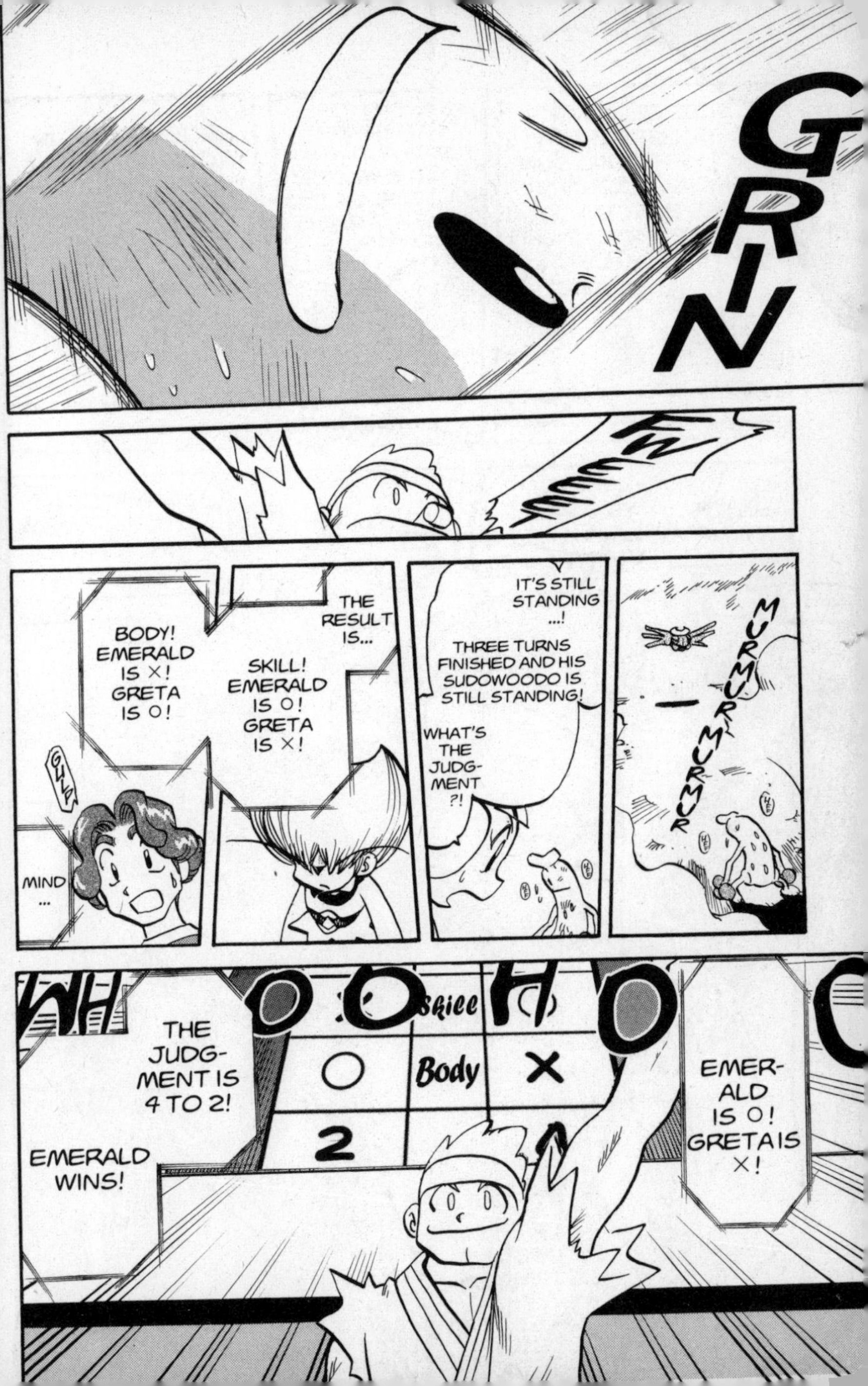
GRIN
FWEEE
MURMUR MURMUR MURMUR
HE HE
IT'S STILL STANDING ...!
THREE TURNS FINISHED AND HIS SUDOWOODO IS STILL STANDING!
WHAT'S THE JUDGMENT ?!
HE HE
THE RESULT IS...
SKILL! EMERALD IS ○! GRETA IS ×!
BODY! EMERALD IS ×! GRETA IS ○!
GULP
MIND ...
WHOOHOOO
Skill
○
Body
×
2
EMERALD IS ○! GRETA IS ×!
THE JUDGMENT IS 4 TO 2!
EMERALD WINS!

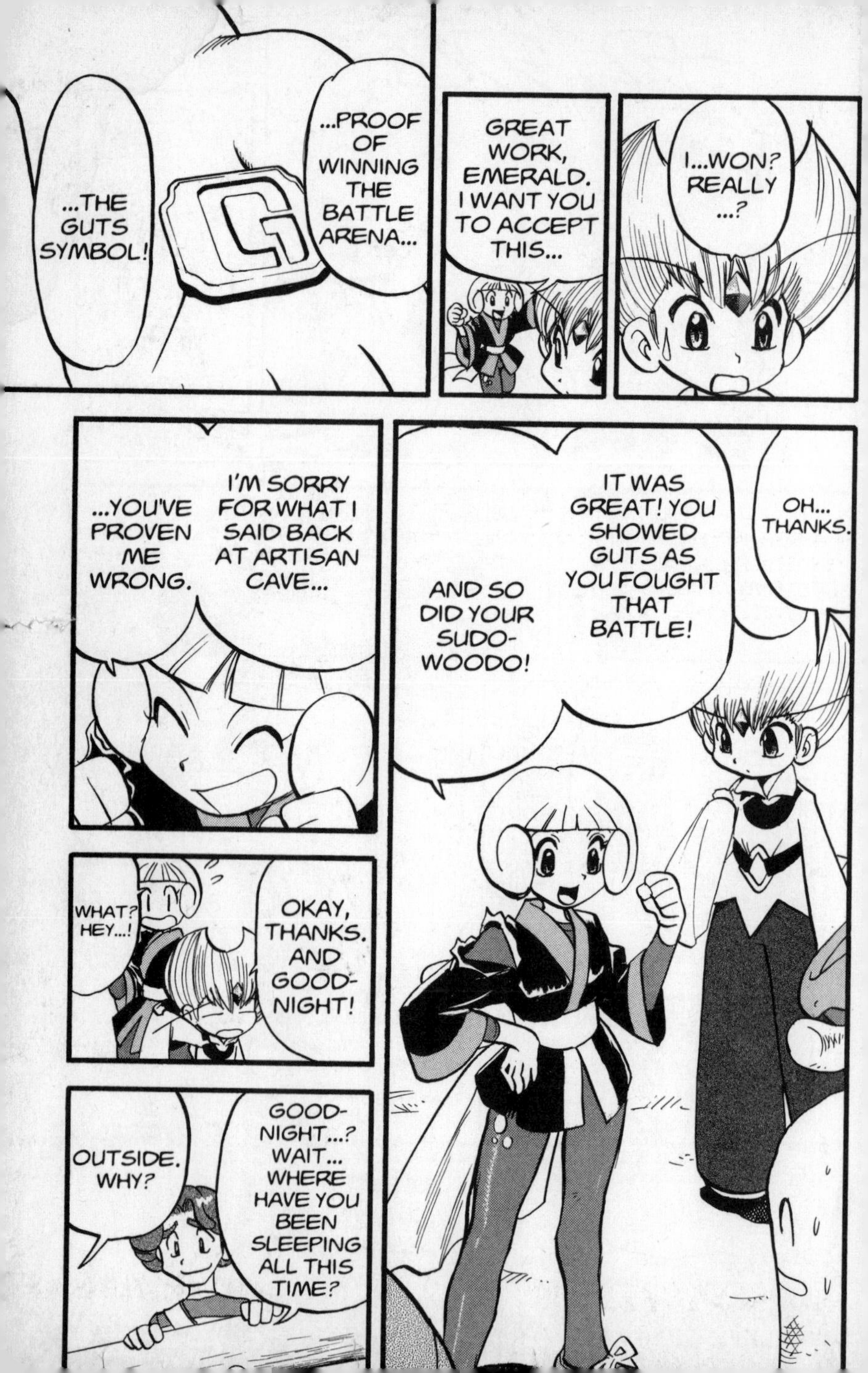
I...WON? REALLY ...?
GREAT WORK, EMERALD. I WANT YOU TO ACCEPT THIS...
...PROOF OF WINNING THE BATTLE ARENA...
...THE GUTS SYMBOL!
OH... THANKS.
IT WAS GREAT! YOU SHOWED GUTS AS YOU FOUGHT THAT BATTLE!
AND SO DID YOUR SUDO-WOODO!
I'M SORRY FOR WHAT I SAID BACK AT ARTISAN CAVE...
...YOU'VE PROVEN ME WRONG.
OKAY, THANKS. AND GOOD-NIGHT!
WHAT? HEY...!
GOOD-NIGHT...? WAIT... WHERE HAVE YOU BEEN SLEEPING ALL THIS TIME?
OUTSIDE. WHY?

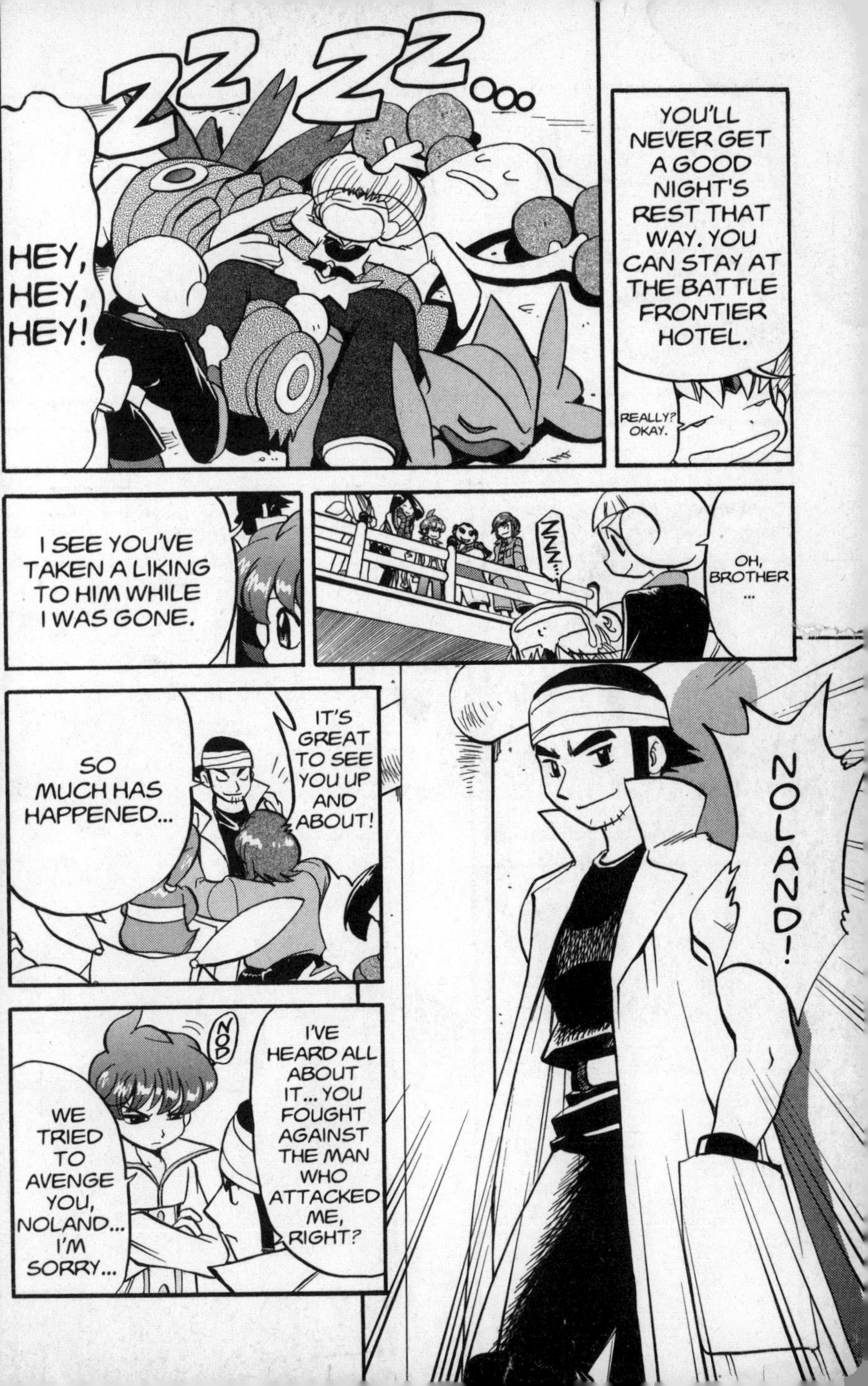
YOU'LL NEVER GET A GOOD NIGHT'S REST THAT WAY. YOU CAN STAY AT THE BATTLE FRONTIER HOTEL.
REALLY? OKAY.
ZZ, ZZZ...
HEY, HEY, HEY!
OH, BROTHER...
ZZZ...
I SEE YOU'VE TAKEN A LIKING TO HIM WHILE I WAS GONE.
NOLAND!
IT'S GREAT TO SEE YOU UP AND ABOUT!
SO MUCH HAS HAPPENED...
I'VE HEARD ALL ABOUT IT... YOU FOUGHT AGAINST THE MAN WHO ATTACKED ME, RIGHT?
NOD
WE TRIED TO AVENGE YOU, NOLAND... I'M SORRY...

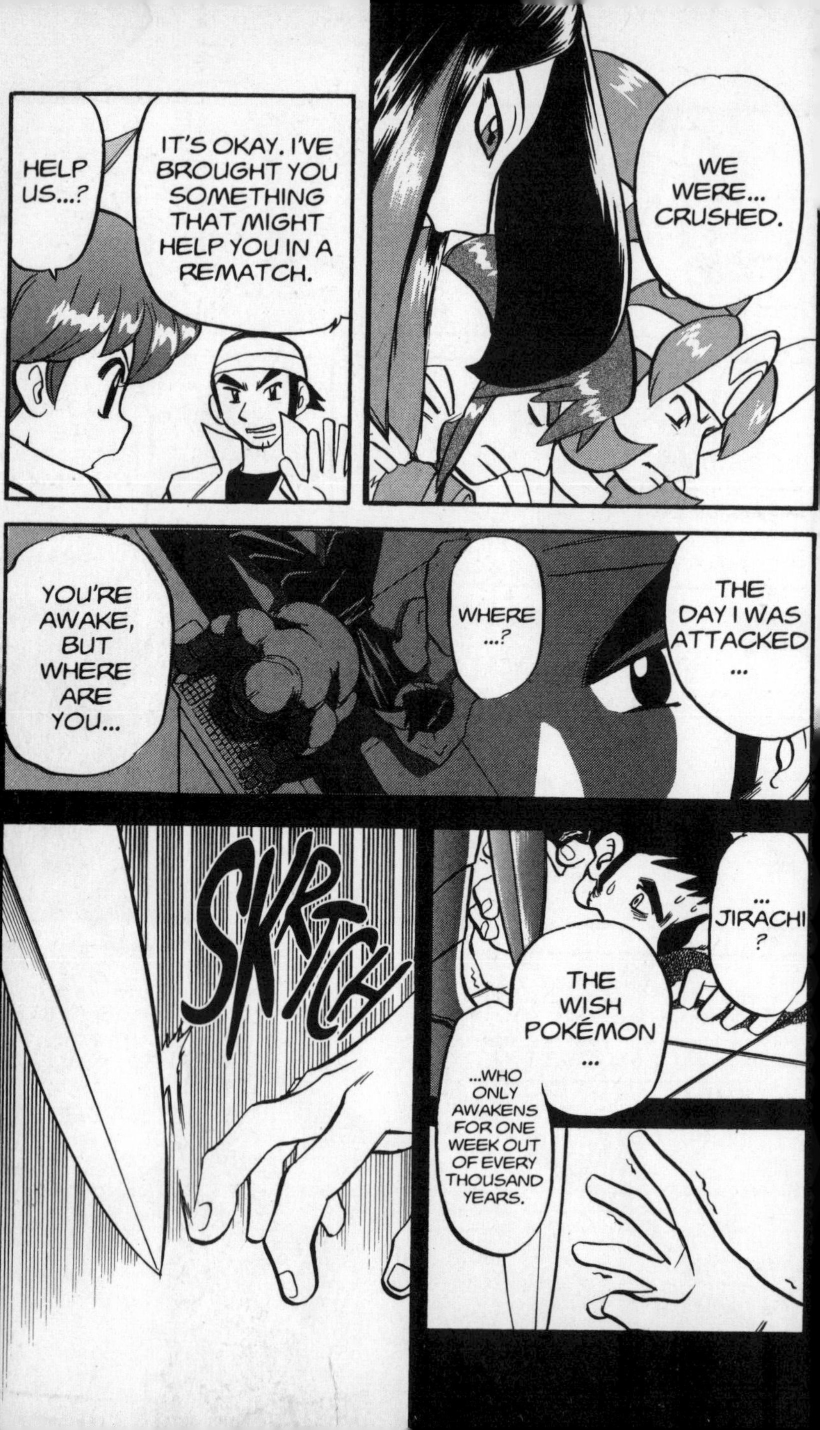
WE WERE... CRUSHED.
IT'S OKAY. I'VE BROUGHT YOU SOMETHING THAT MIGHT HELP YOU IN A REMATCH.
HELP US...?
THE DAY I WAS ATTACKED ...
WHERE ...?
YOU'RE AWAKE, BUT WHERE ARE YOU...
... JIRACHI ?
THE WISH POKÉMON ...
...WHO ONLY AWAKENS FOR ONE WEEK OUT OF EVERY THOUSAND YEARS.
SKRTCH

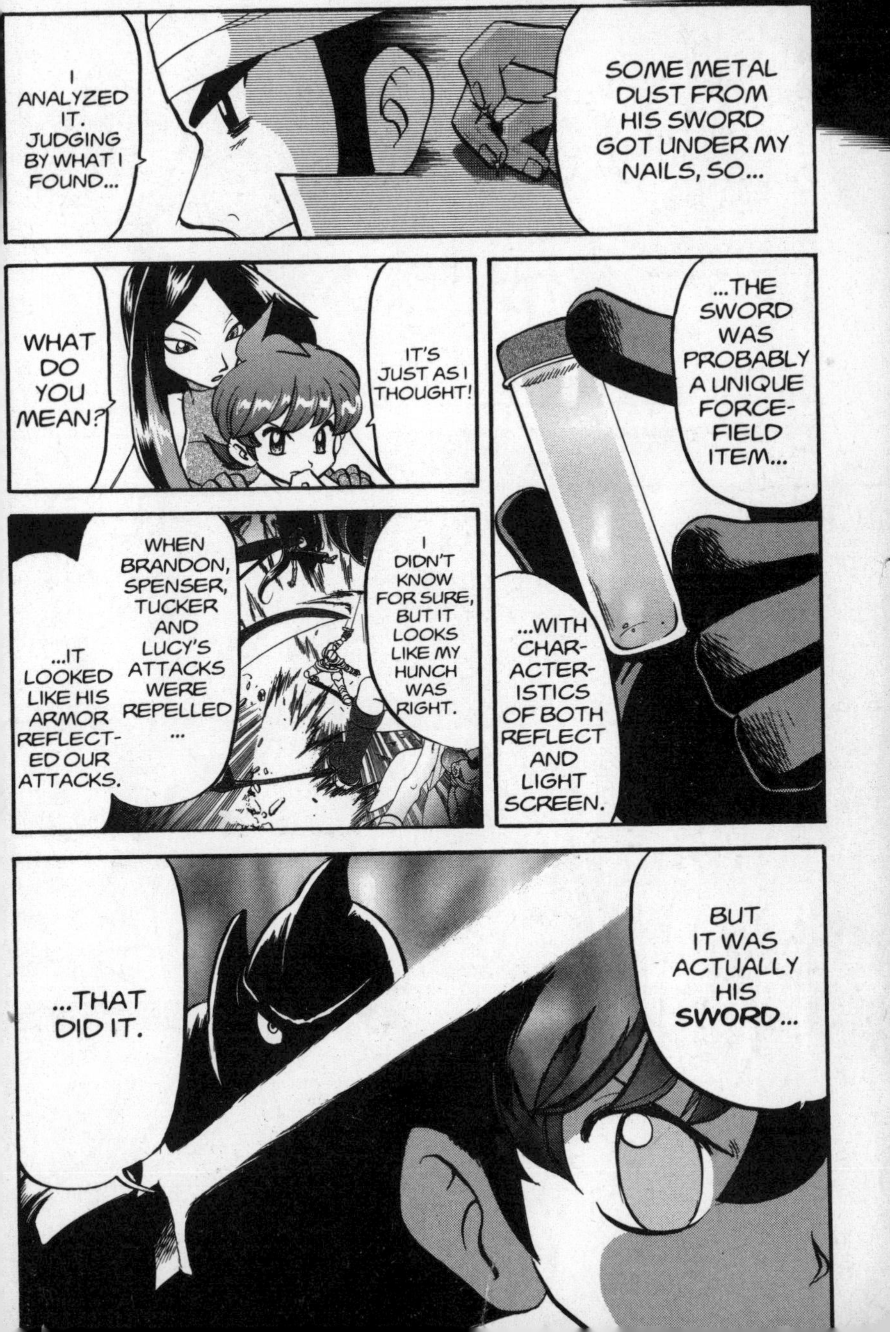
SOME METAL DUST FROM HIS SWORD GOT UNDER MY NAILS, SO...
I ANALYZED IT. JUDGING BY WHAT I FOUND...
...THE SWORD WAS PROBABLY A UNIQUE FORCE-FIELD ITEM...
...WITH CHAR-ACTER-ISTICS OF BOTH REFLECT AND LIGHT SCREEN.
IT'S JUST AS I THOUGHT!
WHAT DO YOU MEAN?
I DIDN'T KNOW FOR SURE, BUT IT LOOKS LIKE MY HUNCH WAS RIGHT.
WHEN BRANDON, SPENSER, TUCKER AND LUCY'S ATTACKS WERE REPELLED...
...IT LOOKED LIKE HIS ARMOR REFLECT-ED OUR ATTACKS.
BUT IT WAS ACTUALLY HIS **SWORD**...
...THAT DID IT.

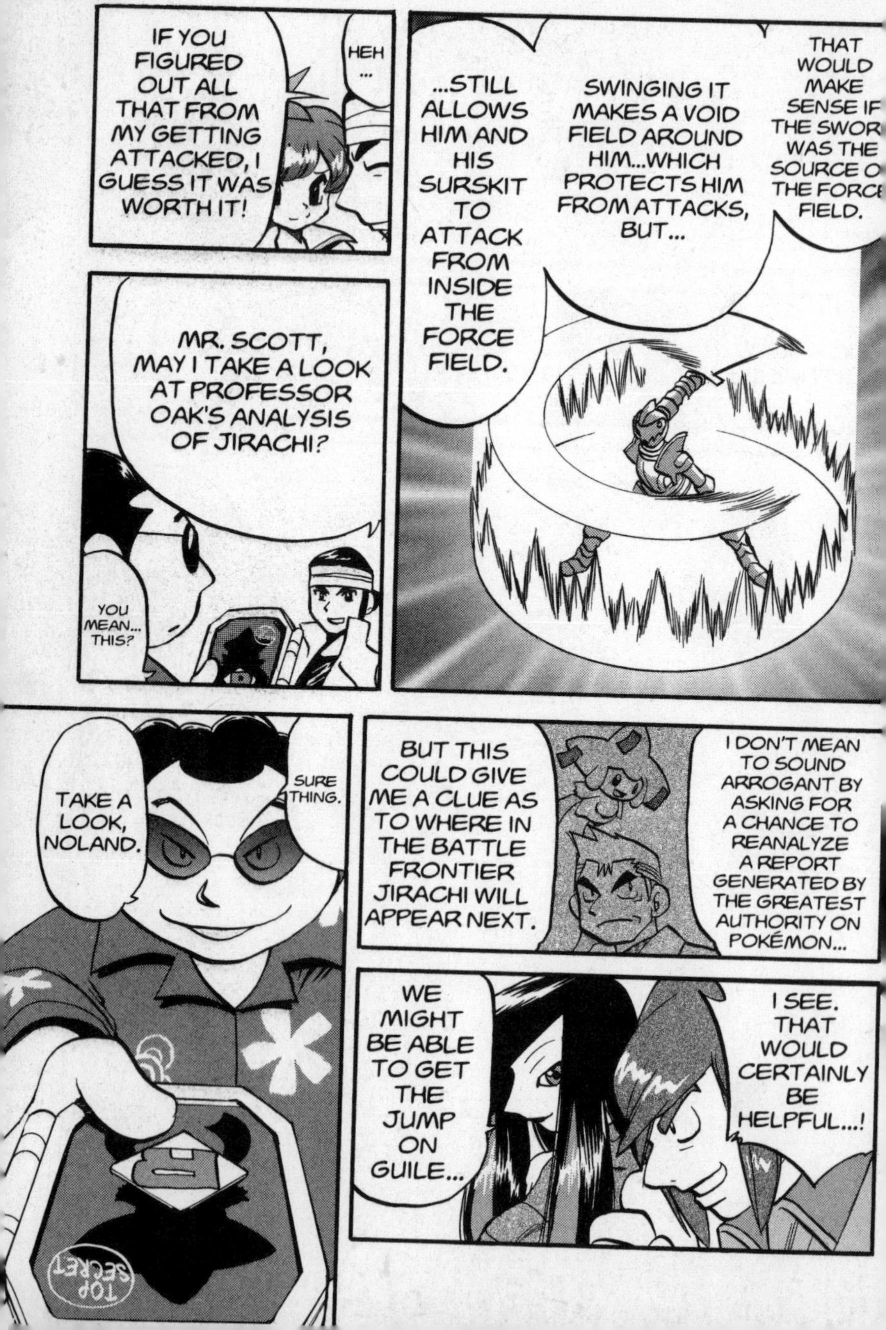
THAT WOULD MAKE SENSE IF THE SWOR WAS THE SOURCE O THE FORCE FIELD.
SWINGING IT MAKES A VOID FIELD AROUND HIM...WHICH PROTECTS HIM FROM ATTACKS, BUT...
...STILL ALLOWS HIM AND HIS SURSKIT TO ATTACK FROM INSIDE THE FORCE FIELD.
HEH...
IF YOU FIGURED OUT ALL THAT FROM MY GETTING ATTACKED, I GUESS IT WAS WORTH IT!
MR. SCOTT, MAY I TAKE A LOOK AT PROFESSOR OAK'S ANALYSIS OF JIRACHI?
YOU MEAN... THIS?
I DON'T MEAN TO SOUND ARROGANT BY ASKING FOR A CHANCE TO REANALYZE A REPORT GENERATED BY THE GREATEST AUTHORITY ON POKÉMON...
BUT THIS COULD GIVE ME A CLUE AS TO WHERE IN THE BATTLE FRONTIER JIRACHI WILL APPEAR NEXT.
I SEE. THAT WOULD CERTAINLY BE HELPFUL...!
WE MIGHT BE ABLE TO GET THE JUMP ON GUILE...
SURE THING.
TAKE A LOOK, NOLAND.
TOP SECRET

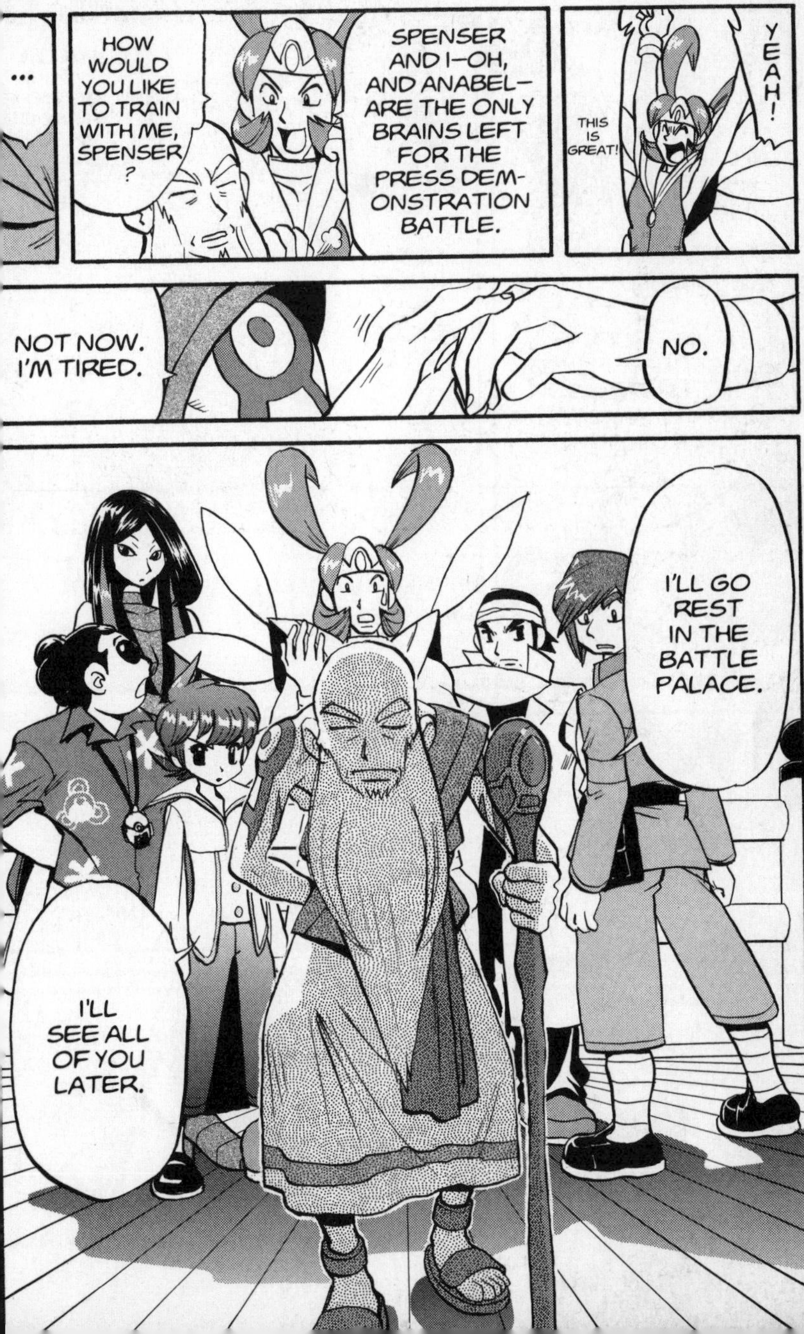
YEAH!
THIS IS GREAT!
SPENSER AND I—OH, AND ANABEL—ARE THE ONLY BRAINS LEFT FOR THE PRESS DEMONSTRATION BATTLE.
HOW WOULD YOU LIKE TO TRAIN WITH ME, SPENSER?
...
NO.
NOT NOW. I'M TIRED.
I'LL GO REST IN THE BATTLE PALACE.
I'LL SEE ALL OF YOU LATER.

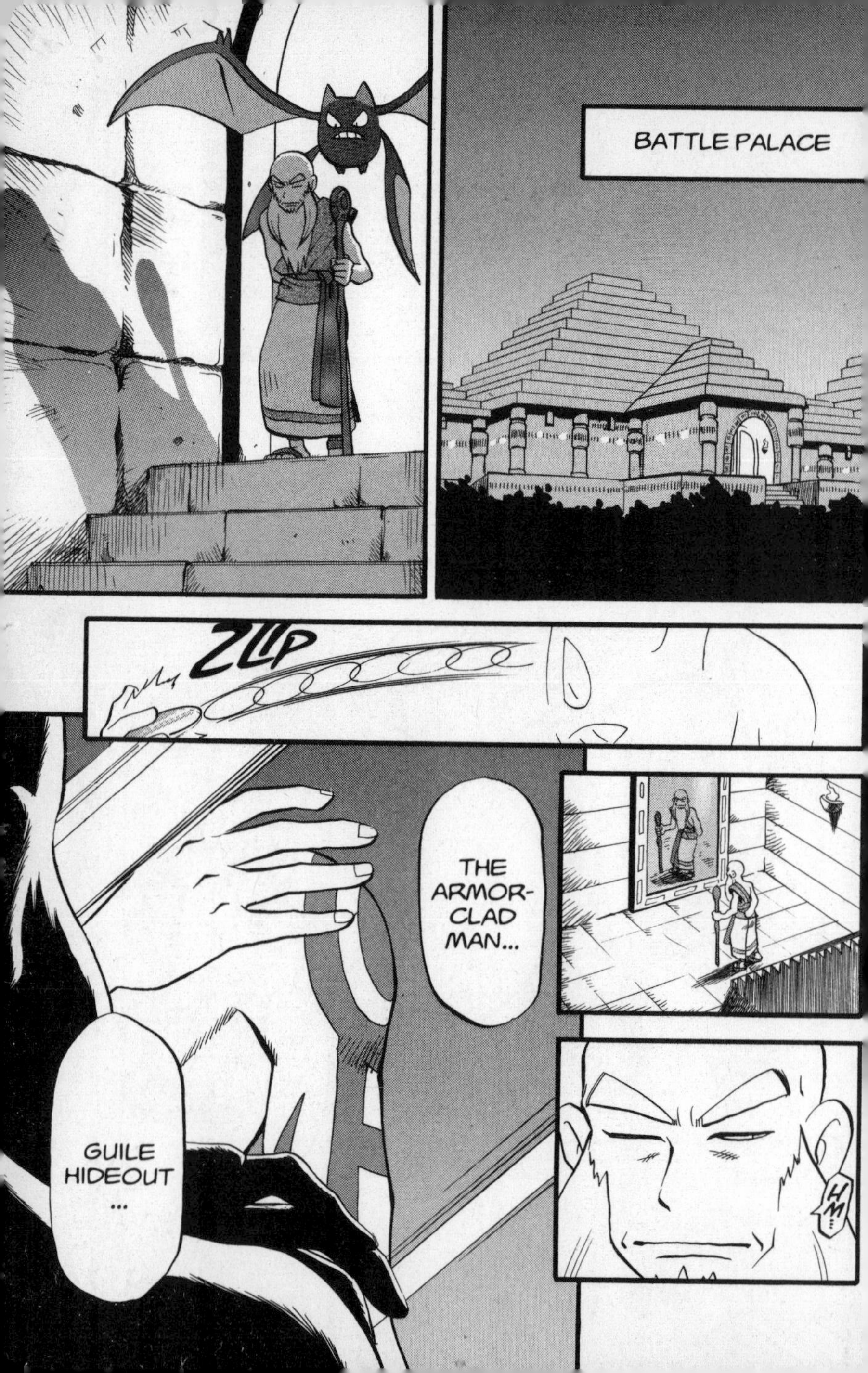
BATTLE PALACE
ZLIP
HM...
THE ARMOR-CLAD MAN...
GUILE HIDEOUT ...

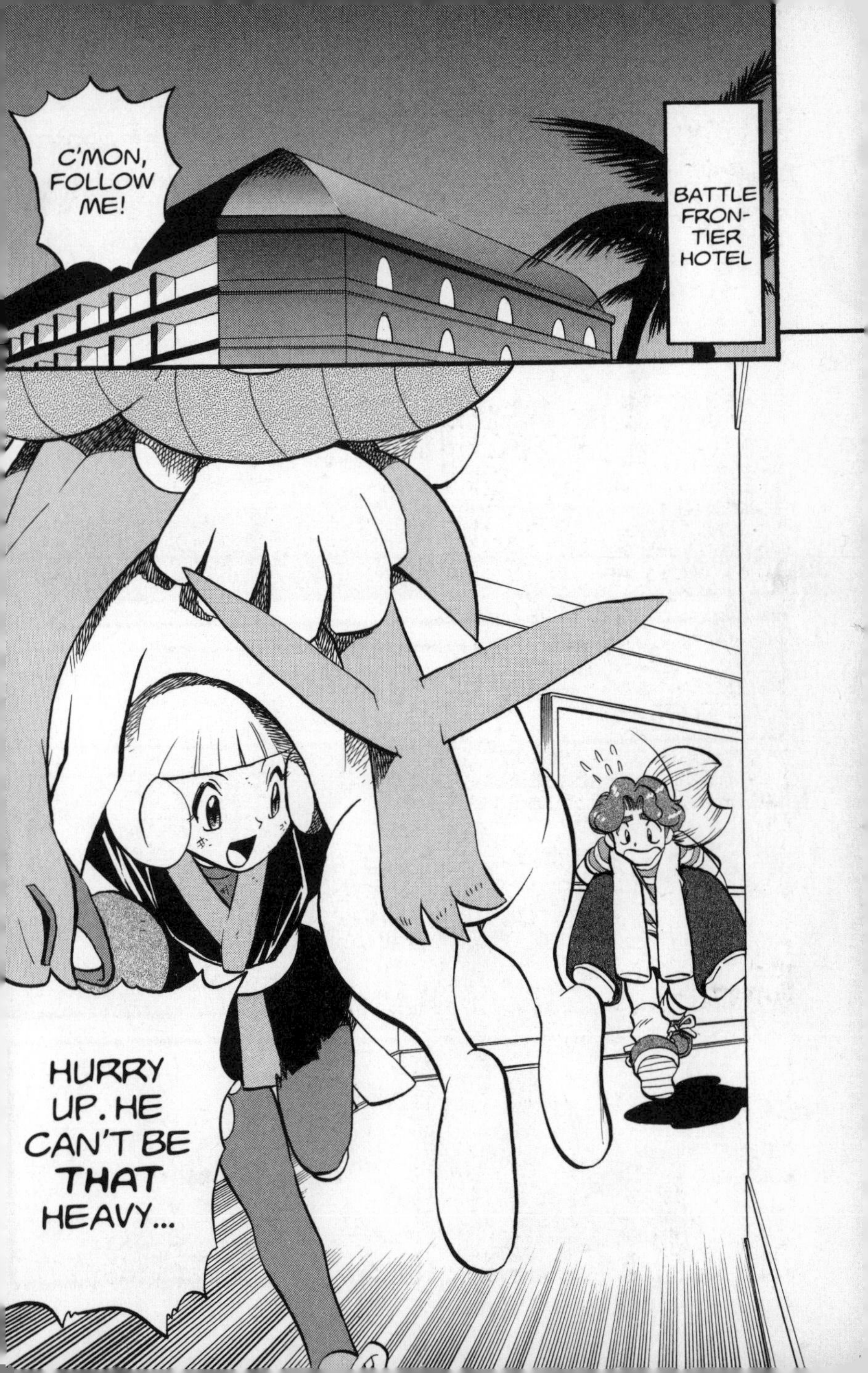
BATTLE FRON-TIER HOTEL
C'MON, FOLLOW ME!
HURRY UP. HE CAN'T BE THAT HEAVY...

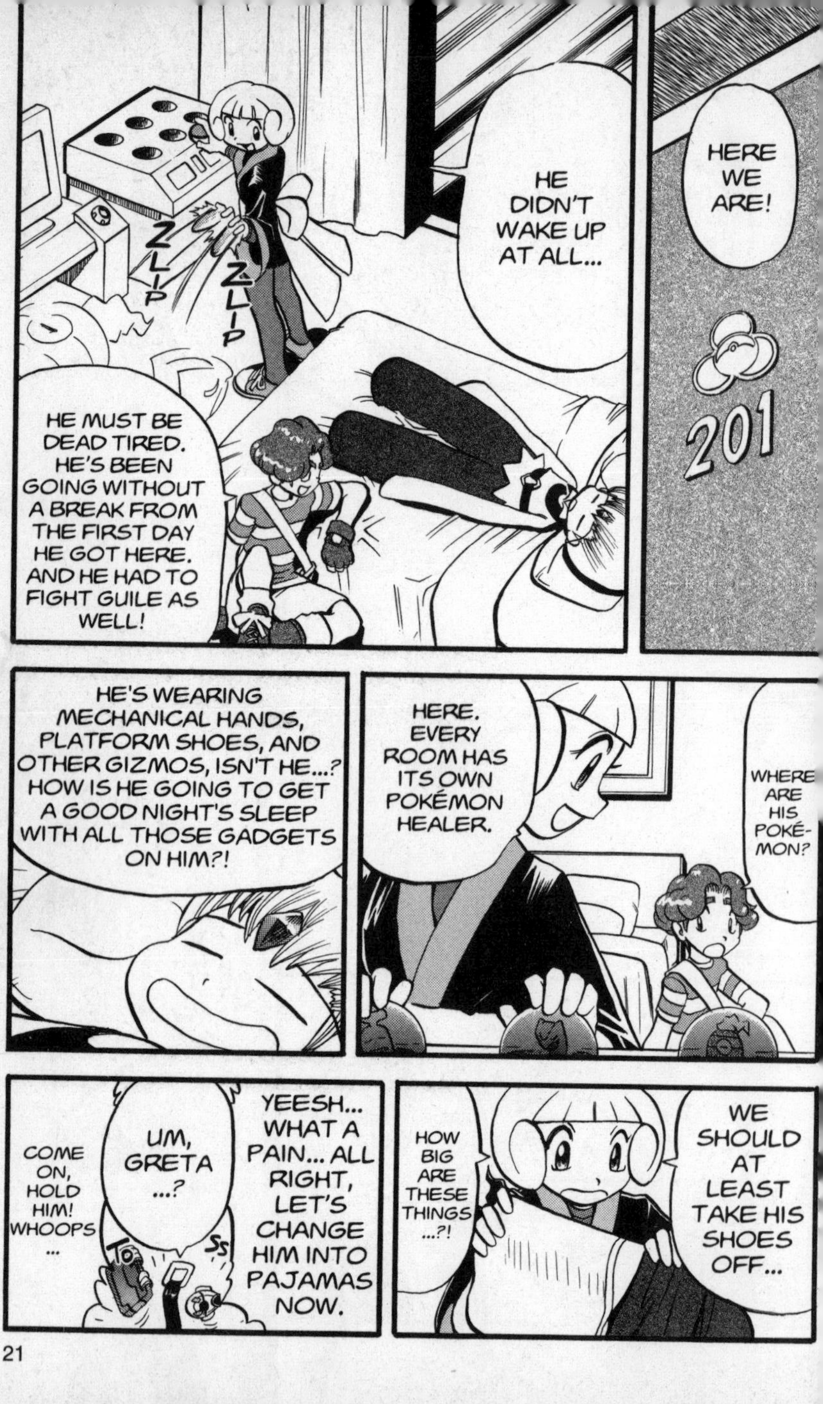
HERE WE ARE!
201
HE DIDN'T WAKE UP AT ALL...
ZLIP
ZLIP
HE MUST BE DEAD TIRED. HE'S BEEN GOING WITHOUT A BREAK FROM THE FIRST DAY HE GOT HERE. AND HE HAD TO FIGHT GUILE AS WELL!
WHERE ARE HIS POKÉ-MON?
HERE. EVERY ROOM HAS ITS OWN POKÉMON HEALER.
HE'S WEARING MECHANICAL HANDS, PLATFORM SHOES, AND OTHER GIZMOS, ISN'T HE...? HOW IS HE GOING TO GET A GOOD NIGHT'S SLEEP WITH ALL THOSE GADGETS ON HIM?!
WE SHOULD AT LEAST TAKE HIS SHOES OFF...
HOW BIG ARE THESE THINGS ...?!
YEESH... WHAT A PAIN... ALL RIGHT, LET'S CHANGE HIM INTO PAJAMAS NOW.
UM, GRETA ...?
SS
TO
COME ON, HOLD HIM! WHOOPS ...

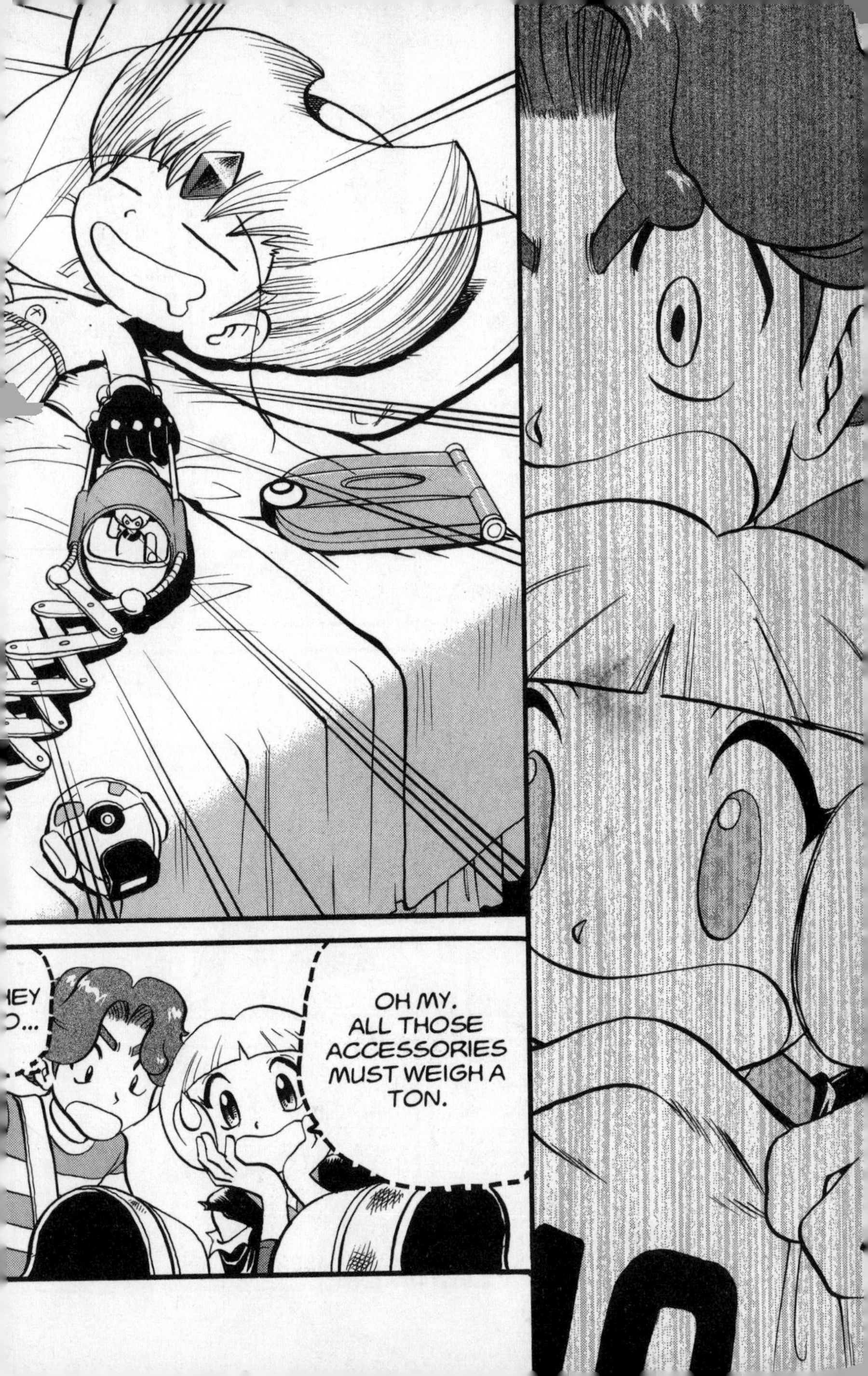
OH MY. ALL THOSE ACCESSORIES MUST WEIGH A TON.

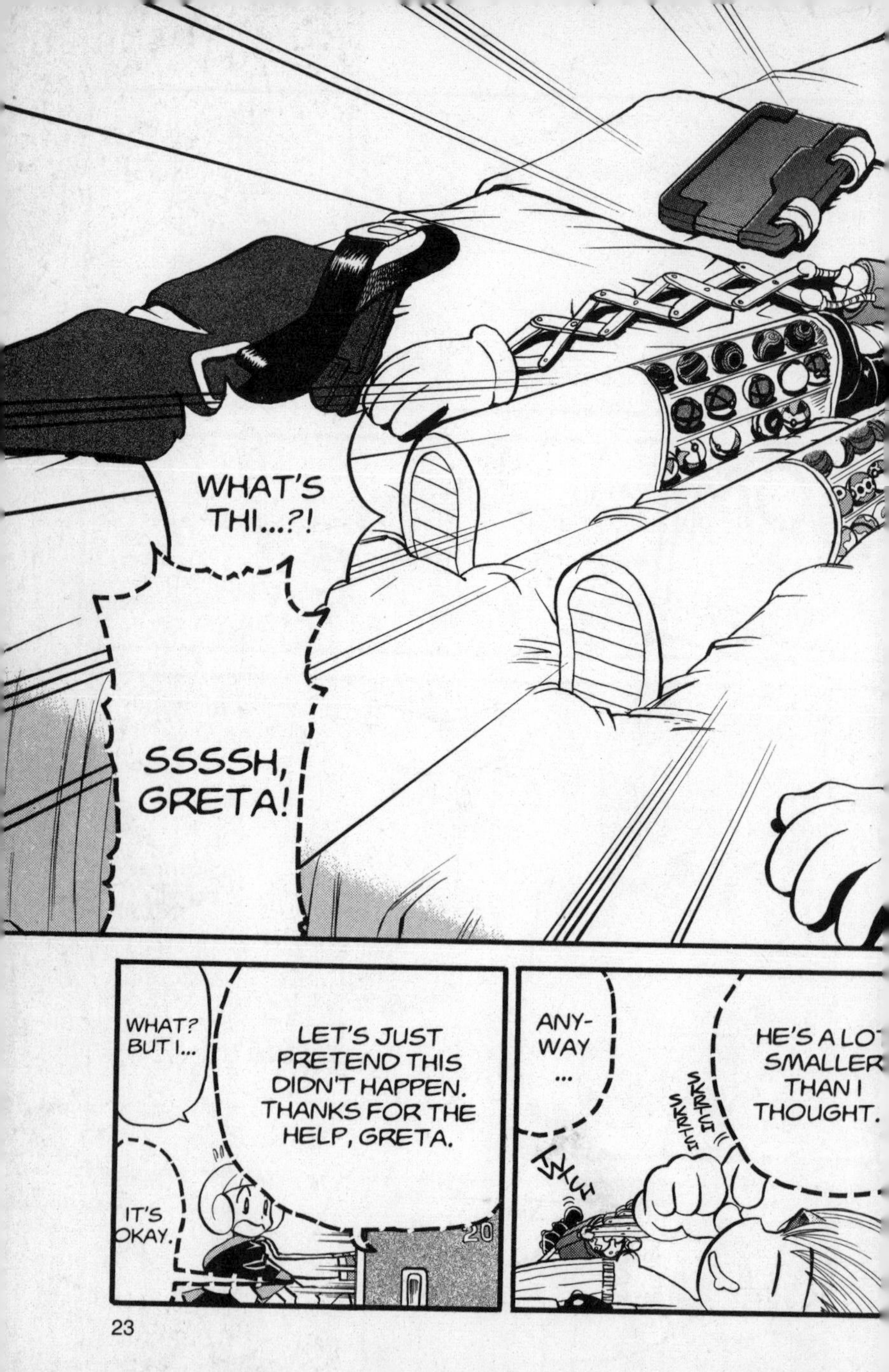
WHAT'S THI...?!
SSSSH, GRETA!
HE'S A LOT SMALLER THAN I THOUGHT.
SKRTCH SKRTCH
ANY-WAY ...
LET'S JUST PRETEND THIS DIDN'T HAPPEN. THANKS FOR THE HELP, GRETA.
WHAT? BUT I...
IT'S OKAY.
20

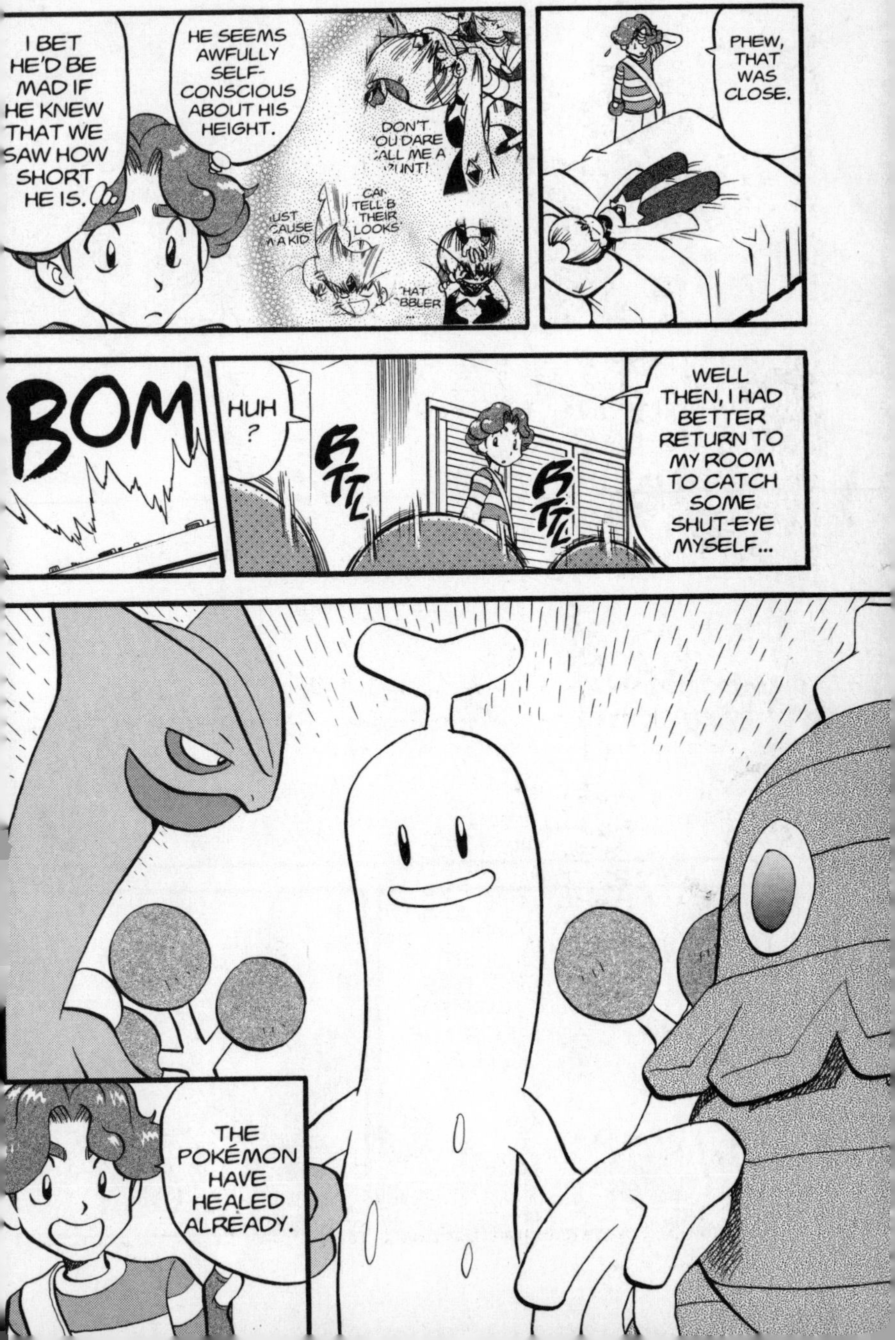
PHEW, THAT WAS CLOSE.
HE SEEMS AWFULLY SELF-CONSCIOUS ABOUT HIS HEIGHT.
I BET HE'D BE MAD IF HE KNEW THAT WE SAW HOW SHORT HE IS.
WELL THEN, I HAD BETTER RETURN TO MY ROOM TO CATCH SOME SHUT-EYE MYSELF...
RTTL
RTTL
HUH?
BOM
THE POKÉMON HAVE HEALED ALREADY.

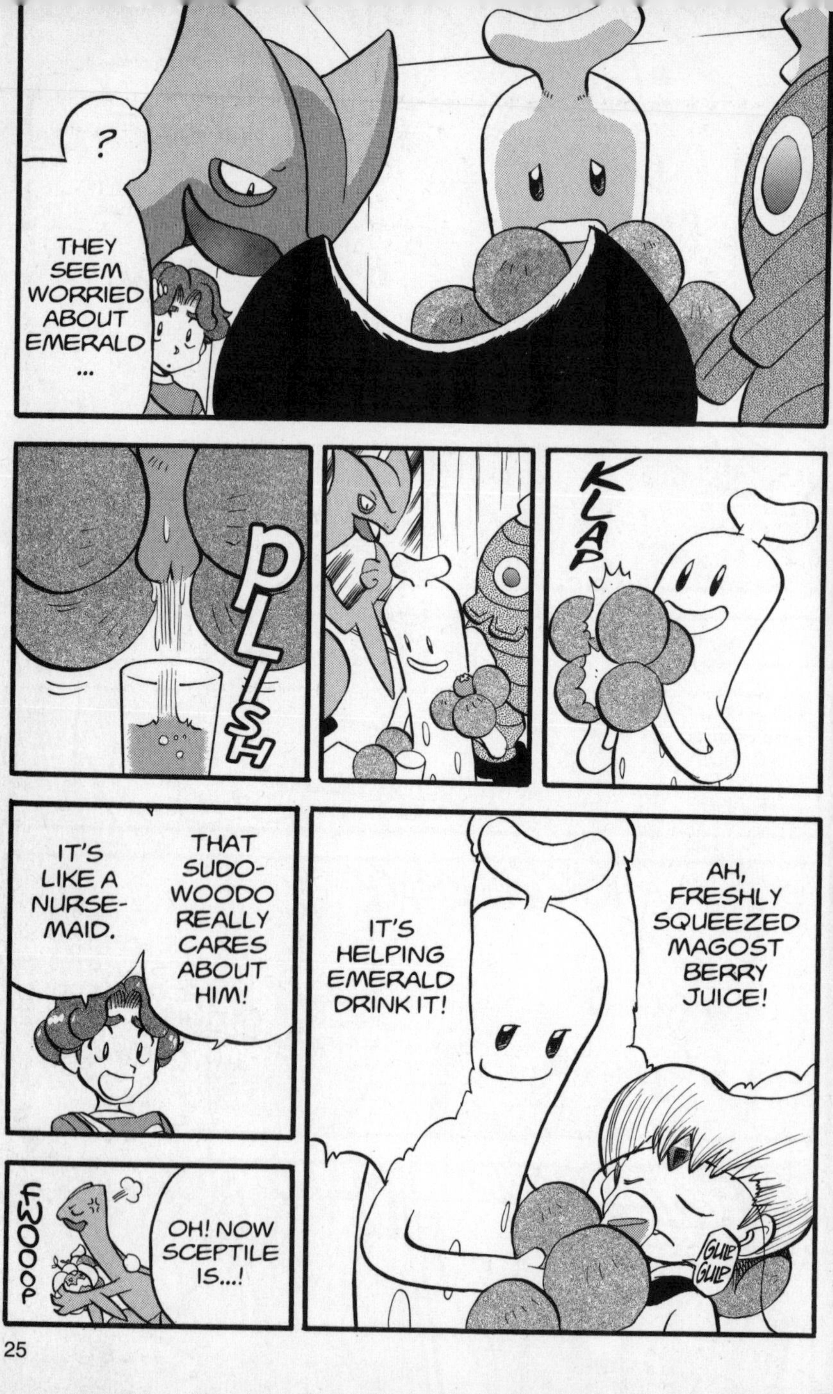
?
THEY SEEM WORRIED ABOUT EMERALD ...
KLAP
PLISH
AH, FRESHLY SQUEEZED MAGOST BERRY JUICE!
IT'S HELPING EMERALD DRINK IT!
GULP GULP
THAT SUDO-WOODO REALLY CARES ABOUT HIM!
IT'S LIKE A NURSE-MAID.
OH! NOW SCEPTILE IS...!
FWOOOP

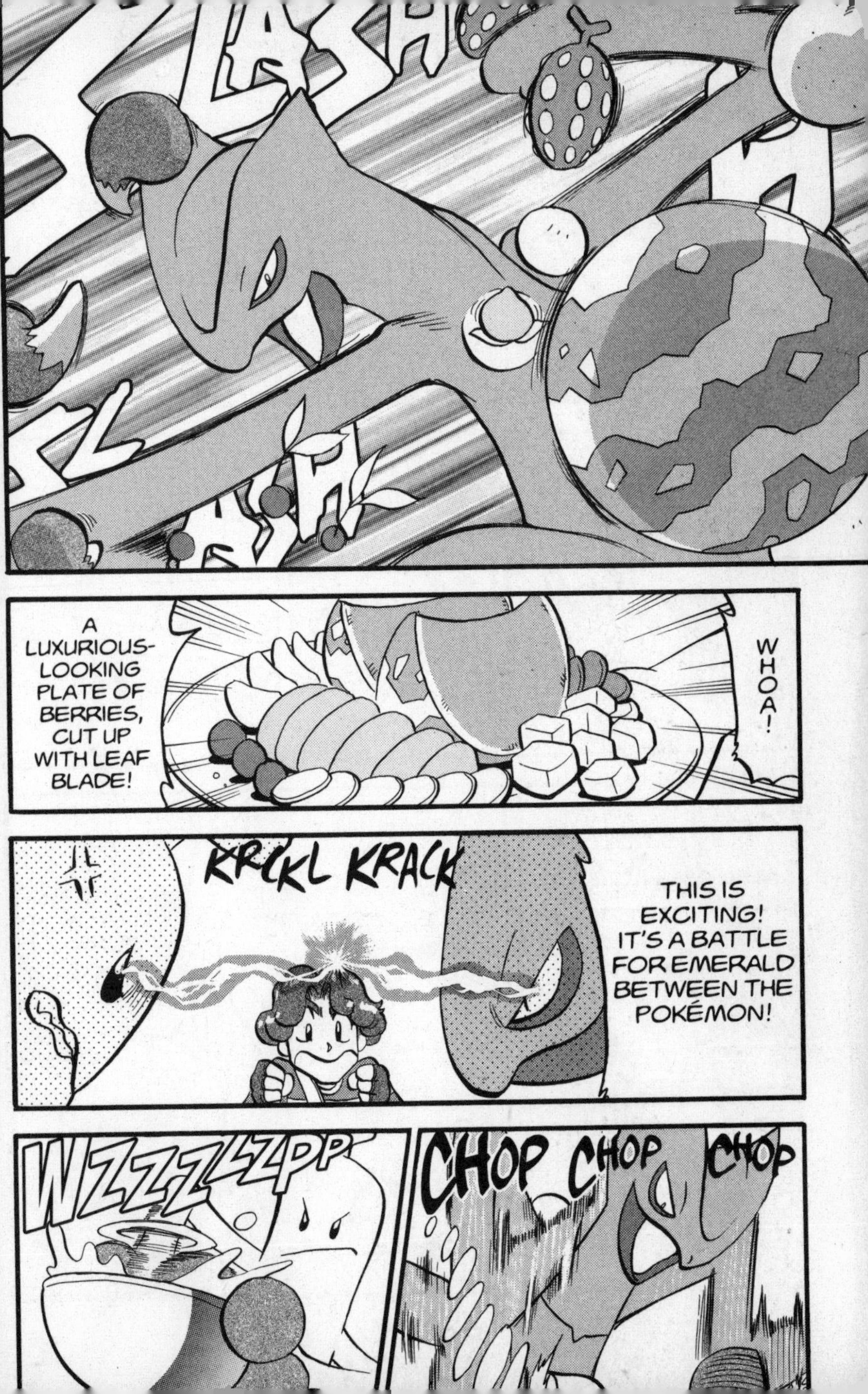
WHOA!
A LUXURIOUS-LOOKING PLATE OF BERRIES, CUT UP WITH LEAF BLADE!
KRCKL KRACK
THIS IS EXCITING! IT'S A BATTLE FOR EMERALD BETWEEN THE POKÉMON!
CHOP CHOP CHOP
WZZZZZPP

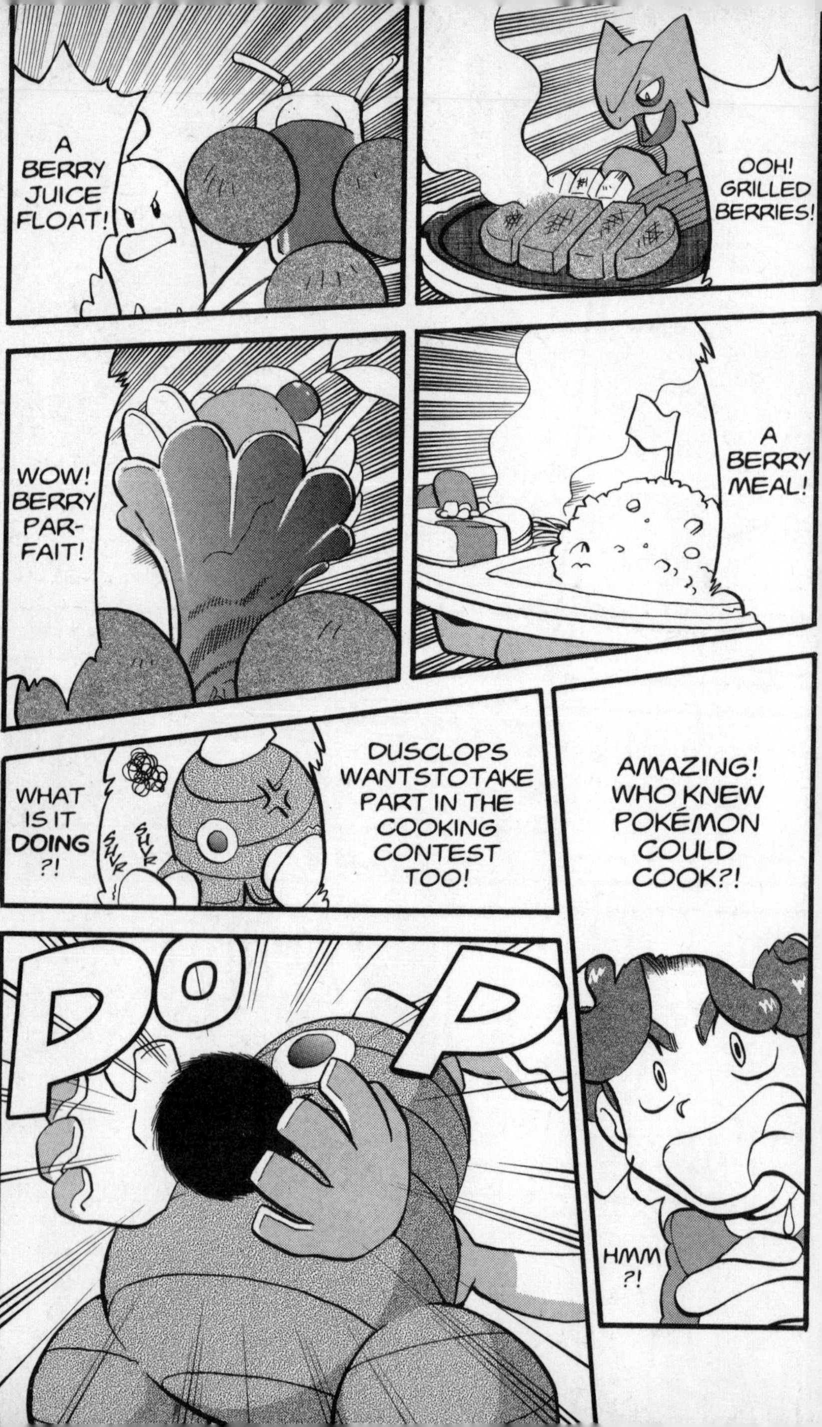
OOH! GRILLED BERRIES!
A BERRY JUICE FLOAT!
A BERRY MEAL!
WOW! BERRY PAR-FAIT!
AMAZING! WHO KNEW POKÉMON COULD COOK?!
HMM ?!
DUSCLOPS WANTSTOTAKE PART IN THE COOKING CONTEST TOO!
WHAT IS IT **DOING** ?!
SHVR
SHVR
POP

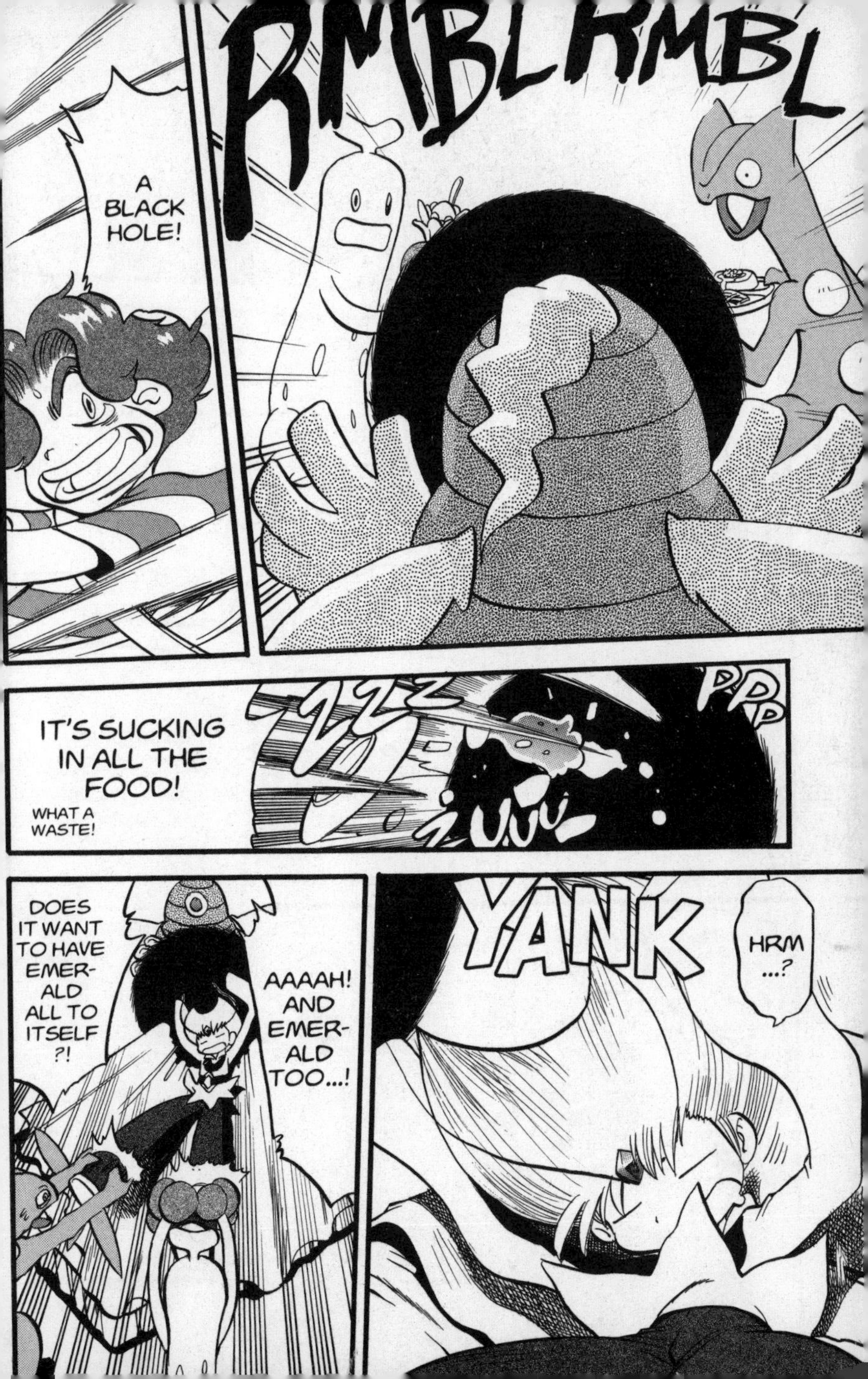
RMBLRMBL
A BLACK HOLE!
PPP
IT'S SUCKING IN ALL THE FOOD!
WHAT A WASTE!
YANK
HRM ...?
AAAAH! AND EMER-ALD TOO...!
DOES IT WANT TO HAVE EMER-ALD ALL TO ITSELF ?!

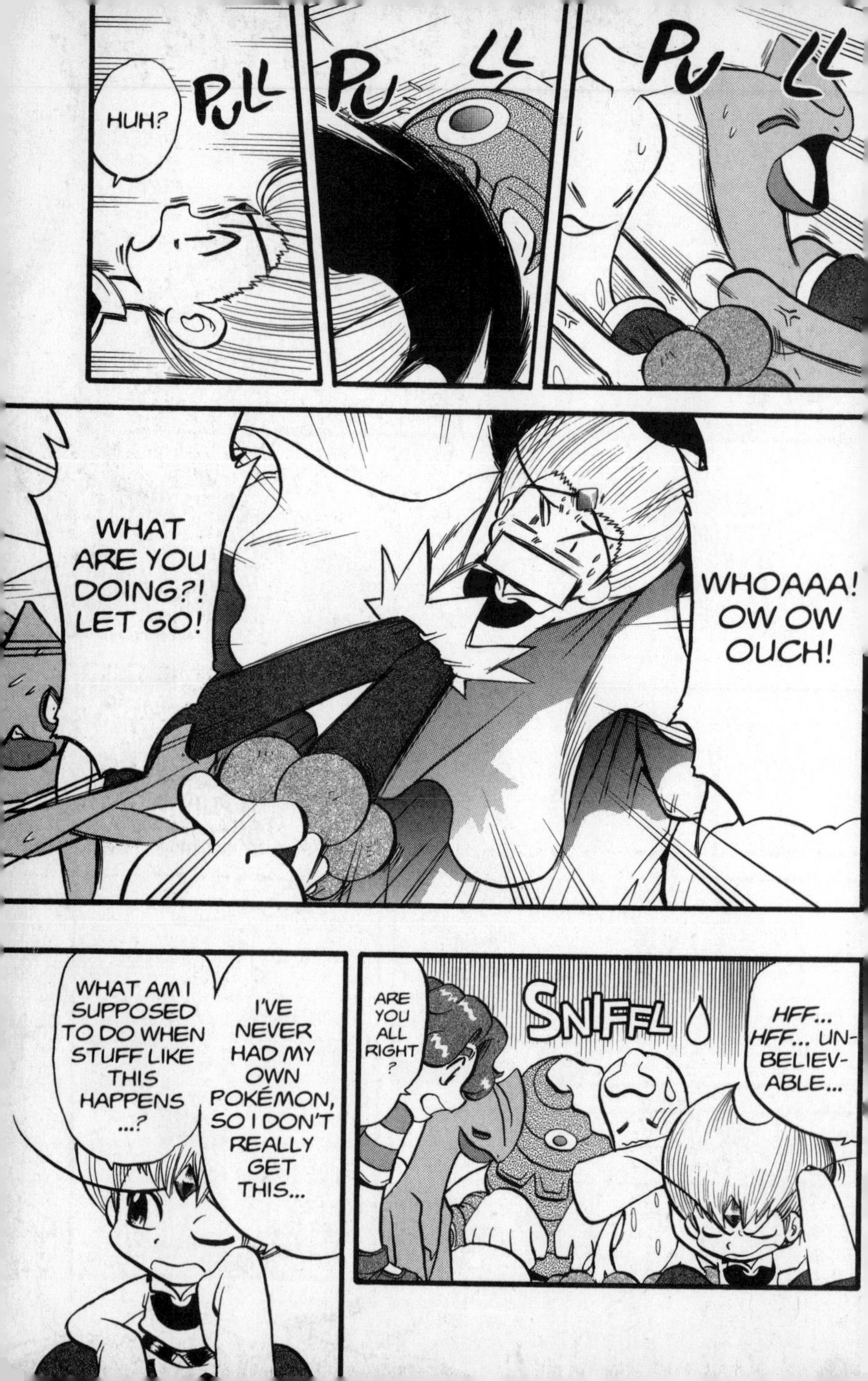
PULL
PULL
HUH?
PULL
WHOAAA! OW OW OUCH!
WHAT ARE YOU DOING?! LET GO!
HFF... HFF... UN-BELIEVABLE...
SNIFFL
ARE YOU ALL RIGHT?
I'VE NEVER HAD MY OWN POKÉMON, SO I DON'T REALLY GET THIS...
WHAT AM I SUPPOSED TO DO WHEN STUFF LIKE THIS HAPPENS...?

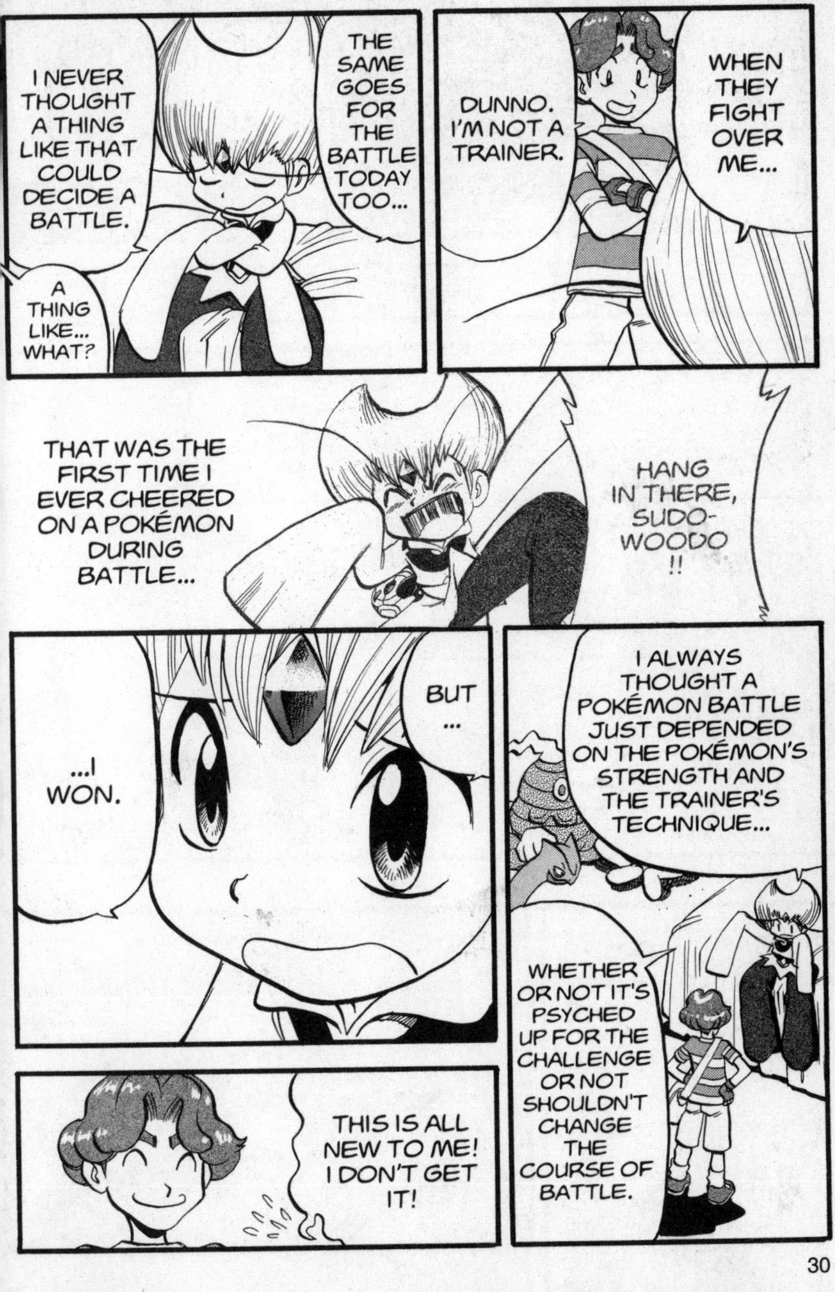
WHEN THEY FIGHT OVER ME...
DUNNO. I'M NOT A TRAINER.
THE SAME GOES FOR THE BATTLE TODAY TOO...
I NEVER THOUGHT A THING LIKE THAT COULD DECIDE A BATTLE.
A THING LIKE... WHAT?
HANG IN THERE, SUDO-WOODO!!
THAT WAS THE FIRST TIME I EVER CHEERED ON A POKÉMON DURING BATTLE...
I ALWAYS THOUGHT A POKÉMON BATTLE JUST DEPENDED ON THE POKÉMON'S STRENGTH AND THE TRAINER'S TECHNIQUE...
WHETHER OR NOT IT'S PSYCHED UP FOR THE CHALLENGE OR NOT SHOULDN'T CHANGE THE COURSE OF BATTLE.
BUT...
...I WON.
THIS IS ALL NEW TO ME! I DON'T GET IT!

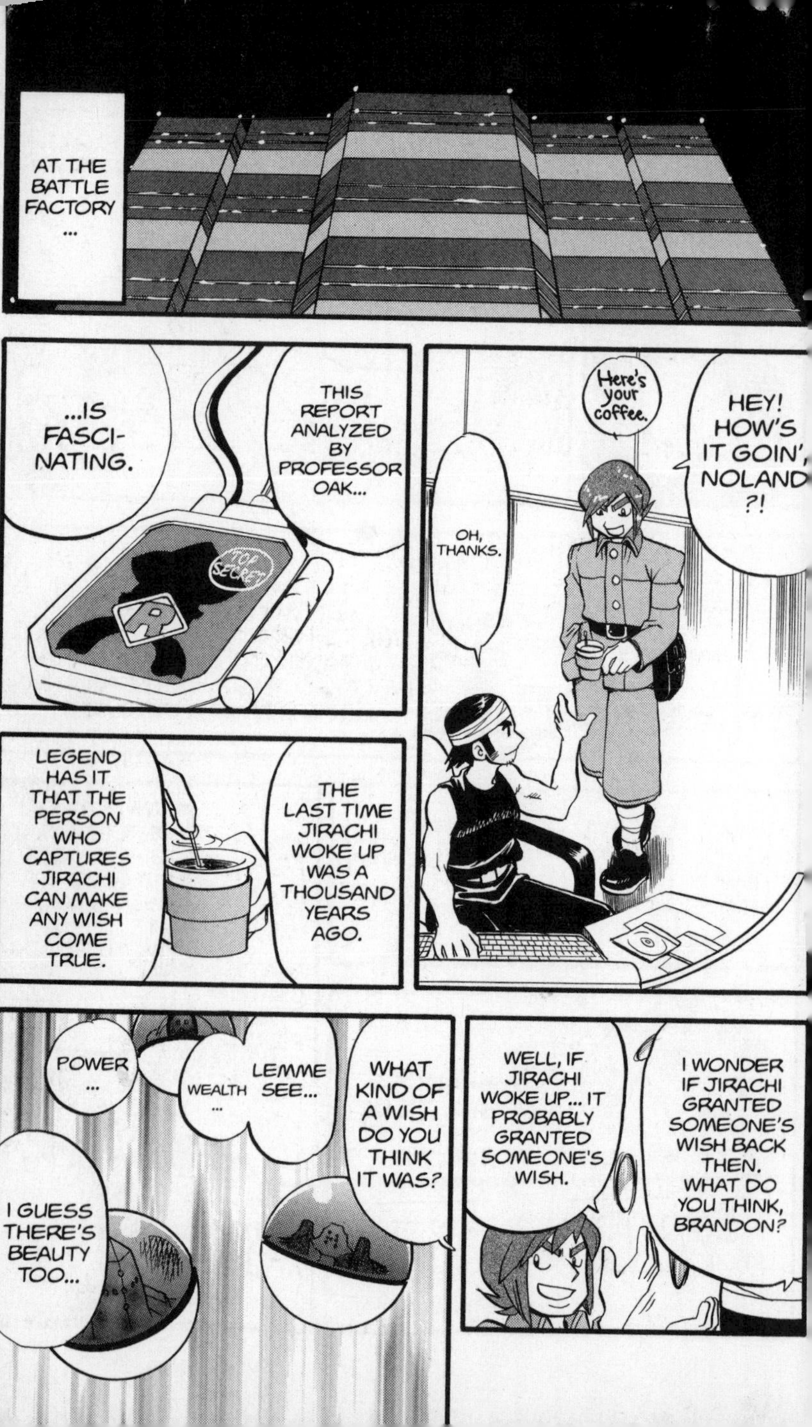
AT THE BATTLE FACTORY ...
HEY! HOW'S IT GOIN', NOLAND?!
Here's your coffee.
OH, THANKS.
THIS REPORT ANALYZED BY PROFESSOR OAK...
...IS FASCINATING.
TOP SECRET
THE LAST TIME JIRACHI WOKE UP WAS A THOUSAND YEARS AGO.
LEGEND HAS IT THAT THE PERSON WHO CAPTURES JIRACHI CAN MAKE ANY WISH COME TRUE.
I WONDER IF JIRACHI GRANTED SOMEONE'S WISH BACK THEN. WHAT DO YOU THINK, BRANDON?
WELL, IF JIRACHI WOKE UP... IT PROBABLY GRANTED SOMEONE'S WISH.
WHAT KIND OF A WISH DO YOU THINK IT WAS?
LEMME SEE...
WEALTH ...
POWER ...
I GUESS THERE'S BEAUTY TOO...

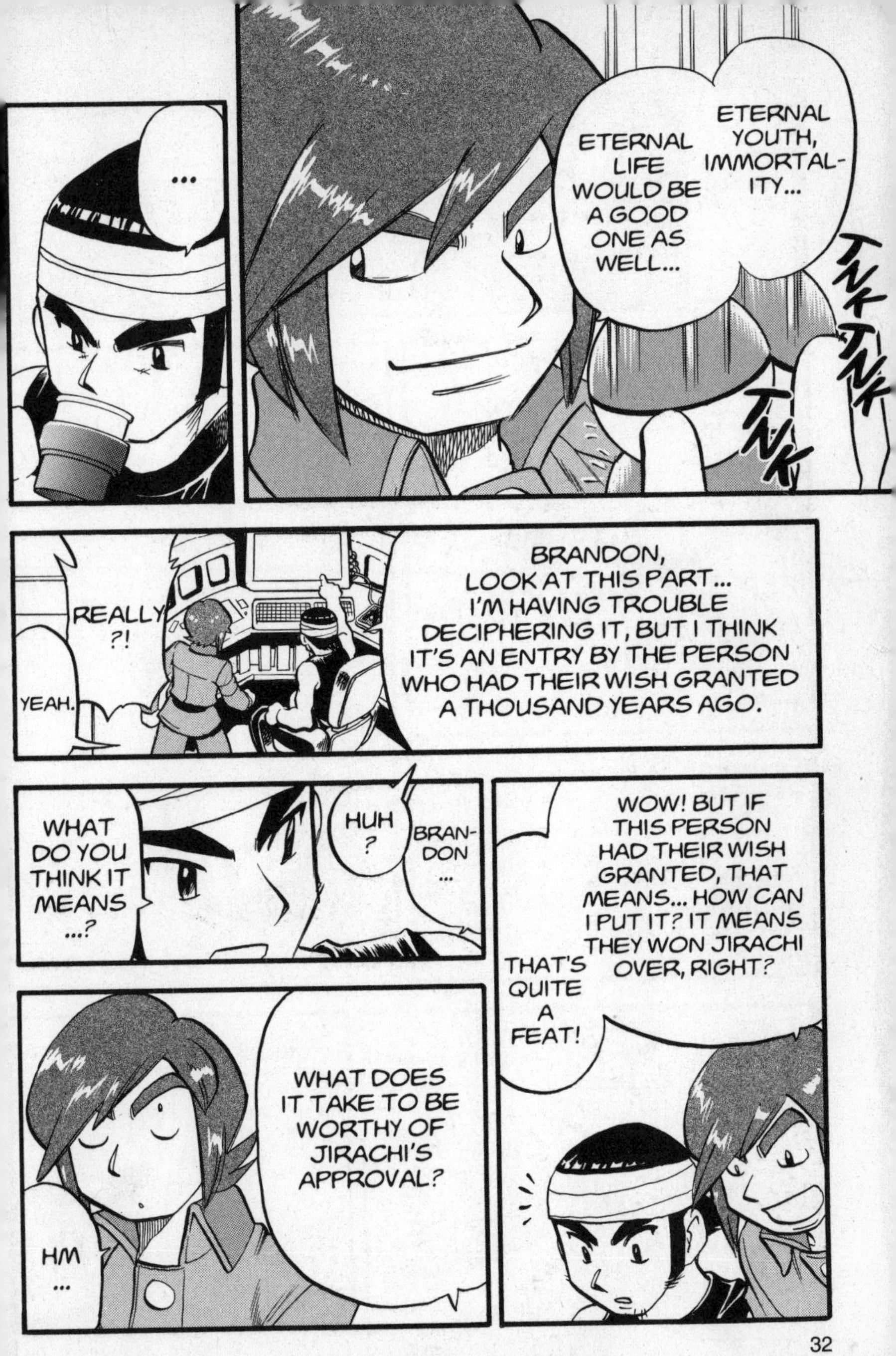
ETERNAL YOUTH, IMMORTAL-ITY...
ETERNAL LIFE WOULD BE A GOOD ONE AS WELL...
TNK TNK TNK
...
BRANDON, LOOK AT THIS PART... I'M HAVING TROUBLE DECIPHERING IT, BUT I THINK IT'S AN ENTRY BY THE PERSON WHO HAD THEIR WISH GRANTED A THOUSAND YEARS AGO.
REALLY?!
YEAH.
WOW! BUT IF THIS PERSON HAD THEIR WISH GRANTED, THAT MEANS... HOW CAN I PUT IT? IT MEANS THEY WON JIRACHI OVER, RIGHT?
THAT'S QUITE A FEAT!
HUH?
BRAN-DON...
WHAT DO YOU THINK IT MEANS...?
WHAT DOES IT TAKE TO BE WORTHY OF JIRACHI'S APPROVAL?
HM...

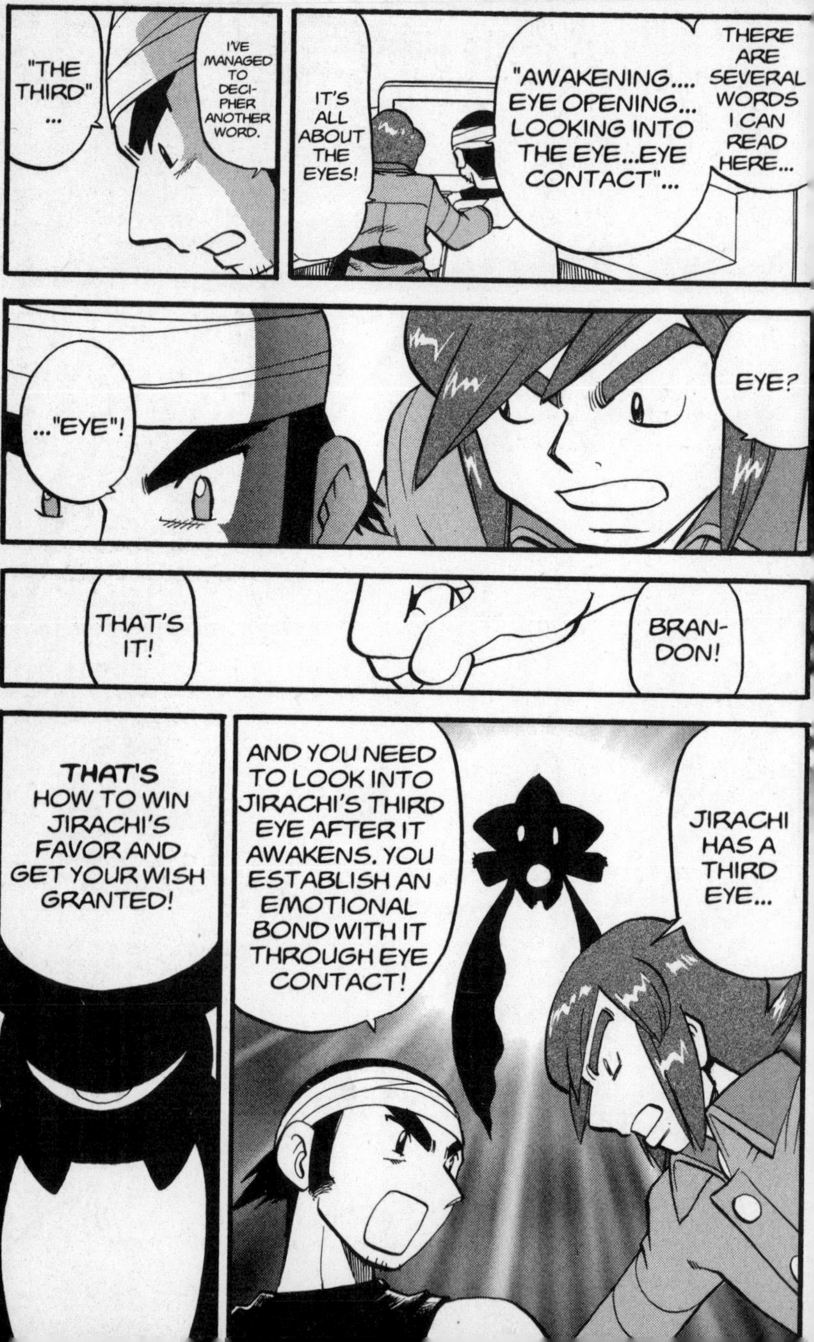
THERE ARE SEVERAL WORDS I CAN READ HERE...
"AWAKENING.... EYE OPENING... LOOKING INTO THE EYE...EYE CONTACT"...
IT'S ALL ABOUT THE EYES!
I'VE MANAGED TO DECI-PHER ANOTHER WORD.
"THE THIRD" ...
EYE?
..."EYE"!
BRAN-DON!
THAT'S IT!
JIRACHI HAS A THIRD EYE...
AND YOU NEED TO LOOK INTO JIRACHI'S THIRD EYE AFTER IT AWAKENS. YOU ESTABLISH AN EMOTIONAL BOND WITH IT THROUGH EYE CONTACT!
THAT'S HOW TO WIN JIRACHI'S FAVOR AND GET YOUR WISH GRANTED!

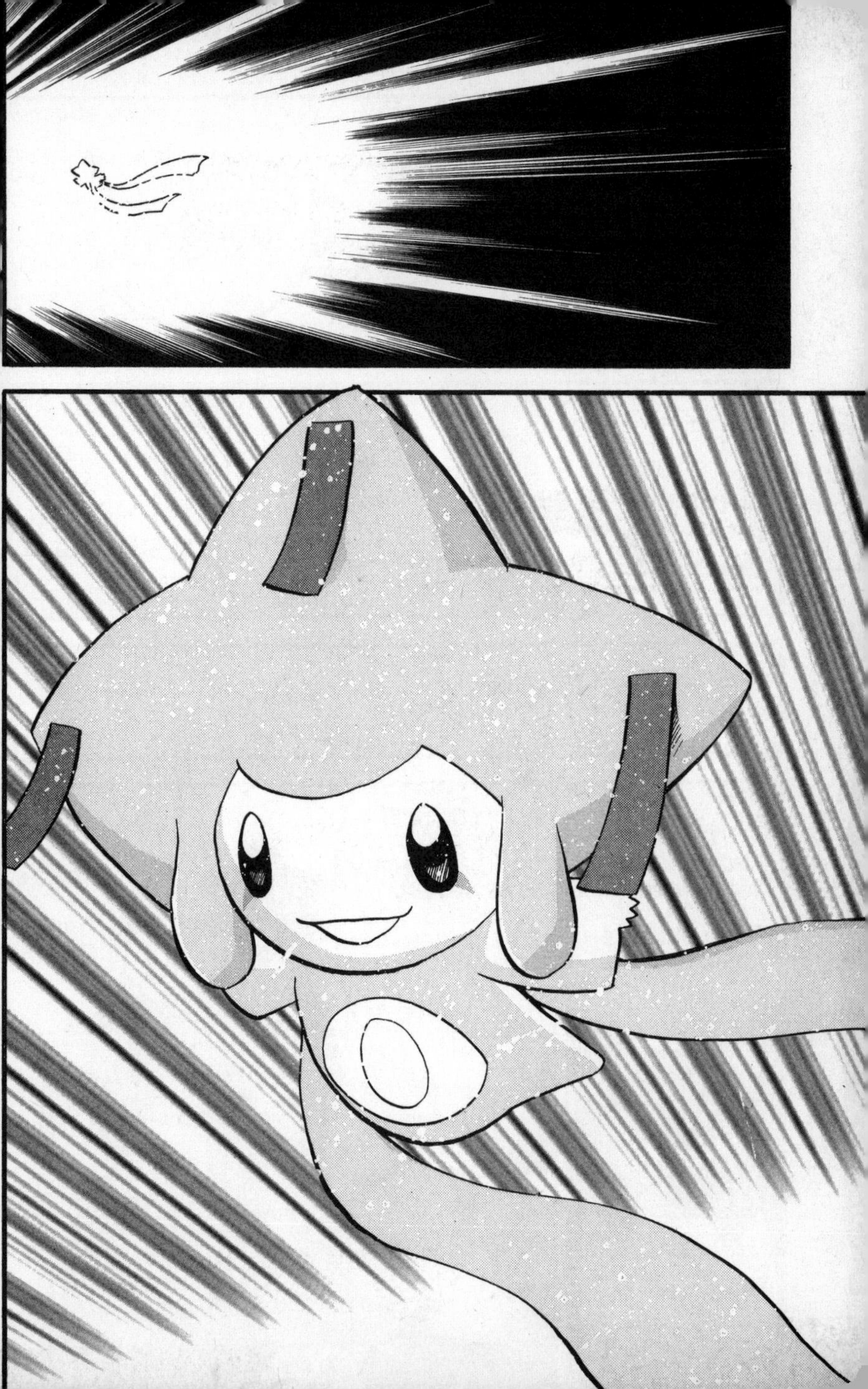

DEAR MEMBERS OF THE PRESS...

Thank you for visiting the Battle Frontier today. Permit me to continue explaining the rules of this facility...

OWNER: SCOTT

FACILITY RULES
BATTLE DOME 2

■ DETAILS OF THE BATTLE CARD ■
The challenger may learn about their opponents at the Battle Dome by reviewing their opponents' battle card.

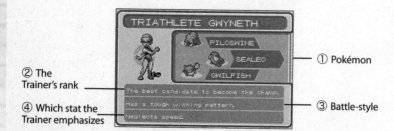

② The Trainer's rank

④ Which stat the Trainer emphasizes

TRIATHLETE GWYNETH

① Pokémon

③ Battle-style

The best candidate to become the champ. Has a tough winning pattern. Neglects speed.

PILOSWINE
SEALEO
QWILFISH

① Pokémon
The Trainer's three Pokémon.

② The Trainer's rank.
The Trainer's rank compared to the rank of the opponent. Represents the Trainer's rank in relation to the stats of the opponent's Pokémon.

③ Battle-style
The type of battle-style this Trainer excels in. (The sentence here will differ depending on the type of Pokémon Moves.)

④ Which stat the Trainer emphasizes.
The stats of the Pokémon. You may also learn how the Nature of the Pokémon affects the stats.

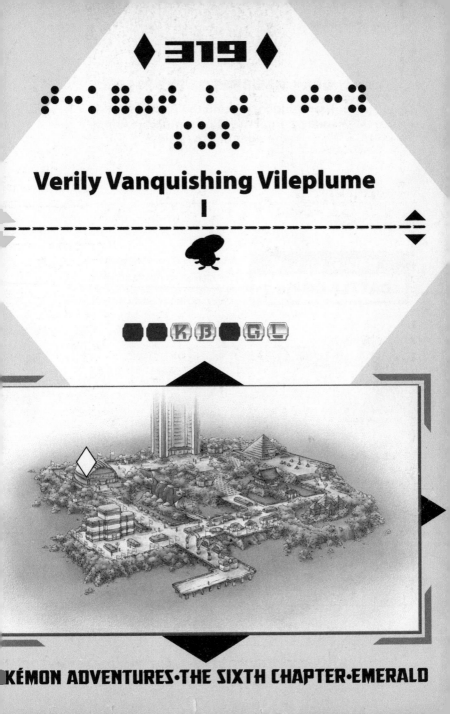

◆ ᗱ1ᑫ ◆

Verily Vanquishing Vileplume
I

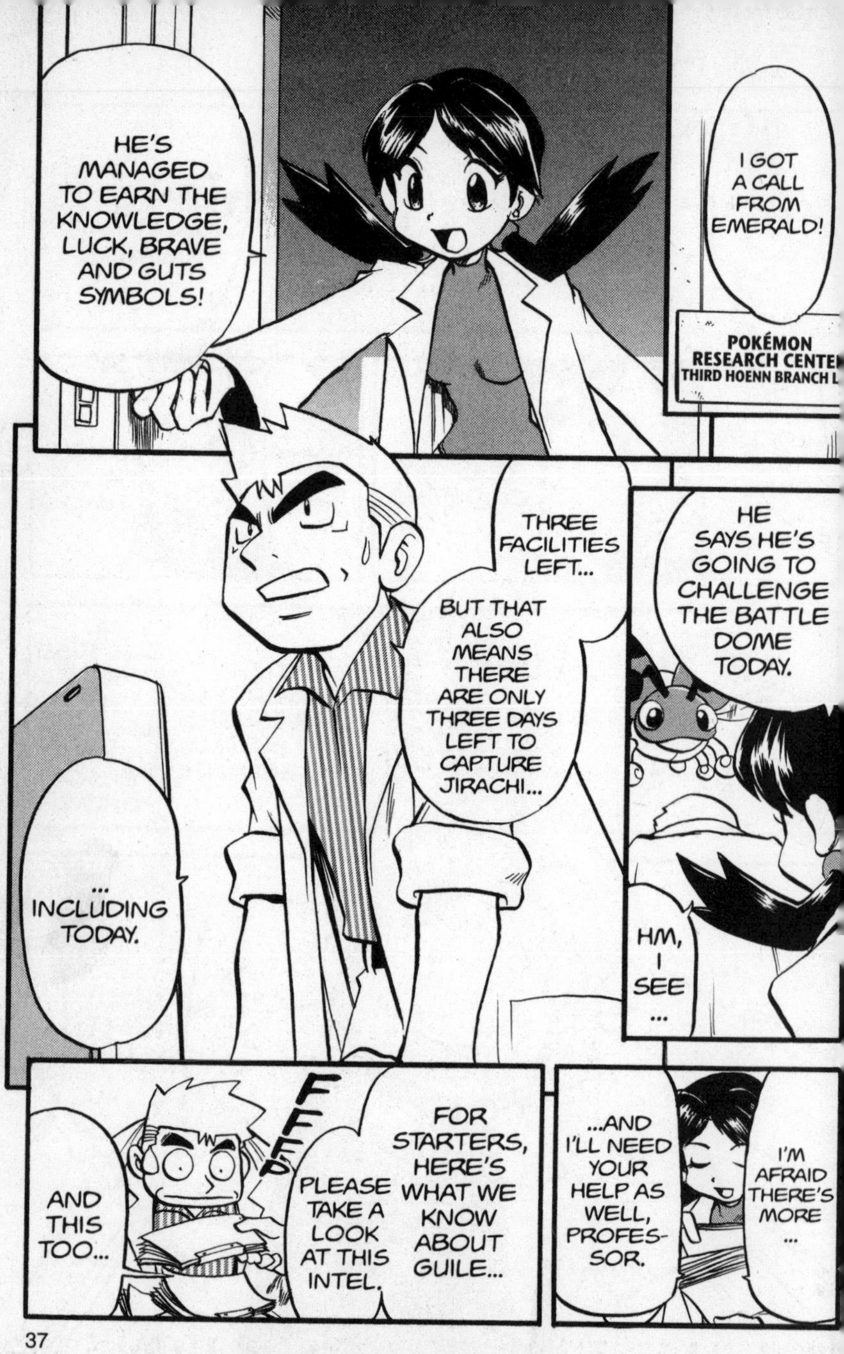
I GOT A CALL FROM EMERALD!
POKÉMON
RESEARCH CENTE
THIRD HOENN BRANCH L
HE'S MANAGED TO EARN THE KNOWLEDGE, LUCK, BRAVE AND GUTS SYMBOLS!
HE SAYS HE'S GOING TO CHALLENGE THE BATTLE DOME TODAY.
HM, I SEE...
THREE FACILITIES LEFT...
BUT THAT ALSO MEANS THERE ARE ONLY THREE DAYS LEFT TO CAPTURE JIRACHI...
...INCLUDING TODAY.
I'M AFRAID THERE'S MORE...
...AND I'LL NEED YOUR HELP AS WELL, PROFES-SOR.
FOR STARTERS, HERE'S WHAT WE KNOW ABOUT GUILE...
PLEASE TAKE A LOOK AT THIS INTEL.
FFFP
AND THIS TOO...

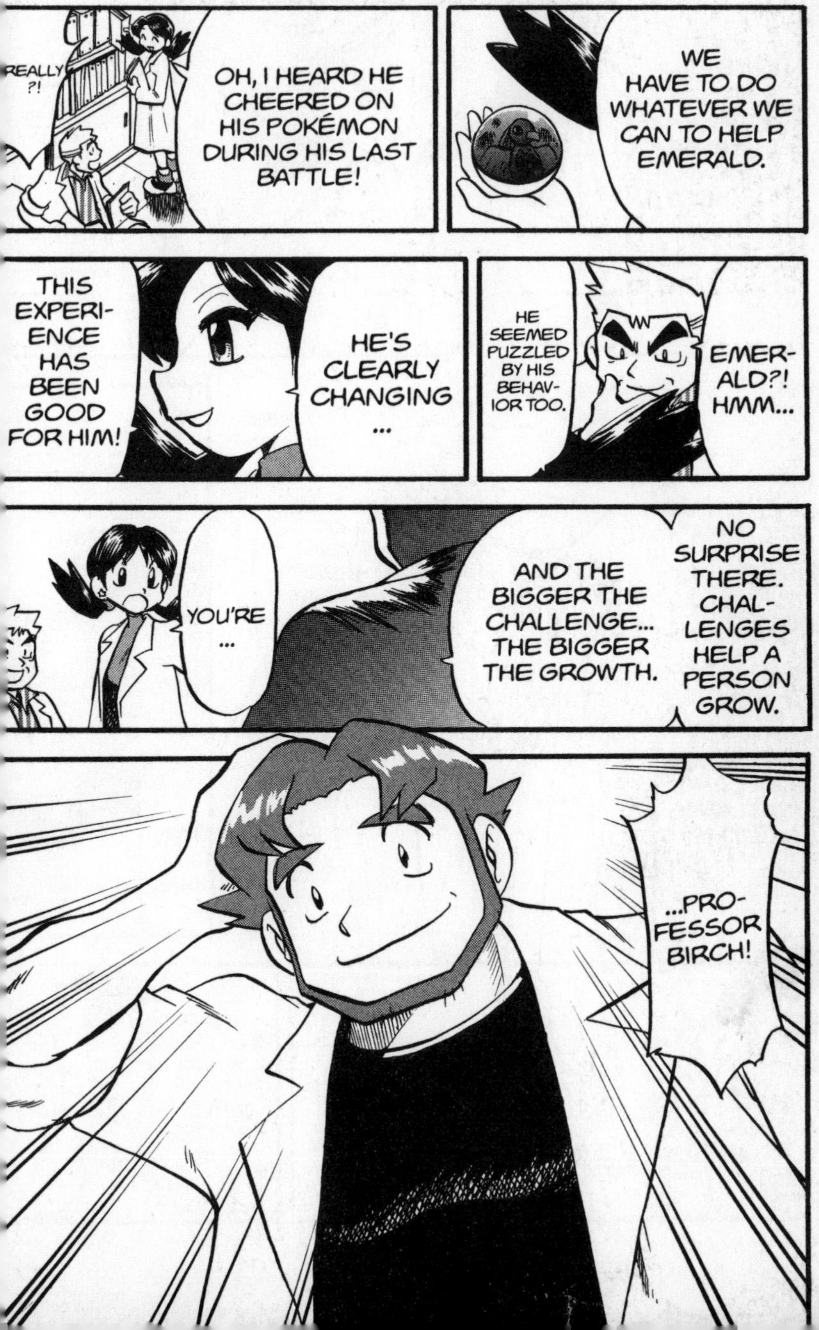

WE HAVE TO DO WHATEVER WE CAN TO HELP EMERALD.
OH, I HEARD HE CHEERED ON HIS POKÉMON DURING HIS LAST BATTLE!
REALLY?!
EMERALD?! HMM...
HE SEEMED PUZZLED BY HIS BEHAVIOR TOO.
HE'S CLEARLY CHANGING...
THIS EXPERIENCE HAS BEEN GOOD FOR HIM!
NO SURPRISE THERE. CHALLENGES HELP A PERSON GROW.
AND THE BIGGER THE CHALLENGE... THE BIGGER THE GROWTH.
YOU'RE...
...PROFESSOR BIRCH!

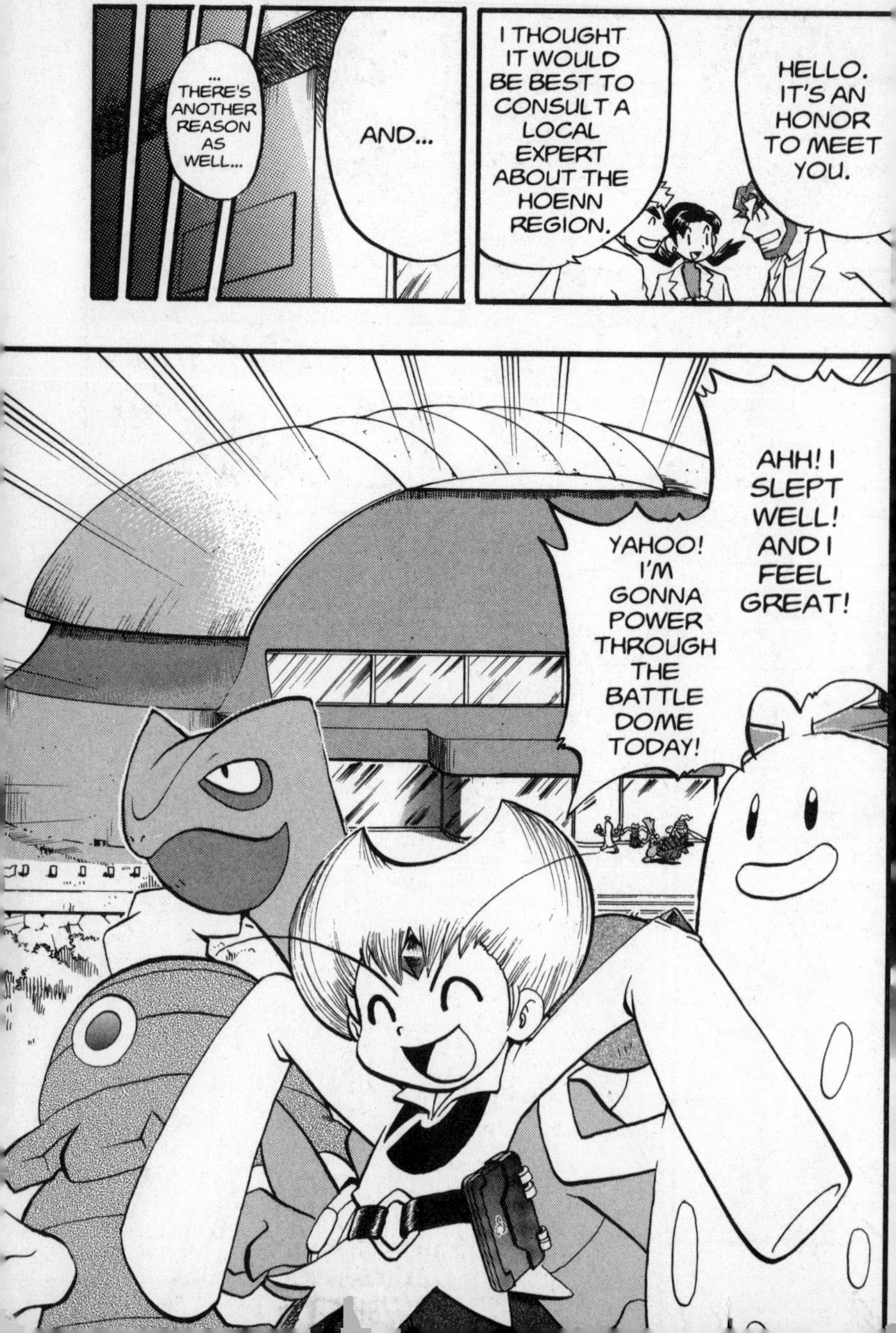
HELLO. IT'S AN HONOR TO MEET YOU.
I THOUGHT IT WOULD BE BEST TO CONSULT A LOCAL EXPERT ABOUT THE HOENN REGION.
AND...
... THERE'S ANOTHER REASON AS WELL...
AHH! I SLEPT WELL! AND I FEEL GREAT!
YAHOO! I'M GONNA POWER THROUGH THE BATTLE DOME TODAY!

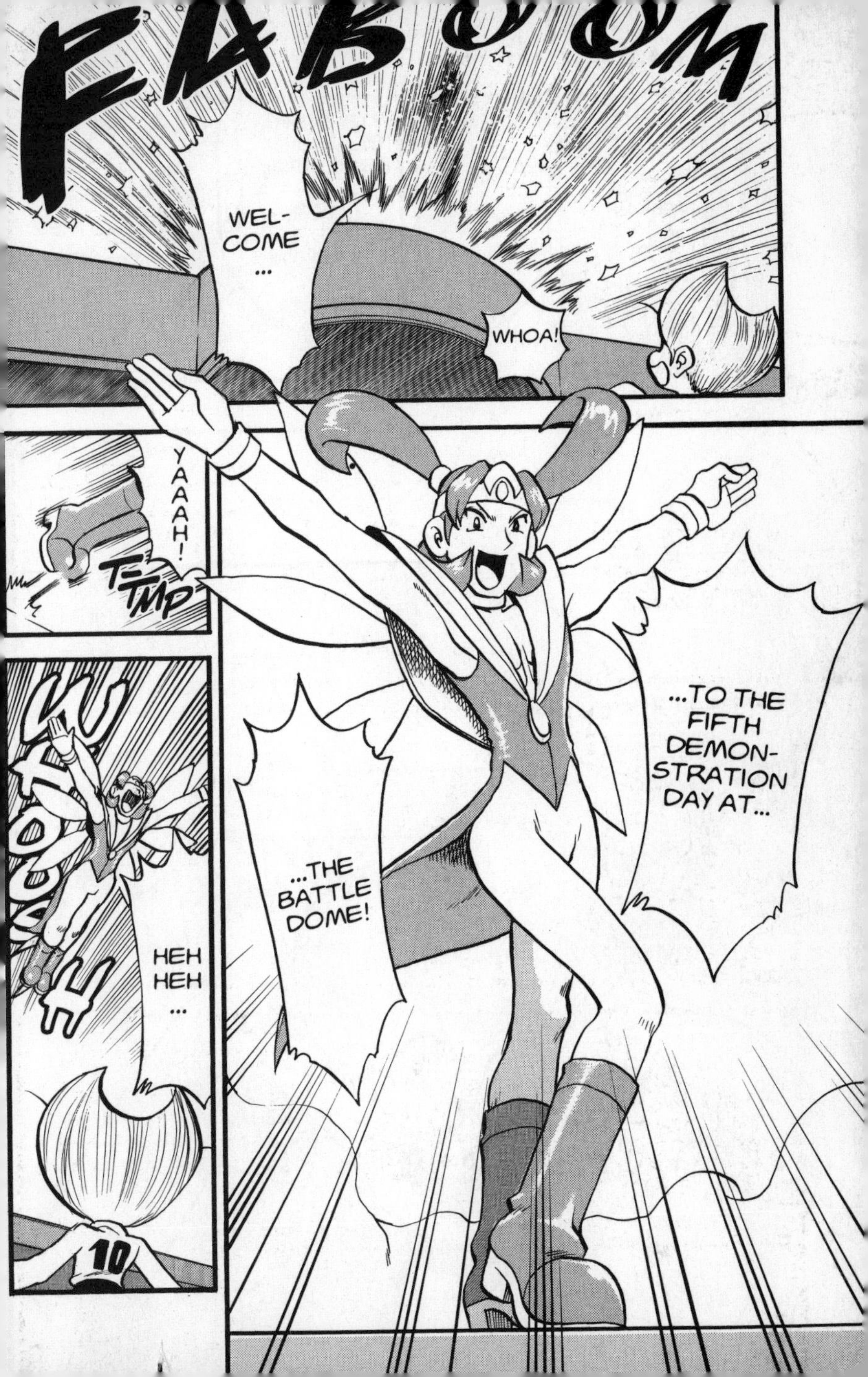
FABOOM
WEL-
COME
...
WHOA!
...TO THE FIFTH DEMON-STRATION DAY AT...
...THE BATTLE DOME!
YAAAAH!
T-TMP
WHOOSH
HEH HEH
...
10

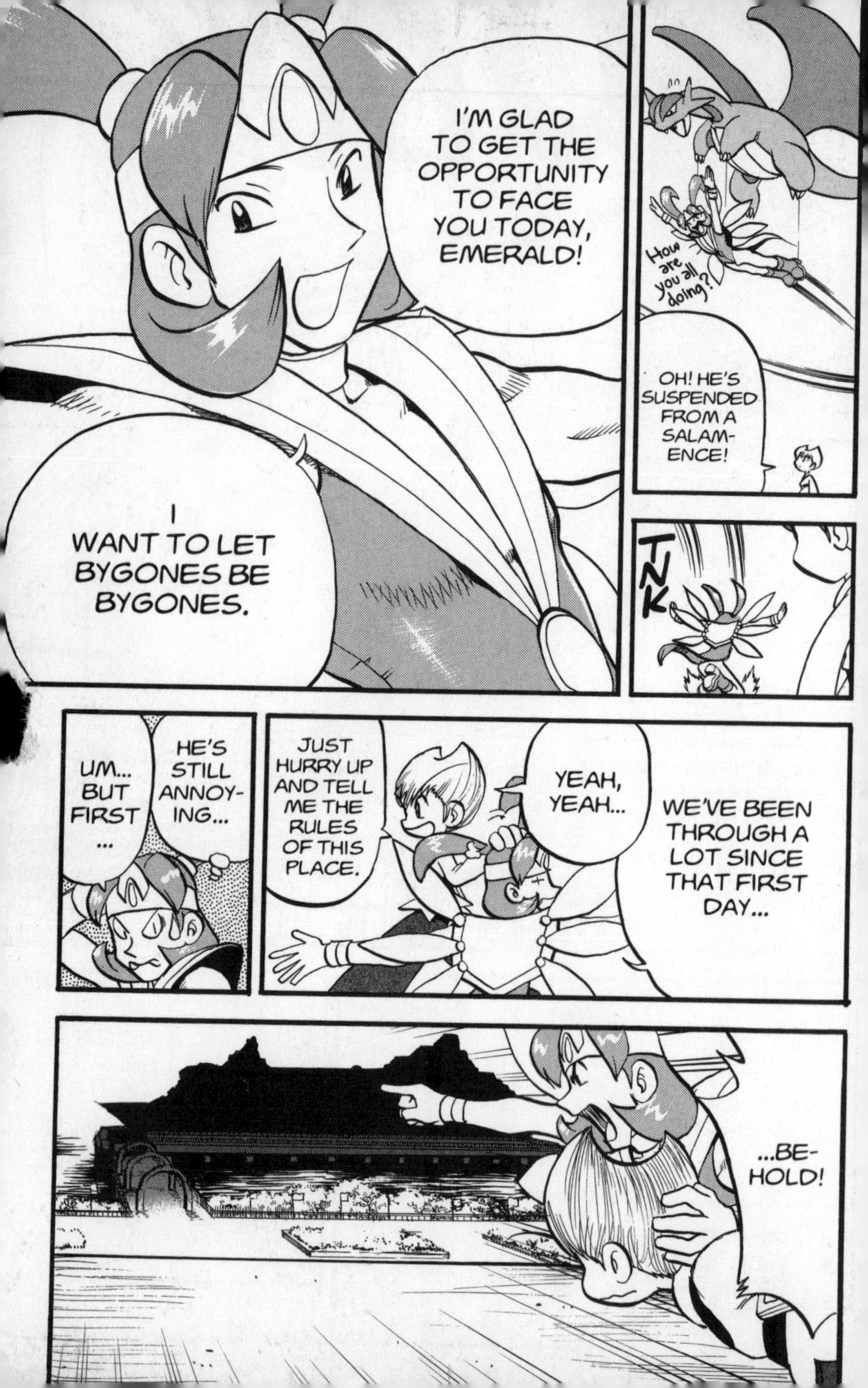
How are you all doing?
OH! HE'S SUSPENDED FROM A SALAM-ENCE!
TNK
I'M GLAD TO GET THE OPPORTUNITY TO FACE YOU TODAY, EMERALD!
I WANT TO LET BYGONES BE BYGONES.
WE'VE BEEN THROUGH A LOT SINCE THAT FIRST DAY...
YEAH, YEAH...
JUST HURRY UP AND TELL ME THE RULES OF THIS PLACE.
HE'S STILL ANNOY-ING...
UM... BUT FIRST ...
...BE-HOLD!

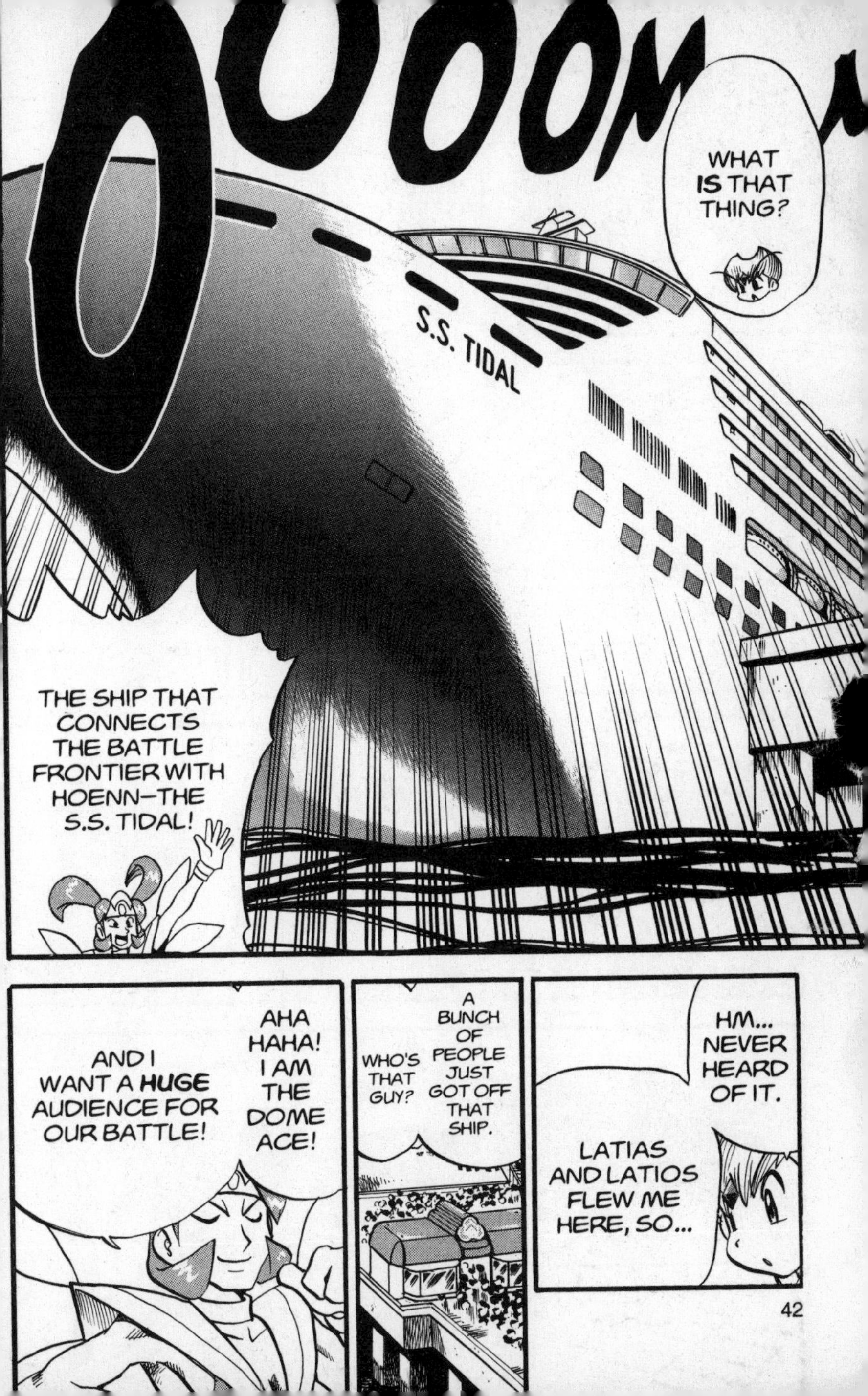
OOOOM
WHAT IS THAT THING?
S.S. TIDAL
THE SHIP THAT CONNECTS THE BATTLE FRONTIER WITH HOENN—THE S.S. TIDAL!
HM... NEVER HEARD OF IT.
LATIAS AND LATIOS FLEW ME HERE, SO...
A BUNCH OF PEOPLE JUST GOT OFF THAT SHIP.
WHO'S THAT GUY?
AHA HAHA! I AM THE DOME ACE!
AND I WANT A HUGE AUDIENCE FOR OUR BATTLE!

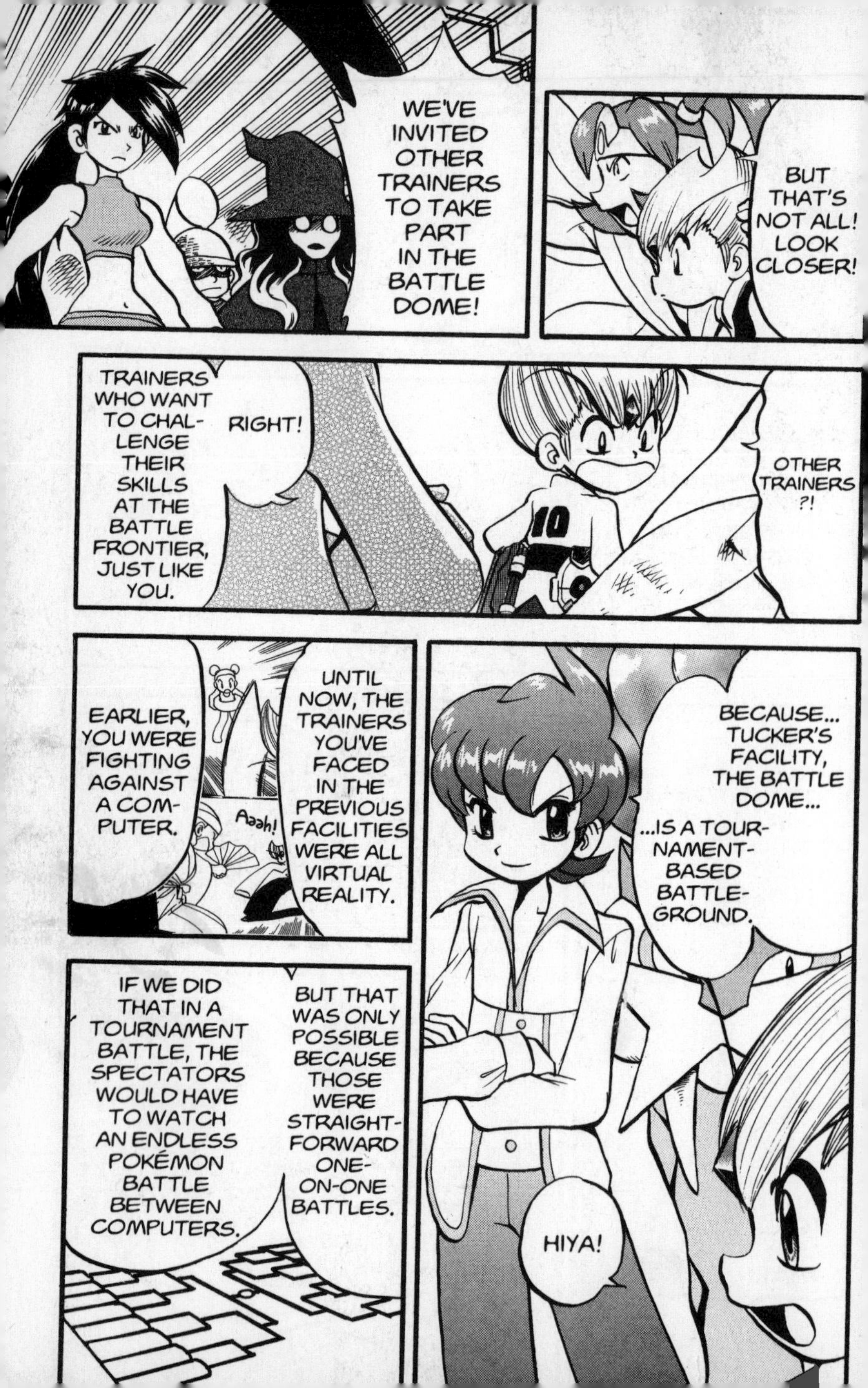
BUT THAT'S NOT ALL! LOOK CLOSER!
WE'VE INVITED OTHER TRAINERS TO TAKE PART IN THE BATTLE DOME!
OTHER TRAINERS?!
RIGHT!
TRAINERS WHO WANT TO CHAL-LENGE THEIR SKILLS AT THE BATTLE FRONTIER, JUST LIKE YOU.
BECAUSE... TUCKER'S FACILITY, THE BATTLE DOME...
...IS A TOUR-NAMENT-BASED BATTLE-GROUND.
HIYA!
UNTIL NOW, THE TRAINERS YOU'VE FACED IN THE PREVIOUS FACILITIES WERE ALL VIRTUAL REALITY.
Aaah!
EARLIER, YOU WERE FIGHTING AGAINST A COM-PUTER.
BUT THAT WAS ONLY POSSIBLE BECAUSE THOSE WERE STRAIGHT-FORWARD ONE-ON-ONE BATTLES.
IF WE DID THAT IN A TOURNAMENT BATTLE, THE SPECTATORS WOULD HAVE TO WATCH AN ENDLESS POKÉMON BATTLE BETWEEN COMPUTERS.

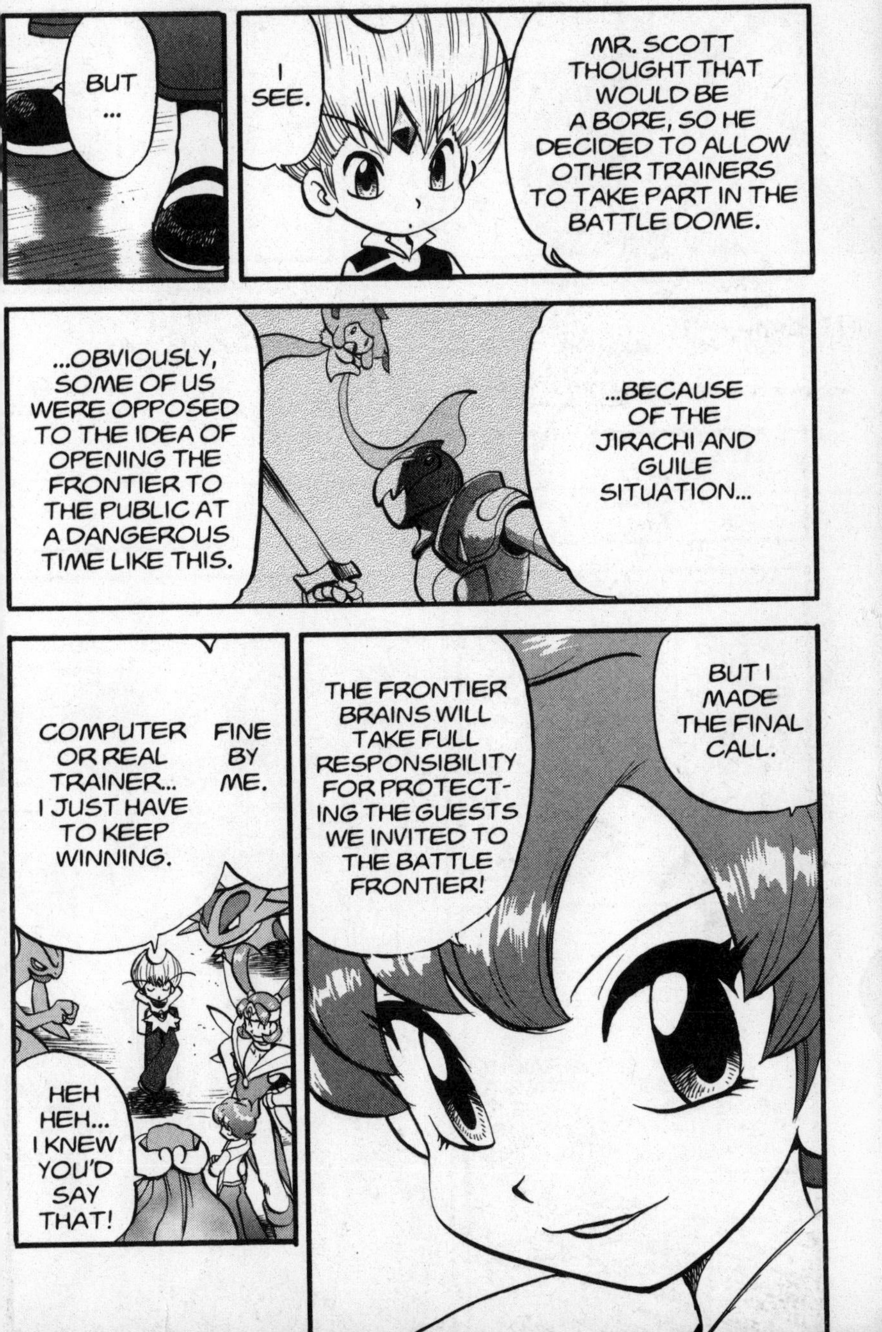
MR. SCOTT THOUGHT THAT WOULD BE A BORE, SO HE DECIDED TO ALLOW OTHER TRAINERS TO TAKE PART IN THE BATTLE DOME.
I SEE.
BUT ...
...BECAUSE OF THE JIRACHI AND GUILE SITUATION...
...OBVIOUSLY, SOME OF US WERE OPPOSED TO THE IDEA OF OPENING THE FRONTIER TO THE PUBLIC AT A DANGEROUS TIME LIKE THIS.
BUT I MADE THE FINAL CALL.
THE FRONTIER BRAINS WILL TAKE FULL RESPONSIBILITY FOR PROTECTING THE GUESTS WE INVITED TO THE BATTLE FRONTIER!
FINE BY ME.
COMPUTER OR REAL TRAINER... I JUST HAVE TO KEEP WINNING.
HEH HEH... I KNEW YOU'D SAY THAT!

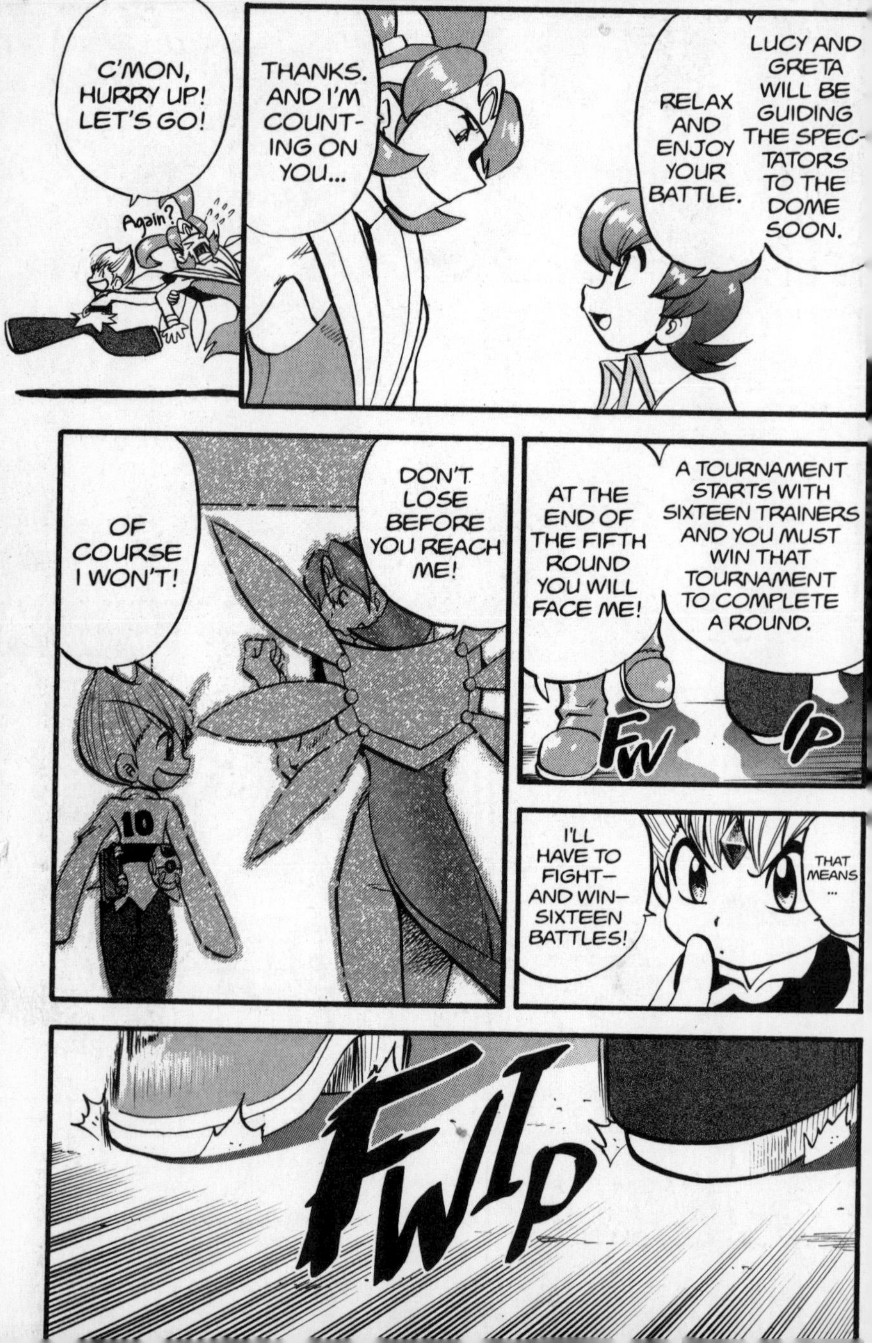
LUCY AND GRETA WILL BE GUIDING THE SPECTATORS TO THE DOME SOON.
RELAX AND ENJOY YOUR BATTLE.
THANKS. AND I'M COUNTING ON YOU...
C'MON, HURRY UP! LET'S GO!
Again?
A TOURNAMENT STARTS WITH SIXTEEN TRAINERS AND YOU MUST WIN THAT TOURNAMENT TO COMPLETE A ROUND.
AT THE END OF THE FIFTH ROUND YOU WILL FACE ME!
FWIP
THAT MEANS...
I'LL HAVE TO FIGHT—AND WIN—SIXTEEN BATTLES!
DON'T LOSE BEFORE YOU REACH ME!
OF COURSE I WON'T!
FWIP

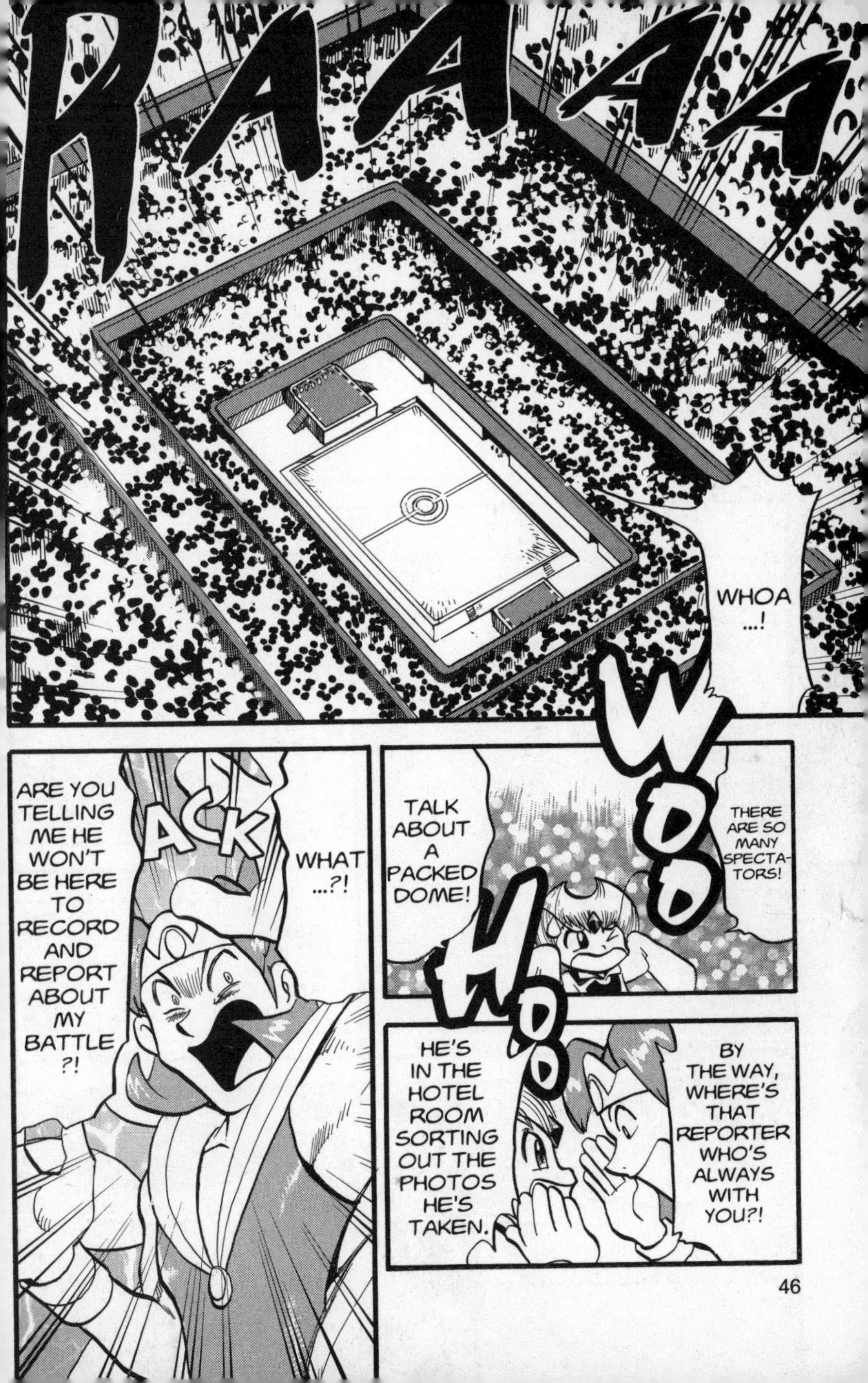
RAAAAA
WHOA ...!
WOOHOO
THERE ARE SO MANY SPECTATORS!
TALK ABOUT A PACKED DOME!
BY THE WAY, WHERE'S THAT REPORTER WHO'S ALWAYS WITH YOU?!
HE'S IN THE HOTEL ROOM SORTING OUT THE PHOTOS HE'S TAKEN.
WHAT ...?!
ACK
ARE YOU TELLING ME HE WON'T BE HERE TO RECORD AND REPORT ABOUT MY BATTLE ?!

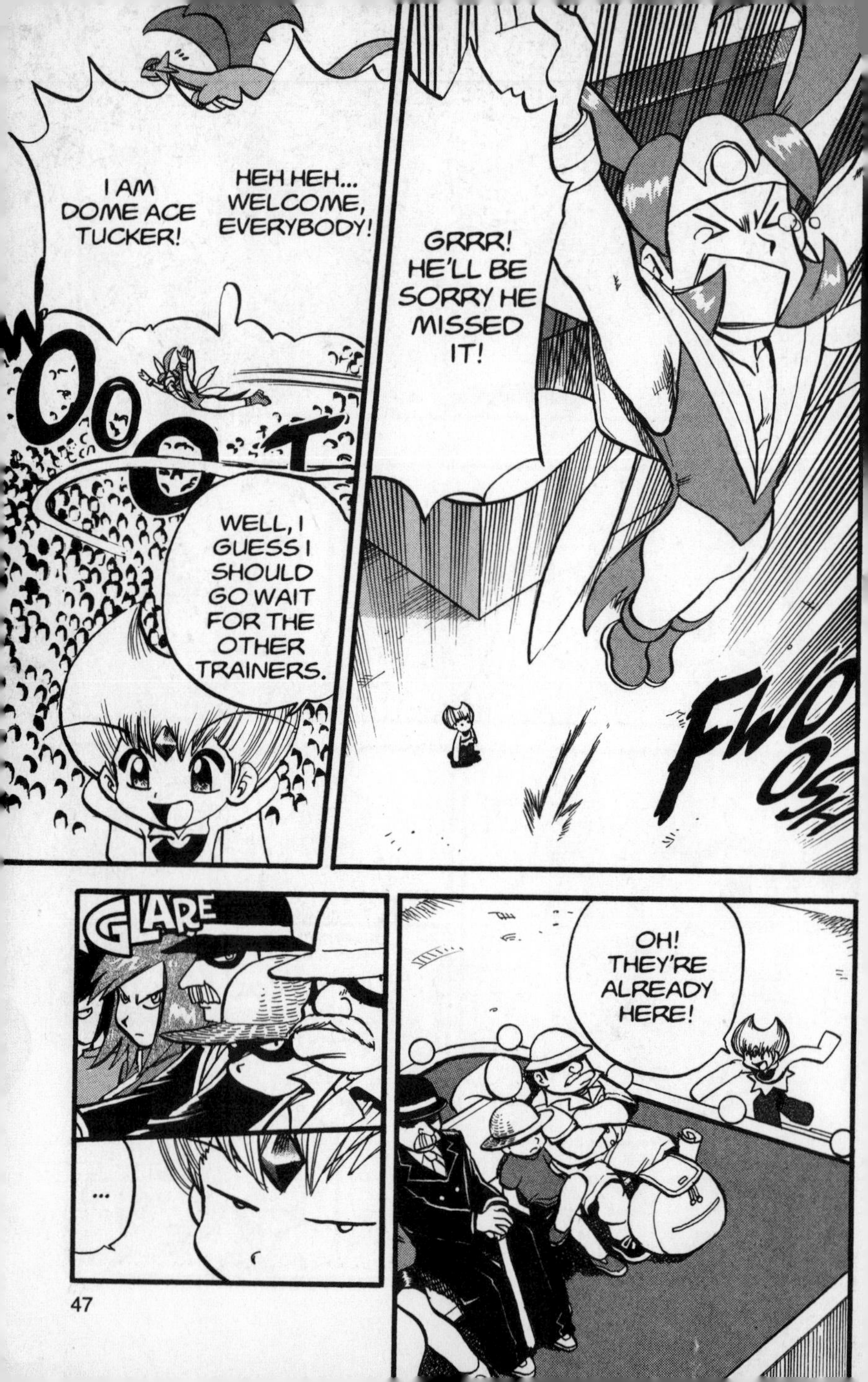
GRRR! HE'LL BE SORRY HE MISSED IT!
FWOOOSH
HEH HEH... WELCOME, EVERYBODY!
I AM DOME ACE TUCKER!
WOOOT
WELL, I GUESS I SHOULD GO WAIT FOR THE OTHER TRAINERS.
OH! THEY'RE ALREADY HERE!
GLARE
...

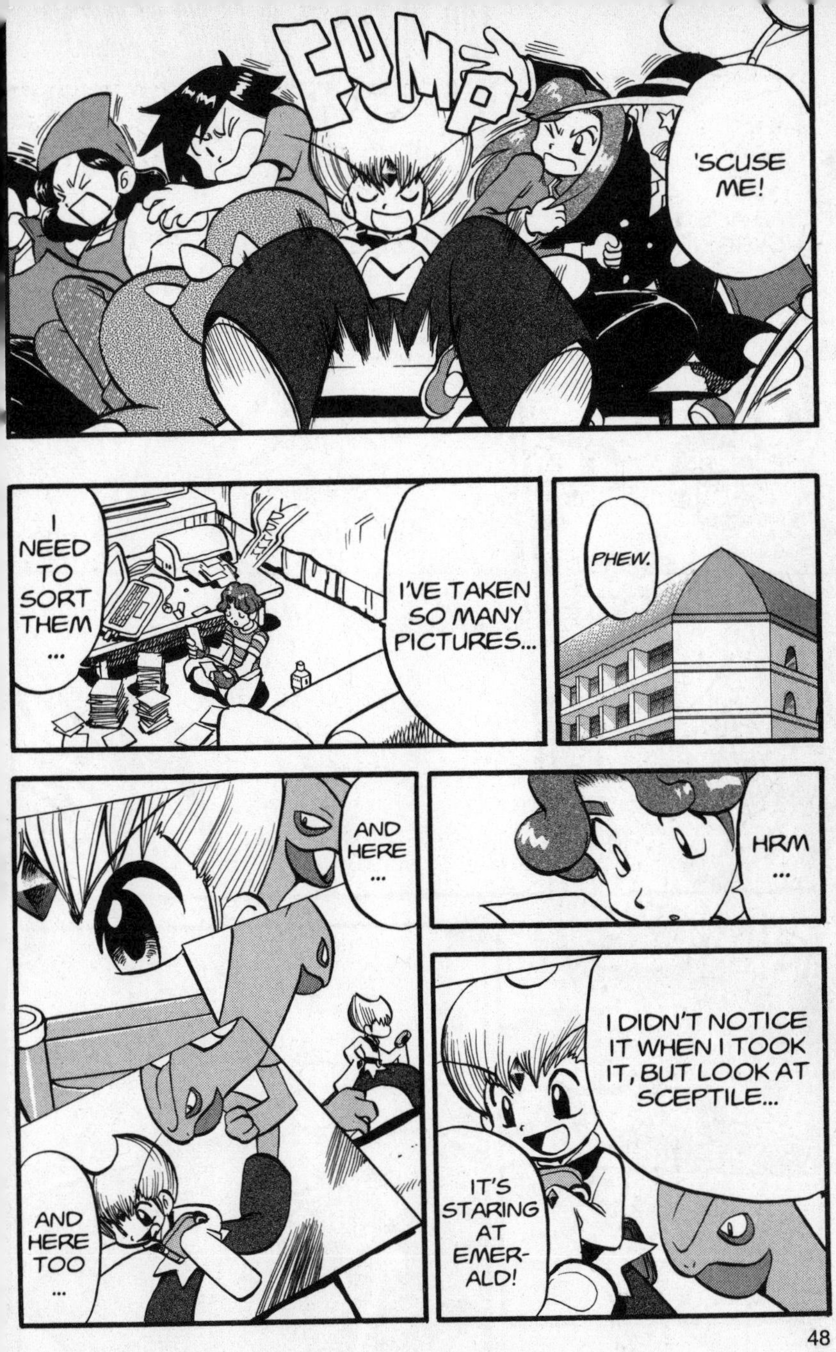
FUMP
'SCUSE ME!
PHEW.
I'VE TAKEN SO MANY PICTURES...
I NEED TO SORT THEM ...
HRM ...
I DIDN'T NOTICE IT WHEN I TOOK IT, BUT LOOK AT SCEPTILE...
IT'S STARING AT EMER-ALD!
AND HERE ...
AND HERE TOO ...

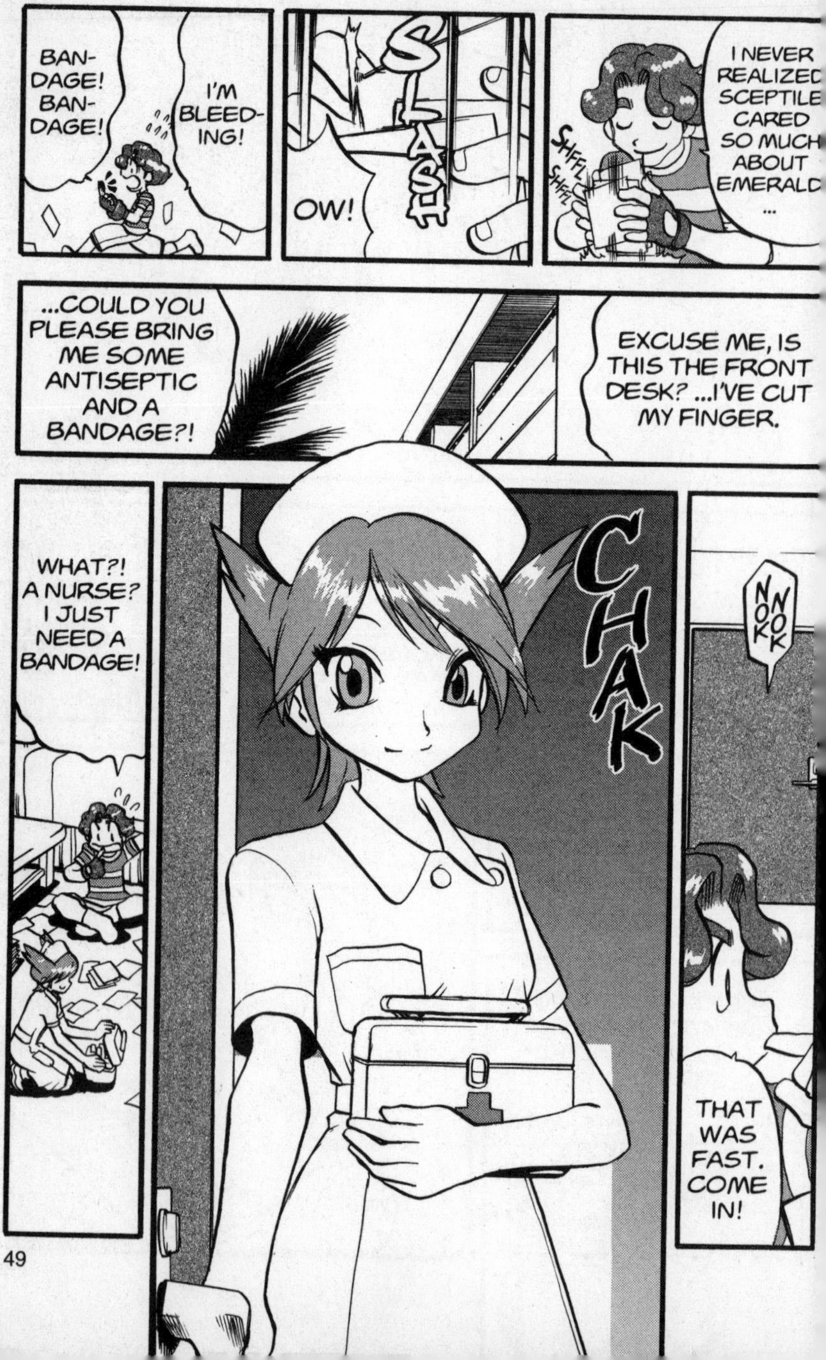
I NEVER REALIZED SCEPTILE CARED SO MUCH ABOUT EMERALD ...
SHFFL SHFFL
SLASH
OW!
I'M BLEED-ING!
BAN-DAGE! BAN-DAGE!
EXCUSE ME, IS THIS THE FRONT DESK? ...I'VE CUT MY FINGER.
...COULD YOU PLEASE BRING ME SOME ANTISEPTIC AND A BANDAGE?!
NOK NOK
THAT WAS FAST. COME IN!
CHAK
WHAT?! A NURSE? I JUST NEED A BANDAGE!

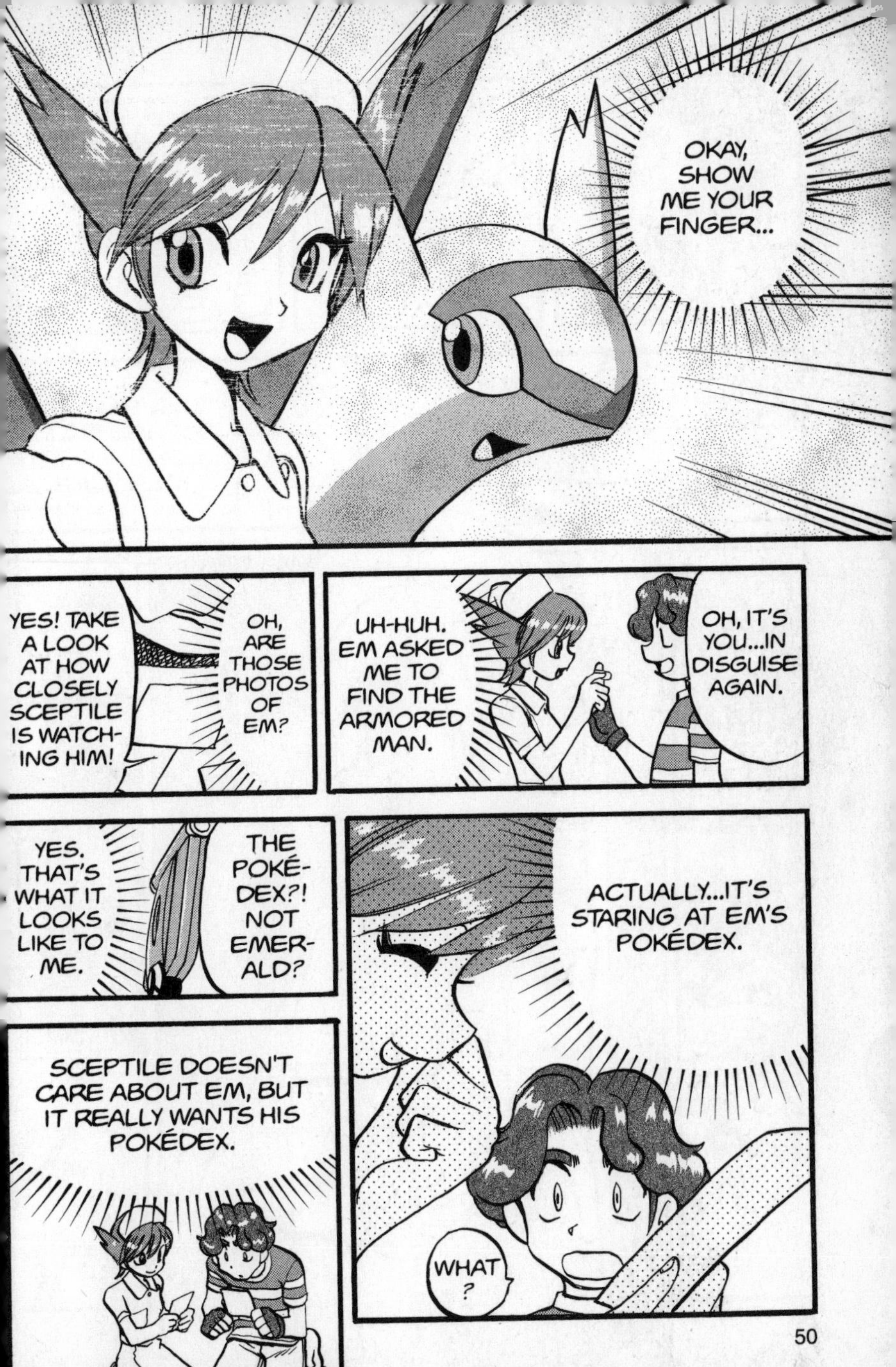
OKAY, SHOW ME YOUR FINGER...
OH, IT'S YOU...IN DISGUISE AGAIN.
UH-HUH. EM ASKED ME TO FIND THE ARMORED MAN.
OH, ARE THOSE PHOTOS OF EM?
YES! TAKE A LOOK AT HOW CLOSELY SCEPTILE IS WATCHING HIM!
ACTUALLY...IT'S STARING AT EM'S POKÉDEX.
WHAT?
THE POKÉDEX?! NOT EMERALD?
YES. THAT'S WHAT IT LOOKS LIKE TO ME.
SCEPTILE DOESN'T CARE ABOUT EM, BUT IT REALLY WANTS HIS POKÉDEX.

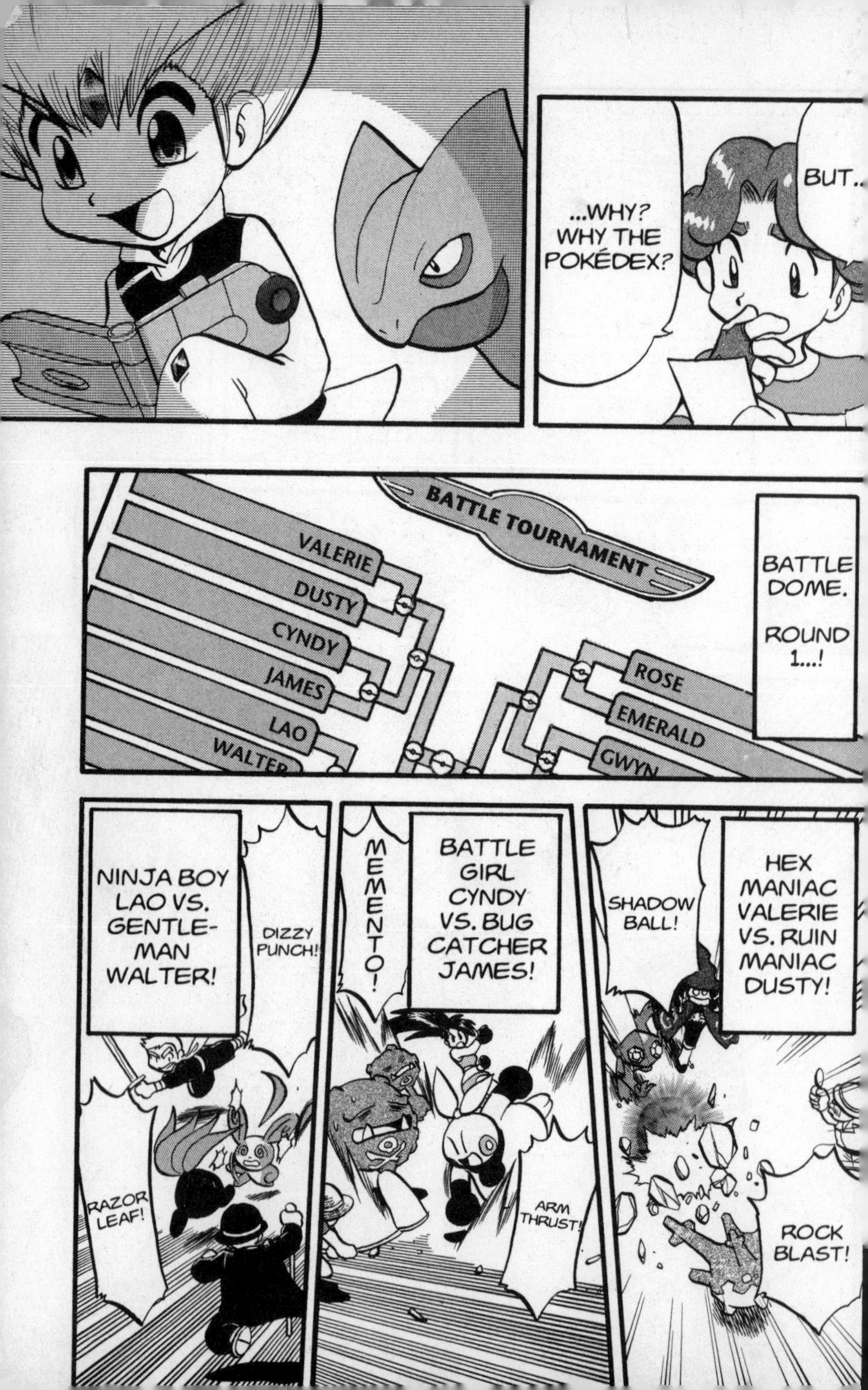
BUT...
...WHY? WHY THE POKÉDEX?
BATTLE DOME. ROUND 1...!
BATTLE TOURNAMENT
VALERIE
DUSTY
CYNDY
JAMES
LAO
WALTER
ROSE
EMERALD
HEX MANIAC VALERIE VS. RUIN MANIAC DUSTY!
SHADOW BALL!
ROCK BLAST!
BATTLE GIRL CYNDY VS. BUG CATCHER JAMES!
MEMENTO!
ARM THRUST!
DIZZY PUNCH!
NINJA BOY LAO VS. GENTLEMAN WALTER!
RAZOR LEAF!

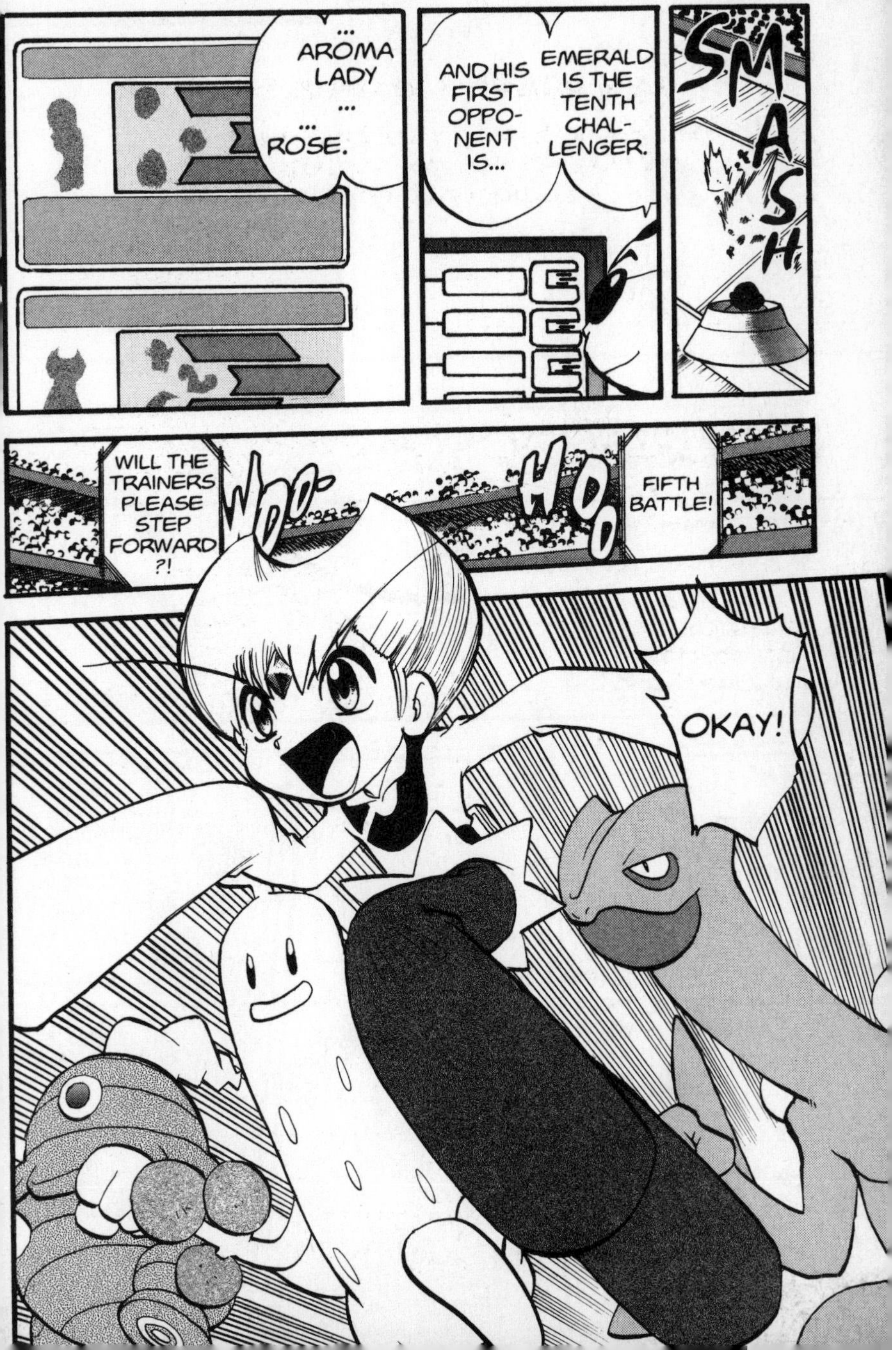
SMASH
EMERALD IS THE TENTH CHALLENGER.
AND HIS FIRST OPPONENT IS...
... AROMA LADY ... ... ROSE.
FIFTH BATTLE!
WOO-HOO
WILL THE TRAINERS PLEASE STEP FORWARD ?!
OKAY!

DEAR MEMBERS OF THE PRESS...

Thank you for visiting the Battle Frontier today. Permit me to continue explaining the rules of this facility...

OWNER: SCOTT

FACILITY RULES

BATTLE DOME 3

■ ABOUT THE TRAINER RANK ■

Trainer Rank: The first line on the Trainer card describes the rank of the opposing Trainer.

➡ Please refer to the chart on the right during the tournament.

↑ High Ranking	- The best candidate to be the champ
	- A sure-finalist team
	- A likely top-three finisher
	- A team with top-class potential
	- A candidate to finish first
	- The dark horse team this tournament
	- A better-than-average team
	- This tournament's average team
	- A team with average potential
	- A weaker-than-average team
	- A team looking for its first win
	- One win will make this team proud
	- Overall, a weak team
	- A team with very low potential
Low Ranking ↓	- A team unlikely to win the tournament
	- The team most unlikely to win

■ DOUBLE KNOCKOUT ■

In the Battle Dome, if both Trainers are knocked out, the Trainer who is ranked highest wins the battle.

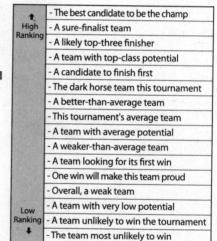

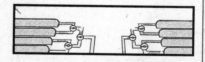

320

Verily Vanquishing Vileplume II

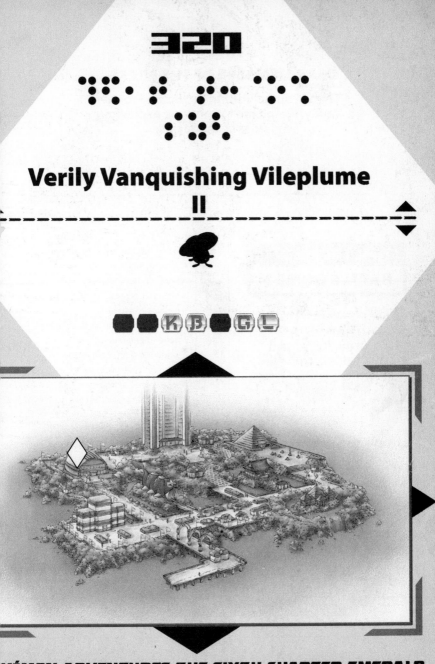

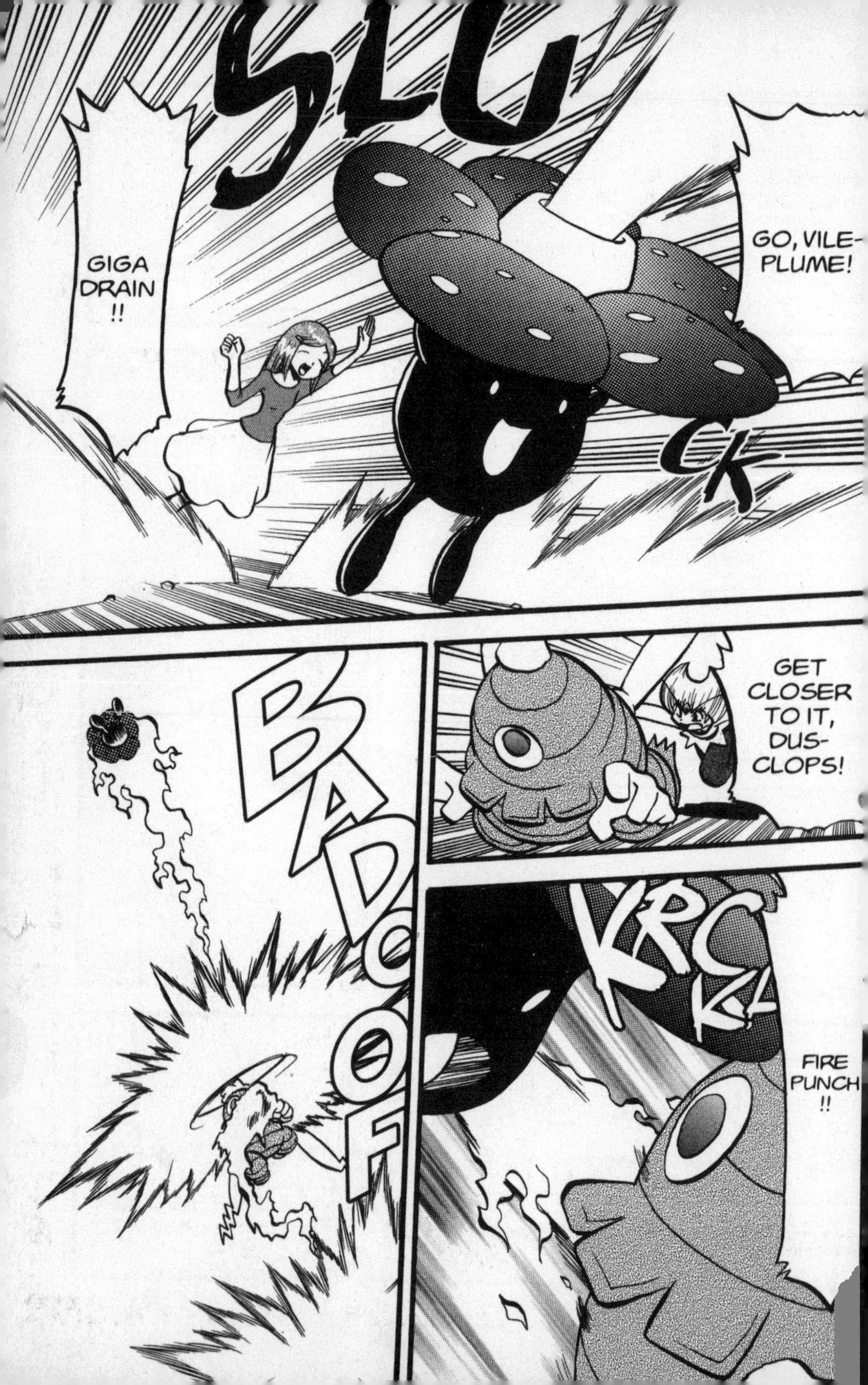
GO, VILE-PLUME!
SLU
CK
GIGA DRAIN !!
GET CLOSER TO IT, DUS-CLOPS!
KRC
KL
FIRE PUNCH !!
BADOOOF

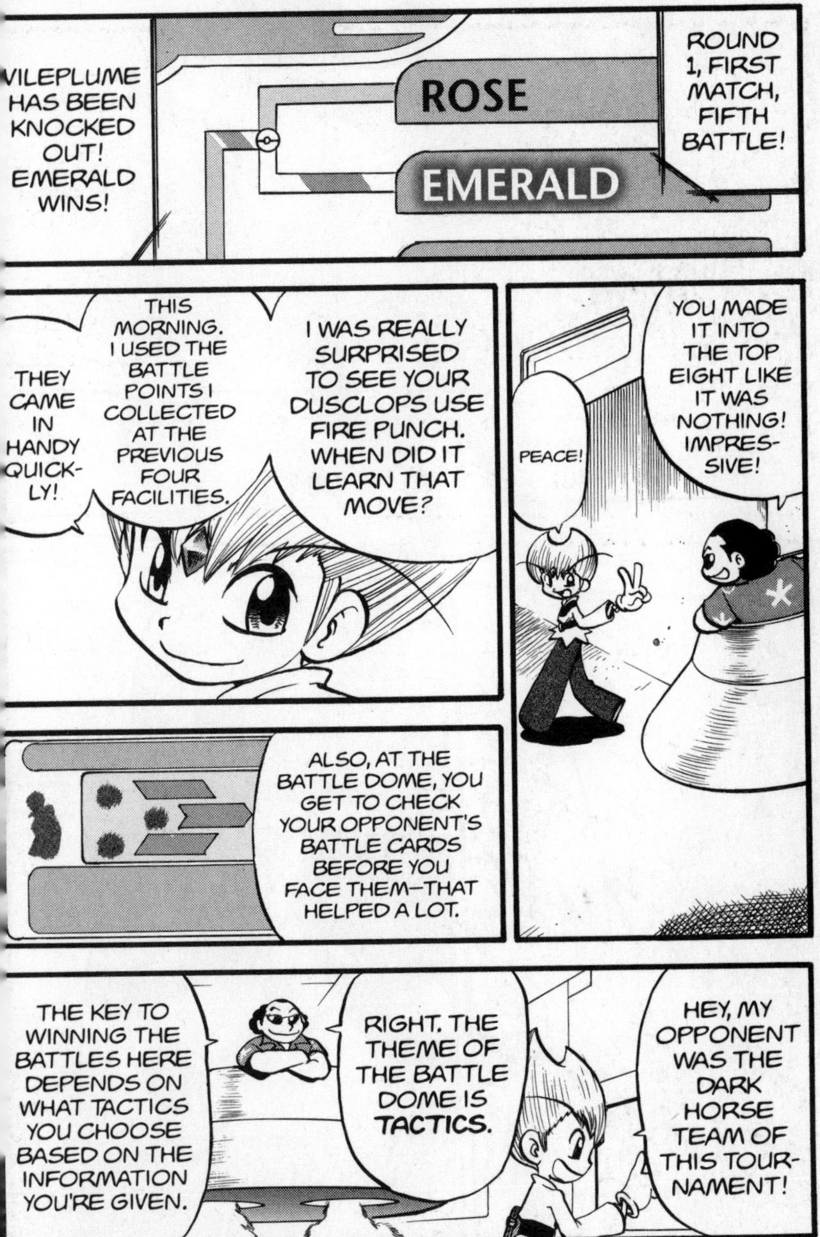
ROUND 1, FIRST MATCH, FIFTH BATTLE!
ROSE
EMERALD
VILEPLUME HAS BEEN KNOCKED OUT! EMERALD WINS!
YOU MADE IT INTO THE TOP EIGHT LIKE IT WAS NOTHING! IMPRES-SIVE!
PEACE!
I WAS REALLY SURPRISED TO SEE YOUR DUSCLOPS USE FIRE PUNCH. WHEN DID IT LEARN THAT MOVE?
THIS MORNING. I USED THE BATTLE POINTS I COLLECTED AT THE PREVIOUS FOUR FACILITIES.
THEY CAME IN HANDY QUICK-LY!
ALSO, AT THE BATTLE DOME, YOU GET TO CHECK YOUR OPPONENT'S BATTLE CARDS BEFORE YOU FACE THEM—THAT HELPED A LOT.
HEY, MY OPPONENT WAS THE DARK HORSE TEAM OF THIS TOUR-NAMENT!
RIGHT. THE THEME OF THE BATTLE DOME IS **TACTICS.**
THE KEY TO WINNING THE BATTLES HERE DEPENDS ON WHAT TACTICS YOU CHOOSE BASED ON THE INFORMATION YOU'RE GIVEN.

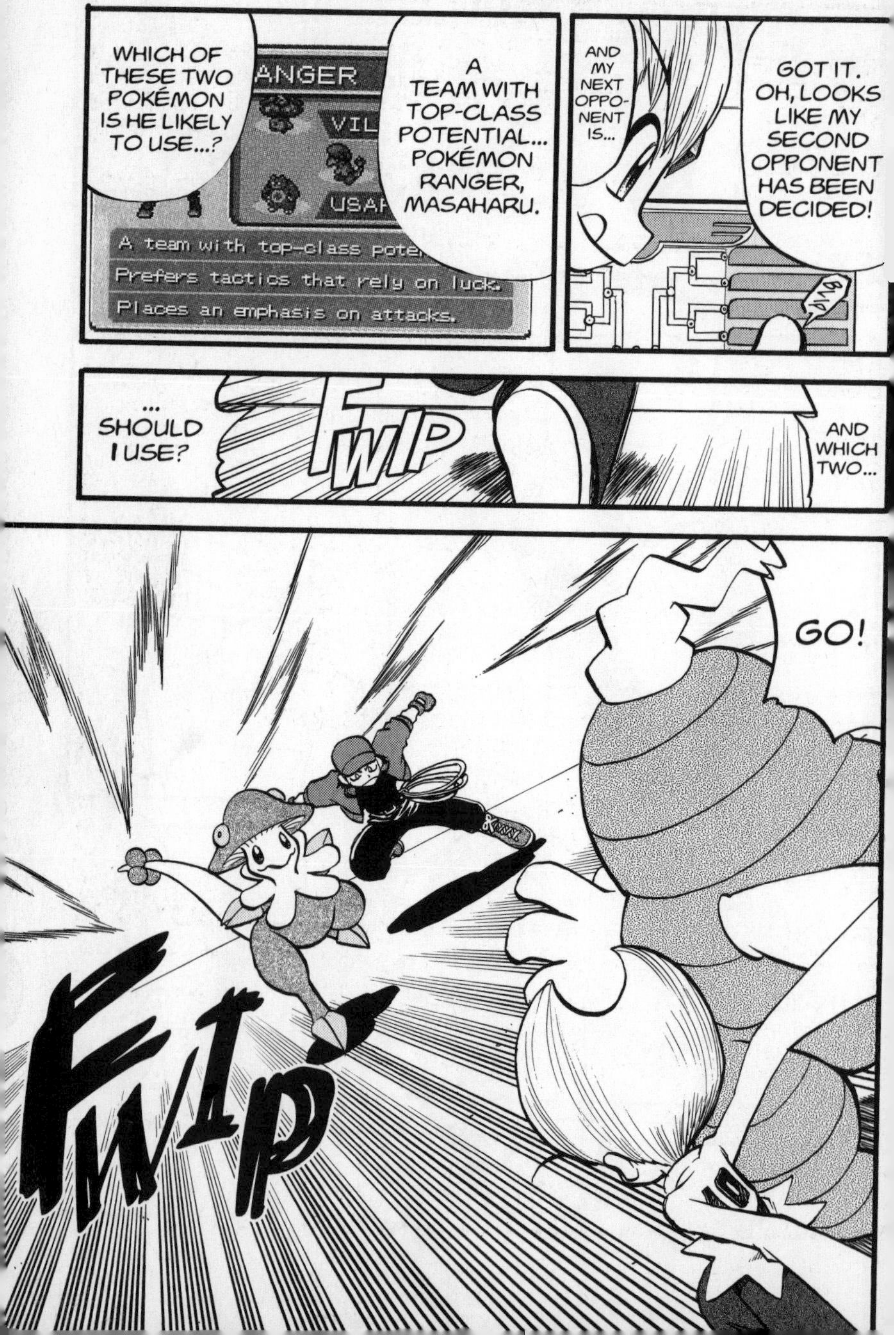
GOT IT. OH, LOOKS LIKE MY SECOND OPPONENT HAS BEEN DECIDED!
AND MY NEXT OPPO-NENT IS...
A TEAM WITH TOP-CLASS POTENTIAL... POKÉMON RANGER, MASAHARU.
WHICH OF THESE TWO POKÉMON IS HE LIKELY TO USE...?
ANGER
VIL
USA
A team with top-class poten
Prefers tactics that rely on luck.
Places an emphasis on attacks.
AND WHICH TWO...
FWIP
... SHOULD I USE?
GO!
FWIP

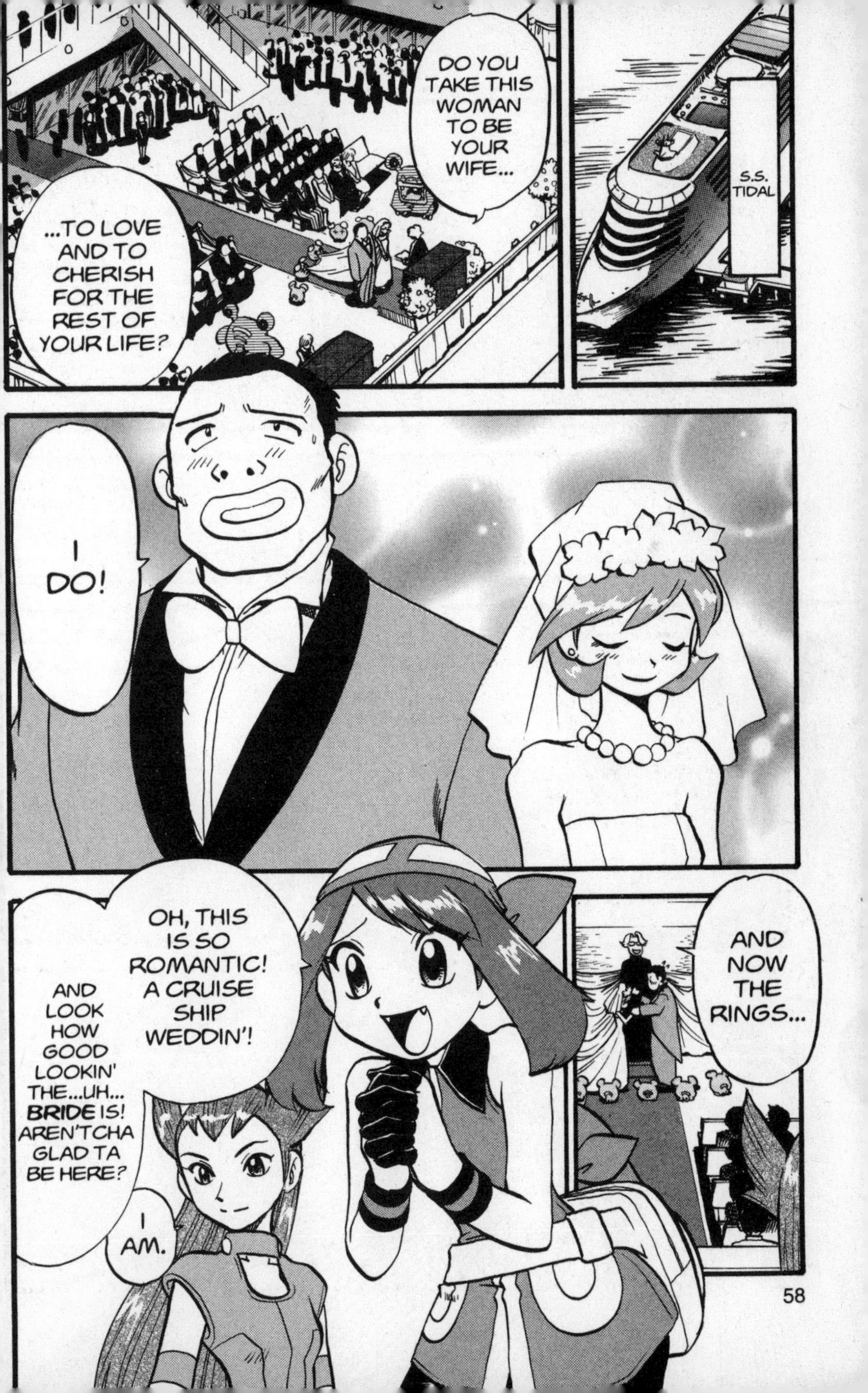
S.S. TIDAL
DO YOU TAKE THIS WOMAN TO BE YOUR WIFE...
...TO LOVE AND TO CHERISH FOR THE REST OF YOUR LIFE?
I DO!
AND NOW THE RINGS...
OH, THIS IS SO ROMANTIC! A CRUISE SHIP WEDDIN'!
AND LOOK HOW GOOD LOOKIN' THE...UH... **BRIDE** IS! AREN'TCHA GLAD TA BE HERE?
I AM.

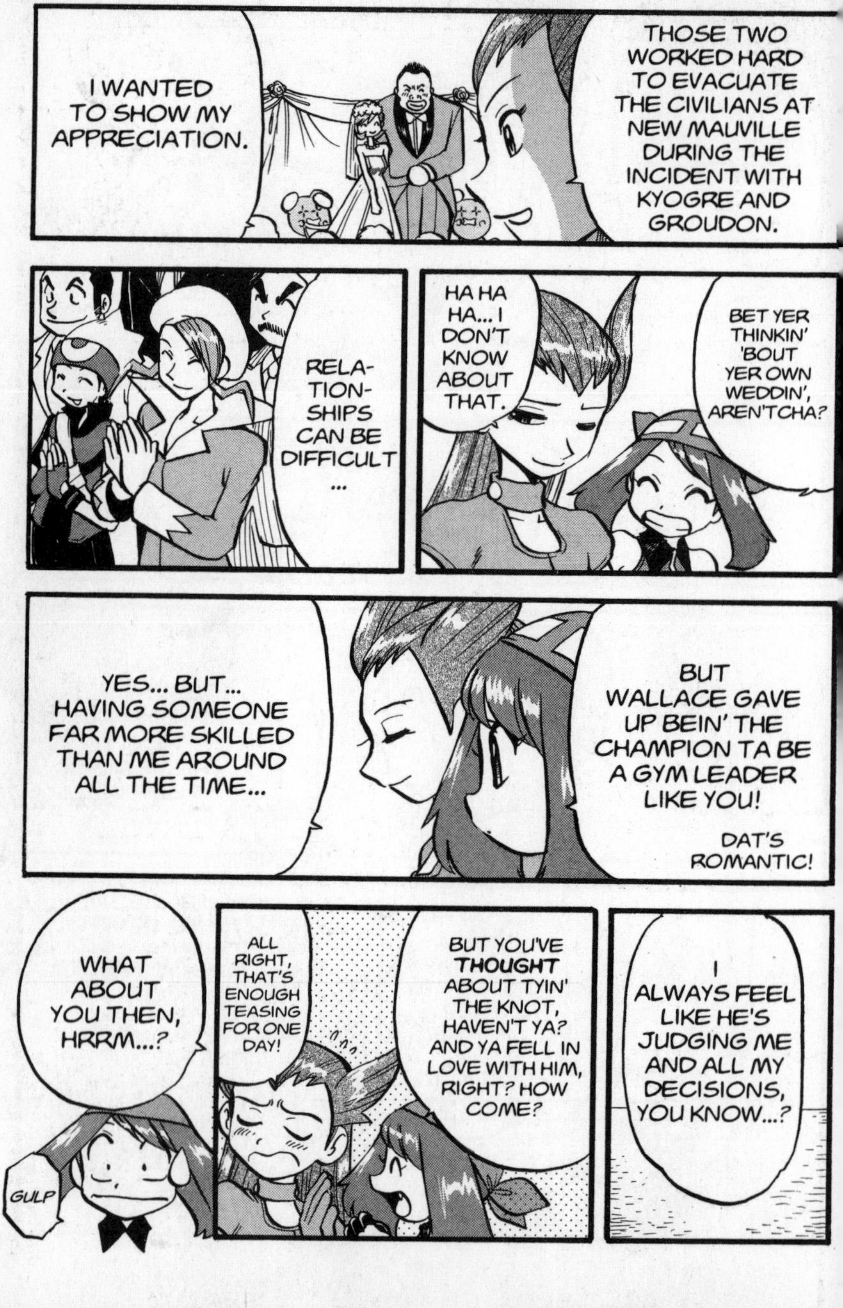
THOSE TWO WORKED HARD TO EVACUATE THE CIVILIANS AT NEW MAUVILLE DURING THE INCIDENT WITH KYOGRE AND GROUDON.
I WANTED TO SHOW MY APPRECIATION.
BET YER THINKIN' 'BOUT YER OWN WEDDIN', AREN'TCHA?
HA HA HA... I DON'T KNOW ABOUT THAT.
RELA-TION-SHIPS CAN BE DIFFICULT ...
BUT WALLACE GAVE UP BEIN' THE CHAMPION TA BE A GYM LEADER LIKE YOU!
DAT'S ROMANTIC!
YES... BUT... HAVING SOMEONE FAR MORE SKILLED THAN ME AROUND ALL THE TIME...
I ALWAYS FEEL LIKE HE'S JUDGING ME AND ALL MY DECISIONS, YOU KNOW...?
BUT YOU'VE THOUGHT ABOUT TYIN' THE KNOT, HAVEN'T YA? AND YA FELL IN LOVE WITH HIM, RIGHT? HOW COME?
ALL RIGHT, THAT'S ENOUGH TEASING FOR ONE DAY!
WHAT ABOUT YOU THEN, HRRM...?
GULP

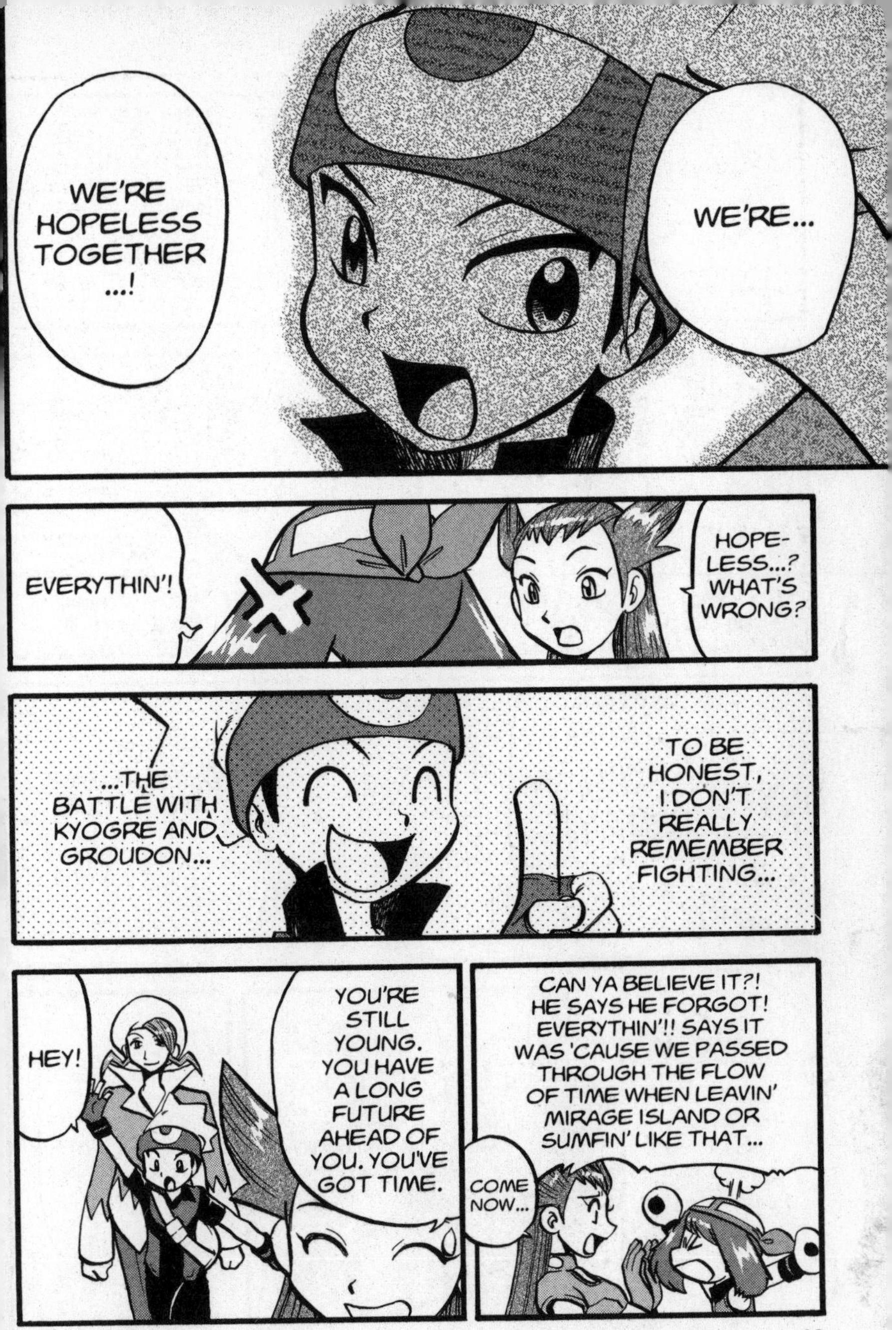
WE'RE...
WE'RE HOPELESS TOGETHER ...!
HOPE-LESS...? WHAT'S WRONG?
EVERYTHIN'!
TO BE HONEST, I DON'T REALLY REMEMBER FIGHTING...
...THE BATTLE WITH KYOGRE AND GROUDON...
CAN YA BELIEVE IT?! HE SAYS HE FORGOT! EVERYTHIN'!! SAYS IT WAS 'CAUSE WE PASSED THROUGH THE FLOW OF TIME WHEN LEAVIN' MIRAGE ISLAND OR SUMFIN' LIKE THAT...
COME NOW...
YOU'RE STILL YOUNG. YOU HAVE A LONG FUTURE AHEAD OF YOU. YOU'VE GOT TIME.
HEY!

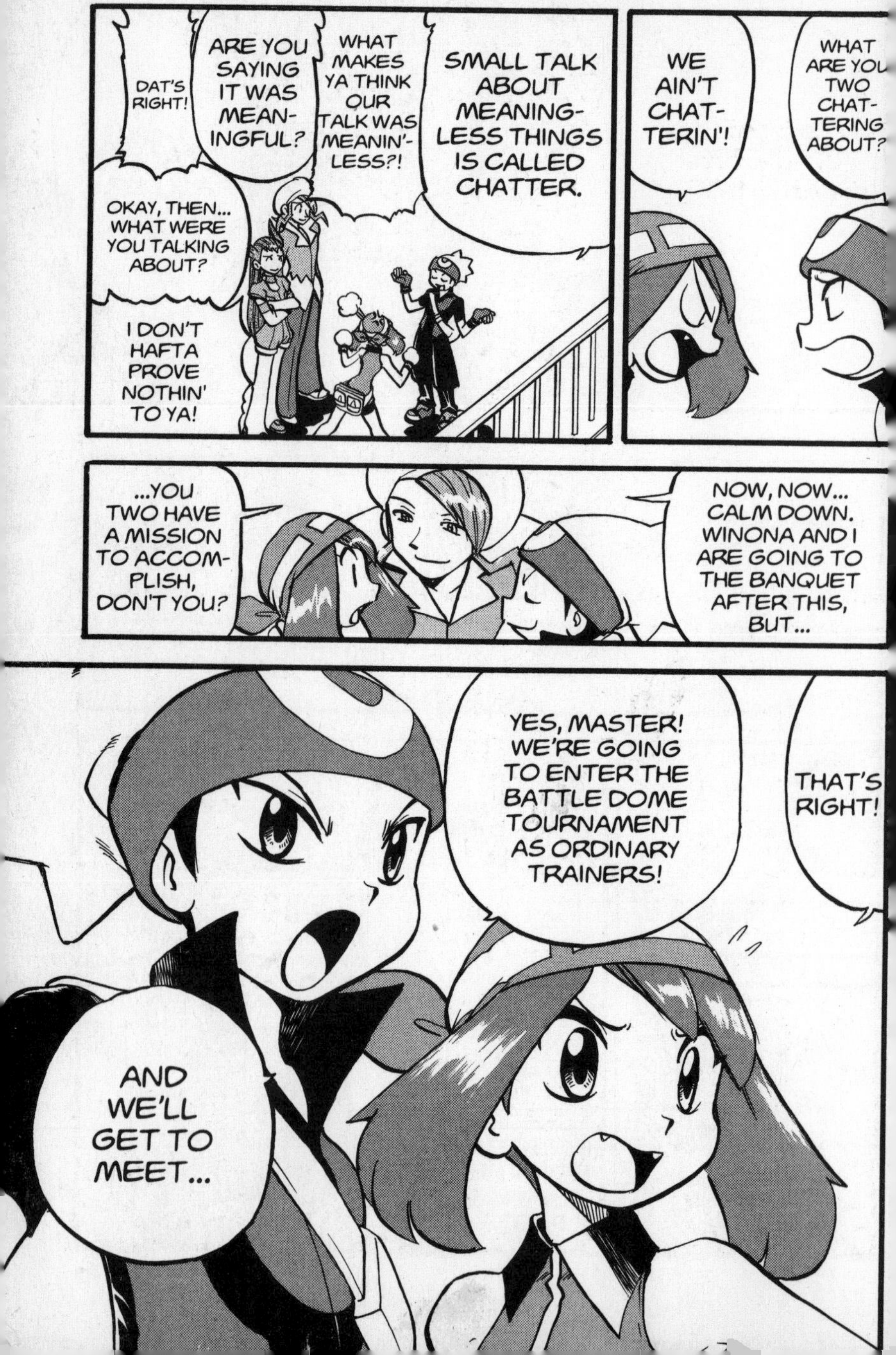
WHAT ARE YOU TWO CHATTERING ABOUT?
WE AIN'T CHATTERIN'!
SMALL TALK ABOUT MEANINGLESS THINGS IS CALLED CHATTER.
WHAT MAKES YA THINK OUR TALK WAS MEANIN'LESS?!
ARE YOU SAYING IT WAS MEANINGFUL?
DAT'S RIGHT!
OKAY, THEN... WHAT WERE YOU TALKING ABOUT?
I DON'T HAFTA PROVE NOTHIN' TO YA!
NOW, NOW... CALM DOWN. WINONA AND I ARE GOING TO THE BANQUET AFTER THIS, BUT...
...YOU TWO HAVE A MISSION TO ACCOMPLISH, DON'T YOU?
THAT'S RIGHT!
YES, MASTER! WE'RE GOING TO ENTER THE BATTLE DOME TOURNAMENT AS ORDINARY TRAINERS!
AND WE'LL GET TO MEET...

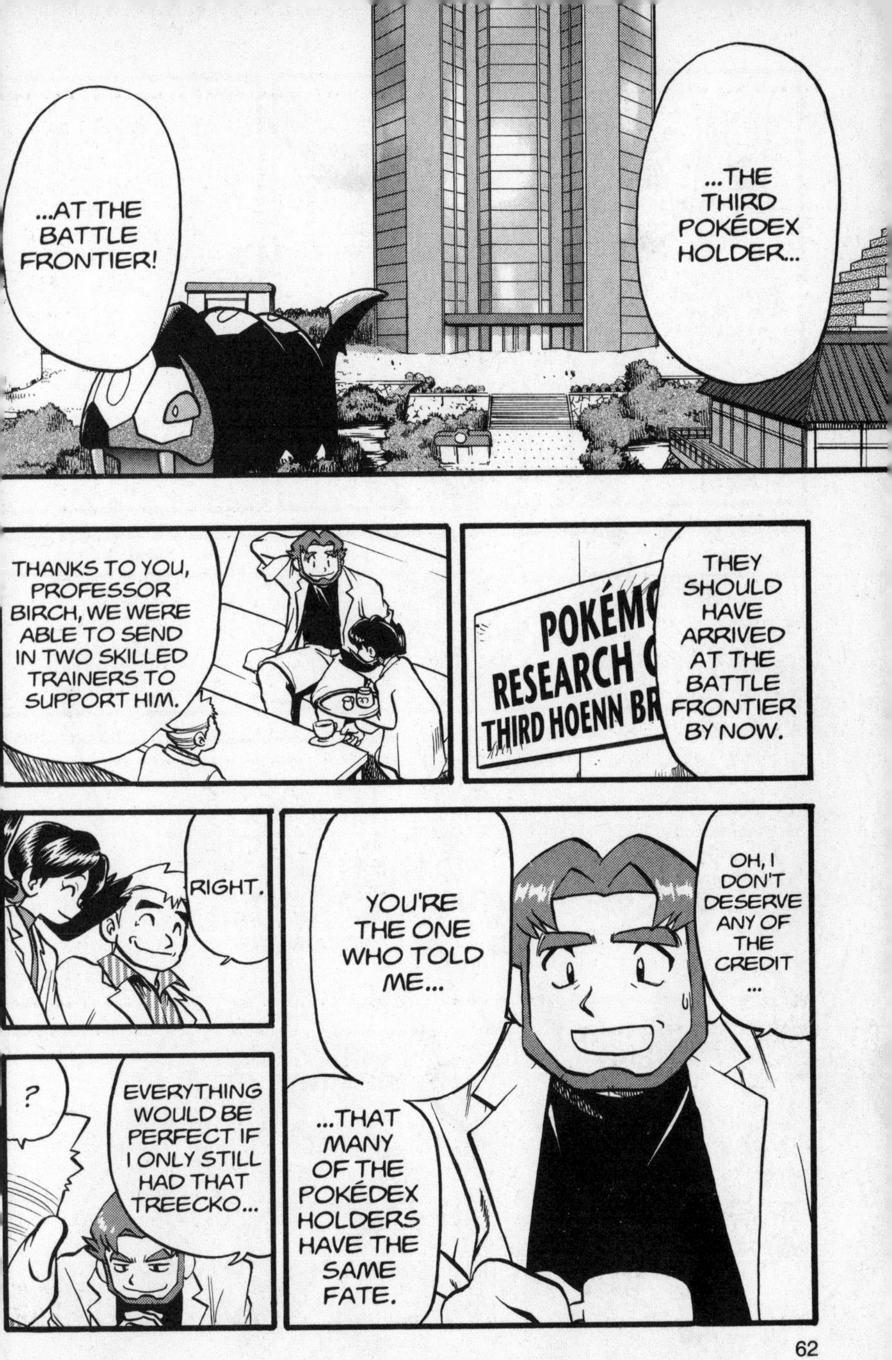
...THE THIRD POKÉDEX HOLDER...
...AT THE BATTLE FRONTIER!
POKÉMO
RESEARCH C
THIRD HOENN BR
THEY SHOULD HAVE ARRIVED AT THE BATTLE FRONTIER BY NOW.
THANKS TO YOU, PROFESSOR BIRCH, WE WERE ABLE TO SEND IN TWO SKILLED TRAINERS TO SUPPORT HIM.
OH, I DON'T DESERVE ANY OF THE CREDIT...
YOU'RE THE ONE WHO TOLD ME...
...THAT MANY OF THE POKÉDEX HOLDERS HAVE THE SAME FATE.
RIGHT.
EVERYTHING WOULD BE PERFECT IF I ONLY STILL HAD THAT TREECKO...
?

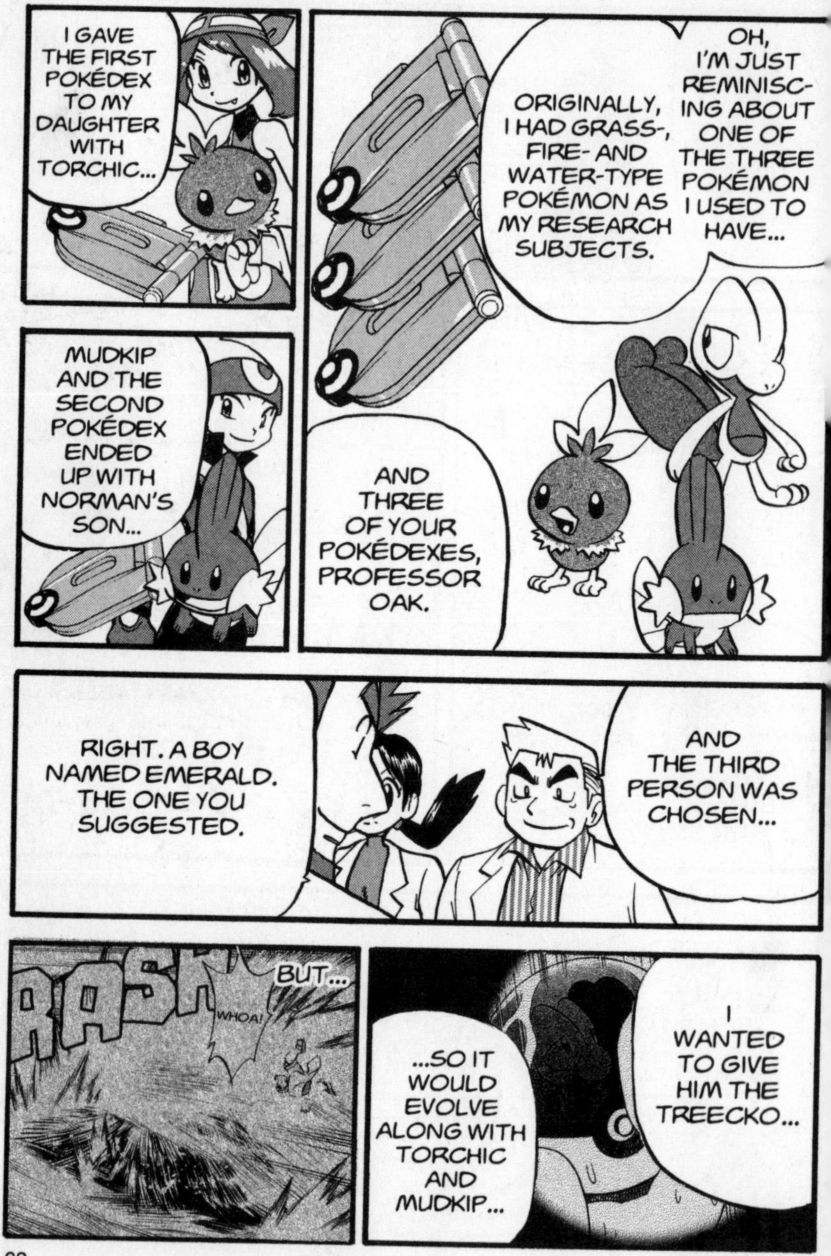
OH, I'M JUST REMINISCING ABOUT ONE OF THE THREE POKÉMON I USED TO HAVE...
ORIGINALLY, I HAD GRASS-, FIRE- AND WATER-TYPE POKÉMON AS MY RESEARCH SUBJECTS.
AND THREE OF YOUR POKÉDEXES, PROFESSOR OAK.
I GAVE THE FIRST POKÉDEX TO MY DAUGHTER WITH TORCHIC...
MUDKIP AND THE SECOND POKÉDEX ENDED UP WITH NORMAN'S SON...
AND THE THIRD PERSON WAS CHOSEN...
RIGHT. A BOY NAMED EMERALD. THE ONE YOU SUGGESTED.
I WANTED TO GIVE HIM THE TREECKO...
...SO IT WOULD EVOLVE ALONG WITH TORCHIC AND MUDKIP...
BUT...
RASH
WHOA!

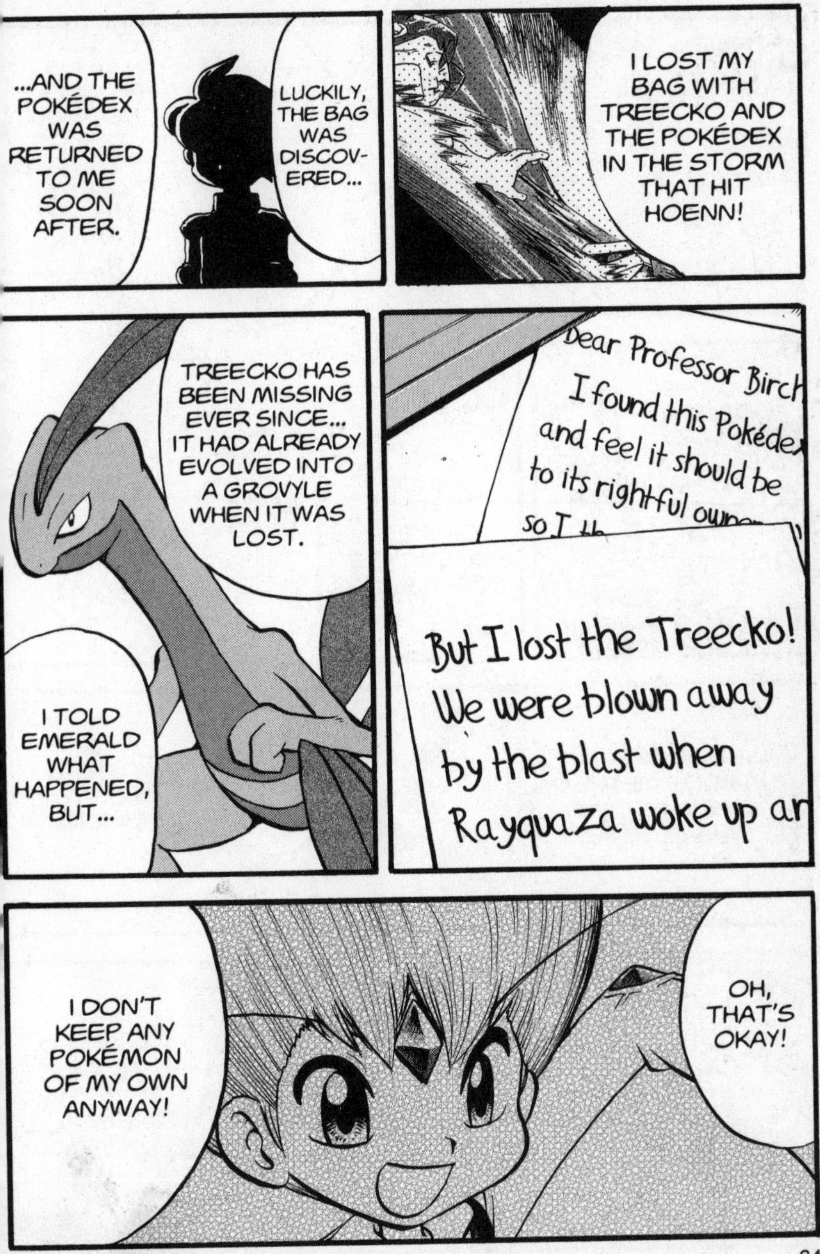
I LOST MY BAG WITH TREECKO AND THE POKÉDEX IN THE STORM THAT HIT HOENN!
LUCKILY, THE BAG WAS DISCOV-ERED...
...AND THE POKÉDEX WAS RETURNED TO ME SOON AFTER.
Dear Professor Birch
I found this Pokéde
and feel it should be
to its rightful
But I lost the Treecko!
We were blown away
by the blast when
Rayquaza woke up a
TREECKO HAS BEEN MISSING EVER SINCE... IT HAD ALREADY EVOLVED INTO A GROVYLE WHEN IT WAS LOST.
I TOLD EMERALD WHAT HAPPENED, BUT...
OH, THAT'S OKAY!
I DON'T KEEP ANY POKÉMON OF MY OWN ANYWAY!

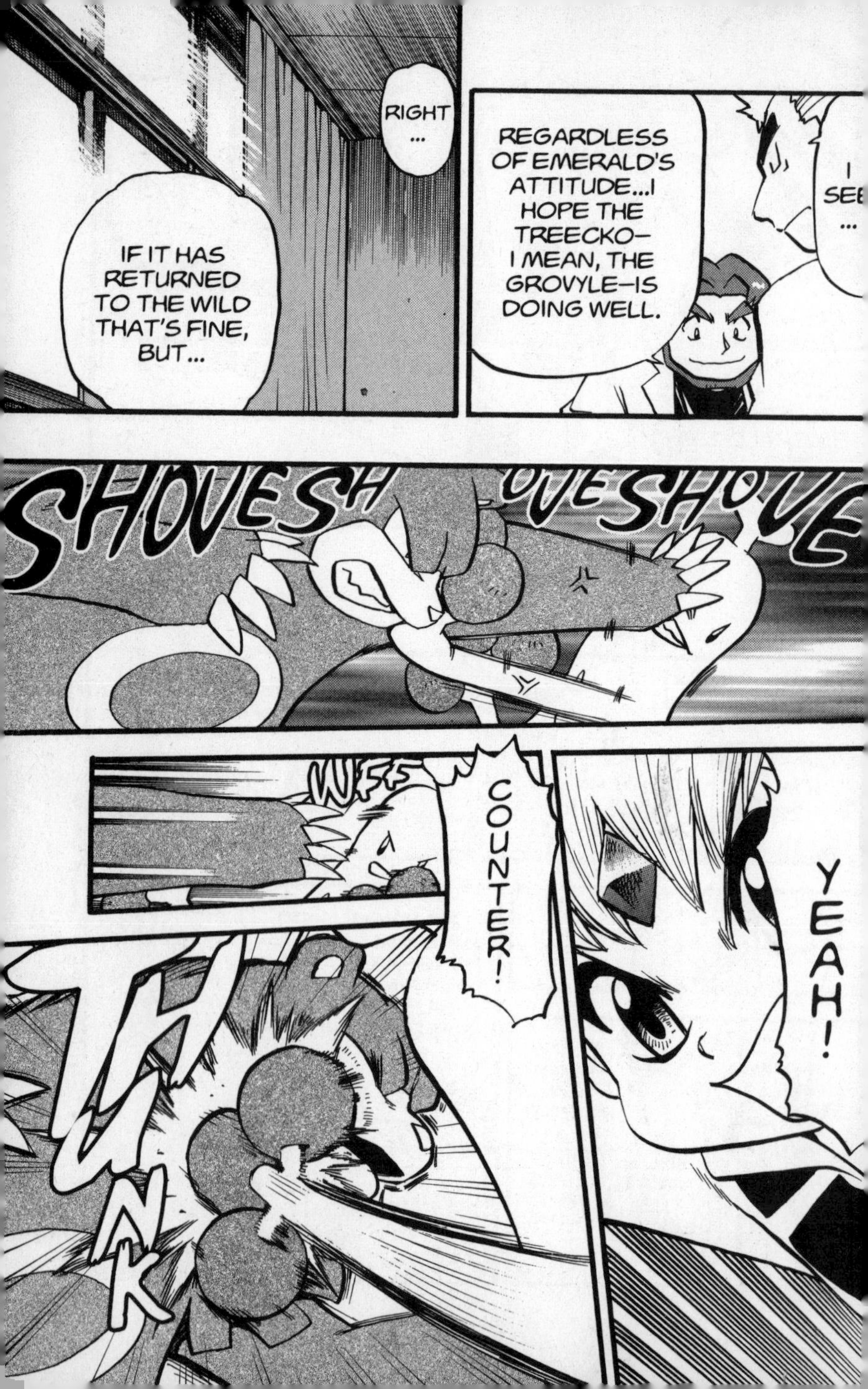
I SEE...
REGARDLESS OF EMERALD'S ATTITUDE...I HOPE THE TREECKO—I MEAN, THE GROVYLE—IS DOING WELL.
RIGHT...
IF IT HAS RETURNED TO THE WILD THAT'S FINE, BUT...
SHOVE SHOVE SHOVE SHOVE
YEAH!
COUNTER!
WFF
THUNK

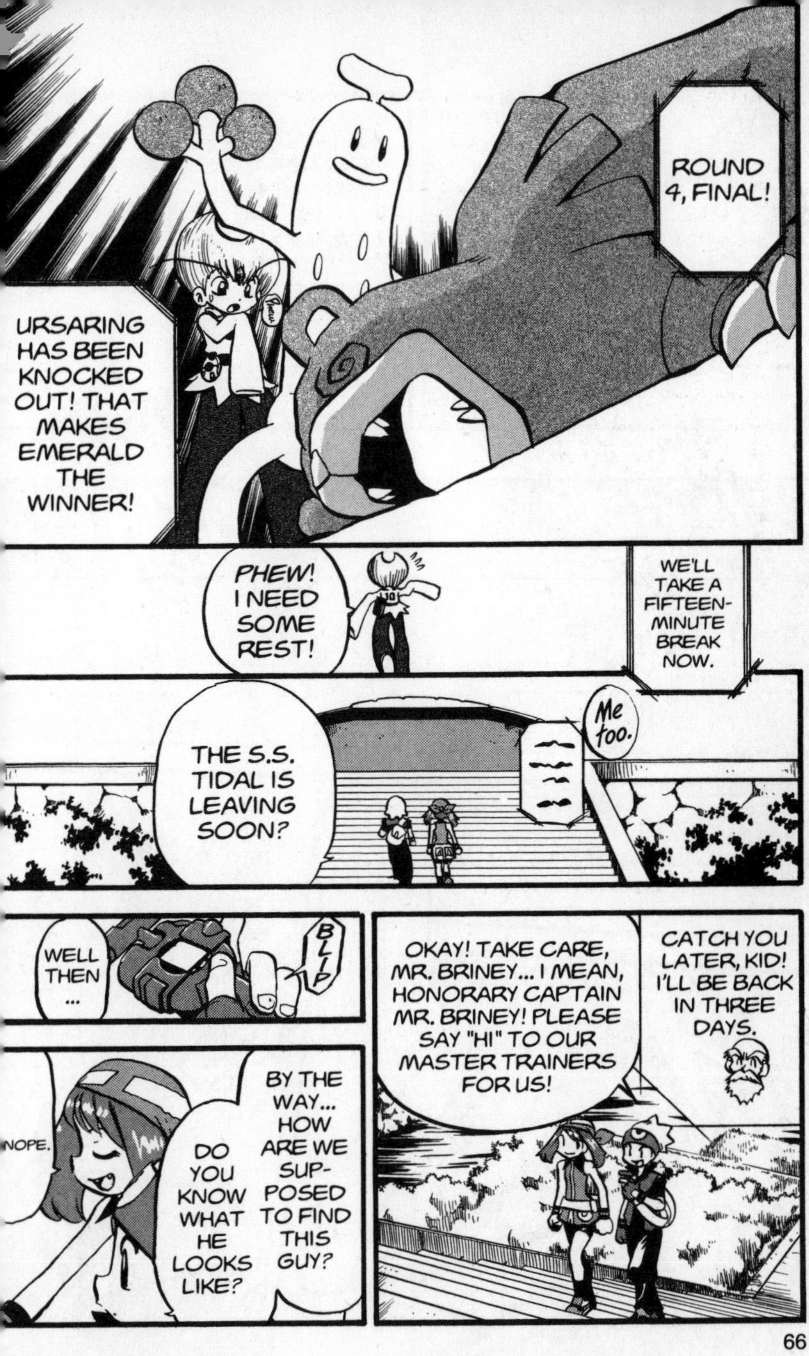
ROUND 4, FINAL!
Phew
URSARING HAS BEEN KNOCKED OUT! THAT MAKES EMERALD THE WINNER!
WE'LL TAKE A FIFTEEN-MINUTE BREAK NOW.
PHEW! I NEED SOME REST!
Me too.
THE S.S. TIDAL IS LEAVING SOON?
CATCH YOU LATER, KID! I'LL BE BACK IN THREE DAYS.
OKAY! TAKE CARE, MR. BRINEY... I MEAN, HONORARY CAPTAIN MR. BRINEY! PLEASE SAY "HI" TO OUR MASTER TRAINERS FOR US!
BLIP
WELL THEN ...
BY THE WAY... HOW ARE WE SUP-POSED TO FIND THIS GUY?
DO YOU KNOW WHAT HE LOOKS LIKE?
NOPE.

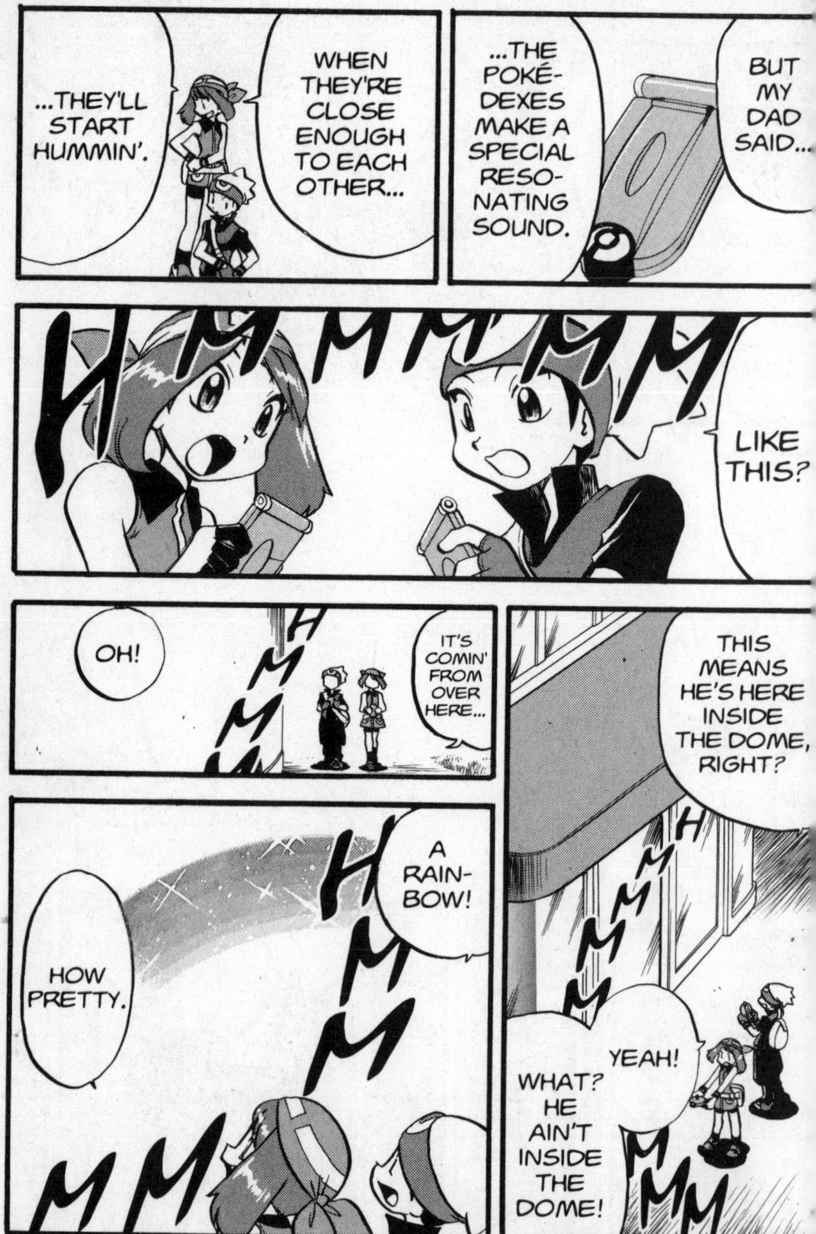
BUT MY DAD SAID...
...THE POKÉ-DEXES MAKE A SPECIAL RESO-NATING SOUND.
WHEN THEY'RE CLOSE ENOUGH TO EACH OTHER...
...THEY'LL START HUMMIN'.
LIKE THIS?
HMMMMMM
THIS MEANS HE'S HERE INSIDE THE DOME, RIGHT?
HMMMMMM
YEAH!
WHAT? HE AIN'T INSIDE THE DOME!
IT'S COMIN' FROM OVER HERE...
HMMM
OH!
A RAIN-BOW!
HMMMMM
HOW PRETTY.

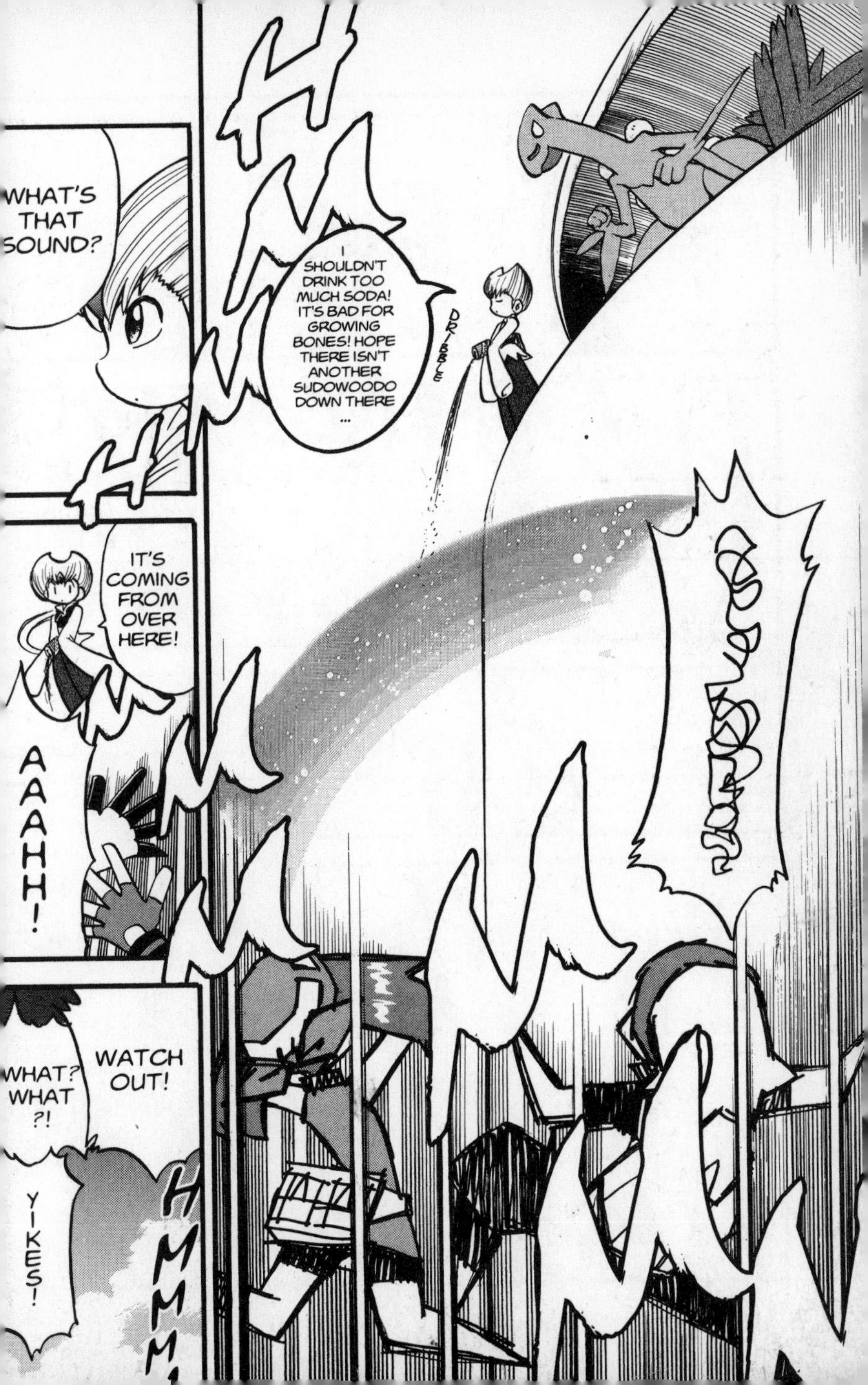
I SHOULDN'T DRINK TOO MUCH SODA! IT'S BAD FOR GROWING BONES! HOPE THERE ISN'T ANOTHER SUDOWOODO DOWN THERE ...
DRIBBLE
WHAT'S THAT SOUND?
IT'S COMING FROM OVER HERE!
AAAAHH!
WATCH OUT!
WHAT? WHAT?!
YIKES!
HMMM

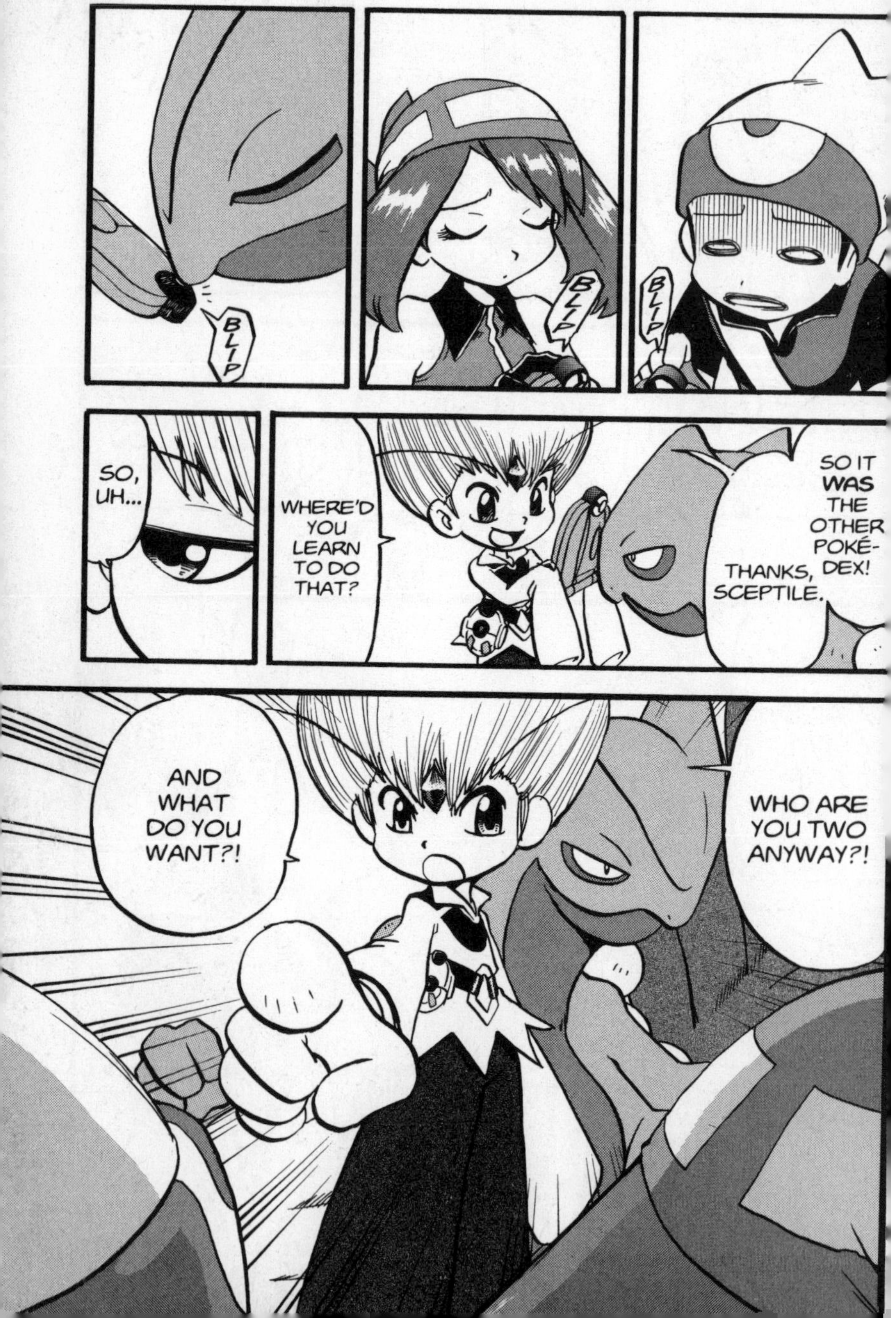
BLIP
BLIP
BLIP
SO IT WAS THE OTHER POKÉ-DEX!
THANKS, SCEPTILE.
WHERE'D YOU LEARN TO DO THAT?
SO, UH...
WHO ARE YOU TWO ANYWAY?!
AND WHAT DO YOU WANT?!

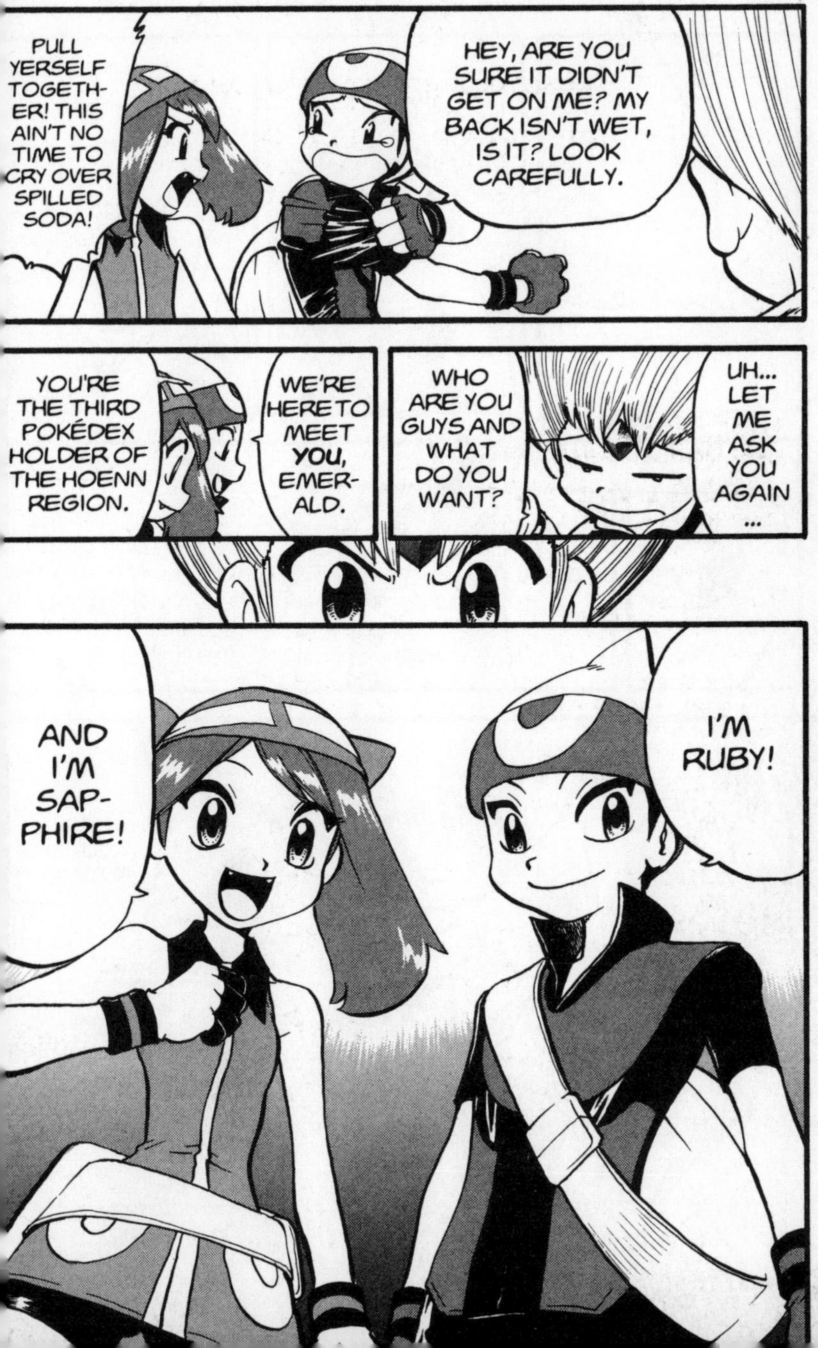
HEY, ARE YOU SURE IT DIDN'T GET ON ME? MY BACK ISN'T WET, IS IT? LOOK CAREFULLY.
PULL YERSELF TOGETHER! THIS AIN'T NO TIME TO CRY OVER SPILLED SODA!
UH... LET ME ASK YOU AGAIN ...
WHO ARE YOU GUYS AND WHAT DO YOU WANT?
WE'RE HERE TO MEET **YOU**, EMERALD.
YOU'RE THE THIRD POKÉDEX HOLDER OF THE HOENN REGION.
I'M RUBY!
AND I'M SAPPHIRE!

DEAR MEMBERS OF THE PRESS...

Thank you for visiting the Battle Frontier today. Permit me to continue explaining the rules of this facility...

OWNER: SCOTT

FACILITY RULES **BATTLE PALACE 1**	Battle-type	Number of Pokémon	Type of Symbol	Wins needed to attain the Symbol
	•Single •Double	3 Pokémon	Spirits	7 Wins × 6 Rounds = 42 Consecutive Wins

At the Battle Palace, battles are fought according to a unique rule: The Trainer is not allowed to give orders to their Pokémon. Pokémon must choose what move to use themselves. So, basically, the Trainer just observes the battle as it unfolds. Since Trainers cannot give orders to their Pokémon, the battles are not as complex as those at other facilities. The Battle Palace is a facility where the Trainers may enjoy a battle centered around the natural instincts of the Pokémon.

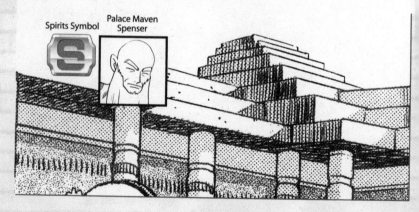

Spirits Symbol

Palace Maven Spenser

321

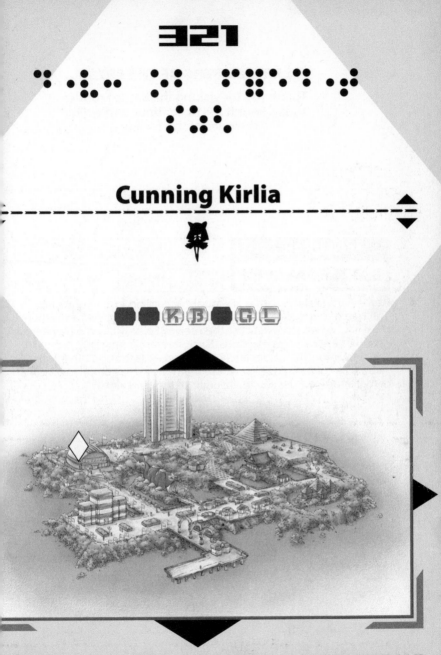

Cunning Kirlia

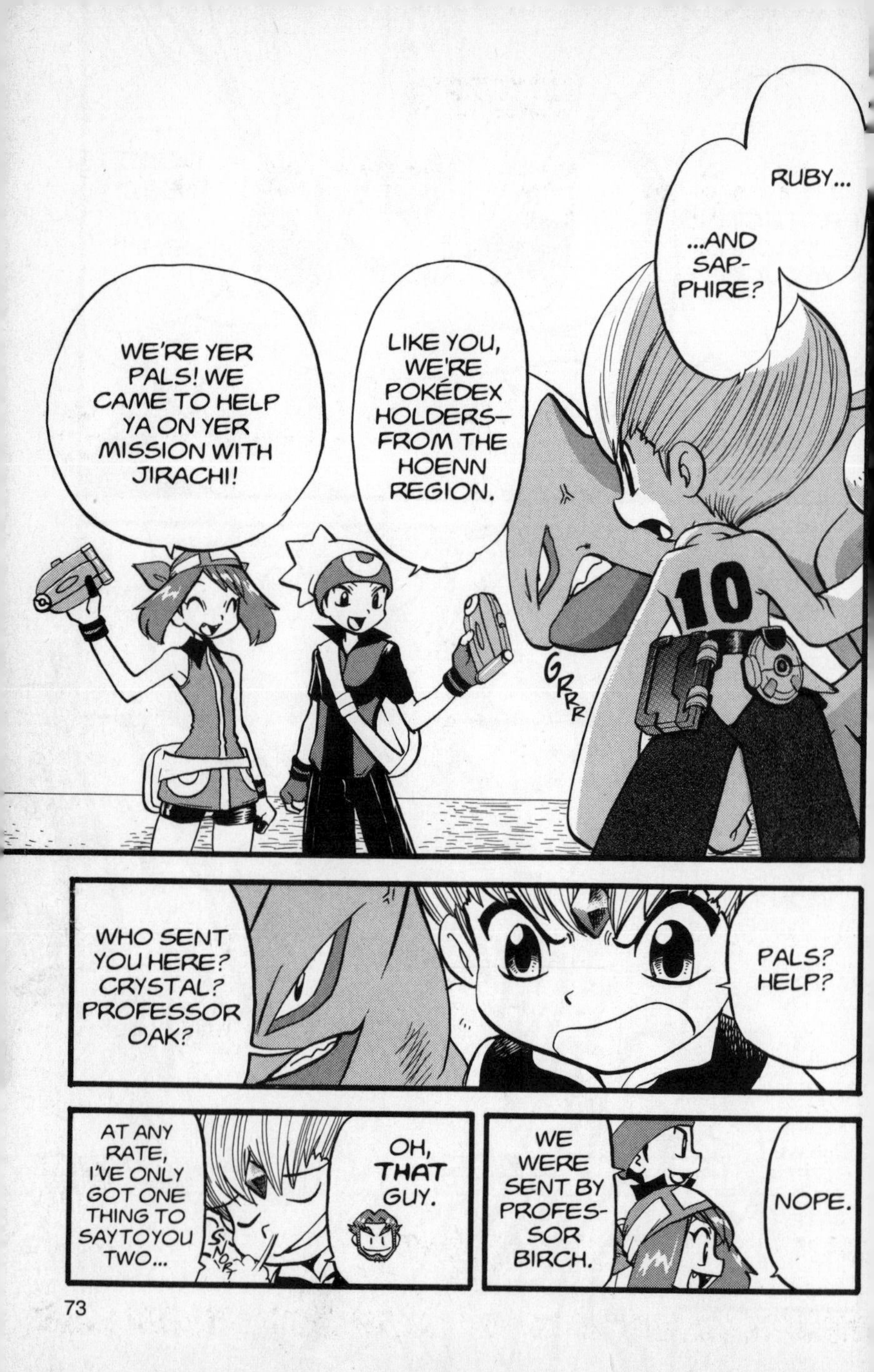
RUBY...
...AND SAPPHIRE?
LIKE YOU, WE'RE POKÉDEX HOLDERS—FROM THE HOENN REGION.
WE'RE YER PALS! WE CAME TO HELP YA ON YER MISSION WITH JIRACHI!
GRRR
PALS? HELP?
WHO SENT YOU HERE? CRYSTAL? PROFESSOR OAK?
NOPE.
WE WERE SENT BY PROFESSOR BIRCH.
OH, THAT GUY.
AT ANY RATE, I'VE ONLY GOT ONE THING TO SAY TO YOU TWO...
SNORT

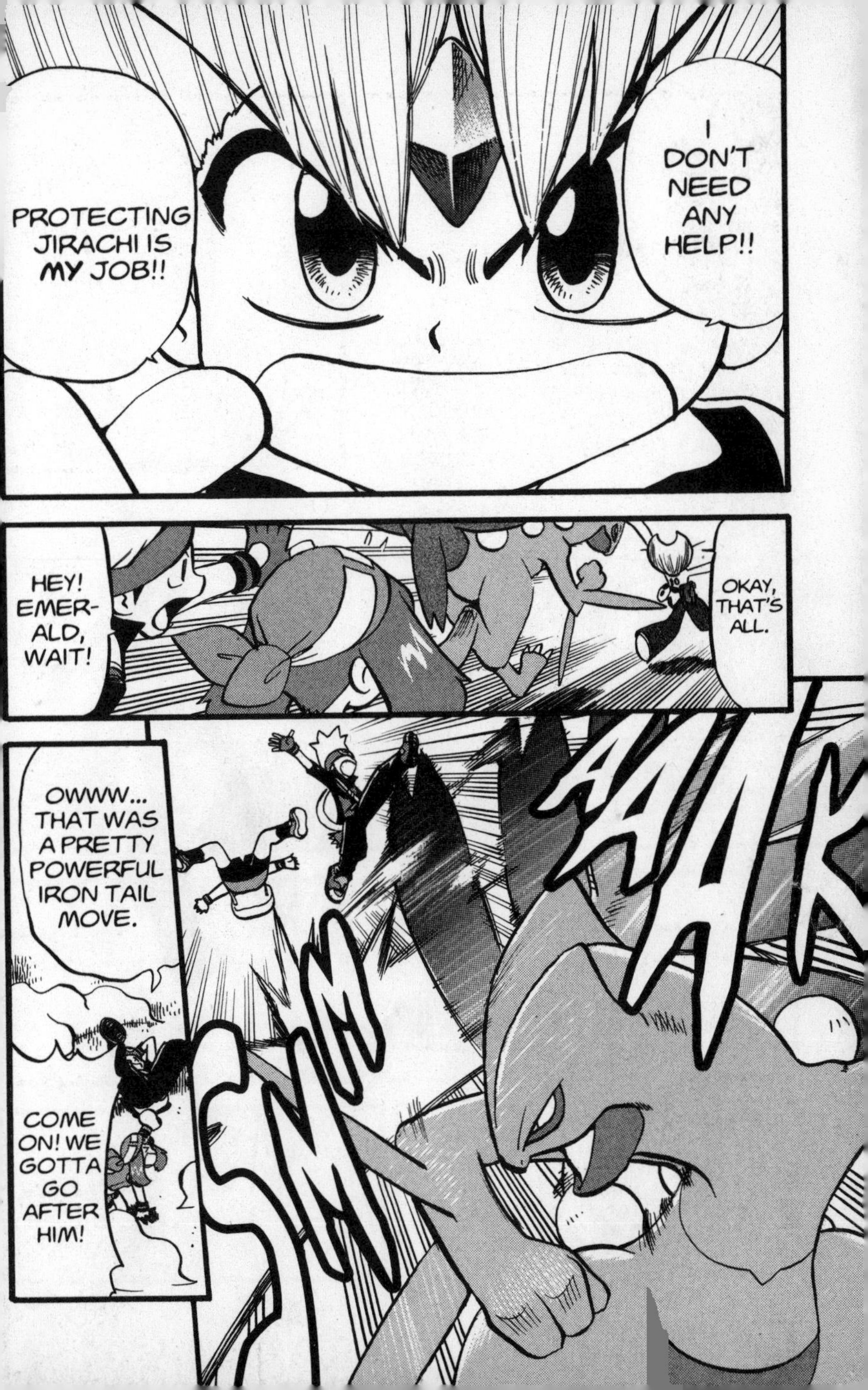
I DON'T NEED ANY HELP!!
PROTECTING JIRACHI IS MY JOB!!
OKAY, THAT'S ALL.
HEY! EMER-ALD, WAIT!
OWWW... THAT WAS A PRETTY POWERFUL IRON TAIL MOVE.
COME ON! WE GOTTA GO AFTER HIM!

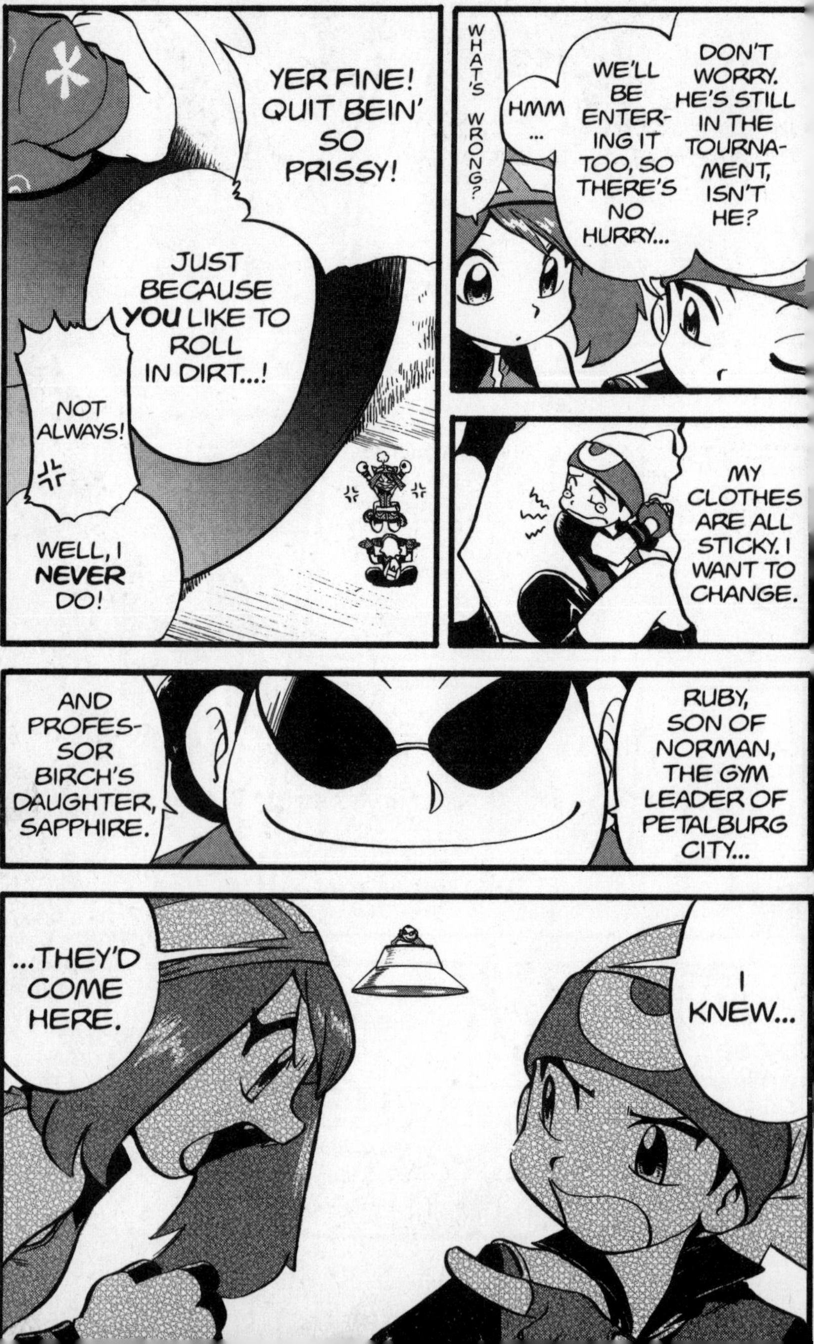
DON'T WORRY. HE'S STILL IN THE TOURNAMENT, ISN'T HE?
WE'LL BE ENTERING IT TOO, SO THERE'S NO HURRY...
HMM ...
WHAT'S WRONG?
MY CLOTHES ARE ALL STICKY. I WANT TO CHANGE.
YER FINE! QUIT BEIN' SO PRISSY!
JUST BECAUSE **YOU** LIKE TO ROLL IN DIRT...!
NOT ALWAYS!
WELL, I **NEVER** DO!
RUBY, SON OF NORMAN, THE GYM LEADER OF PETALBURG CITY...
AND PROFESSOR BIRCH'S DAUGHTER, SAPPHIRE.
I KNEW...
...THEY'D COME HERE.

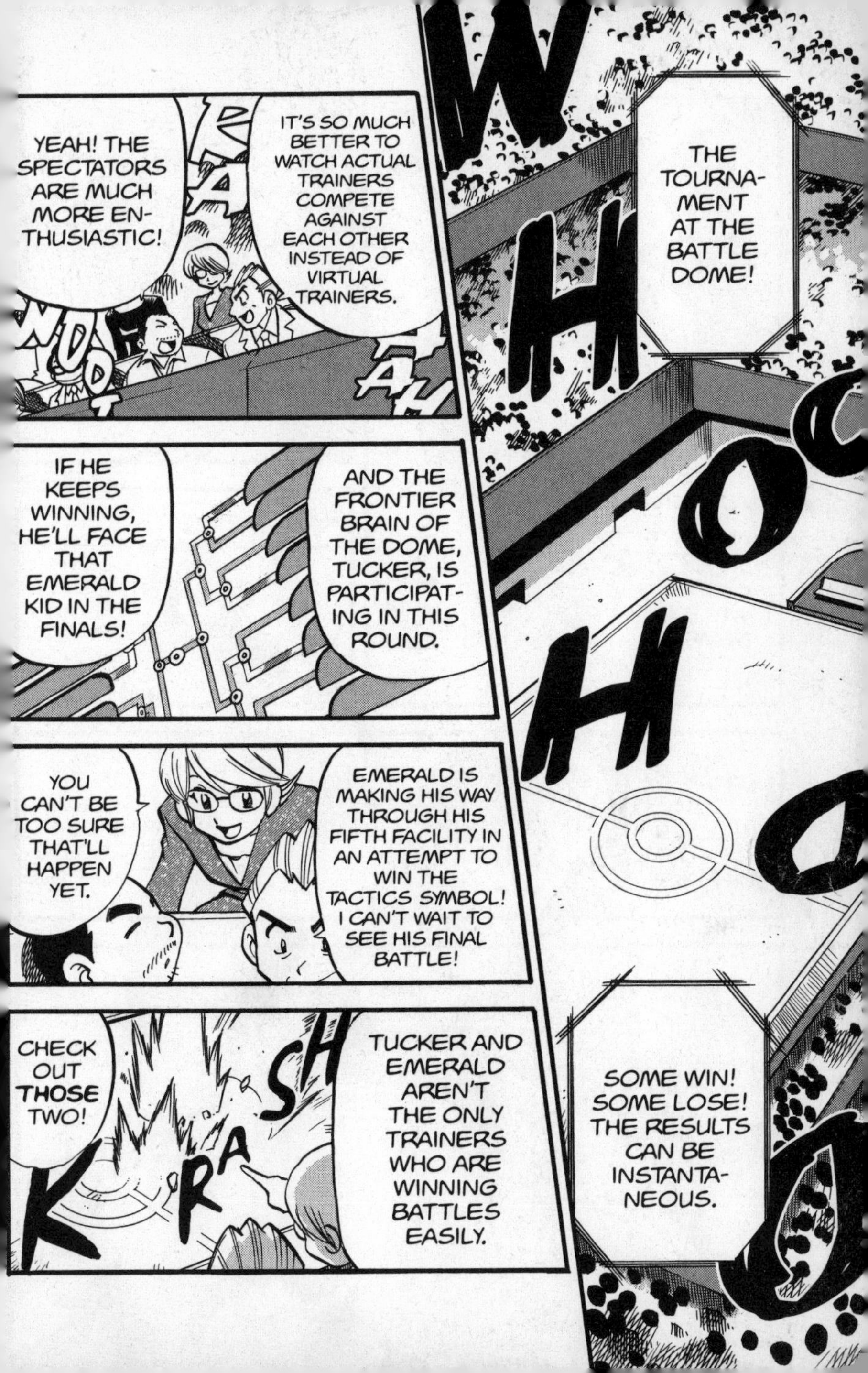
THE TOURNAMENT AT THE BATTLE DOME!
SOME WIN! SOME LOSE! THE RESULTS CAN BE INSTANTANEOUS.
IT'S SO MUCH BETTER TO WATCH ACTUAL TRAINERS COMPETE AGAINST EACH OTHER INSTEAD OF VIRTUAL TRAINERS.
YEAH! THE SPECTATORS ARE MUCH MORE ENTHUSIASTIC!
AND THE FRONTIER BRAIN OF THE DOME, TUCKER, IS PARTICIPATING IN THIS ROUND.
IF HE KEEPS WINNING, HE'LL FACE THAT EMERALD KID IN THE FINALS!
EMERALD IS MAKING HIS WAY THROUGH HIS FIFTH FACILITY IN AN ATTEMPT TO WIN THE TACTICS SYMBOL! I CAN'T WAIT TO SEE HIS FINAL BATTLE!
YOU CAN'T BE TOO SURE THAT'LL HAPPEN YET.
TUCKER AND EMERALD AREN'T THE ONLY TRAINERS WHO ARE WINNING BATTLES EASILY.
CHECK OUT THOSE TWO!
KRASH

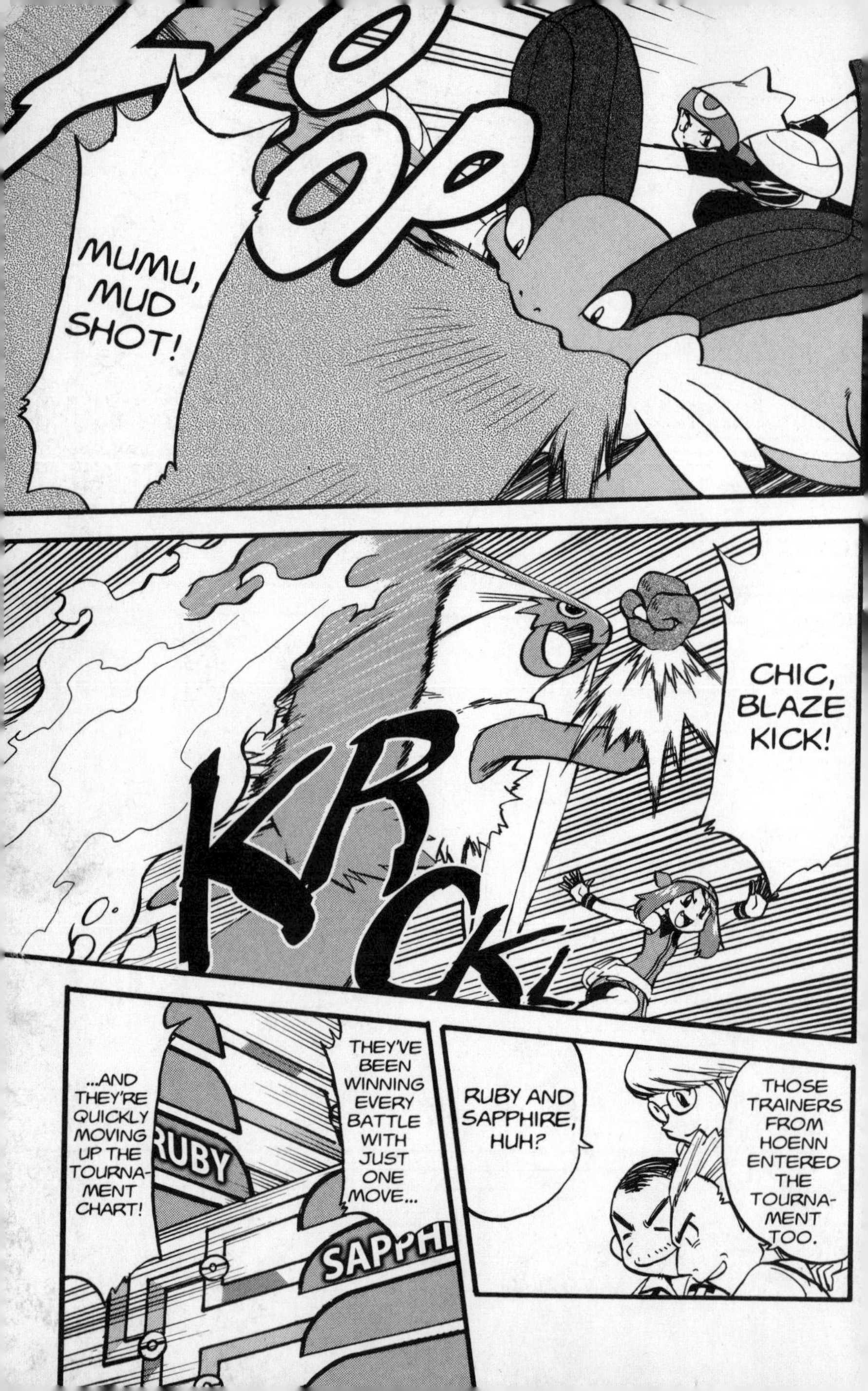
FLOOP
MUMU, MUD SHOT!
CHIC, BLAZE KICK!
KRCKL
THOSE TRAINERS FROM HOENN ENTERED THE TOURNAMENT TOO.
RUBY AND SAPPHIRE, HUH?
THEY'VE BEEN WINNING EVERY BATTLE WITH JUST ONE MOVE...
...AND THEY'RE QUICKLY MOVING UP THE TOURNAMENT CHART!
RUBY
SAPPHI

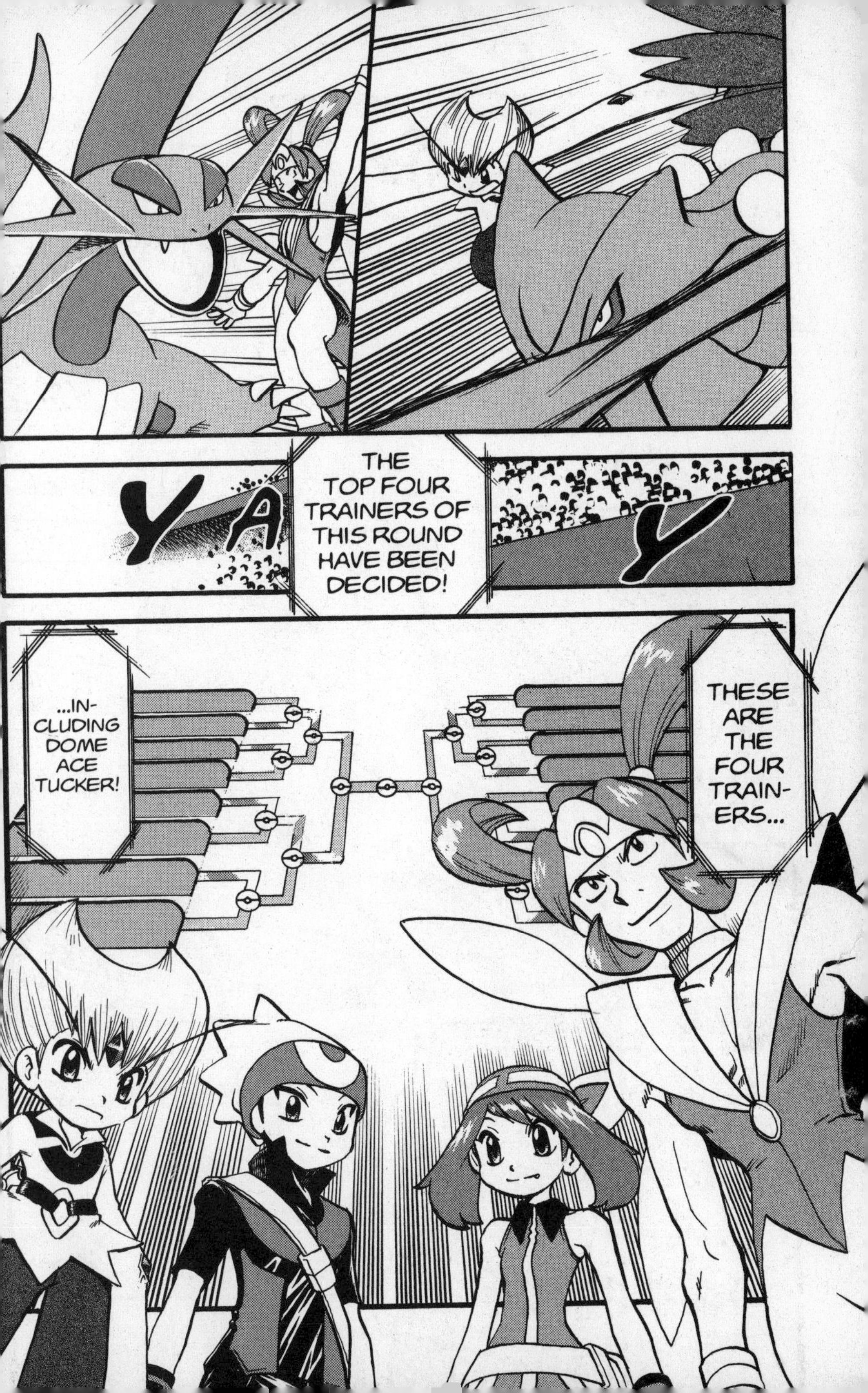
Y
THE TOP FOUR TRAINERS OF THIS ROUND HAVE BEEN DECIDED!
YA
THESE ARE THE FOUR TRAIN-ERS...
...IN-CLUDING DOME ACE TUCKER!

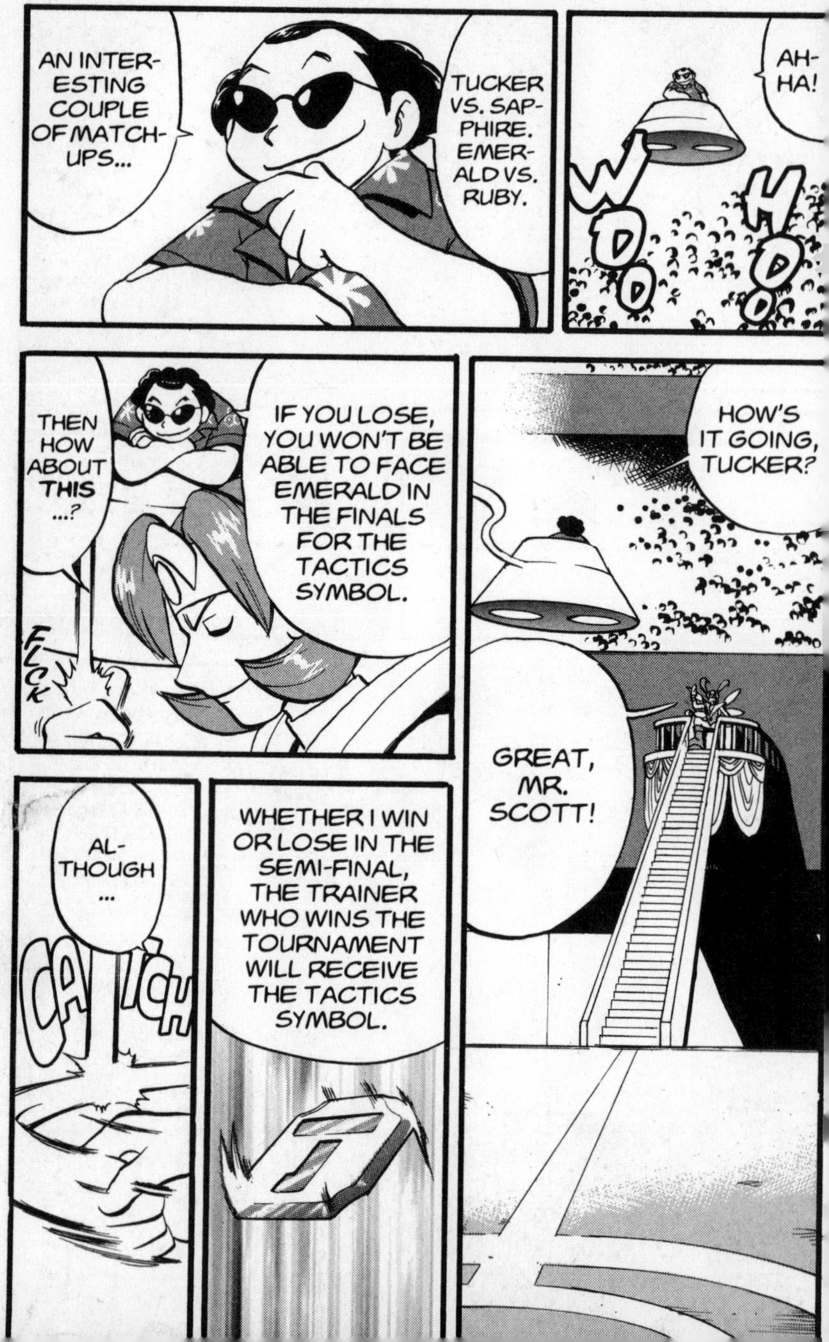
AH-HA!
WHOOO
WHOOO
AN INTERESTING COUPLE OF MATCH-UPS...
TUCKER VS. SAPPHIRE. EMERALD VS. RUBY.
HOW'S IT GOING, TUCKER?
GREAT, MR. SCOTT!
THEN HOW ABOUT THIS ...?
IF YOU LOSE, YOU WON'T BE ABLE TO FACE EMERALD IN THE FINALS FOR THE TACTICS SYMBOL.
FLICK
WHETHER I WIN OR LOSE IN THE SEMI-FINAL, THE TRAINER WHO WINS THE TOURNAMENT WILL RECEIVE THE TACTICS SYMBOL.
AL-THOUGH ...
CATCH

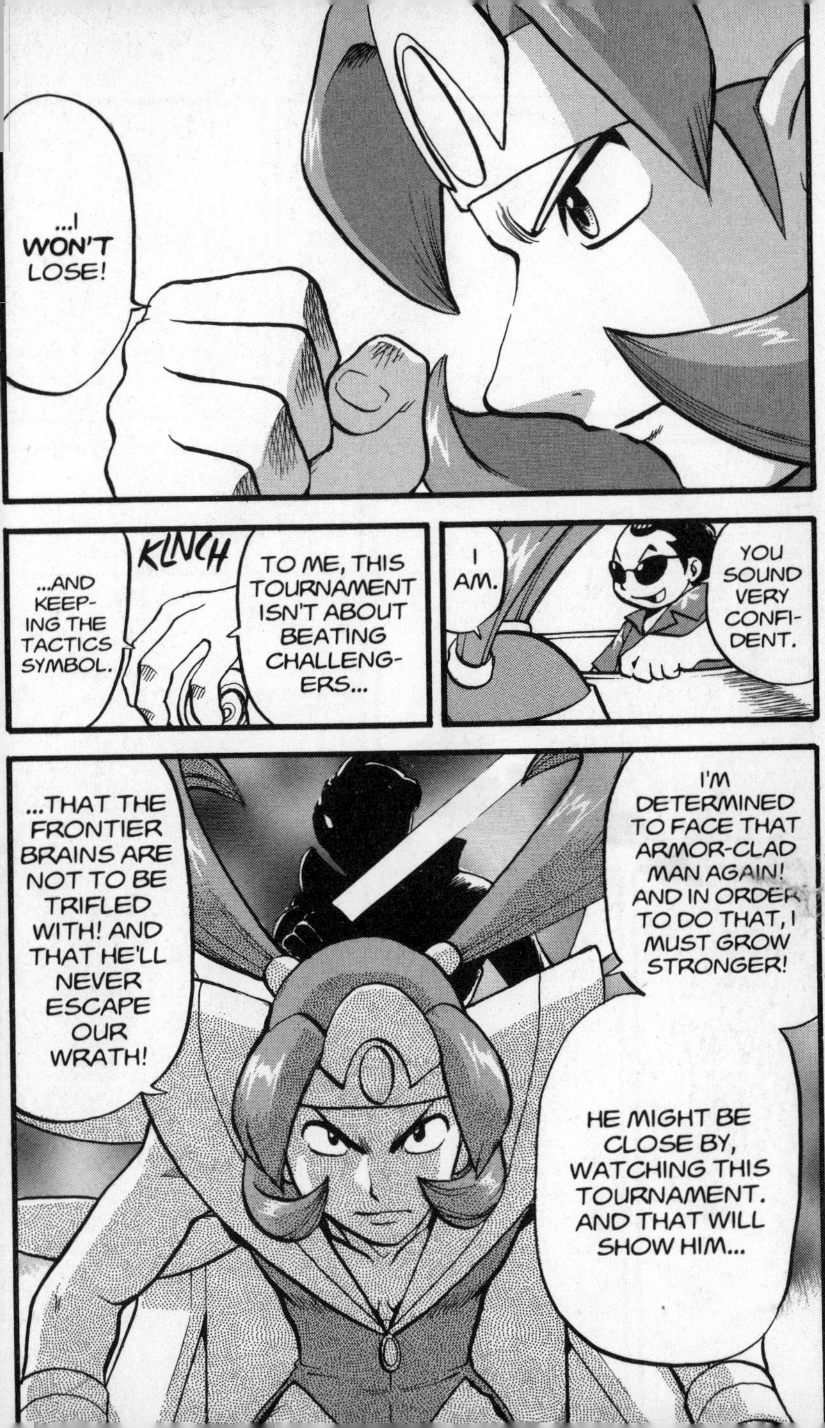
...I WON'T LOSE!
YOU SOUND VERY CONFI-DENT.
I AM.
TO ME, THIS TOURNAMENT ISN'T ABOUT BEATING CHALLENG-ERS...
KLNCH
...AND KEEP-ING THE TACTICS SYMBOL.
I'M DETERMINED TO FACE THAT ARMOR-CLAD MAN AGAIN! AND IN ORDER TO DO THAT, I MUST GROW STRONGER!
HE MIGHT BE CLOSE BY, WATCHING THIS TOURNAMENT. AND THAT WILL SHOW HIM...
...THAT THE FRONTIER BRAINS ARE NOT TO BE TRIFLED WITH! AND THAT HE'LL NEVER ESCAPE OUR WRATH!

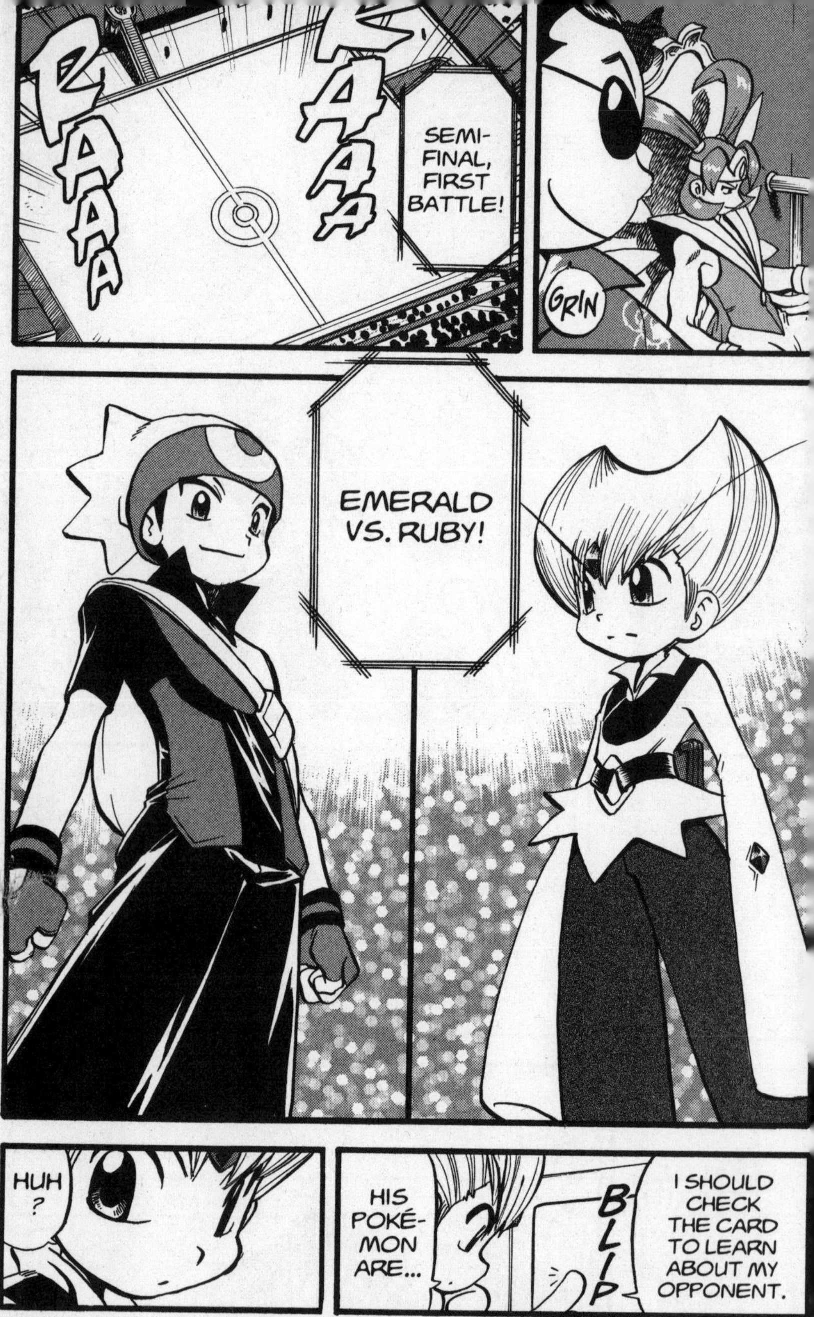
GRIN
AAAA
SEMI-FINAL, FIRST BATTLE!
RAAAA
EMERALD VS. RUBY!
I SHOULD CHECK THE CARD TO LEARN ABOUT MY OPPONENT.
BLIP
HIS POKÉMON ARE...
HUH?

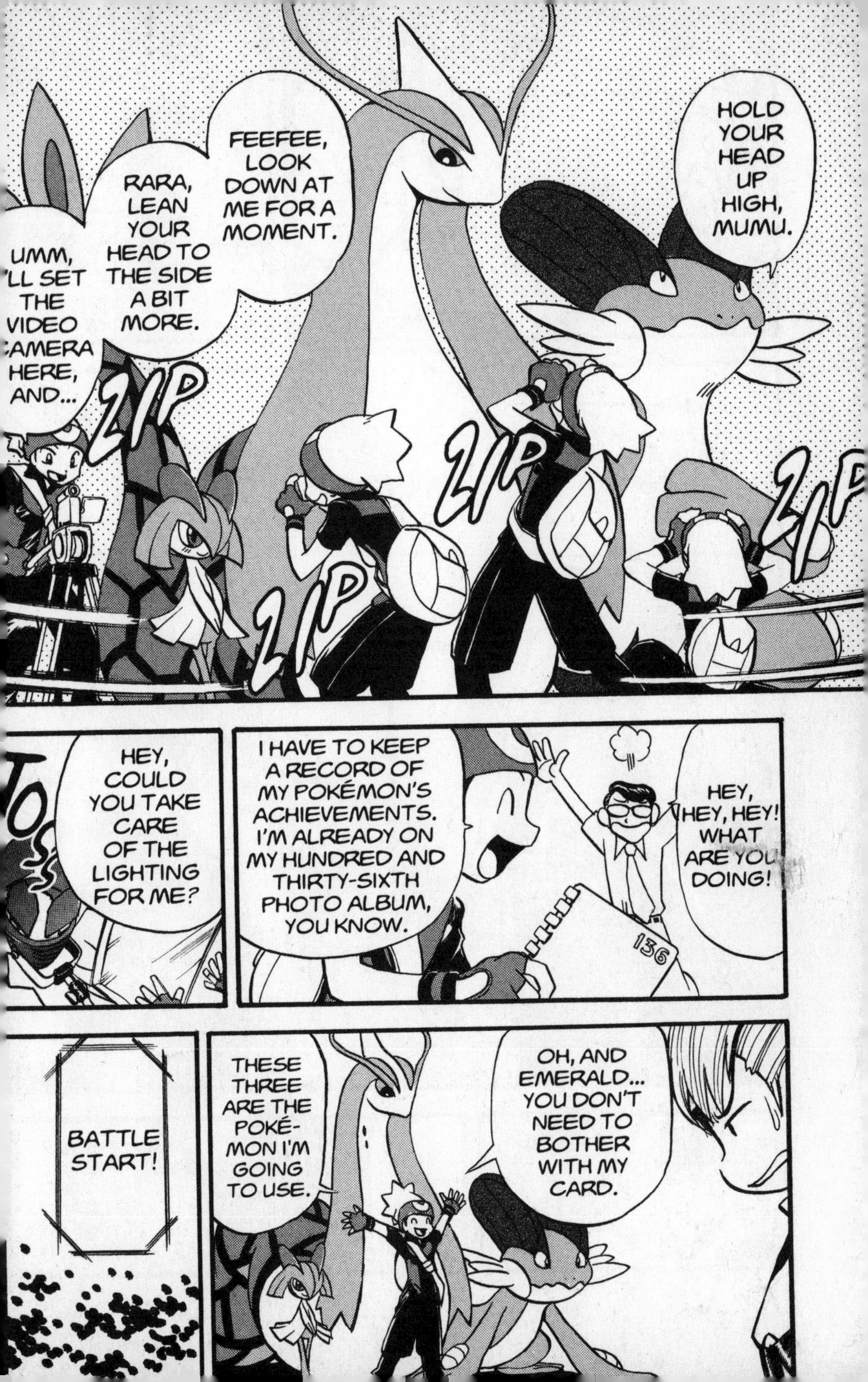
HOLD YOUR HEAD UP HIGH, MUMU.
FEEFEE, LOOK DOWN AT ME FOR A MOMENT.
RARA, LEAN YOUR HEAD TO THE SIDE A BIT MORE.
UMM, 'LL SET THE VIDEO AMERA HERE, AND...
ZIP
ZIP
ZIP
ZIP
ZIP
HEY, HEY, HEY! WHAT ARE YOU DOING!
I HAVE TO KEEP A RECORD OF MY POKÉMON'S ACHIEVEMENTS. I'M ALREADY ON MY HUNDRED AND THIRTY-SIXTH PHOTO ALBUM, YOU KNOW.
136
HEY, COULD YOU TAKE CARE OF THE LIGHTING FOR ME?
OH, AND EMERALD... YOU DON'T NEED TO BOTHER WITH MY CARD.
THESE THREE ARE THE POKÉMON I'M GOING TO USE.
BATTLE START!

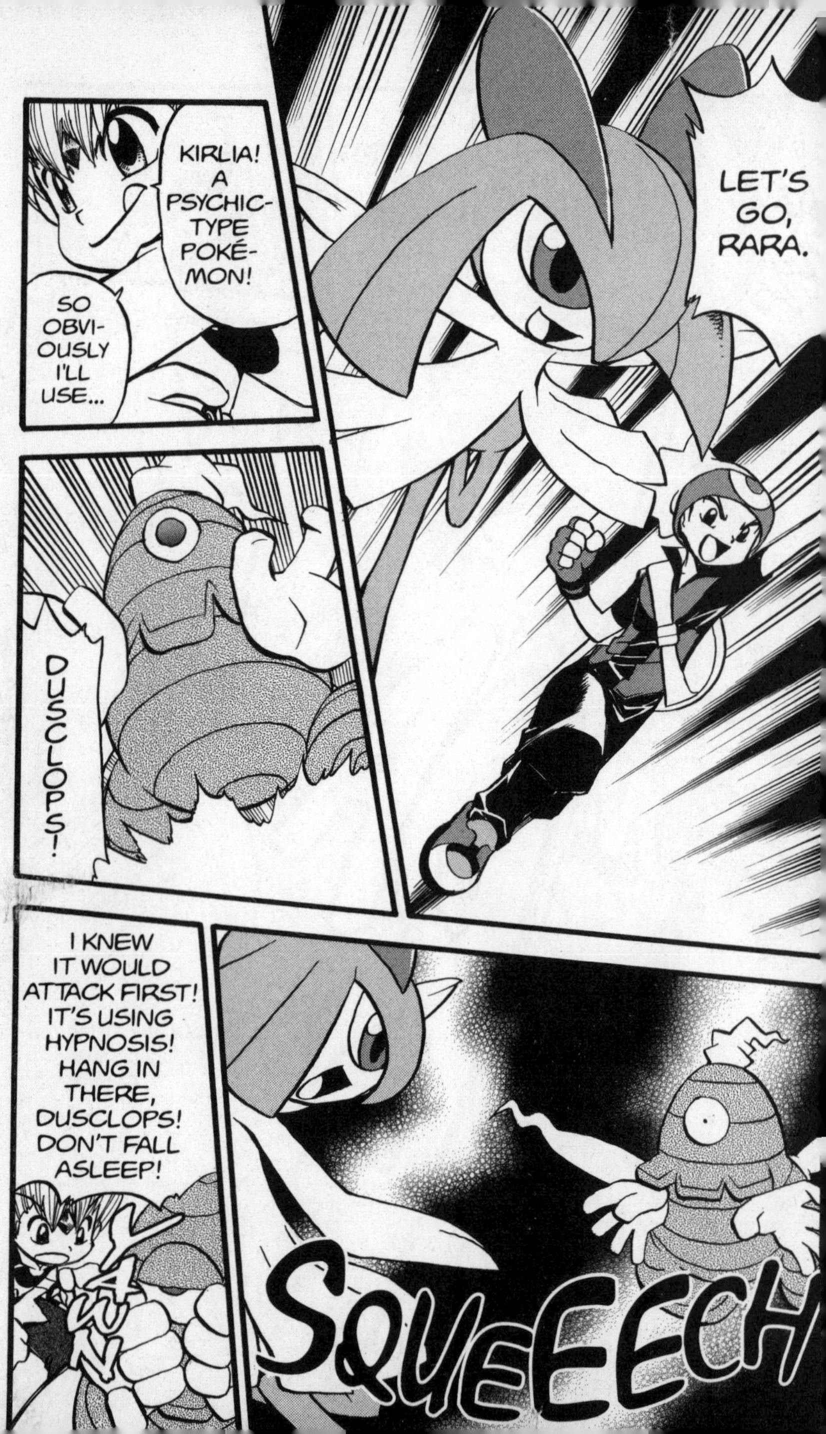
LET'S GO, RARA.
KIRLIA! A PSYCHIC-TYPE POKÉMON!
SO OBVIOUSLY I'LL USE...
DUSCLOPS!
SQUEEECH
I KNEW IT WOULD ATTACK FIRST! IT'S USING HYPNOSIS! HANG IN THERE, DUSCLOPS! DON'T FALL ASLEEP!

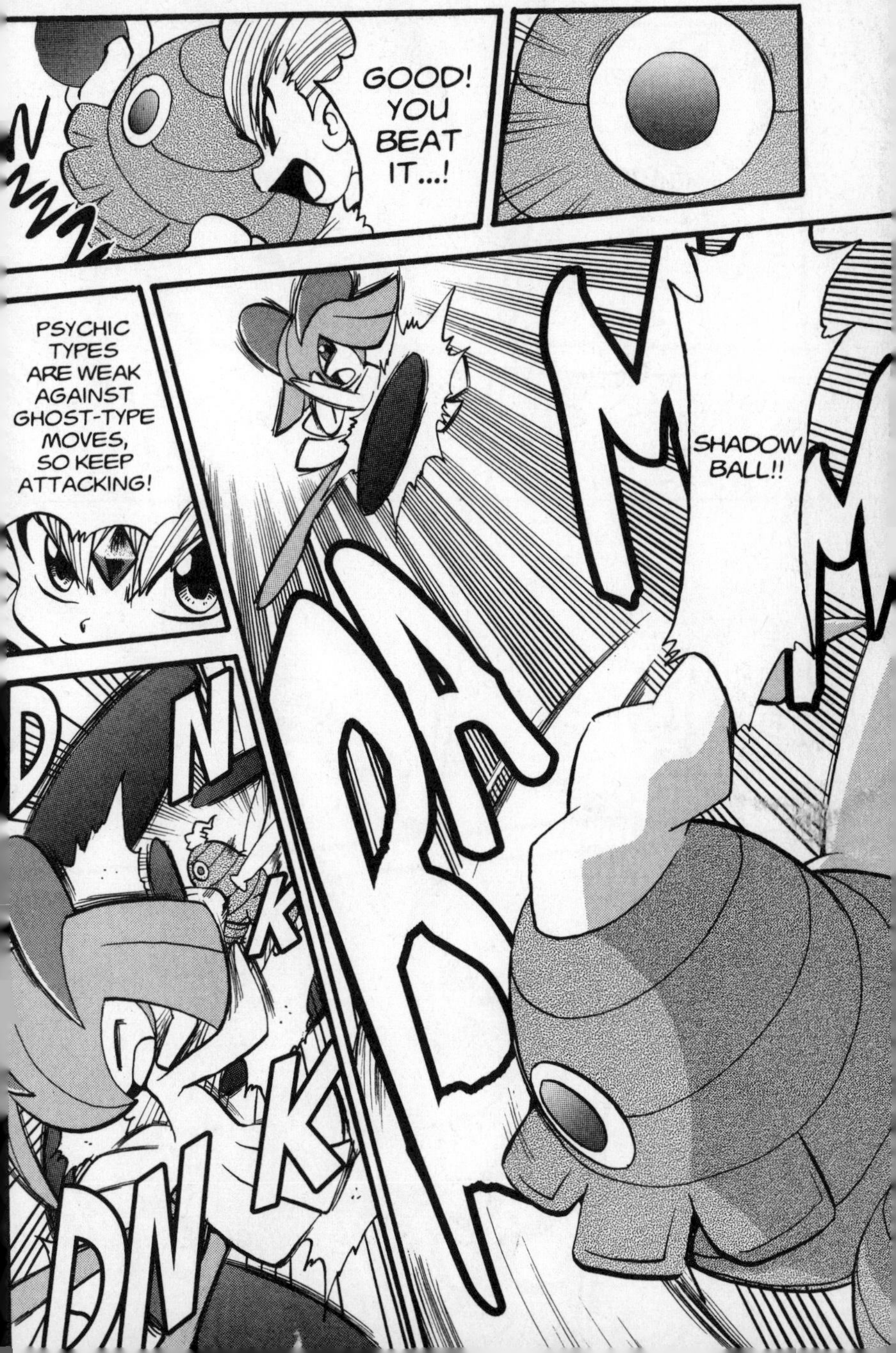
GOOD! YOU BEAT IT...!
SHADOW BALL!!
PSYCHIC TYPES ARE WEAK AGAINST GHOST-TYPE MOVES, SO KEEP ATTACKING!

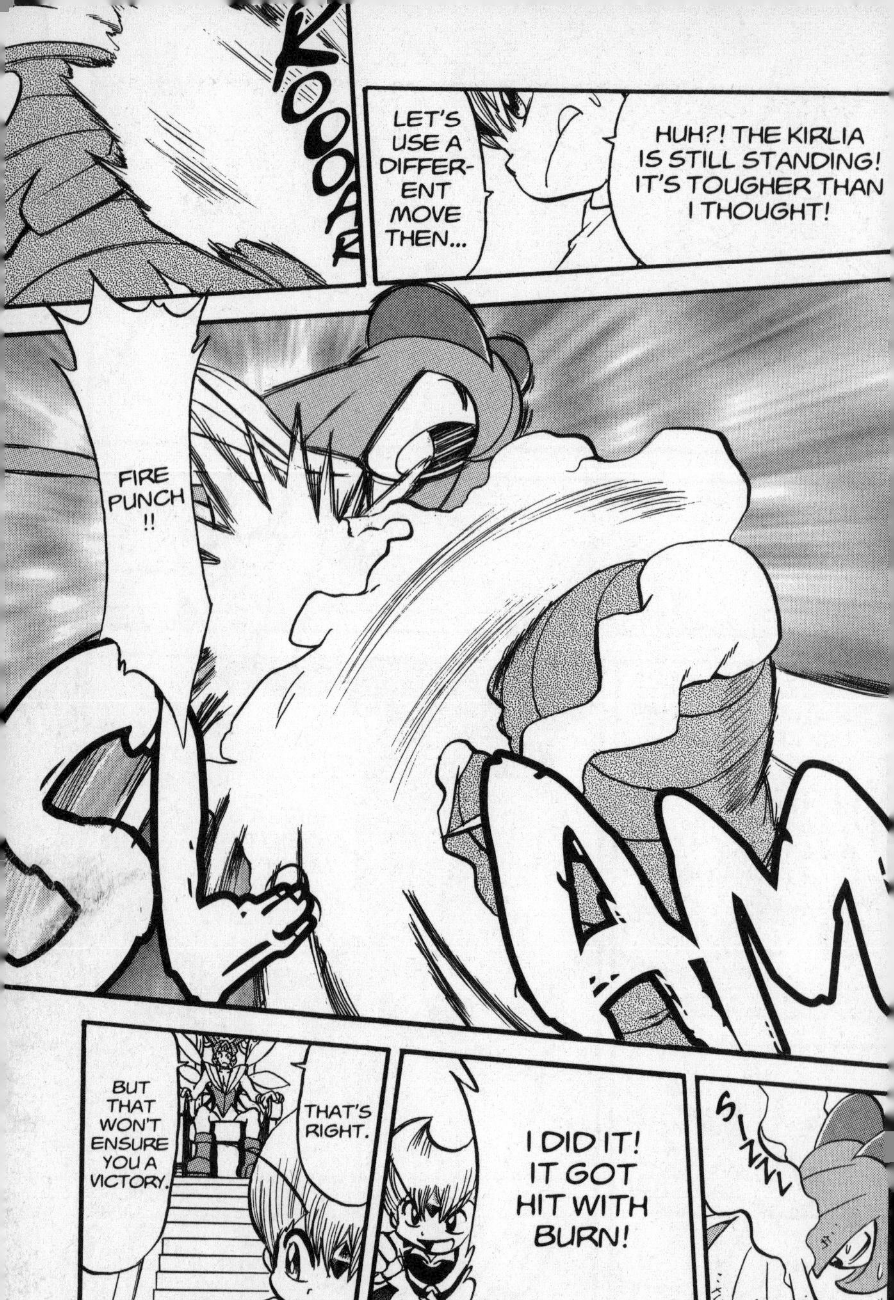
HUH?! THE KIRLIA IS STILL STANDING! IT'S TOUGHER THAN I THOUGHT!
LET'S USE A DIFFER-ENT MOVE THEN...
VOOOAR
FIRE PUNCH!!
S-NNN
I DID IT! IT GOT HIT WITH BURN!
THAT'S RIGHT.
BUT THAT WON'T ENSURE YOU A VICTORY.

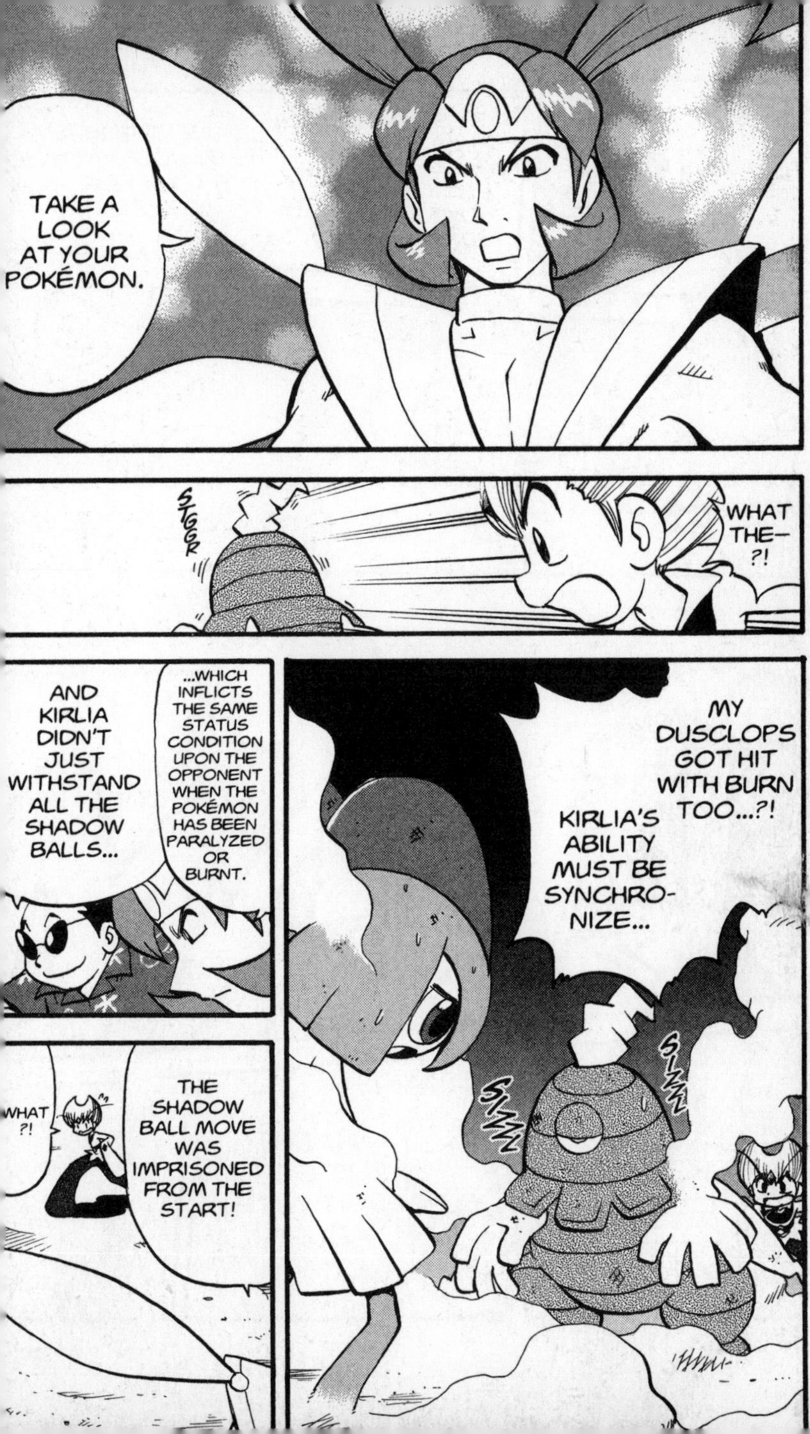
TAKE A LOOK AT YOUR POKÉMON.
WHAT THE—?!
STGGR
MY DUSCLOPS GOT HIT WITH BURN TOO...?!
KIRLIA'S ABILITY MUST BE SYNCHRO-NIZE...
SIZZZ
SIZZZ
...WHICH INFLICTS THE SAME STATUS CONDITION UPON THE OPPONENT WHEN THE POKÉMON HAS BEEN PARALYZED OR BURNT.
AND KIRLIA DIDN'T JUST WITHSTAND ALL THE SHADOW BALLS...
THE SHADOW BALL MOVE WAS IMPRISONED FROM THE START!
WHAT?!

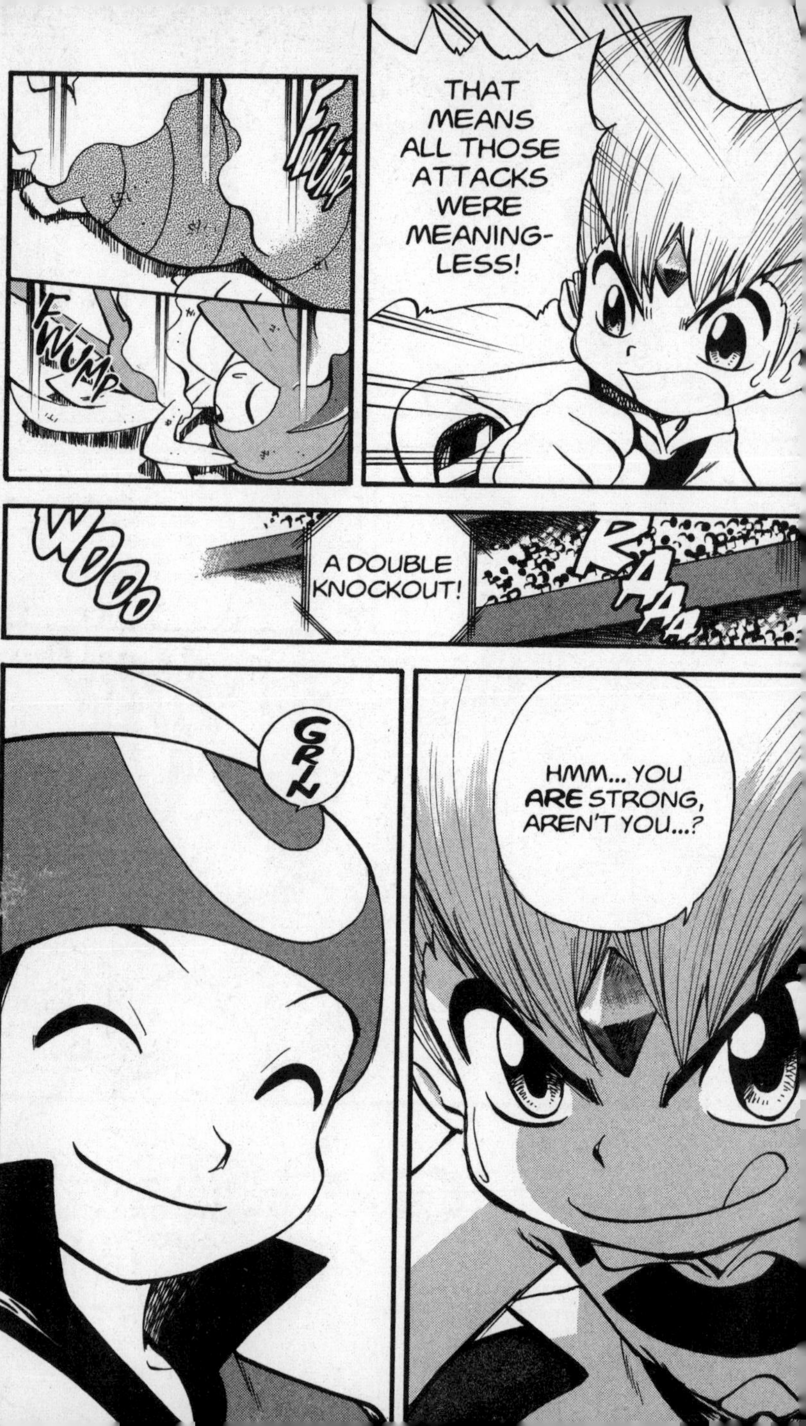
THAT MEANS ALL THOSE ATTACKS WERE MEANING-LESS!
FWUMP
FWUMP
RAAAA
A DOUBLE KNOCKOUT!
WOOOO
HMM... YOU **ARE** STRONG, AREN'T YOU...?
GRLN

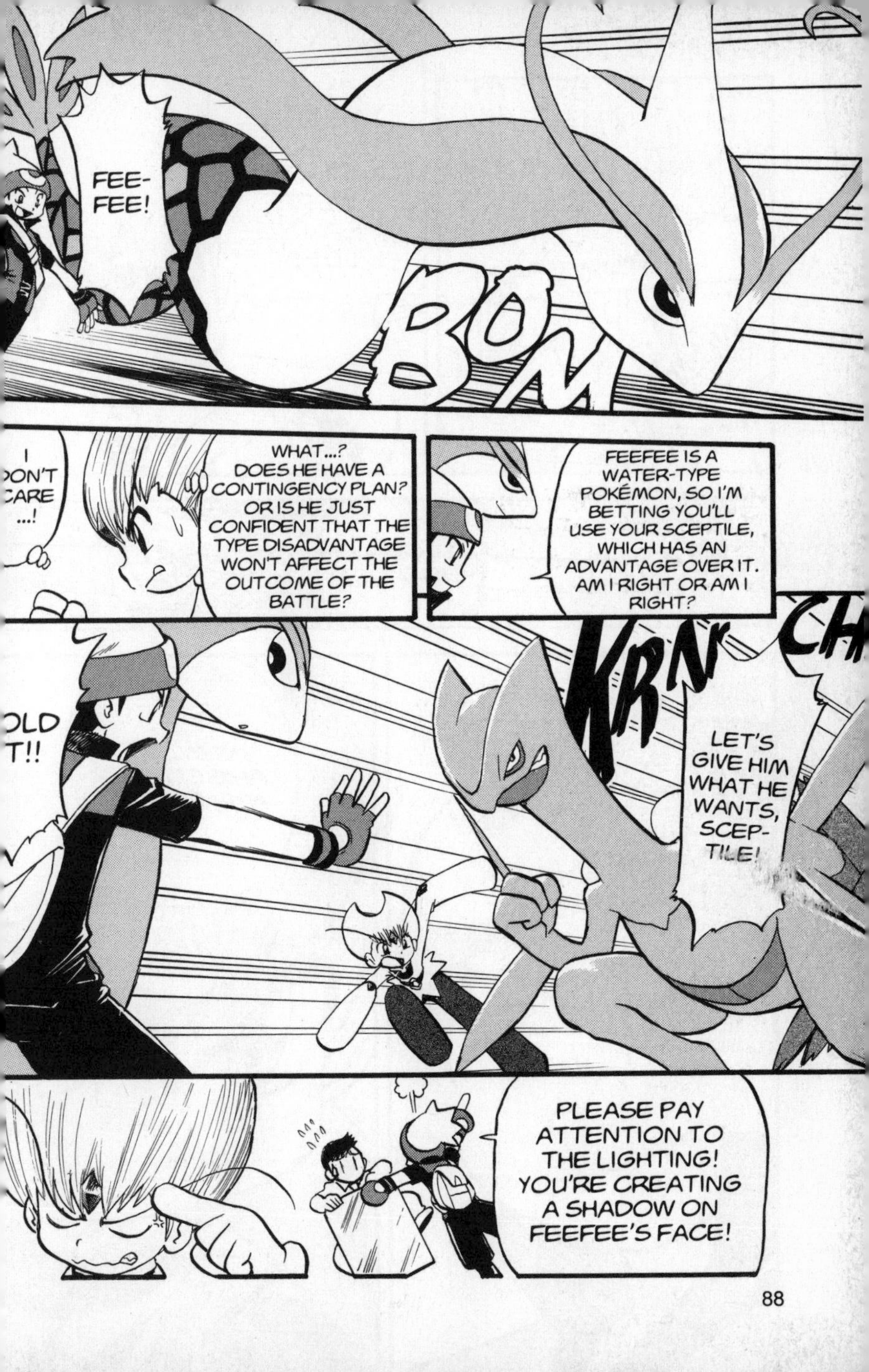
BOM
FEE-FEE!
FEEFEE IS A WATER-TYPE POKÉMON, SO I'M BETTING YOU'LL USE YOUR SCEPTILE, WHICH HAS AN ADVANTAGE OVER IT. AM I RIGHT OR AM I RIGHT?
WHAT...? DOES HE HAVE A CONTINGENCY PLAN? OR IS HE JUST CONFIDENT THAT THE TYPE DISADVANTAGE WON'T AFFECT THE OUTCOME OF THE BATTLE?
KRN
LET'S GIVE HIM WHAT HE WANTS, SCEP-TILE!
PLEASE PAY ATTENTION TO THE LIGHTING! YOU'RE CREATING A SHADOW ON FEEFEE'S FACE!

DEAR MEMBERS OF THE PRESS...

Thank you for visiting the Battle Frontier today. Permit me to continue explaining the rules of this facility...

OWNER: SCOTT

FACILITY RULES

BATTLE PALACE 2

① Watch

After entering the battle area, the Trainer places their Poké Balls with their Pokémon inside in the battle area and moves over to the spectator circle. After that, the Trainers are not allowed to give any orders, but they may watch the battle all the way through.

② Switch

Trainers are not allowed to give orders to their Pokémon, but they may switch out their Pokémon during battle. If a Trainer wishes to switch their Pokémon due to a type disadvantage or status condition, they may request a change through the microphone located in their spectator's seat.

■ TRAINER EXPERIENCE AT THE BATTLE PALACE ■

At the Battle Palace, Trainers must permit their Pokémon to fight as they wish. However, the Trainers are allowed to make the following moves.

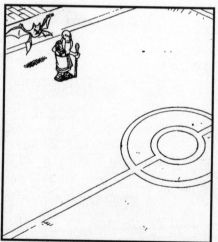

322

Susceptible to Sceptile

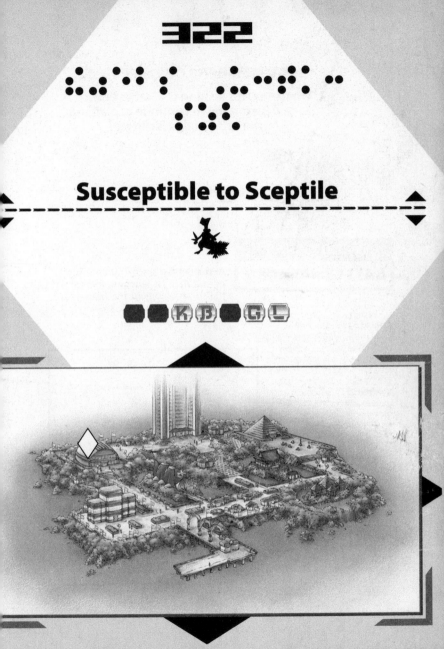

● ● k B O G L

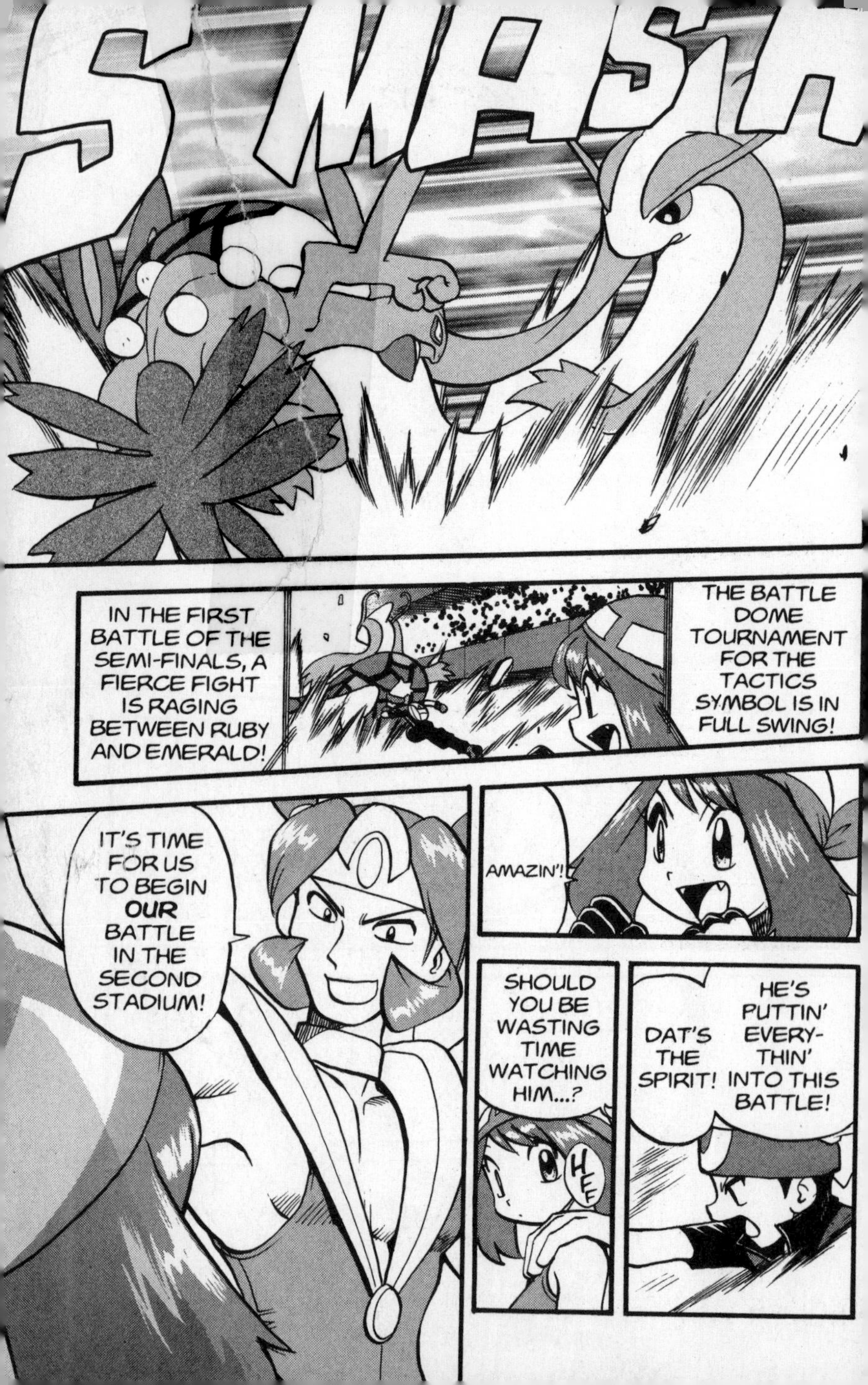
SMASH
THE BATTLE DOME TOURNAMENT FOR THE TACTICS SYMBOL IS IN FULL SWING!
IN THE FIRST BATTLE OF THE SEMI-FINALS, A FIERCE FIGHT IS RAGING BETWEEN RUBY AND EMERALD!
AMAZIN'!
HE'S PUTTIN' EVERY-THIN' INTO THIS BATTLE!
DAT'S THE SPIRIT!
SHOULD YOU BE WASTING TIME WATCHING HIM...?
HEF
IT'S TIME FOR US TO BEGIN **OUR** BATTLE IN THE SECOND STADIUM!

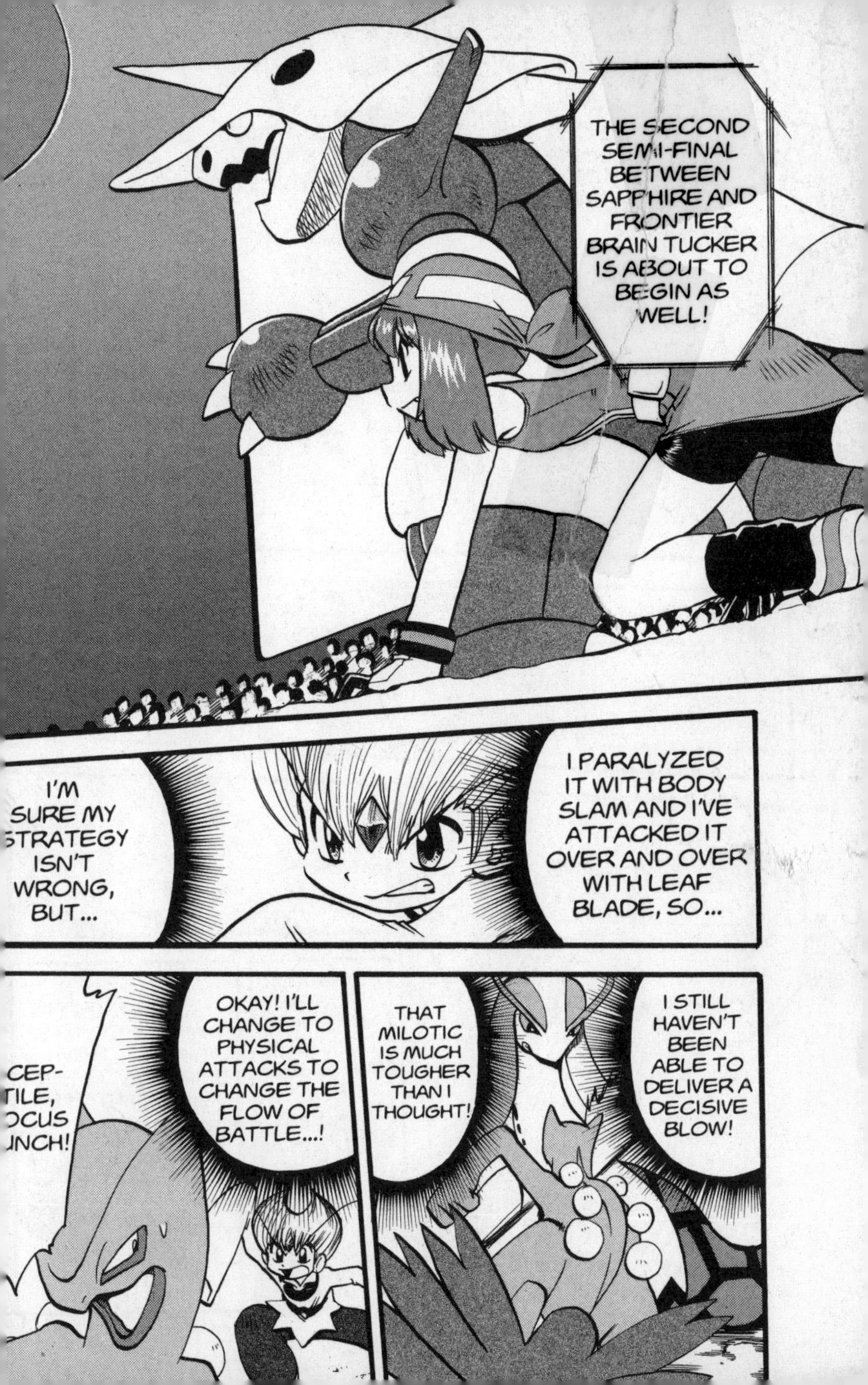
THE SECOND SEMI-FINAL BETWEEN SAPPHIRE AND FRONTIER BRAIN TUCKER IS ABOUT TO BEGIN AS WELL!
I PARALYZED IT WITH BODY SLAM AND I'VE ATTACKED IT OVER AND OVER WITH LEAF BLADE, SO...
I'M SURE MY STRATEGY ISN'T WRONG, BUT...
I STILL HAVEN'T BEEN ABLE TO DELIVER A DECISIVE BLOW!
THAT MILOTIC IS MUCH TOUGHER THAN I THOUGHT!
OKAY! I'LL CHANGE TO PHYSICAL ATTACKS TO CHANGE THE FLOW OF BATTLE...!
CEP- TILE, OCUS UNCH!

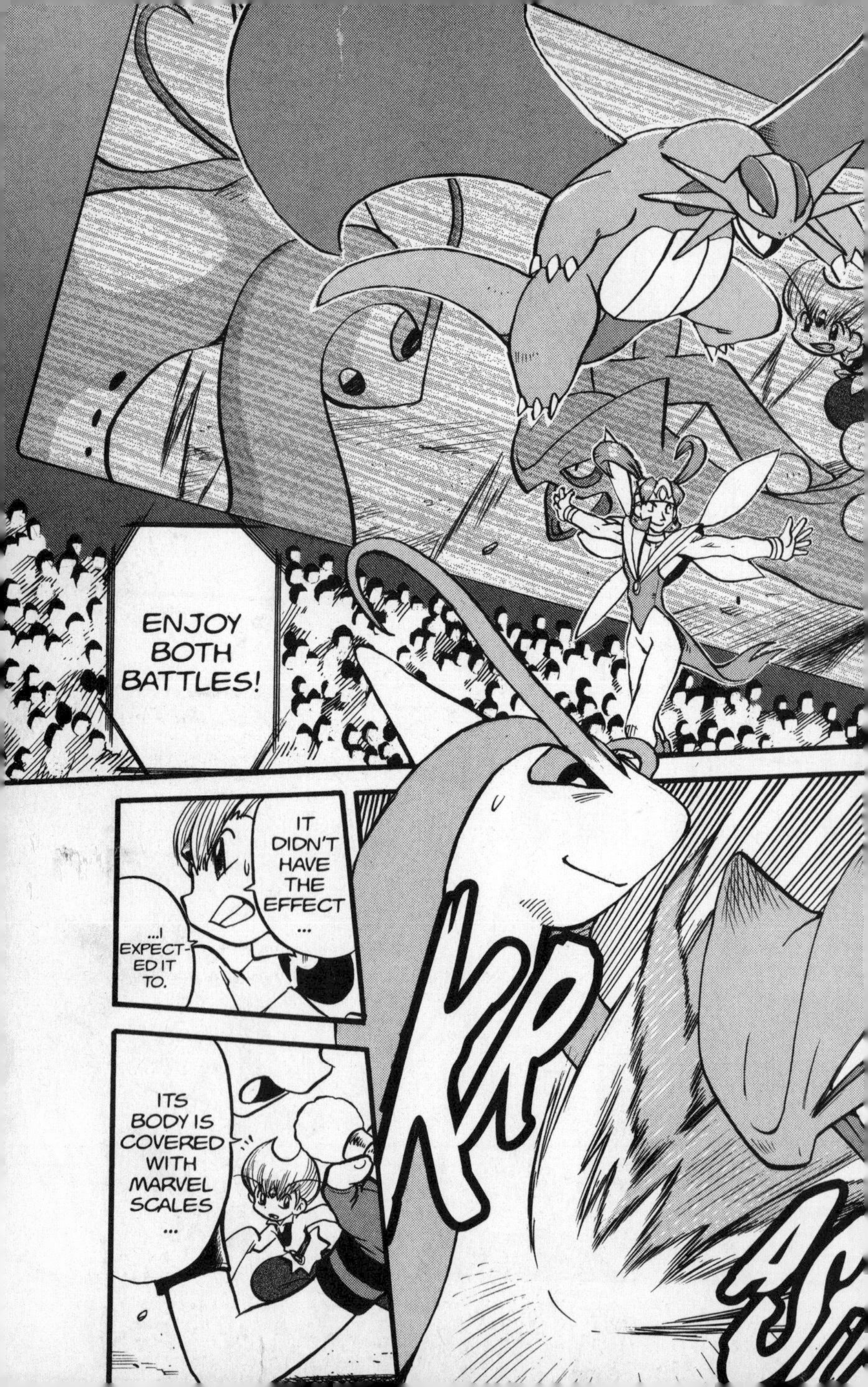
ENJOY BOTH BATTLES!
IT DIDN'T HAVE THE EFFECT...
...I EXPECT-ED IT TO.
ITS BODY IS COVERED WITH MARVEL SCALES...

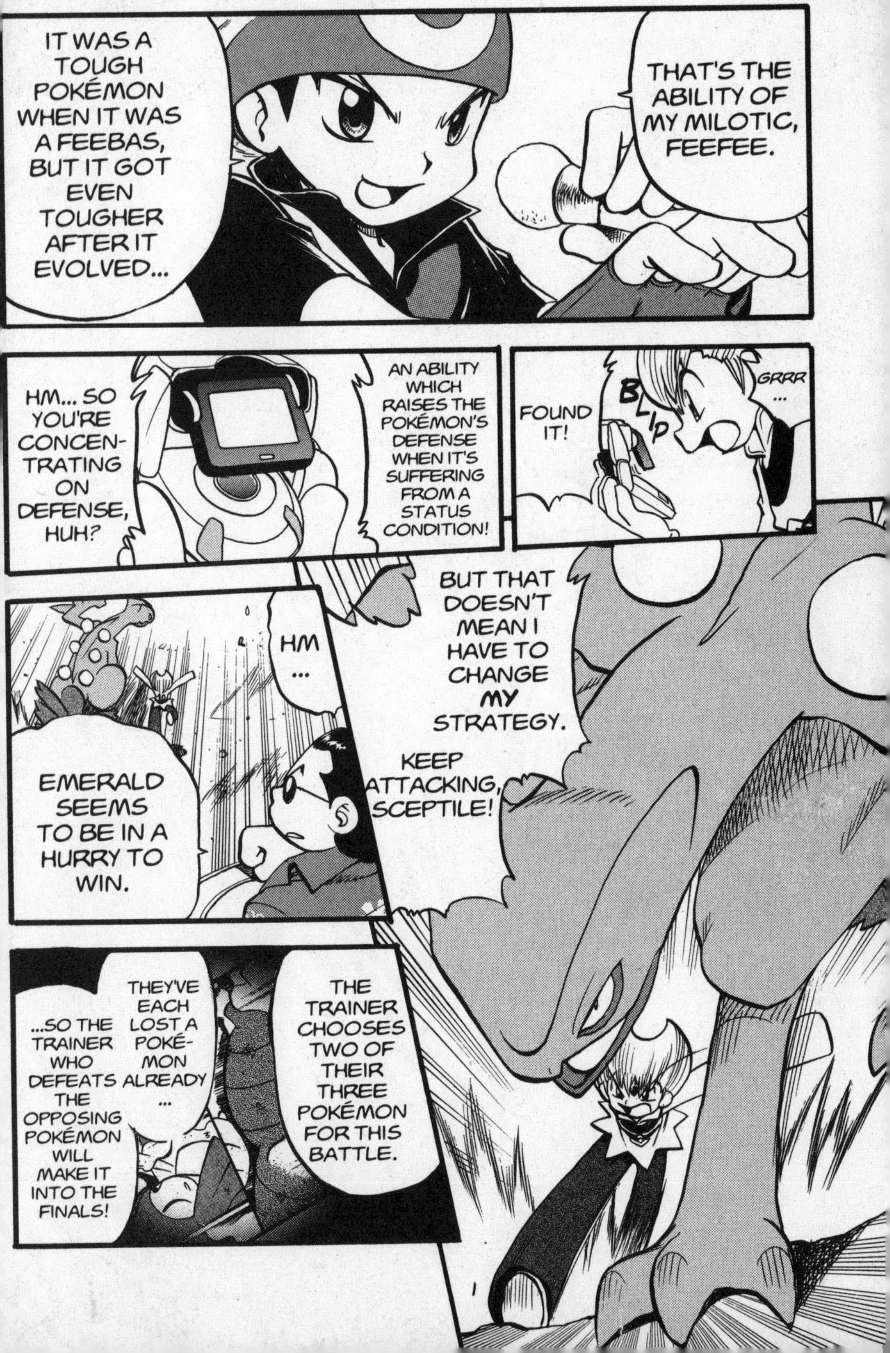
THAT'S THE ABILITY OF MY MILOTIC, FEEFEE.
IT WAS A TOUGH POKÉMON WHEN IT WAS A FEEBAS, BUT IT GOT EVEN TOUGHER AFTER IT EVOLVED...
GRRR ...
BLIP
FOUND IT!
AN ABILITY WHICH RAISES THE POKÉMON'S DEFENSE WHEN IT'S SUFFERING FROM A STATUS CONDITION!
HM... SO YOU'RE CONCEN-TRATING ON DEFENSE, HUH?
BUT THAT DOESN'T MEAN I HAVE TO CHANGE MY STRATEGY.
KEEP ATTACKING, SCEPTILE!
HM ...
EMERALD SEEMS TO BE IN A HURRY TO WIN.
THE TRAINER CHOOSES TWO OF THEIR THREE POKÉMON FOR THIS BATTLE.
THEY'VE EACH LOST A POKÉ-MON ALREADY ...
...SO THE TRAINER WHO DEFEATS THE OPPOSING POKÉMON WILL MAKE IT INTO THE FINALS!

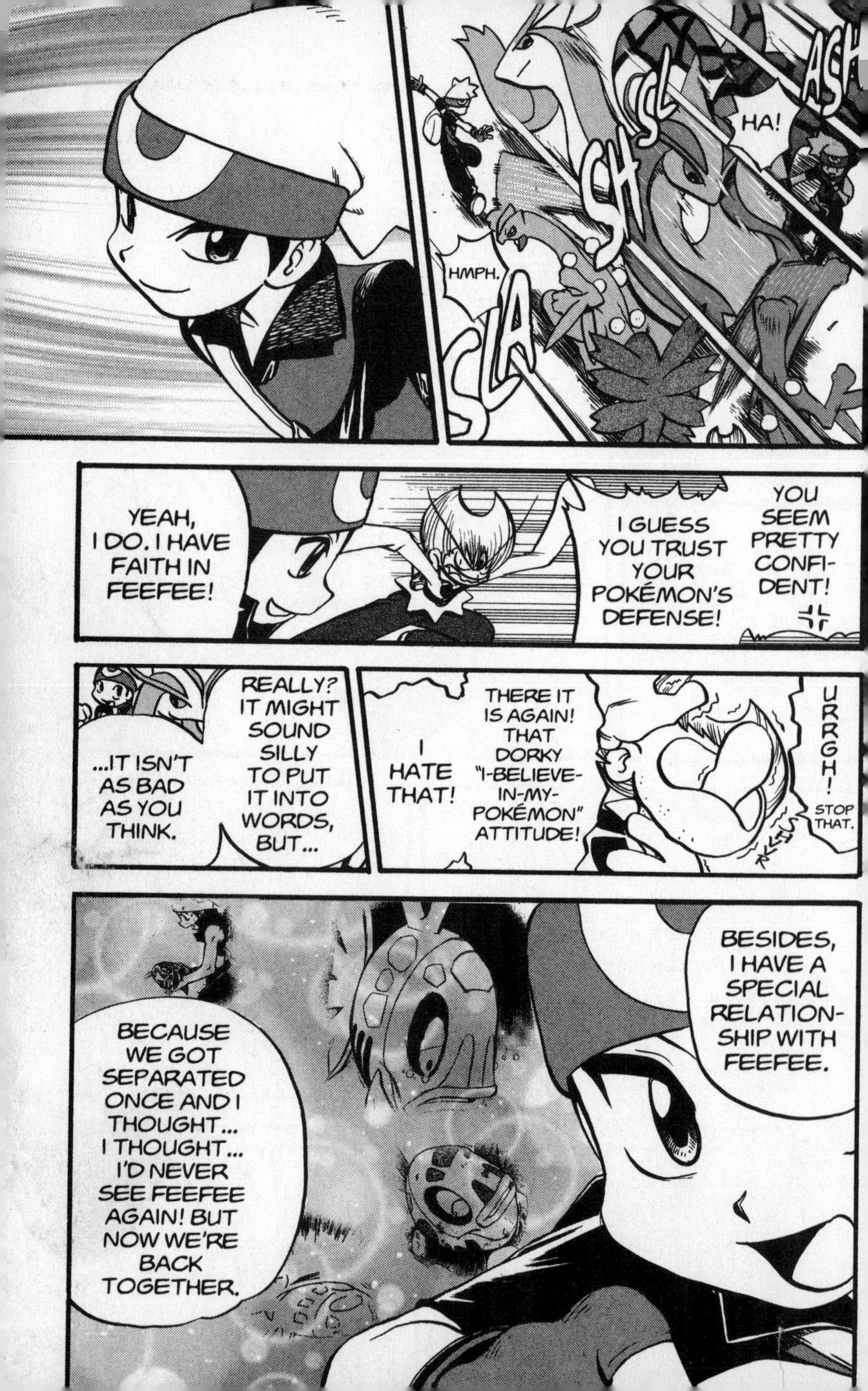
ASH
HA!
HMPH.
YOU SEEM PRETTY CONFIDENT!
I GUESS YOU TRUST YOUR POKÉMON'S DEFENSE!
YEAH, I DO. I HAVE FAITH IN FEEFEE!
URRGH!
STOP THAT.
THERE IT IS AGAIN! THAT DORKY "I-BELIEVE-IN-MY-POKÉMON" ATTITUDE!
I HATE THAT!
REALLY? IT MIGHT SOUND SILLY TO PUT IT INTO WORDS, BUT...
...IT ISN'T AS BAD AS YOU THINK.
BESIDES, I HAVE A SPECIAL RELATIONSHIP WITH FEEFEE.
BECAUSE WE GOT SEPARATED ONCE AND I THOUGHT... I THOUGHT... I'D NEVER SEE FEEFEE AGAIN! BUT NOW WE'RE BACK TOGETHER.

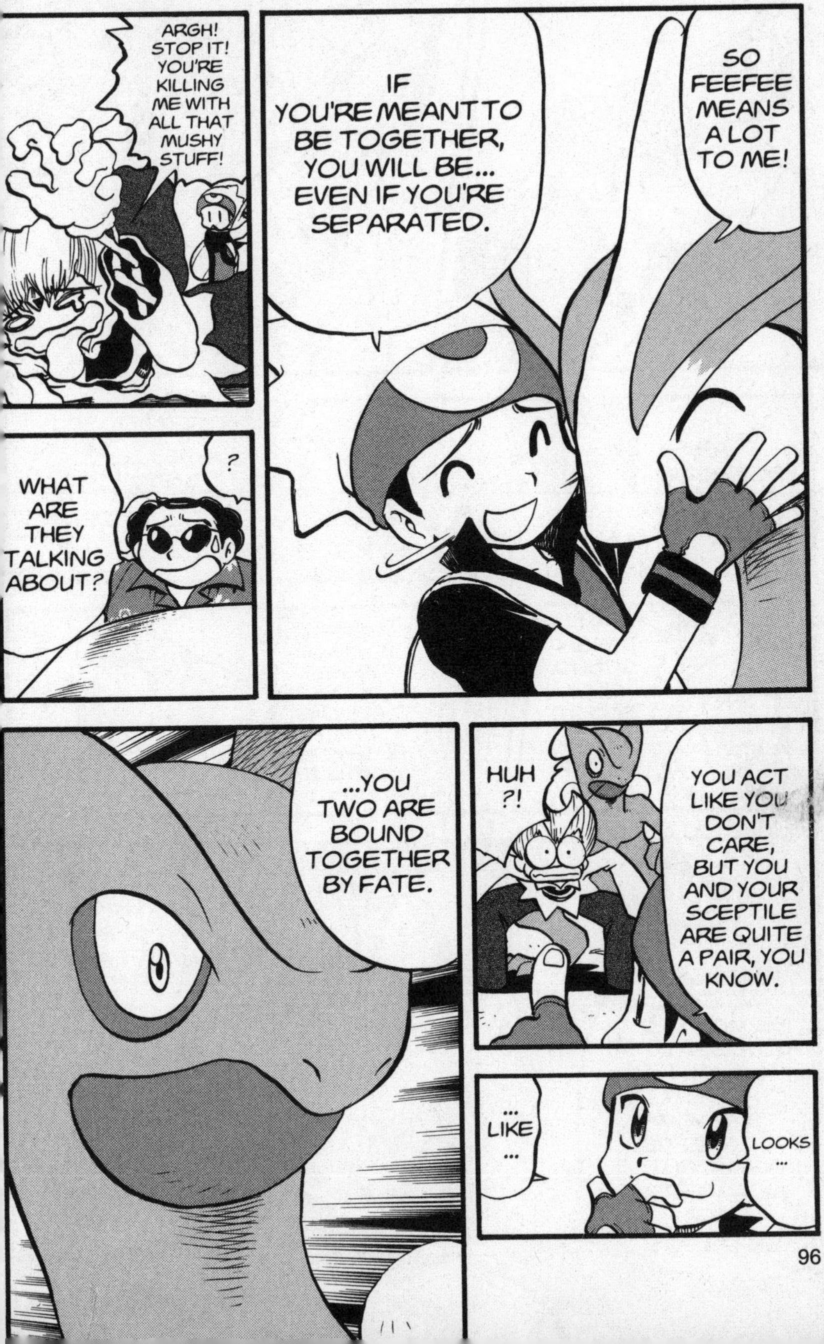
SO FEEFEE MEANS A LOT TO ME!
IF YOU'RE MEANT TO BE TOGETHER, YOU WILL BE... EVEN IF YOU'RE SEPARATED.
ARGH! STOP IT! YOU'RE KILLING ME WITH ALL THAT MUSHY STUFF!
?
WHAT ARE THEY TALKING ABOUT?
YOU ACT LIKE YOU DON'T CARE, BUT YOU AND YOUR SCEPTILE ARE QUITE A PAIR, YOU KNOW.
HUH ?!
LOOKS ...
... LIKE ...
...YOU TWO ARE BOUND TOGETHER BY FATE.

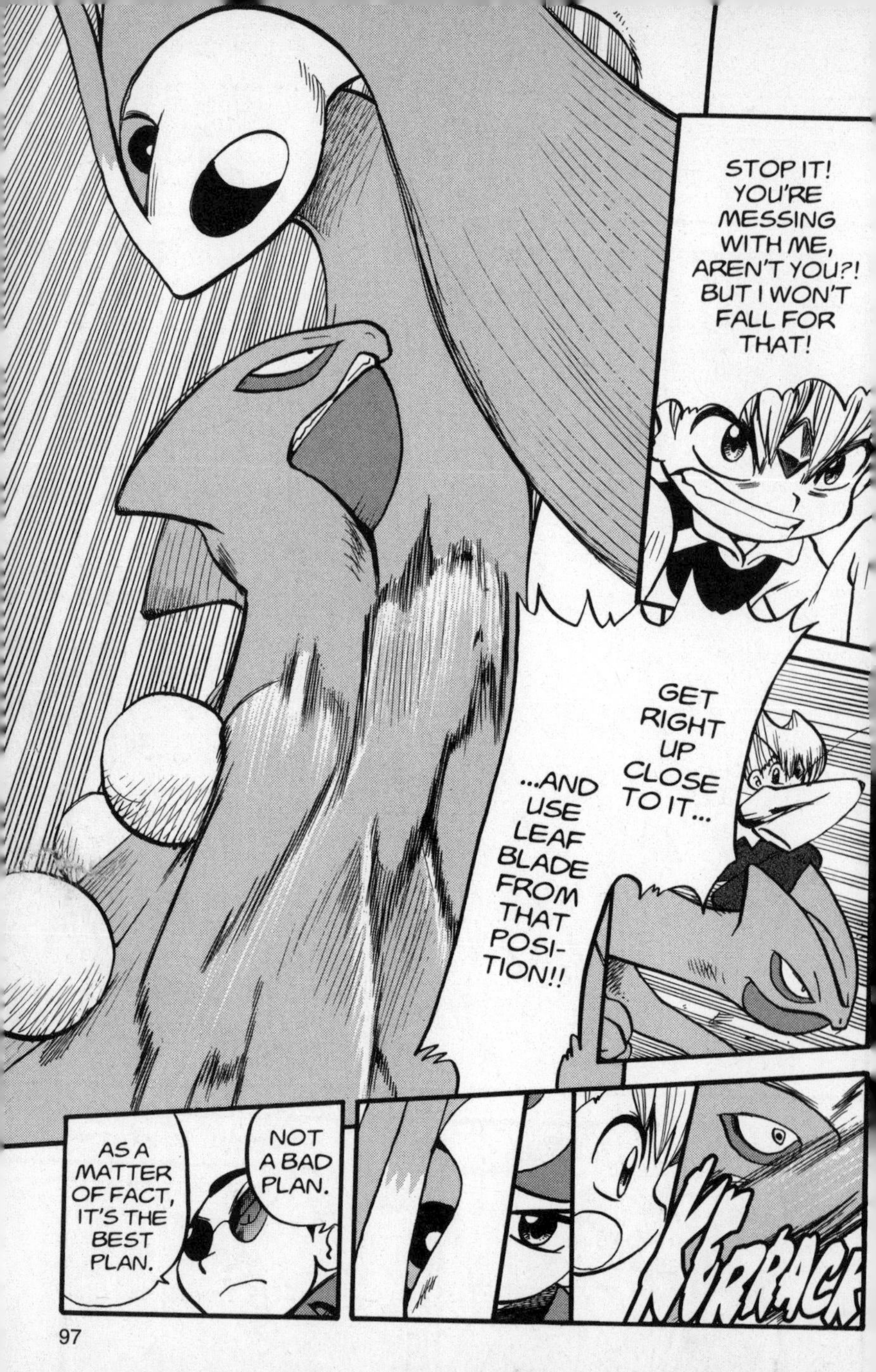
STOP IT! YOU'RE MESSING WITH ME, AREN'T YOU?! BUT I WON'T FALL FOR THAT!
GET RIGHT UP CLOSE TO IT...
...AND USE LEAF BLADE FROM THAT POSI-TION!!
KRRACK
NOT A BAD PLAN.
AS A MATTER OF FACT, IT'S THE BEST PLAN.

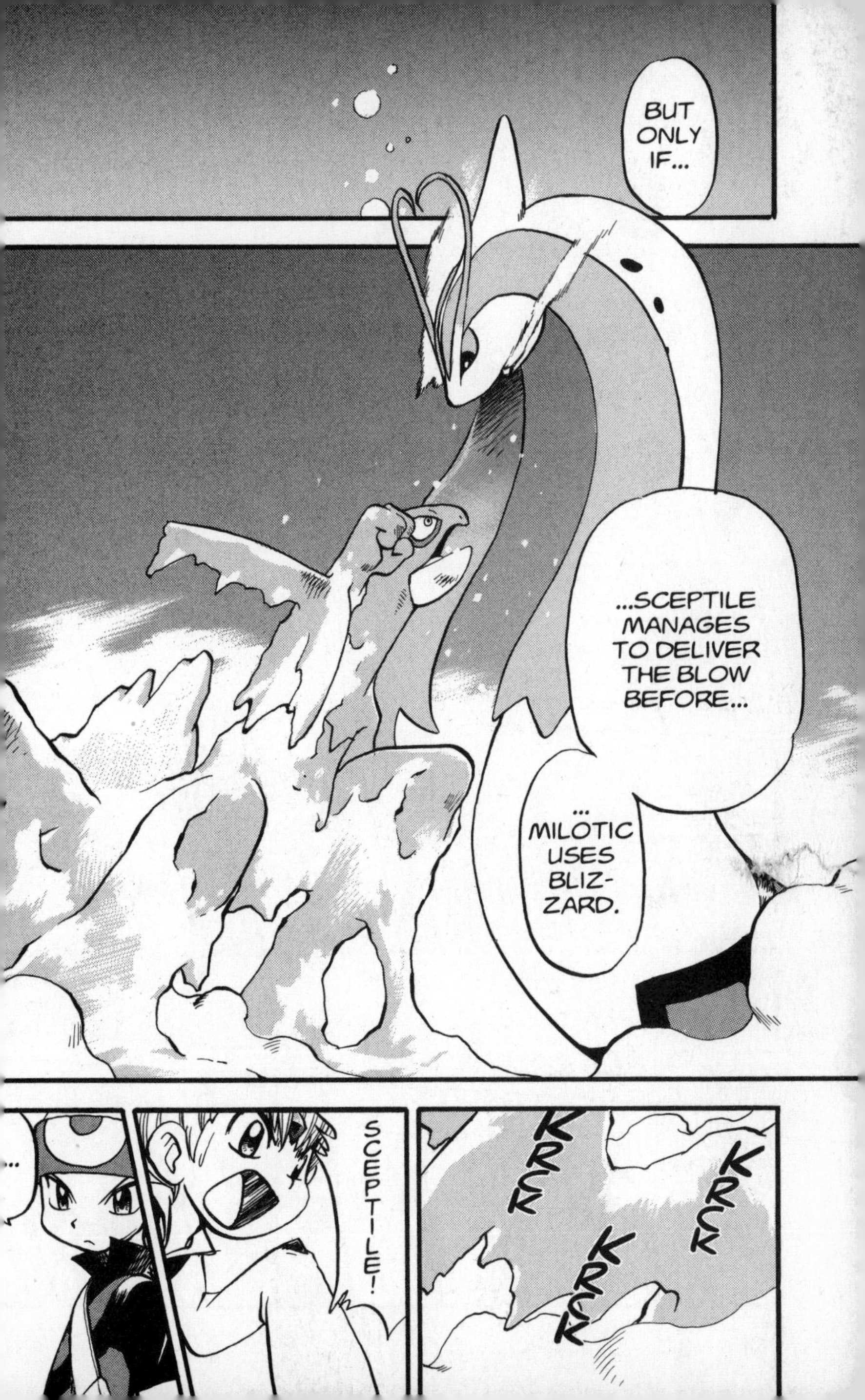
BUT ONLY IF...
...SCEPTILE MANAGES TO DELIVER THE BLOW BEFORE...
... MILOTIC USES BLIZ-ZARD.
KRCK KRCK KRCK
SCEPTILE!
...

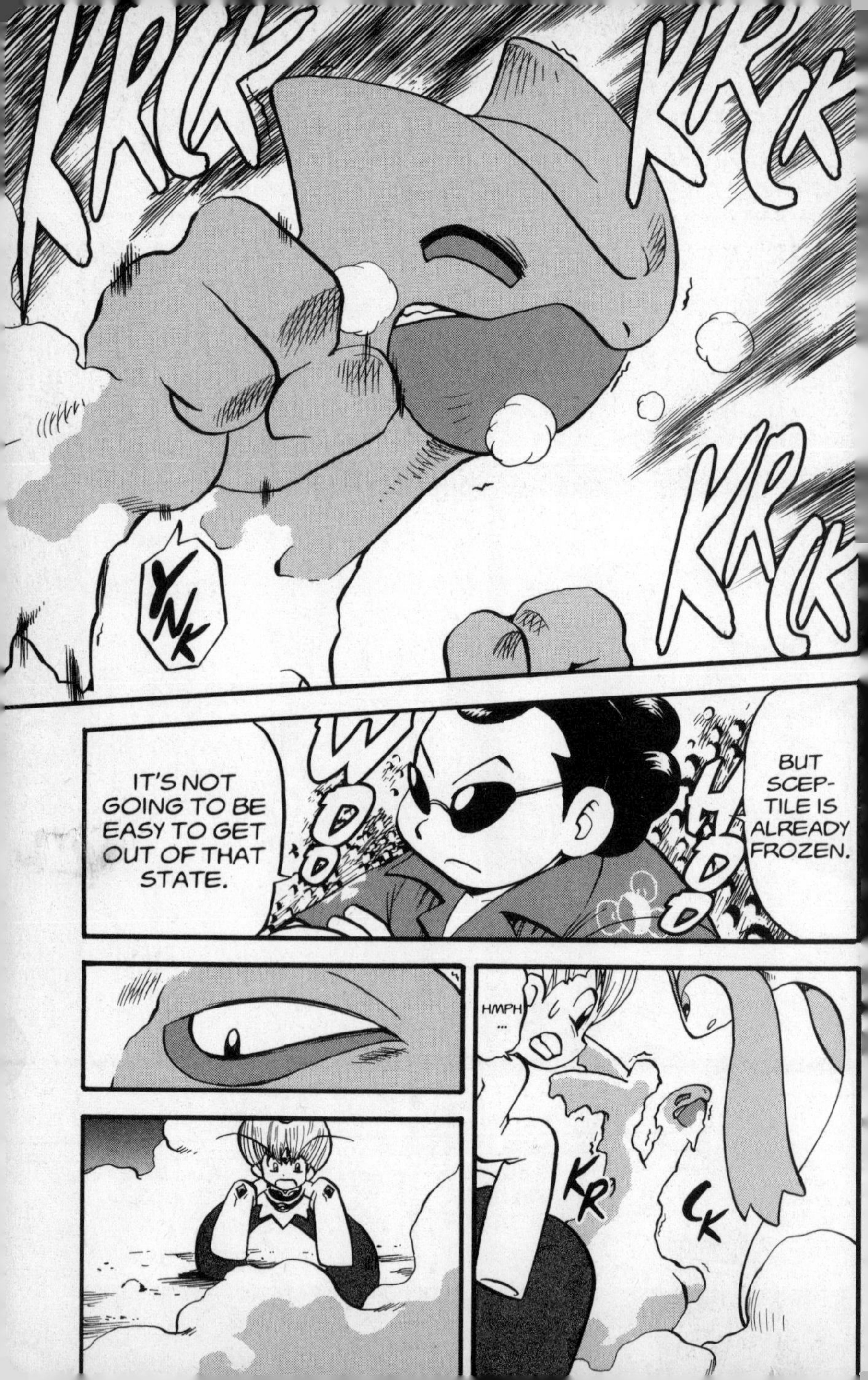
KRCK
KRCK
KRCK
YANK
BUT SCEP-
TILE IS
ALREADY
FROZEN.
IT'S NOT
GOING TO BE
EASY TO GET
OUT OF THAT
STATE.
HMPH
...
KR
CK

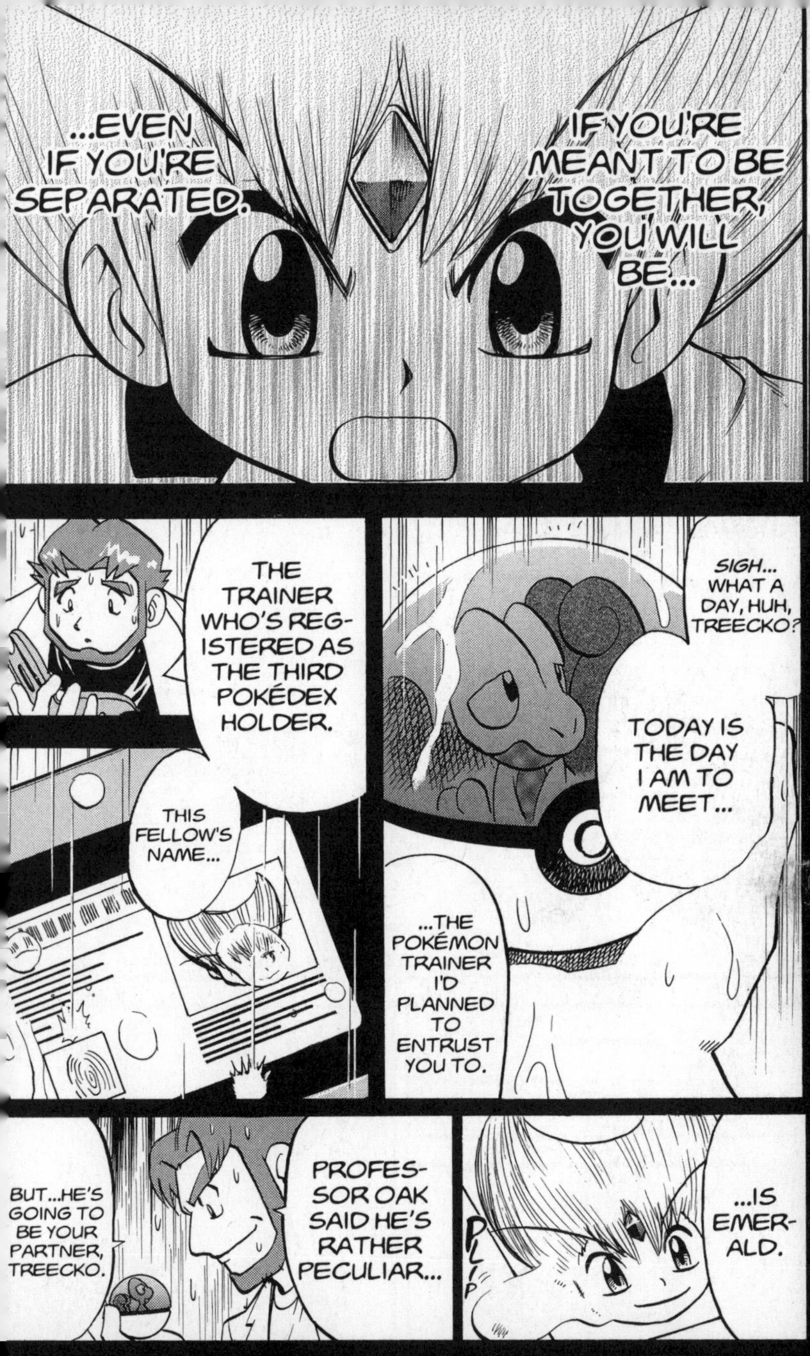
IF YOU'RE MEANT TO BE TOGETHER, YOU WILL BE...
...EVEN IF YOU'RE SEPARATED.
SIGH... WHAT A DAY, HUH, TREECKO?
TODAY IS THE DAY I AM TO MEET...
...THE POKÉMON TRAINER I'D PLANNED TO ENTRUST YOU TO.
THE TRAINER WHO'S REGISTERED AS THE THIRD POKÉDEX HOLDER.
THIS FELLOW'S NAME...
...IS EMERALD.
FLIP
PROFESSOR OAK SAID HE'S RATHER PECULIAR...
BUT...HE'S GOING TO BE YOUR PARTNER, TREECKO.

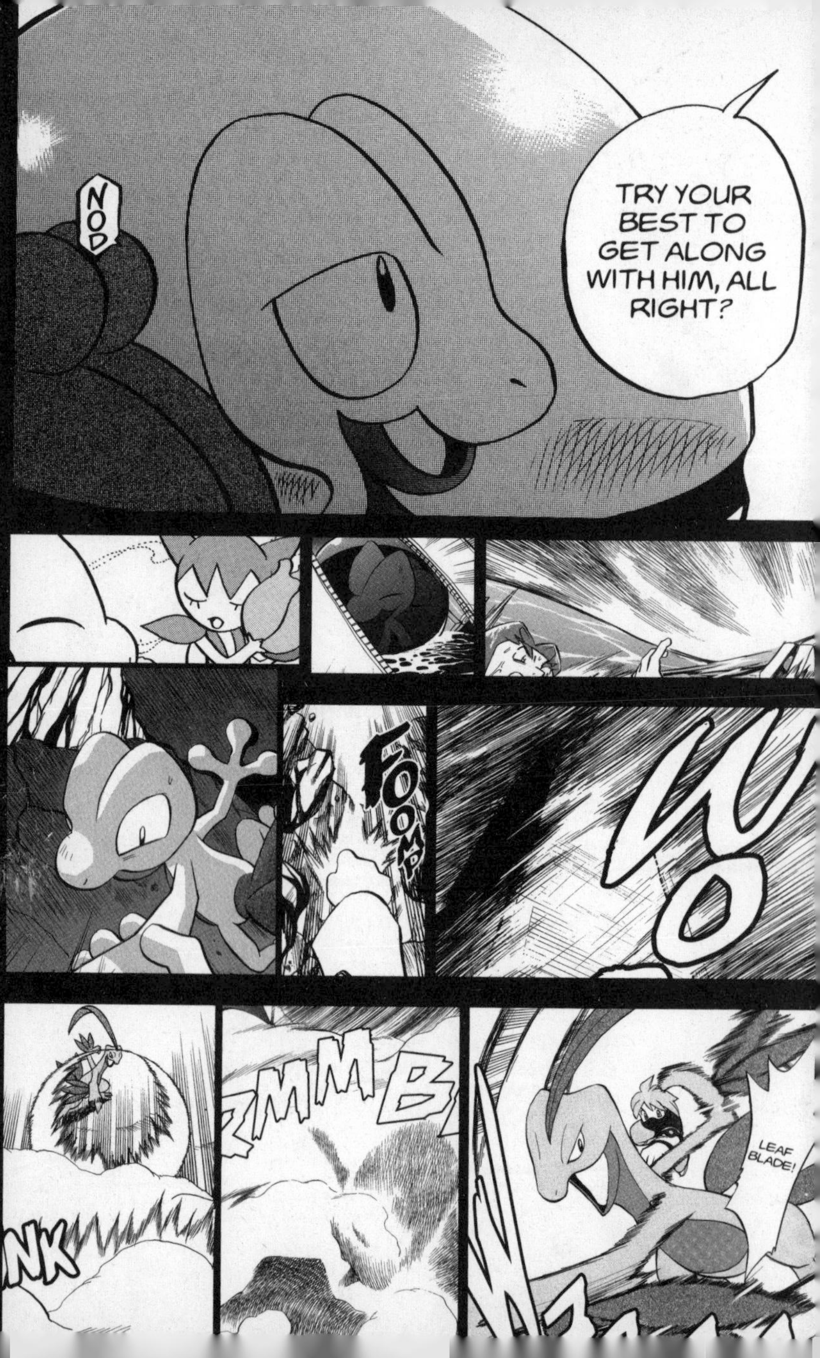
TRY YOUR BEST TO GET ALONG WITH HIM, ALL RIGHT?
NOD
FOOMP
LEAF BLADE!
ZMMMB
NK

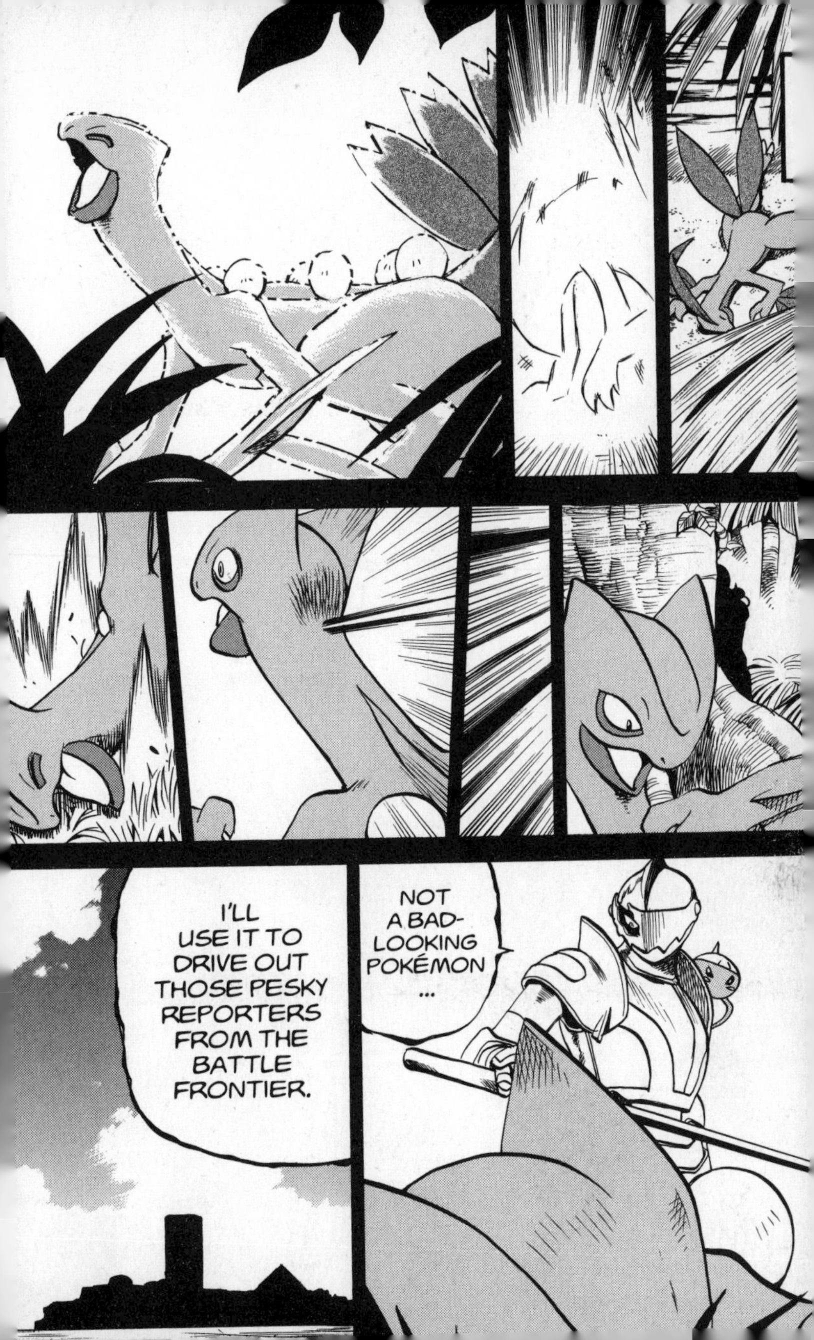
NOT A BAD-LOOKING POKÉMON ...
I'LL USE IT TO DRIVE OUT THOSE PESKY REPORTERS FROM THE BATTLE FRONTIER.

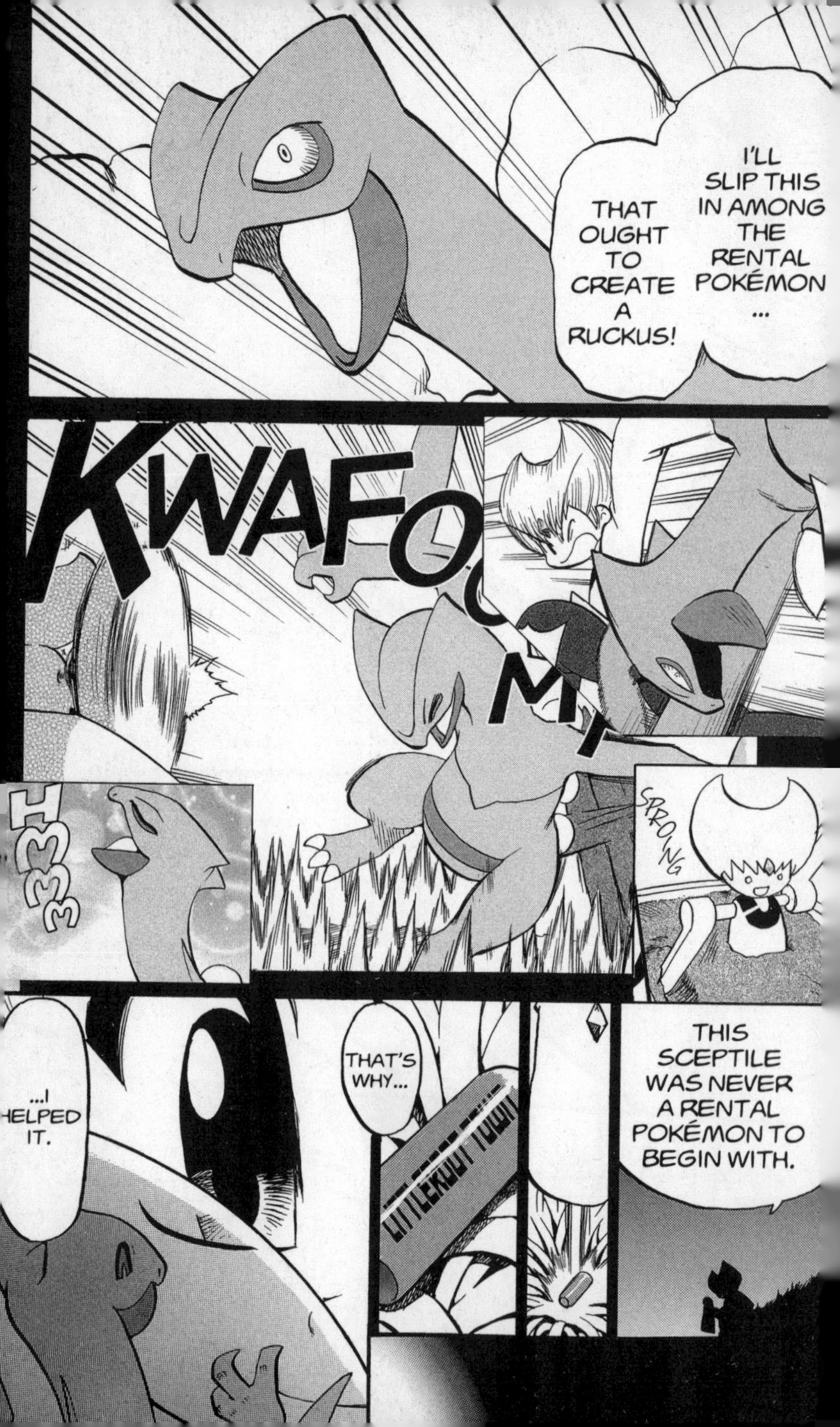
I'LL SLIP THIS IN AMONG THE RENTAL POKÉMON ...
THAT OUGHT TO CREATE A RUCKUS!
KWAFOOMY
SPROING
HMMMM
THIS SCEPTILE WAS NEVER A RENTAL POKÉMON TO BEGIN WITH.
THAT'S WHY...
...I HELPED IT.

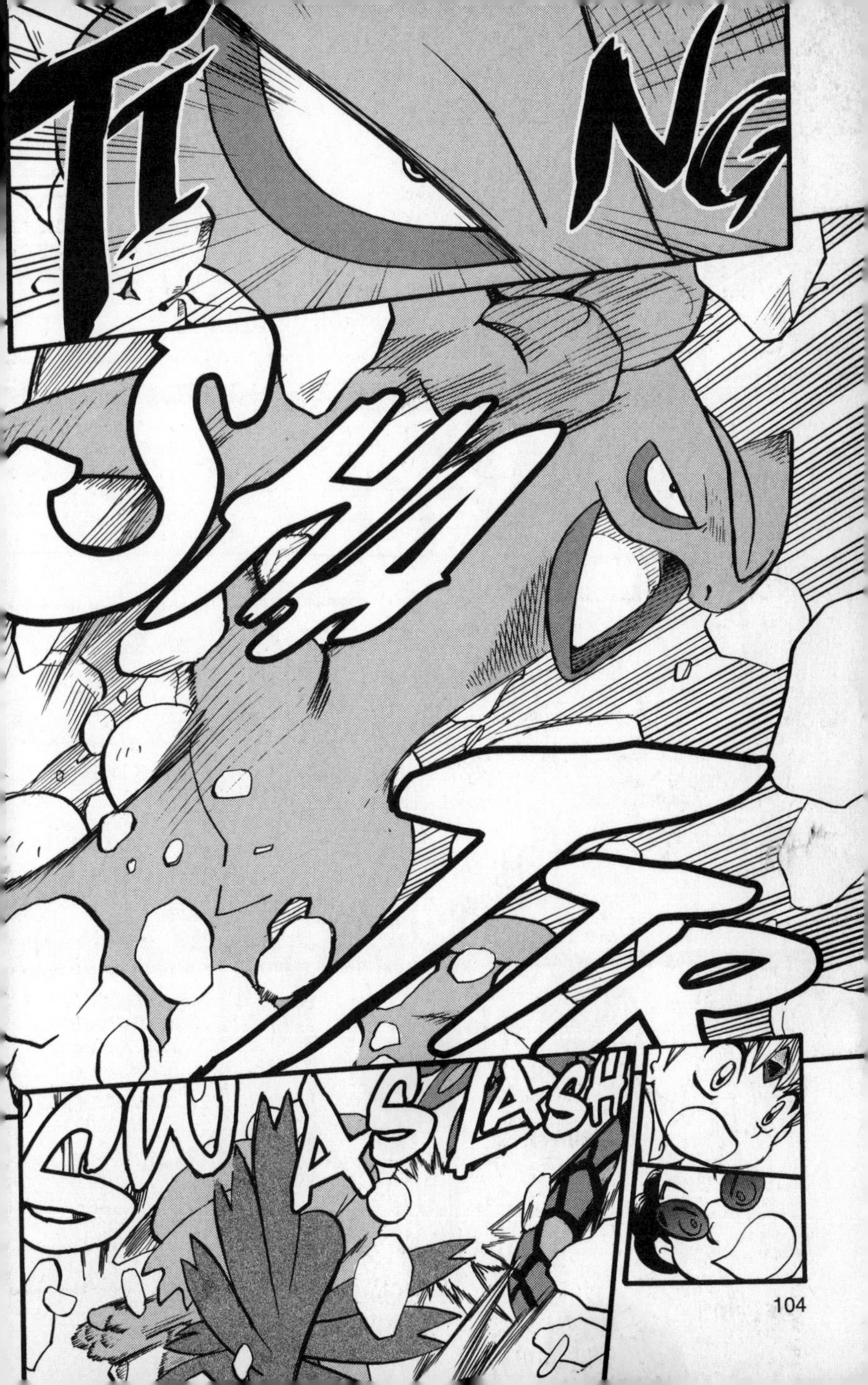
TING
SWASLASH

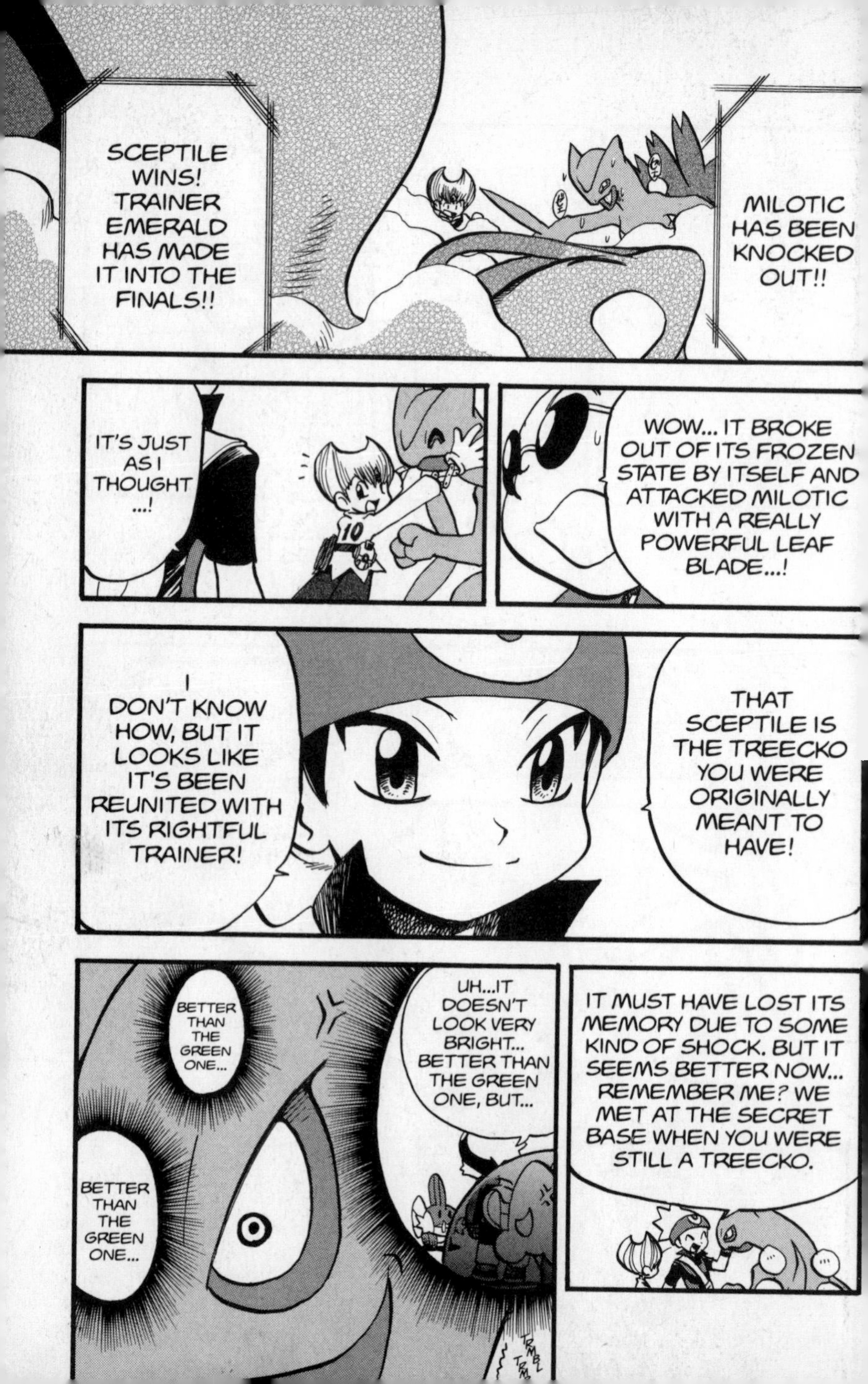
MILOTIC HAS BEEN KNOCKED OUT!!
SCEPTILE WINS! TRAINER EMERALD HAS MADE IT INTO THE FINALS!!
WOW... IT BROKE OUT OF ITS FROZEN STATE BY ITSELF AND ATTACKED MILOTIC WITH A REALLY POWERFUL LEAF BLADE...!
IT'S JUST AS I THOUGHT ...!
THAT SCEPTILE IS THE TREECKO YOU WERE ORIGINALLY MEANT TO HAVE!
I DON'T KNOW HOW, BUT IT LOOKS LIKE IT'S BEEN REUNITED WITH ITS RIGHTFUL TRAINER!
IT MUST HAVE LOST ITS MEMORY DUE TO SOME KIND OF SHOCK. BUT IT SEEMS BETTER NOW... REMEMBER ME? WE MET AT THE SECRET BASE WHEN YOU WERE STILL A TREECKO.
UH...IT DOESN'T LOOK VERY BRIGHT... BETTER THAN THE GREEN ONE, BUT...
BETTER THAN THE GREEN ONE...
BETTER THAN THE GREEN ONE...
TRMBL TRMBL

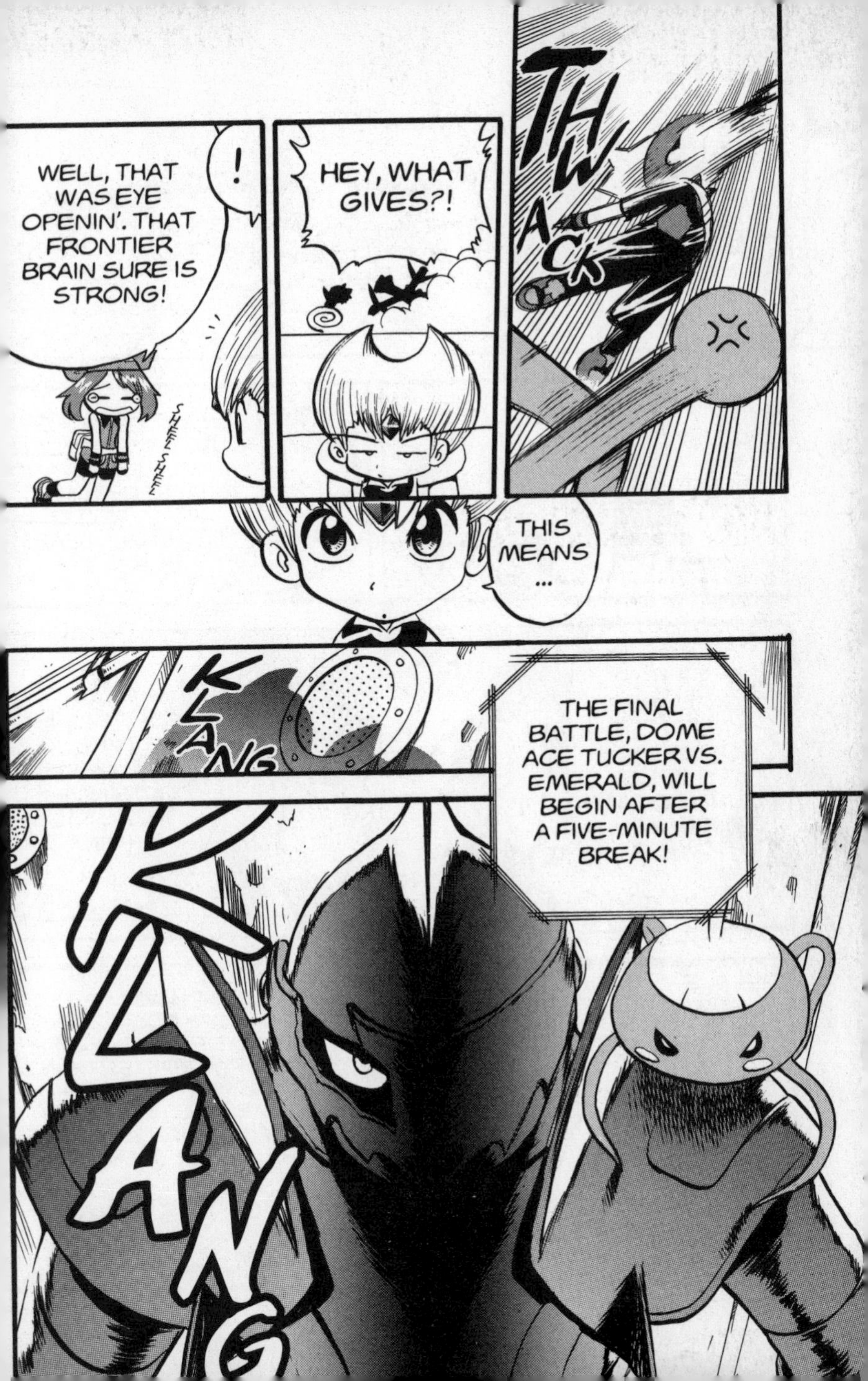
THWACK
HEY, WHAT GIVES?!
!
WELL, THAT WAS EYE OPENIN'. THAT FRONTIER BRAIN SURE IS STRONG!
SHEEL SHEEL
THIS MEANS ...
KLANG
THE FINAL BATTLE, DOME ACE TUCKER VS. EMERALD, WILL BEGIN AFTER A FIVE-MINUTE BREAK!
KLANG

DEAR MEMBERS OF THE PRESS...

Thank you for visiting the Battle Frontier today. Permit me to continue explaining the rules of this facility...

OWNER: SCOTT

FACILITY RULES

BATTLE PALACE 3

■ MOVE CATEGORY ■

All the moves are uniquely categorized at the Battle Palace. These are the three categories.

ATTACK Moves like Iron Tail and Ice Beam that attack and damage an opponent.

DEFENSE Moves like Rest and Swords Dance which boost the Pokémon's stats or heal damage and status conditions.

SUPPORT Moves like Toxic and Charm which lower the opponent's stats or give them status conditions.

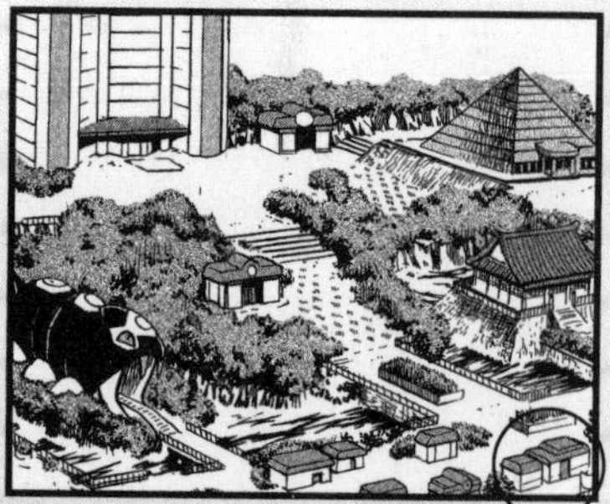

The types of moves used by the Pokémon will depend on their Nature. You can receive help from an avid fan (west of the Battle Palace) who will teach you what kind of moves your Pokémon are inclined to choose when left to their own devices.

323

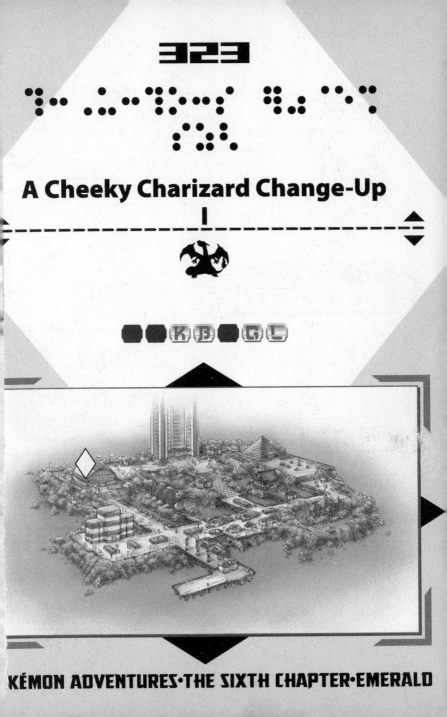

A Cheeky Charizard Change-Up I

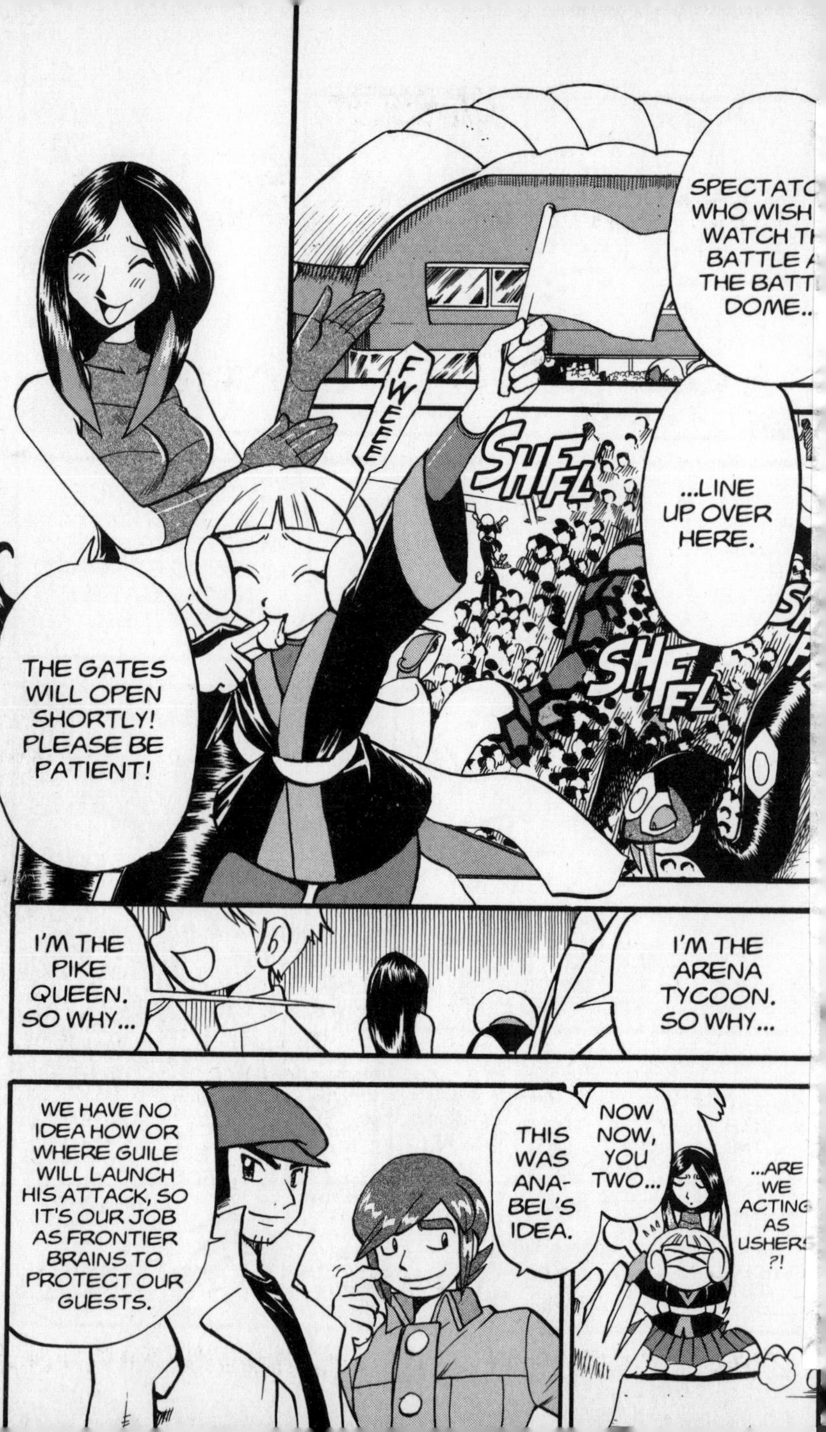
SPECTATO
WHO WISH
WATCH T
BATTLE A
THE BATT
DOME..
...LINE UP OVER HERE.
SHFFL
SHFFL
FWEEE
THE GATES WILL OPEN SHORTLY! PLEASE BE PATIENT!
I'M THE ARENA TYCOON. SO WHY...
I'M THE PIKE QUEEN. SO WHY...
...ARE WE ACTING AS USHERS?!
NOW NOW, YOU TWO...
THIS WAS ANA-BEL'S IDEA.
WE HAVE NO IDEA HOW OR WHERE GUILE WILL LAUNCH HIS ATTACK, SO IT'S OUR JOB AS FRONTIER BRAINS TO PROTECT OUR GUESTS.

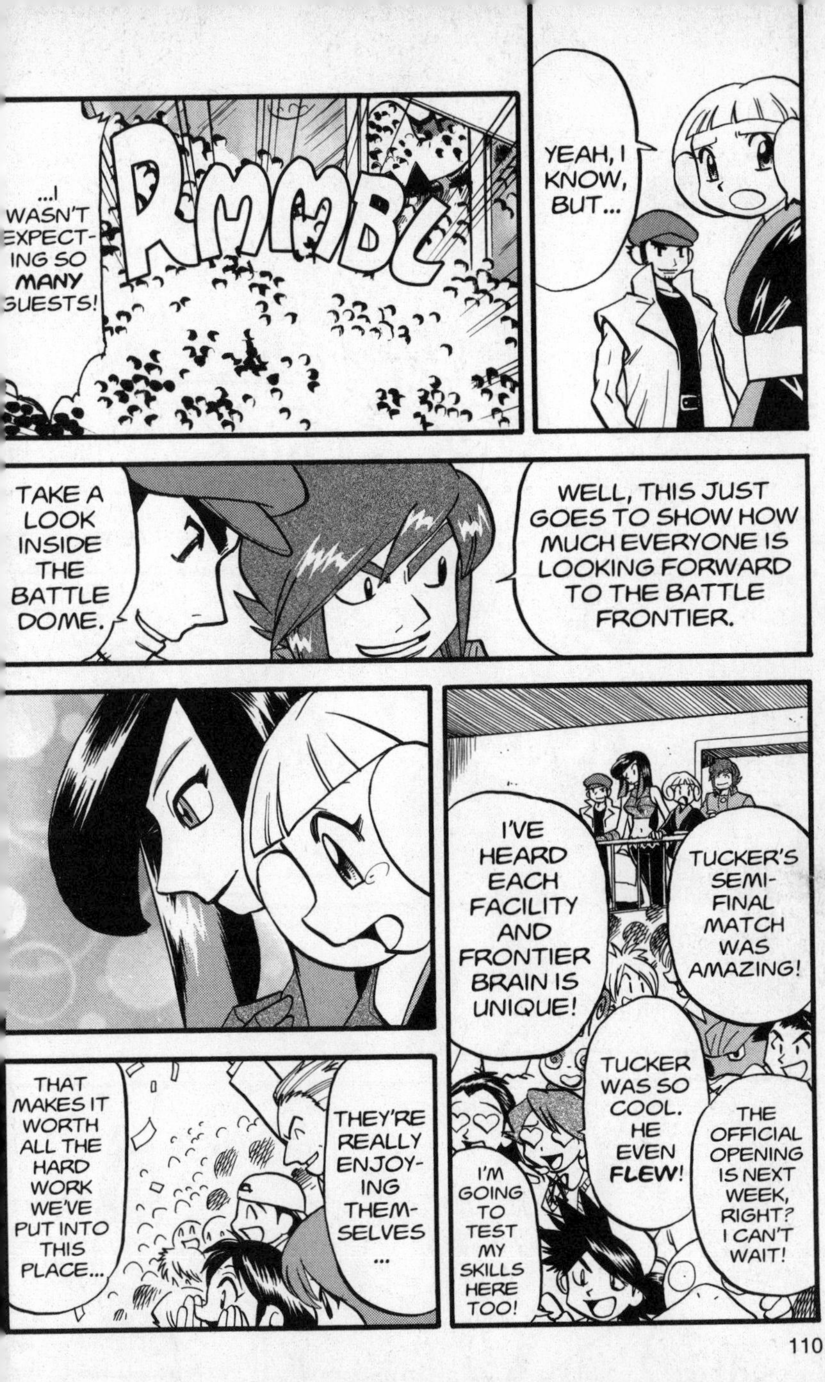
YEAH, I KNOW, BUT...
RMMBL
...I WASN'T EXPECTING SO **MANY** GUESTS!
WELL, THIS JUST GOES TO SHOW HOW MUCH EVERYONE IS LOOKING FORWARD TO THE BATTLE FRONTIER.
TAKE A LOOK INSIDE THE BATTLE DOME.
TUCKER'S SEMI-FINAL MATCH WAS AMAZING!
I'VE HEARD EACH FACILITY AND FRONTIER BRAIN IS UNIQUE!
THE OFFICIAL OPENING IS NEXT WEEK, RIGHT? I CAN'T WAIT!
TUCKER WAS SO COOL. HE EVEN **FLEW**!
I'M GOING TO TEST MY SKILLS HERE TOO!
THEY'RE REALLY ENJOYING THEMSELVES...
THAT MAKES IT WORTH ALL THE HARD WORK WE'VE PUT INTO THIS PLACE...

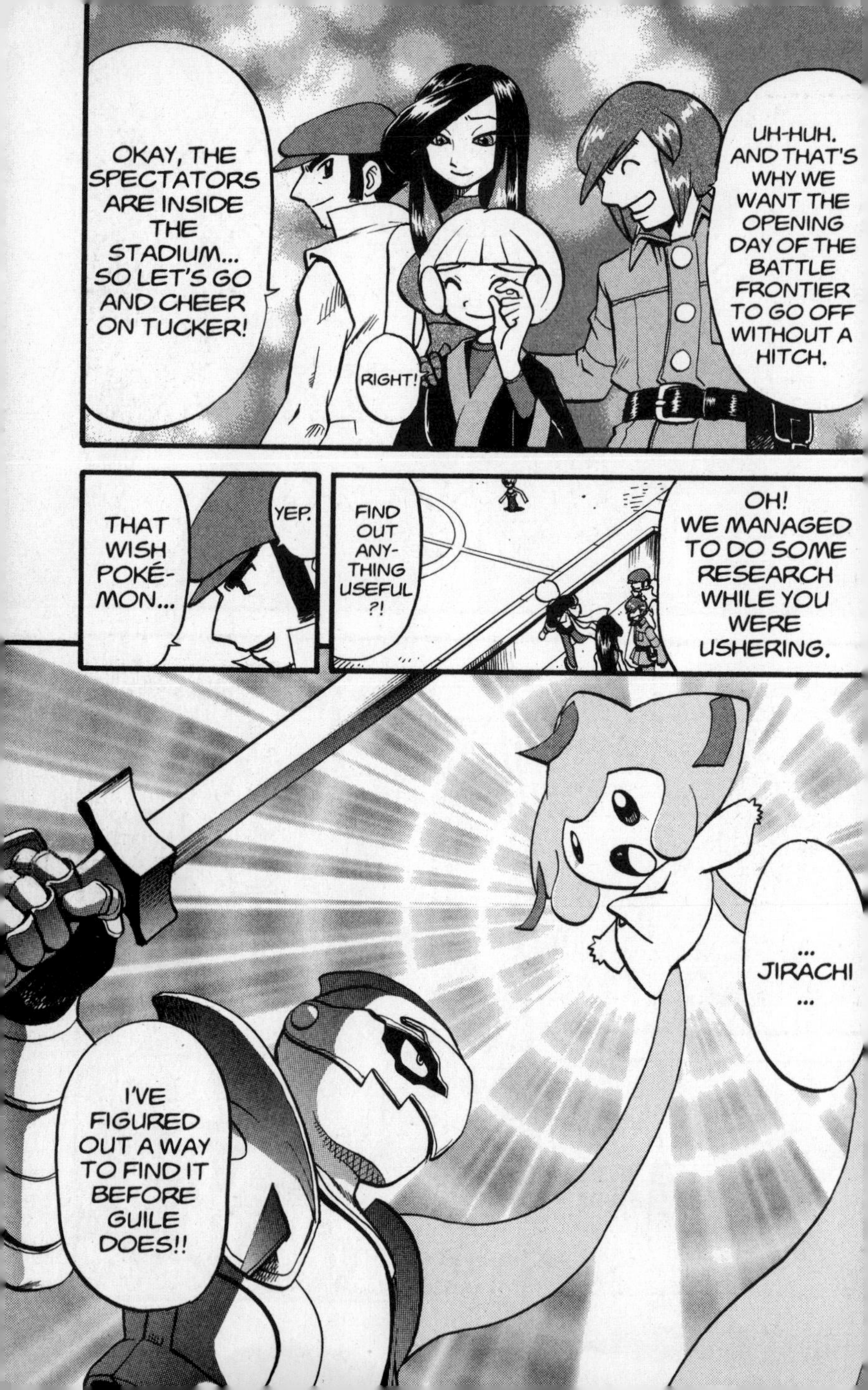
UH-HUH. AND THAT'S WHY WE WANT THE OPENING DAY OF THE BATTLE FRONTIER TO GO OFF WITHOUT A HITCH.
OKAY, THE SPECTATORS ARE INSIDE THE STADIUM... SO LET'S GO AND CHEER ON TUCKER!
RIGHT!
OH! WE MANAGED TO DO SOME RESEARCH WHILE YOU WERE USHERING.
FIND OUT ANYTHING USEFUL?!
YEP.
THAT WISH POKÉMON...
... JIRACHI ...
I'VE FIGURED OUT A WAY TO FIND IT BEFORE GUILE DOES!!

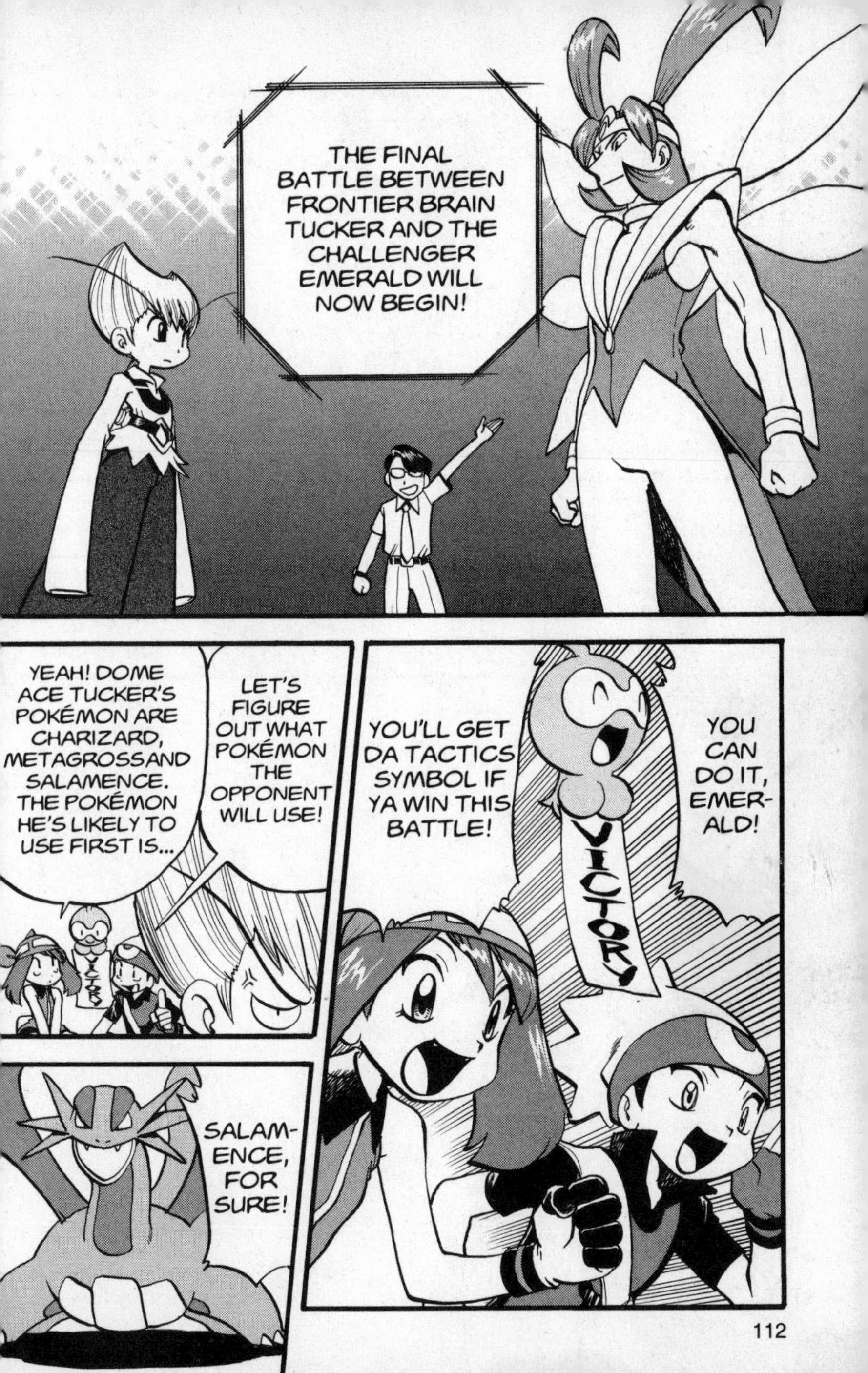
THE FINAL BATTLE BETWEEN FRONTIER BRAIN TUCKER AND THE CHALLENGER EMERALD WILL NOW BEGIN!
YOU CAN DO IT, EMER-ALD!
YOU'LL GET DA TACTICS SYMBOL IF YA WIN THIS BATTLE!
VICTORY!
LET'S FIGURE OUT WHAT POKÉMON THE OPPONENT WILL USE!
YEAH! DOME ACE TUCKER'S POKÉMON ARE CHARIZARD, METAGROSS AND SALAMENCE. THE POKÉMON HE'S LIKELY TO USE FIRST IS...
SALAM-ENCE, FOR SURE!

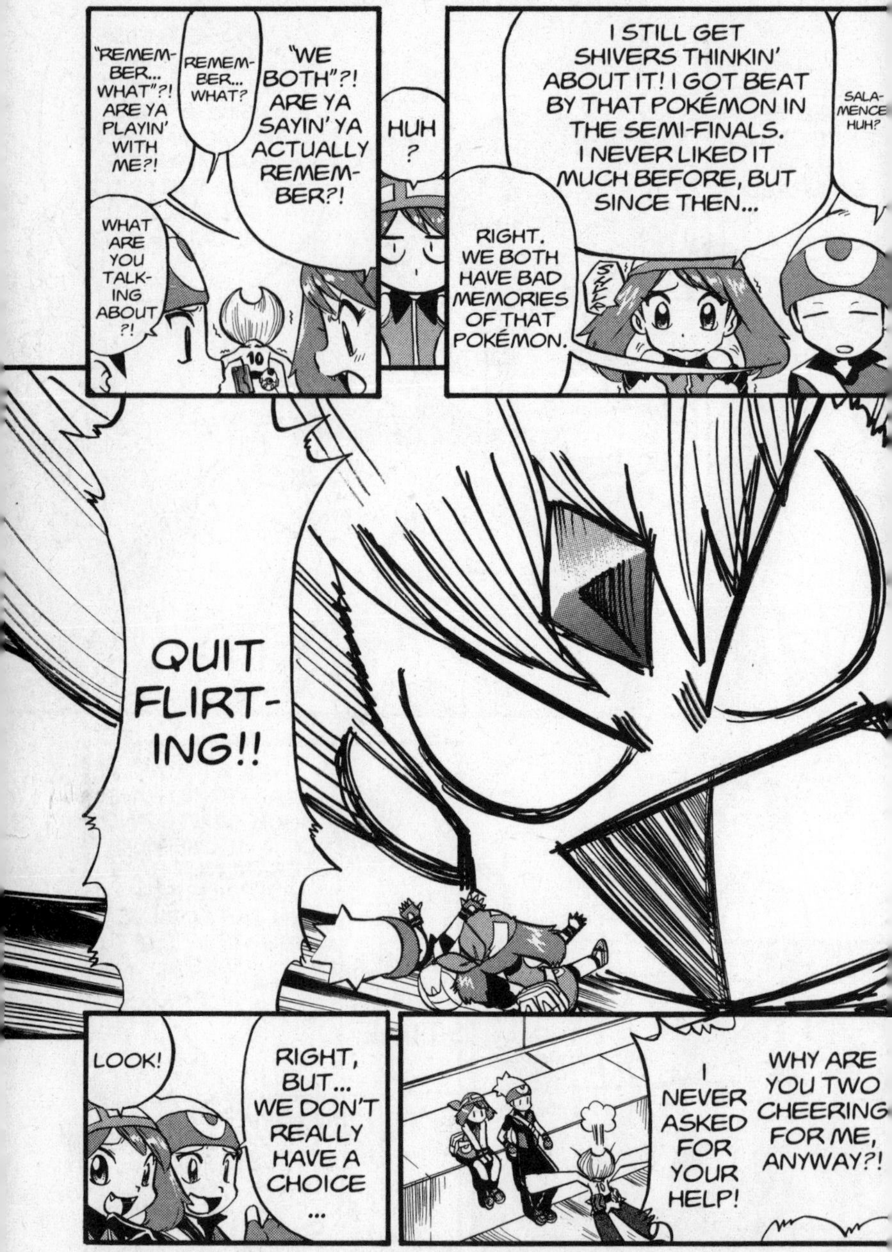
SALAMENCE HUH?
I STILL GET SHIVERS THINKIN' ABOUT IT! I GOT BEAT BY THAT POKÉMON IN THE SEMI-FINALS. I NEVER LIKED IT MUCH BEFORE, BUT SINCE THEN...
RIGHT. WE BOTH HAVE BAD MEMORIES OF THAT POKÉMON.
HUH?
"WE BOTH"?! ARE YA SAYIN' YA ACTUALLY REMEMBER?!
REMEMBER... WHAT?
"REMEMBER... WHAT"?! ARE YA PLAYIN' WITH ME?!
WHAT ARE YOU TALKING ABOUT?!
QUIT FLIRTING!!
WHY ARE YOU TWO CHEERING FOR ME, ANYWAY?!
I NEVER ASKED FOR YOUR HELP!
RIGHT, BUT... WE DON'T REALLY HAVE A CHOICE...
LOOK!

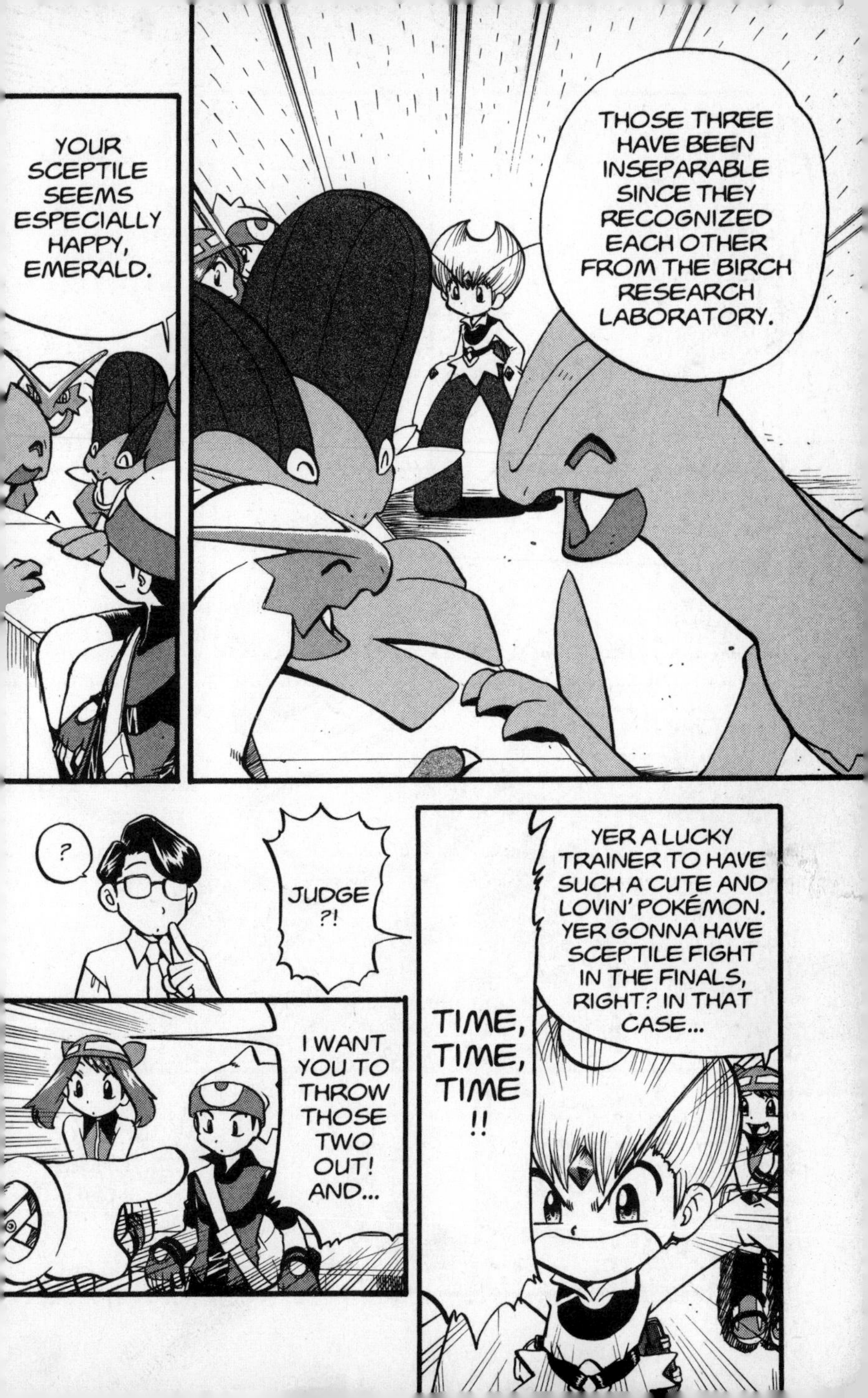
YOUR SCEPTILE SEEMS ESPECIALLY HAPPY, EMERALD.
THOSE THREE HAVE BEEN INSEPARABLE SINCE THEY RECOGNIZED EACH OTHER FROM THE BIRCH RESEARCH LABORATORY.
?
JUDGE ?!
YER A LUCKY TRAINER TO HAVE SUCH A CUTE AND LOVIN' POKÉMON. YER GONNA HAVE SCEPTILE FIGHT IN THE FINALS, RIGHT? IN THAT CASE...
TIME, TIME, TIME !!
I WANT YOU TO THROW THOSE TWO OUT! AND...

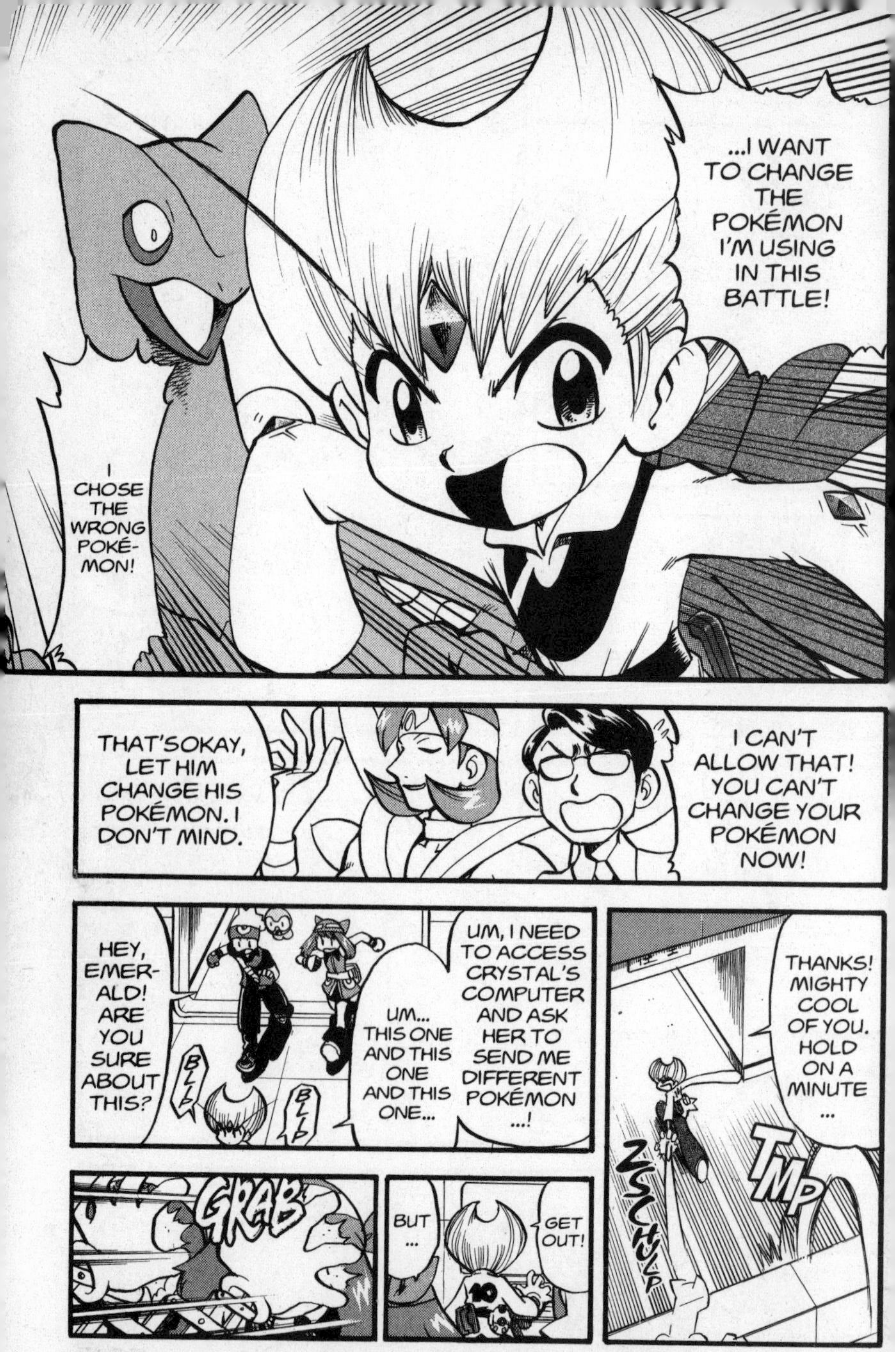
...I WANT TO CHANGE THE POKÉMON I'M USING IN THIS BATTLE!
I CHOSE THE WRONG POKÉ-MON!
I CAN'T ALLOW THAT! YOU CAN'T CHANGE YOUR POKÉMON NOW!
THAT'SOKAY, LET HIM CHANGE HIS POKÉMON. I DON'T MIND.
THANKS! MIGHTY COOL OF YOU. HOLD ON A MINUTE ...
TMP
ZSCHUP
UM, I NEED TO ACCESS CRYSTAL'S COMPUTER AND ASK HER TO SEND ME DIFFERENT POKÉMON ...!
UM... THIS ONE AND THIS ONE AND THIS ONE...
BLIP
BLIP
HEY, EMER-ALD! ARE YOU SURE ABOUT THIS?
GET OUT!
BUT ...
GRAB

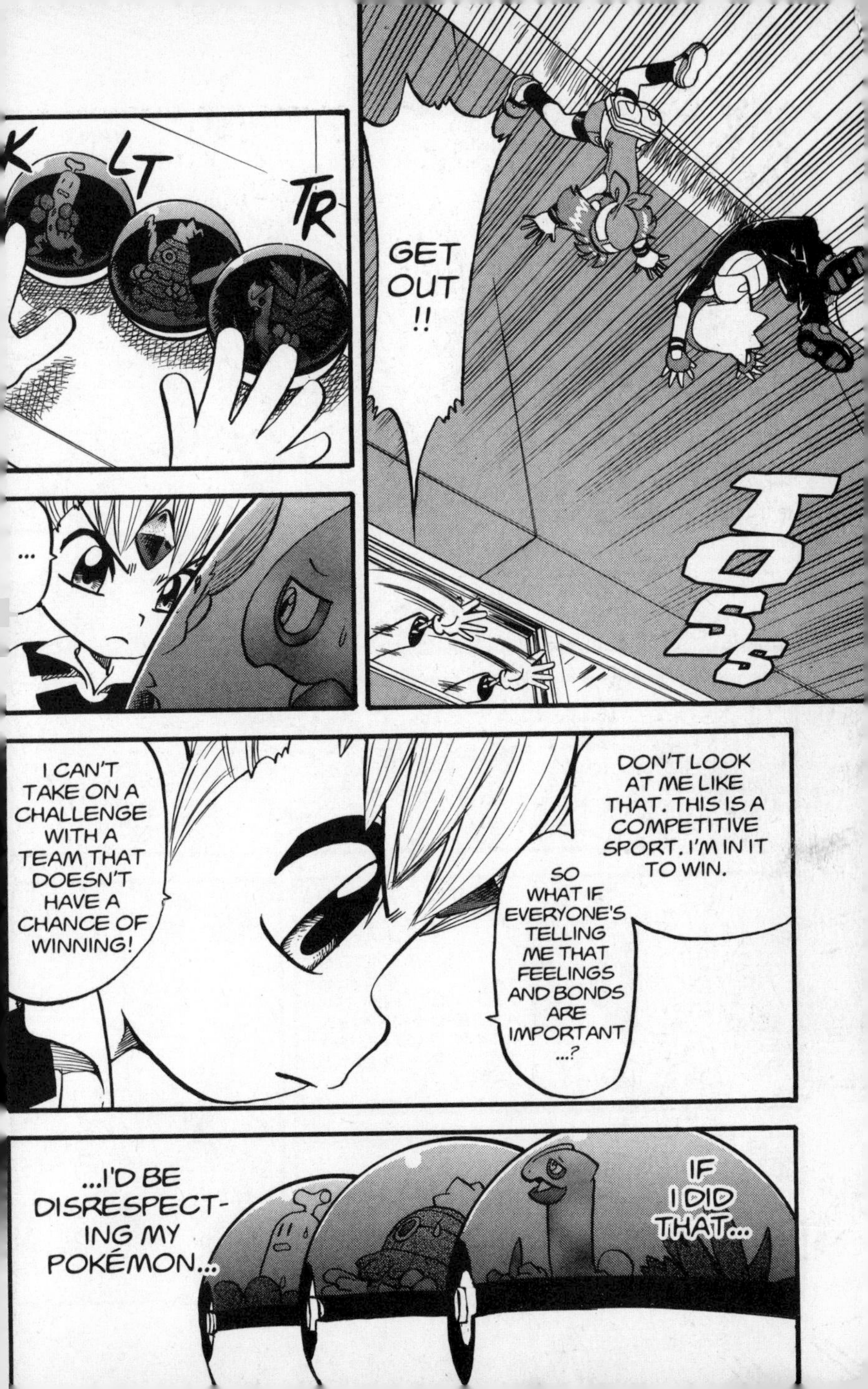
GET OUT !!
TOSS
KLT
TR
...
DON'T LOOK AT ME LIKE THAT. THIS IS A COMPETITIVE SPORT. I'M IN IT TO WIN.
SO WHAT IF EVERYONE'S TELLING ME THAT FEELINGS AND BONDS ARE IMPORTANT ...?
I CAN'T TAKE ON A CHALLENGE WITH A TEAM THAT DOESN'T HAVE A CHANCE OF WINNING!
IF I DID THAT...
...I'D BE DISRESPECT-ING MY POKÉMON...

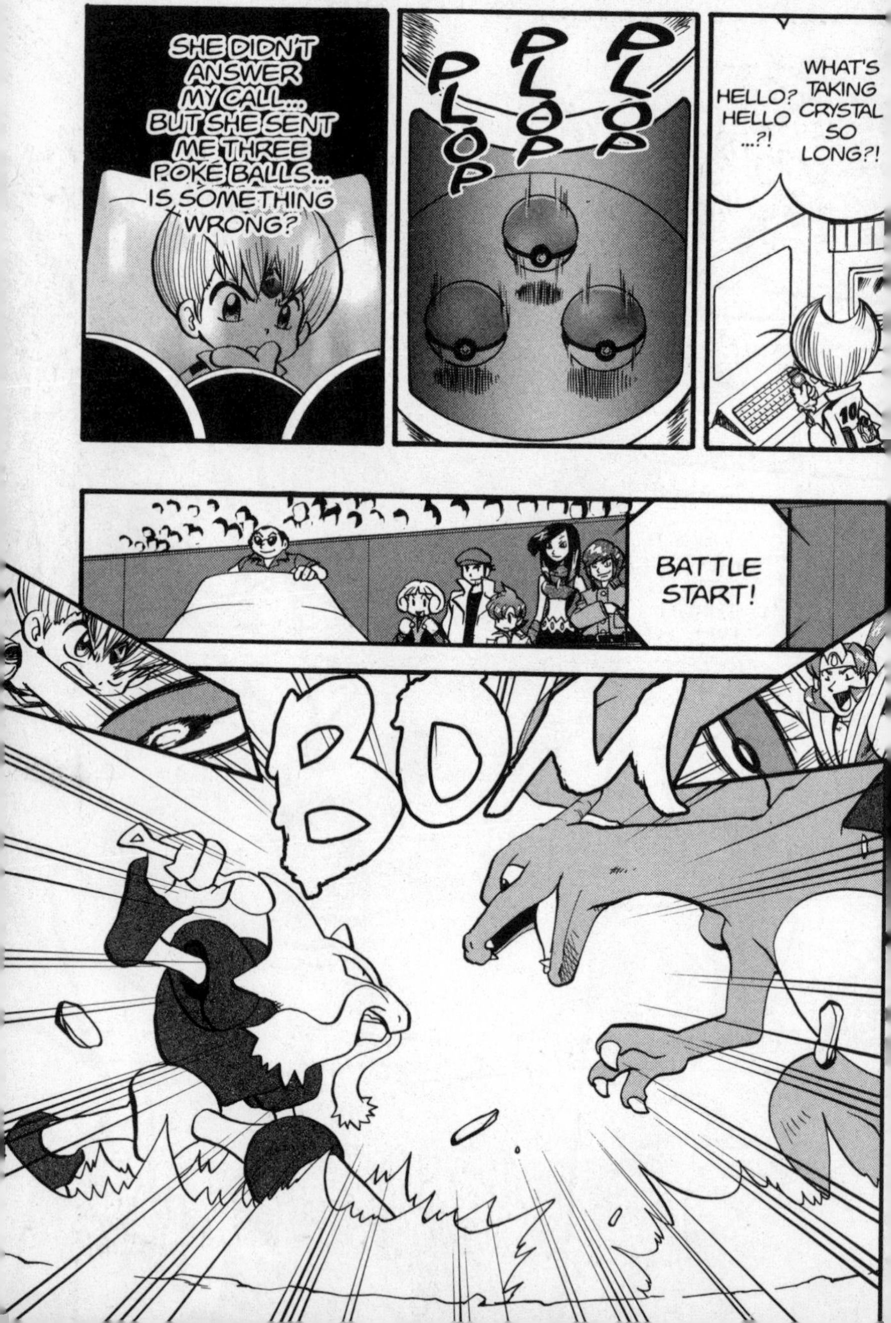
WHAT'S TAKING CRYSTAL SO LONG?!
HELLO? HELLO ...?!
PLOP PLOP PLOP
SHE DIDN'T ANSWER MY CALL... BUT SHE SENT ME THREE POKÉ BALLS... IS SOMETHING WRONG?
BATTLE START!
BOM

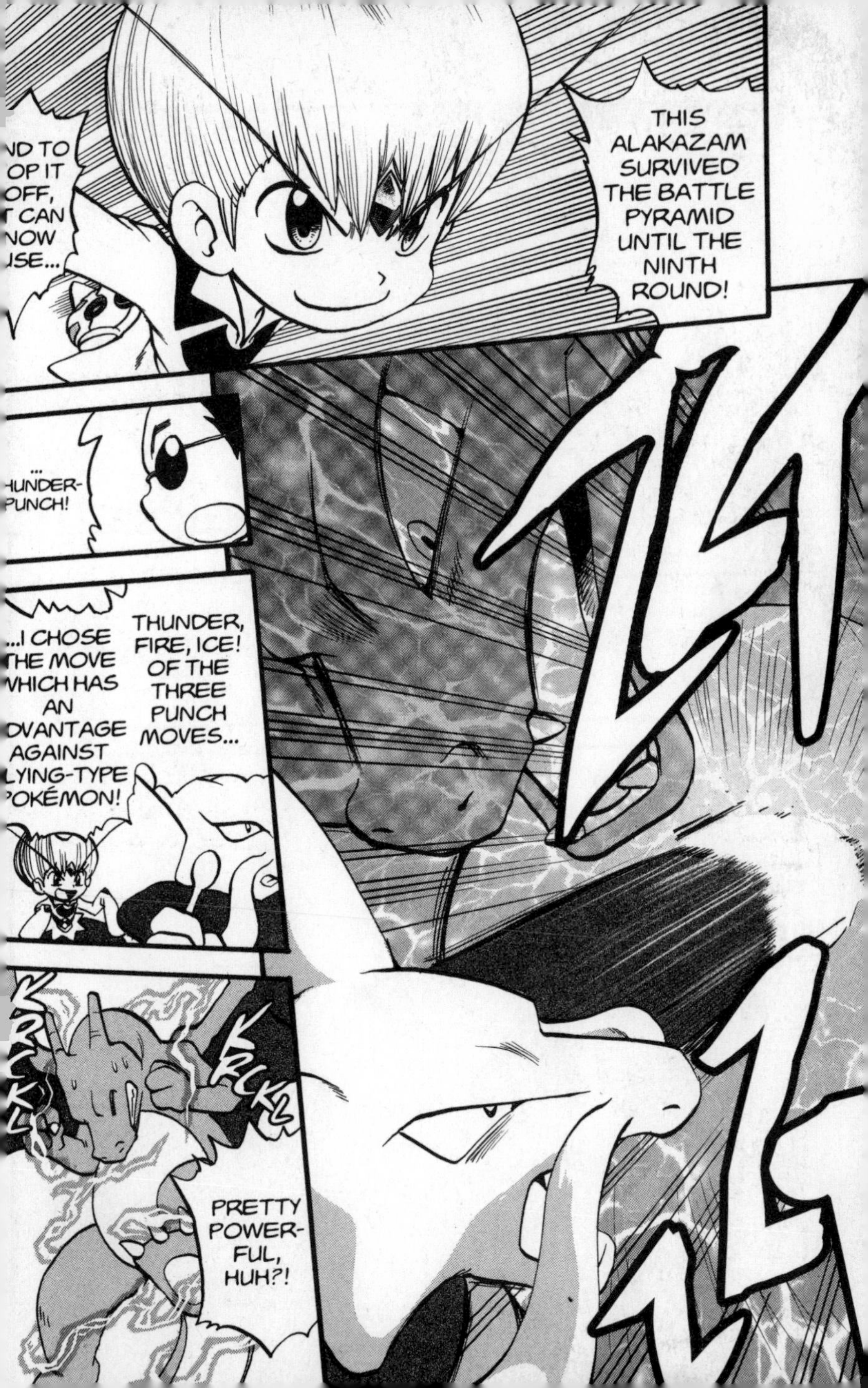
THIS ALAKAZAM SURVIVED THE BATTLE PYRAMID UNTIL THE NINTH ROUND!
ND TO OP IT OFF, T CAN NOW USE...
... HUNDER-PUNCH!
THUNDER, FIRE, ICE! OF THE THREE PUNCH MOVES...
...I CHOSE THE MOVE WHICH HAS AN DVANTAGE AGAINST LYING-TYPE OKÉMON!
PRETTY POWER-FUL, HUH?!

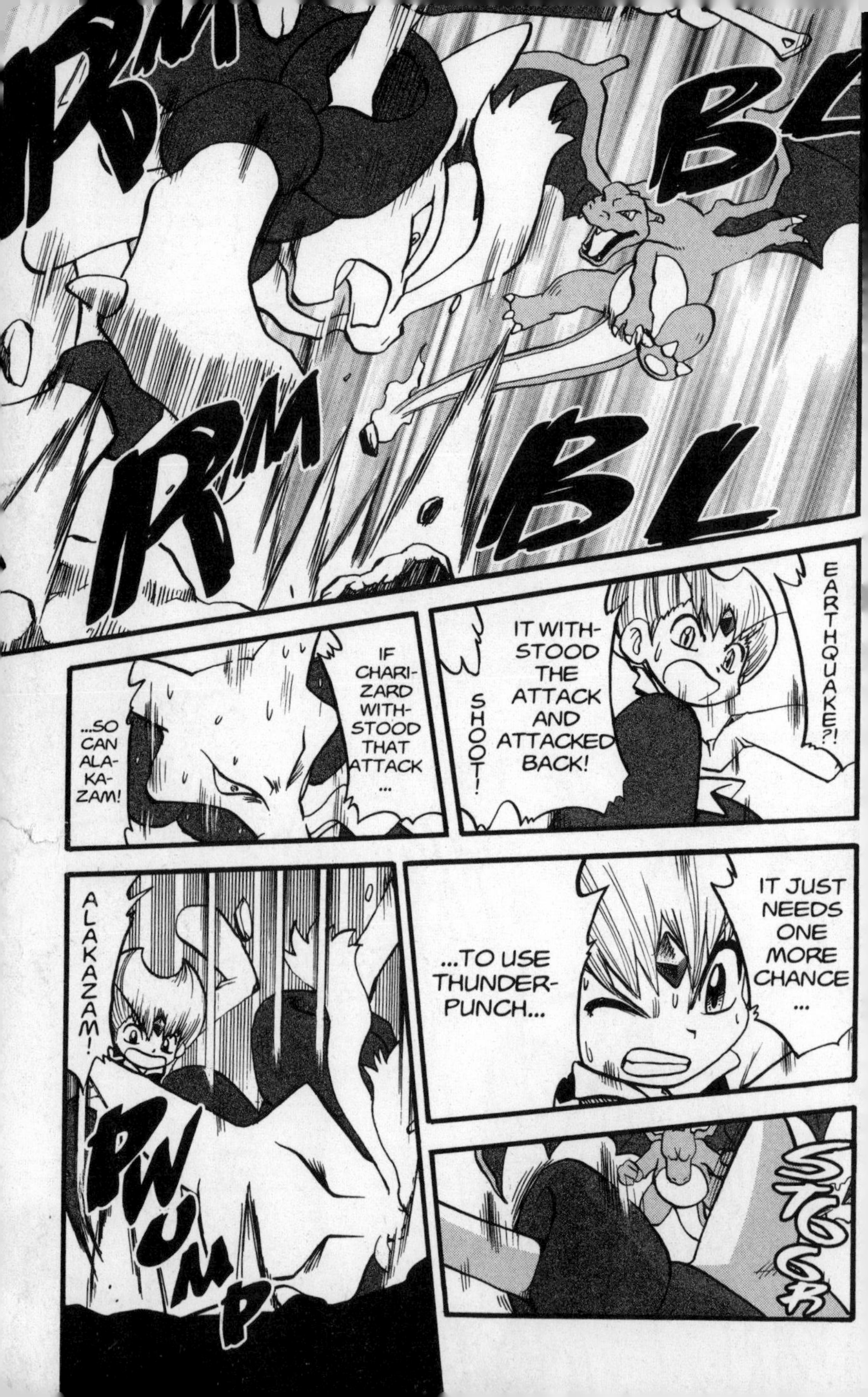
RM
BL
RM
BL
EARTHQUAKE?!
IT WITHSTOOD THE ATTACK AND ATTACKED BACK!
SHOOT!
IF CHARIZARD WITHSTOOD THAT ATTACK...
...SO CAN ALAKAZAM!
IT JUST NEEDS ONE MORE CHANCE...
...TO USE THUNDERPUNCH...
STGGR
ALAKAZAM!
PWUMP

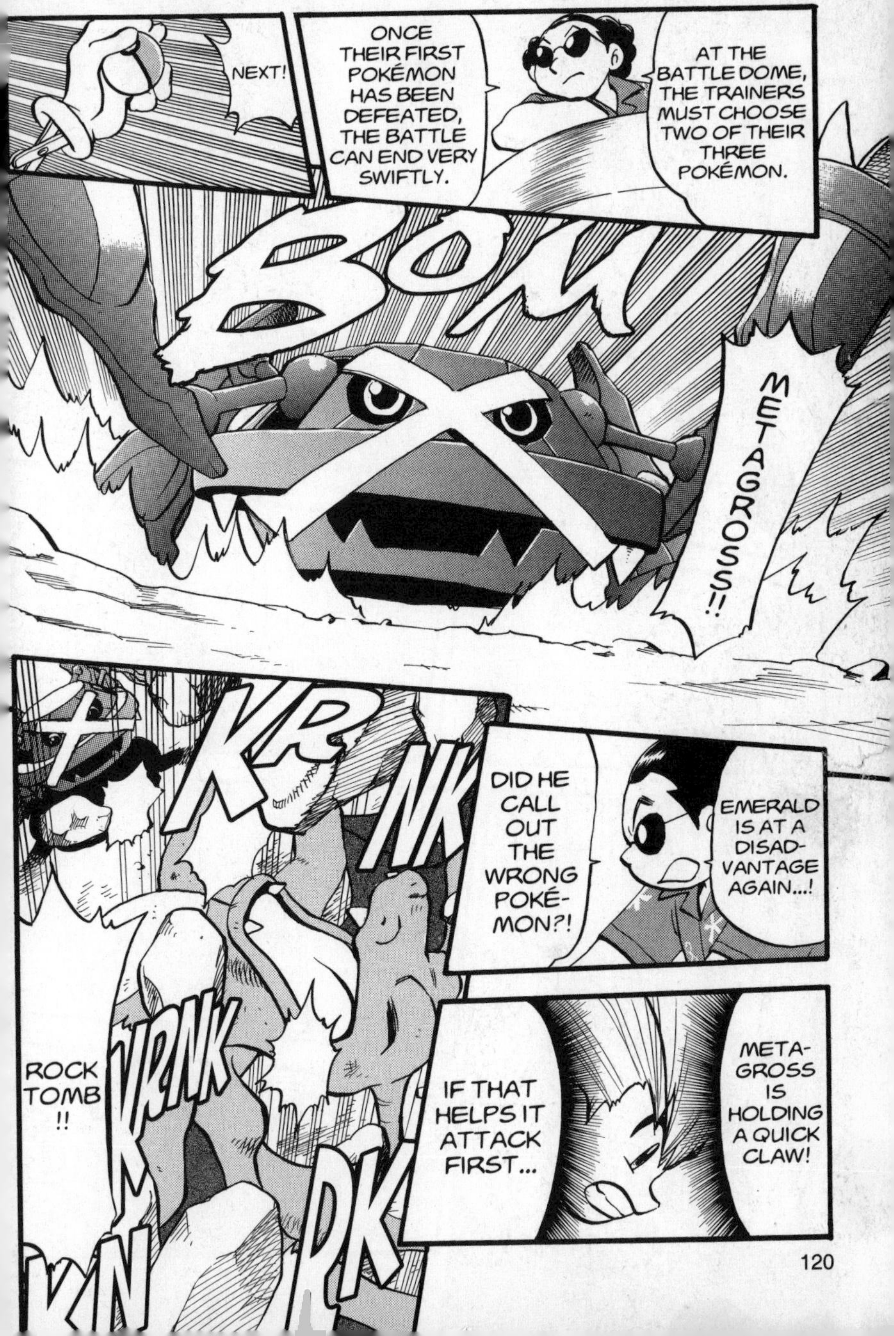
AT THE BATTLE DOME, THE TRAINERS MUST CHOOSE TWO OF THEIR THREE POKÉMON.
ONCE THEIR FIRST POKÉMON HAS BEEN DEFEATED, THE BATTLE CAN END VERY SWIFTLY.
NEXT!
BOM
METAGROSS!!
EMERALD IS AT A DISAD-VANTAGE AGAIN...!
DID HE CALL OUT THE WRONG POKÉ-MON?!
META-GROSS IS HOLDING A QUICK CLAW!
IF THAT HELPS IT ATTACK FIRST...
KRNK
KRNK
ROCK TOMB !!

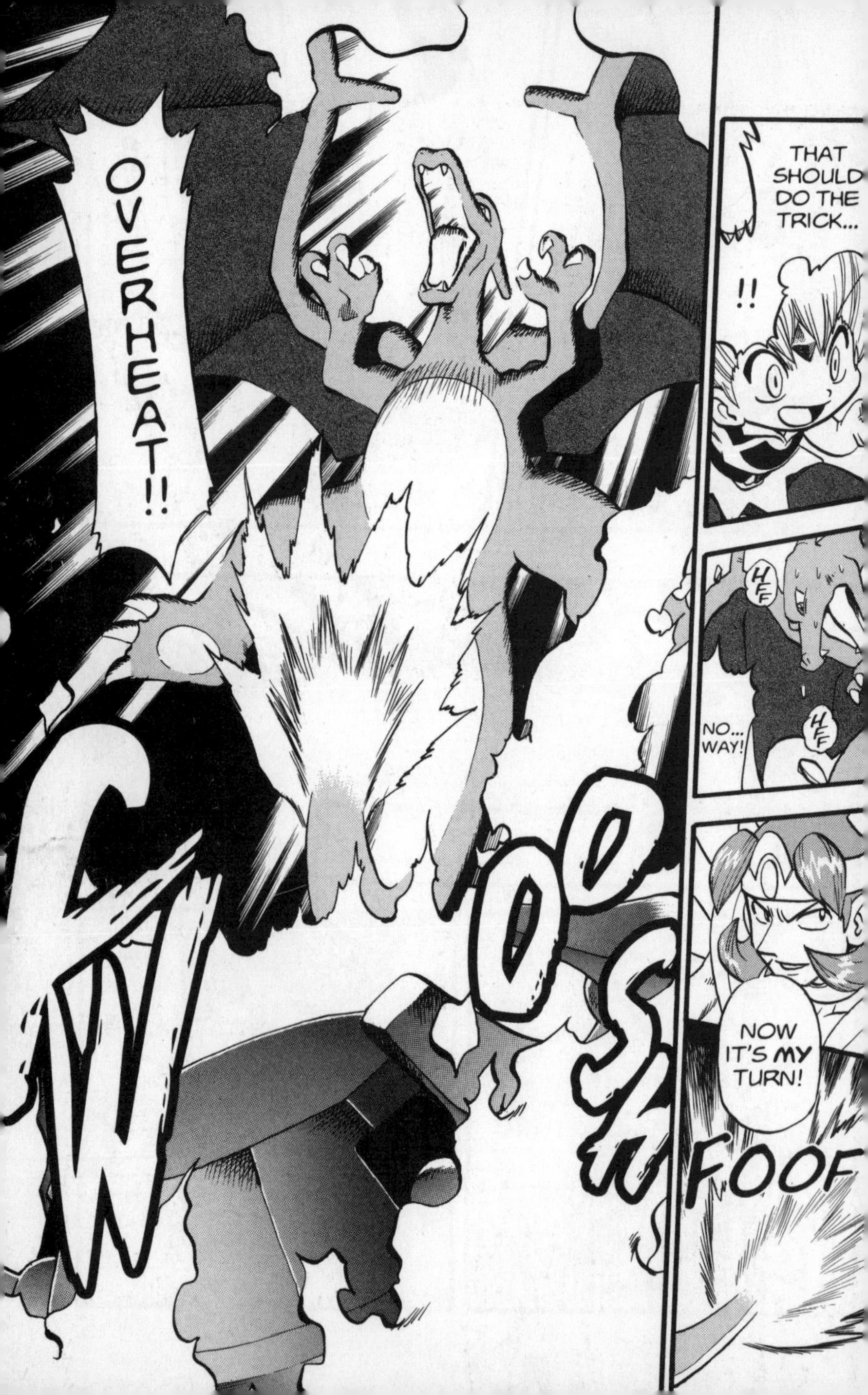
THAT SHOULD DO THE TRICK...
!!
HFF
NO... WAY!
HFF
NOW IT'S **MY** TURN!
FOOF
OVERHEAT!!

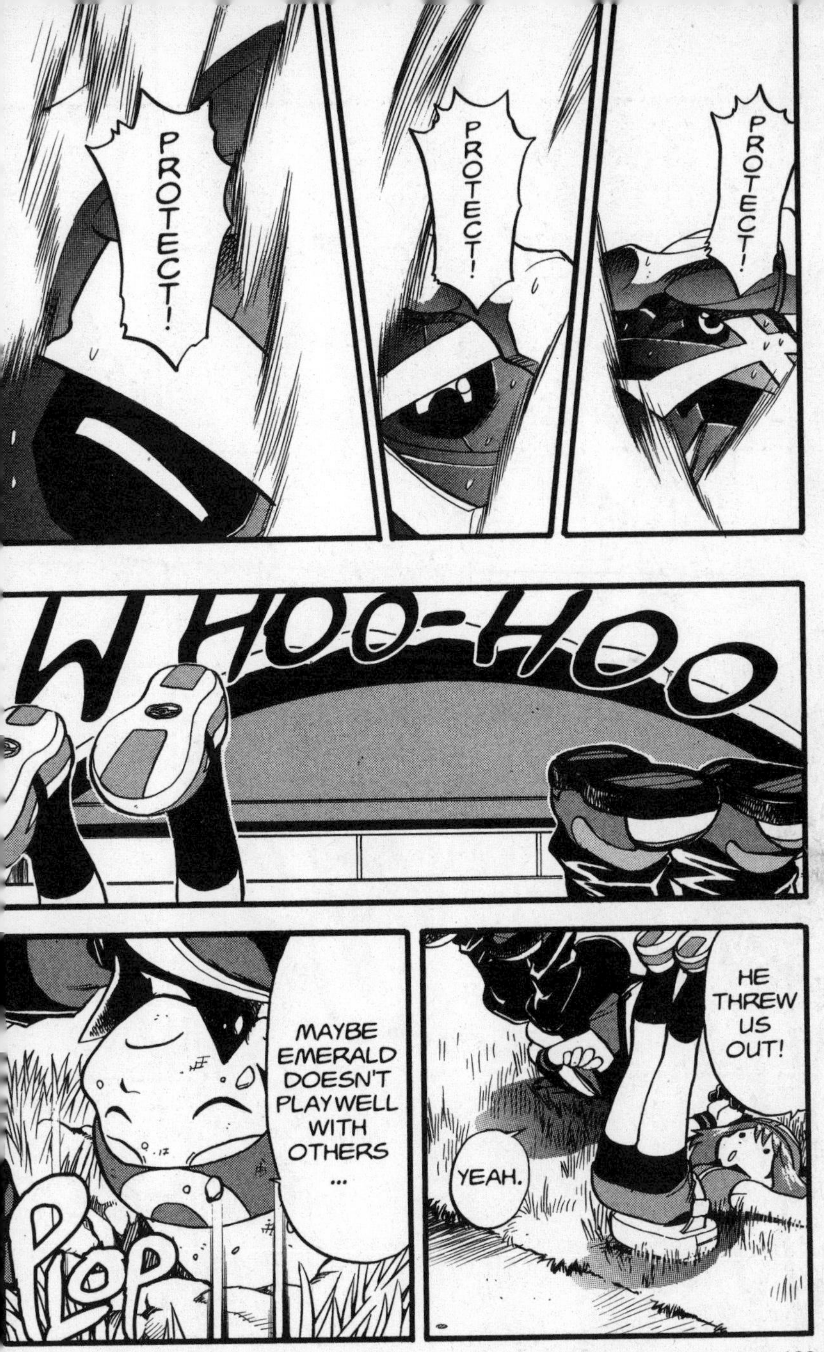
PROTECT!
PROTECT!
PROTECT!
WHOO-HOO
HE THREW US OUT!
YEAH.
MAYBE EMERALD DOESN'T PLAYWELL WITH OTHERS ...
PLOP

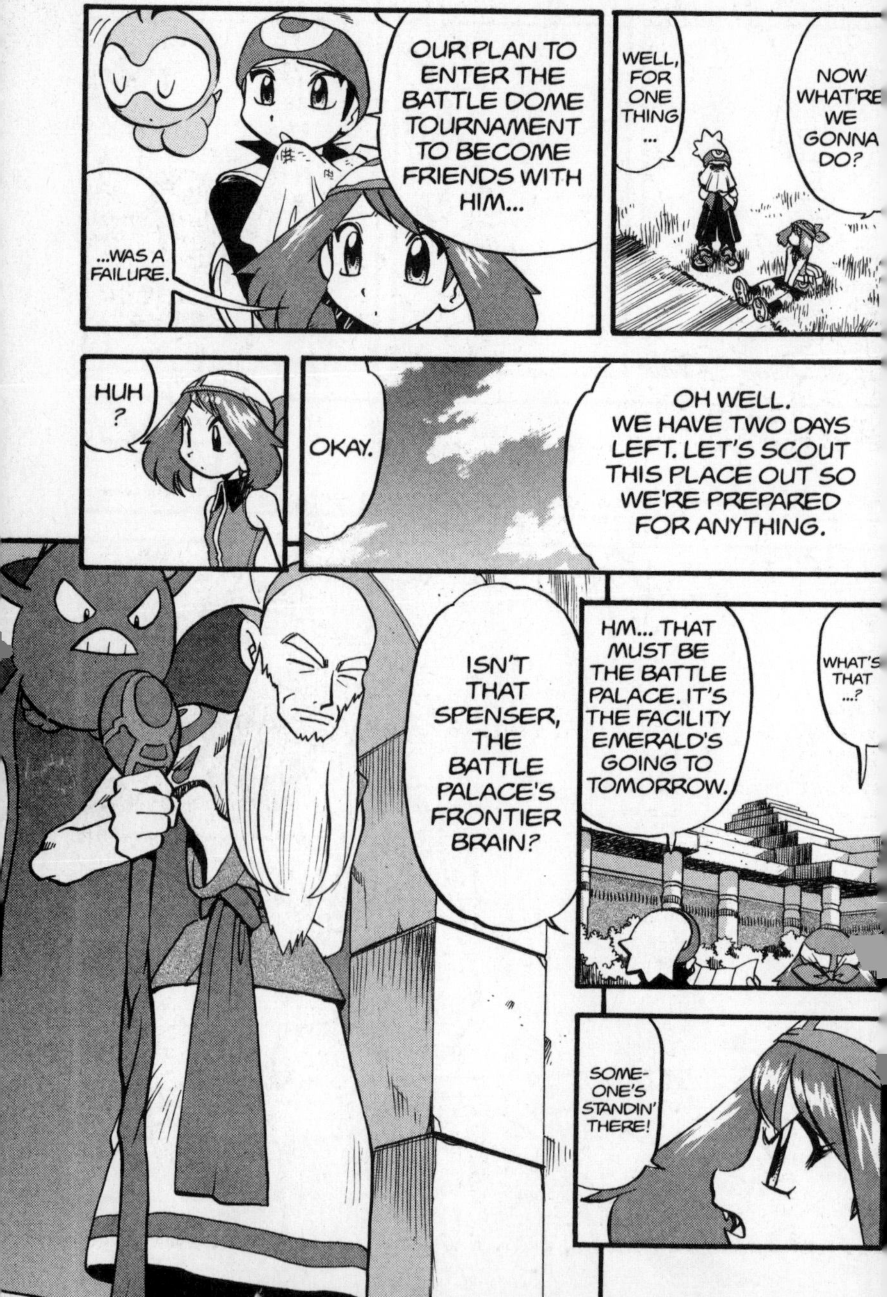
NOW WHAT'RE WE GONNA DO?
WELL, FOR ONE THING ...
OUR PLAN TO ENTER THE BATTLE DOME TOURNAMENT TO BECOME FRIENDS WITH HIM...
...WAS A FAILURE.
OH WELL. WE HAVE TWO DAYS LEFT. LET'S SCOUT THIS PLACE OUT SO WE'RE PREPARED FOR ANYTHING.
OKAY.
HUH?
WHAT'S THAT ...?
HM... THAT MUST BE THE BATTLE PALACE. IT'S THE FACILITY EMERALD'S GOING TO TOMORROW.
SOME-ONE'S STANDIN' THERE!
ISN'T THAT SPENSER, THE BATTLE PALACE'S FRONTIER BRAIN?

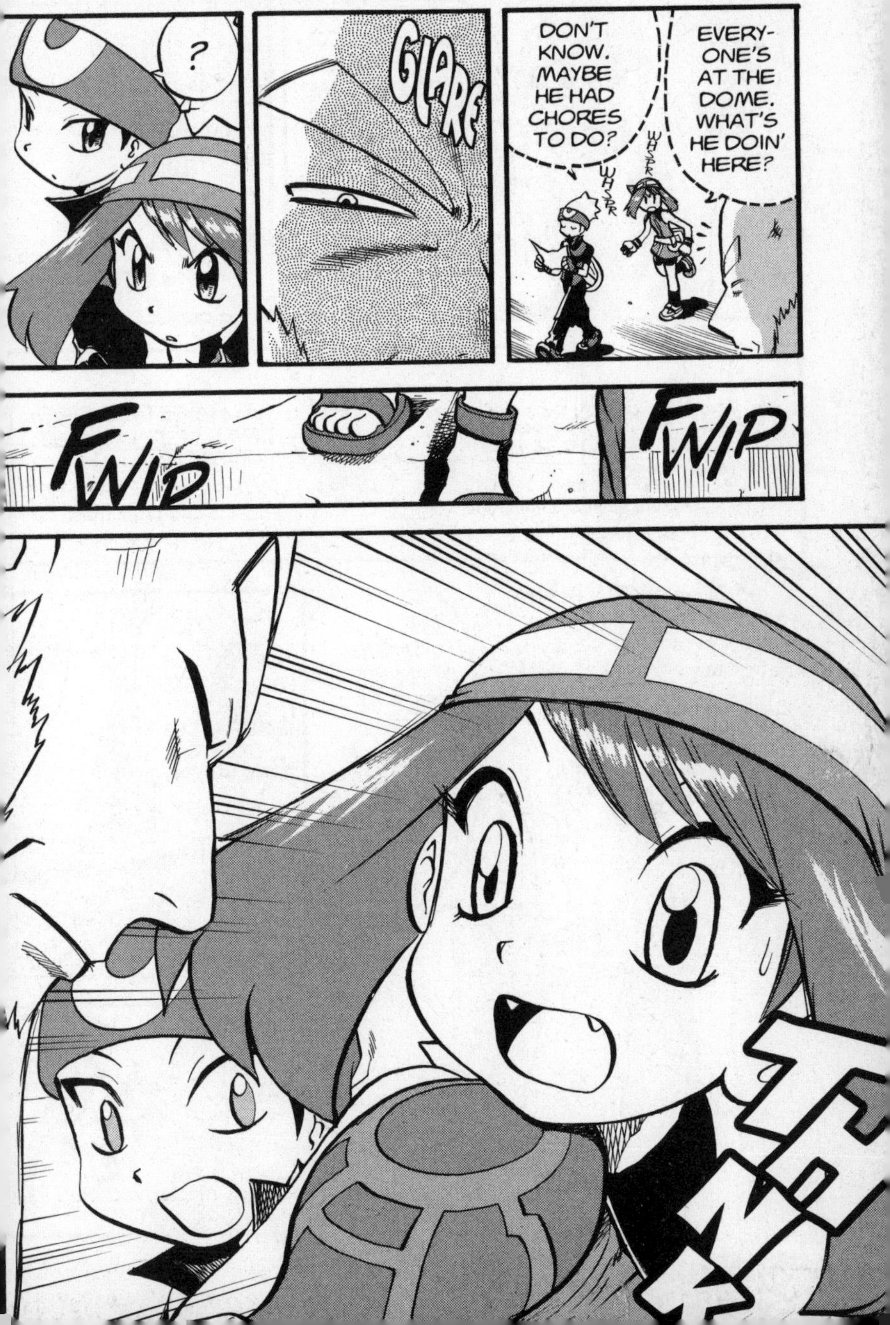

EVERY-ONE'S AT THE DOME. WHAT'S HE DOIN' HERE?
WHSPR
DON'T KNOW. MAYBE HE HAD CHORES TO DO?
WHSPR
GLARE
?
FWIP
FWIP

DEAR MEMBERS OF THE PRESS...

Thank you for visiting the Battle Frontier today. Permit me to continue explaining the rules of this facility...

OWNER: SCOTT

FACILITY RULES

BATTLE TOWER 1

Battle-type	Number of Pokémon	Type of Symbol	Wins needed to attain the Symbol
•Single •Double •Multi	3 Pokémon	Ability	7 Wins × 10 Rounds = 70 Consecutive Wins

The symbol of the Battle Frontier, the large building to the north, is the Battle Tower. This facility existed before the other six facilities were built, so I'm sure you know all about it already. It's a facility for classic Pokémon Battles, so there are no new rules or gimmicks as there are in the other six facilities. Here, the challengers may enjoy a simple battle showing off the Pokémon's and Trainer's skills.

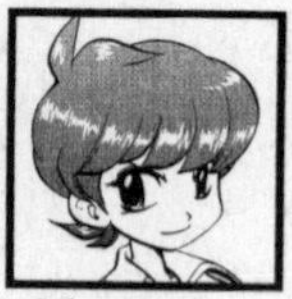

Salon Maiden Anabel

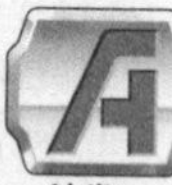

Ability Symbol

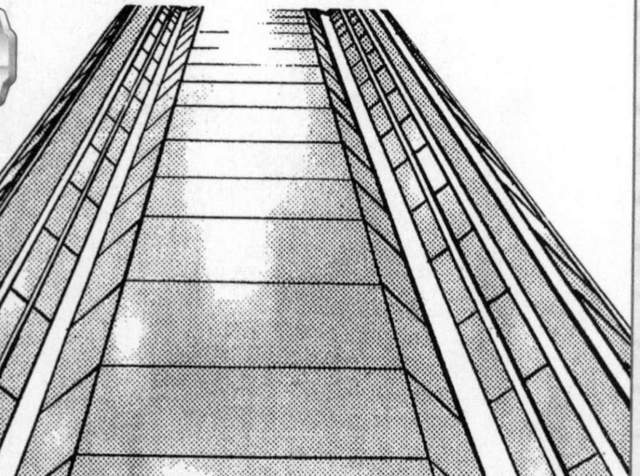

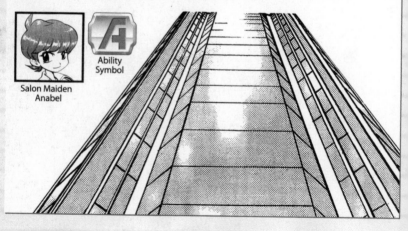

324

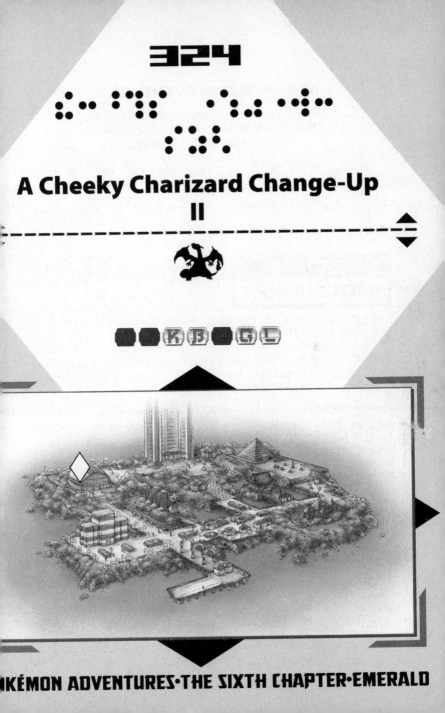

A Cheeky Charizard Change-Up II

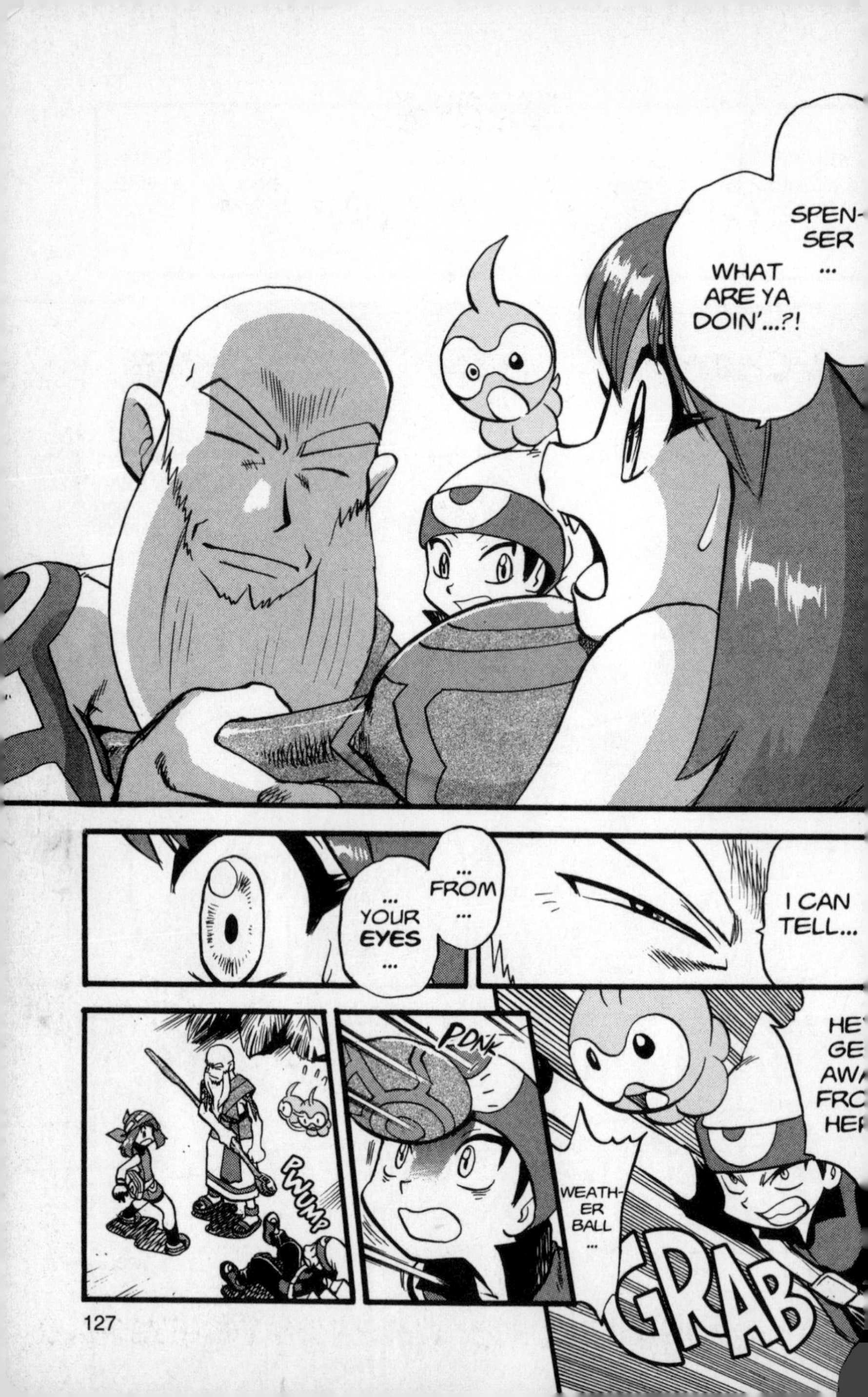
SPEN-SER ...
WHAT ARE YA DOIN'...?!
I CAN TELL...
... FROM ...
... YOUR EYES ...
HE' GE AW FRO HE
GRAB
WEATH-ER BALL ...
P-DNK
PWUMP

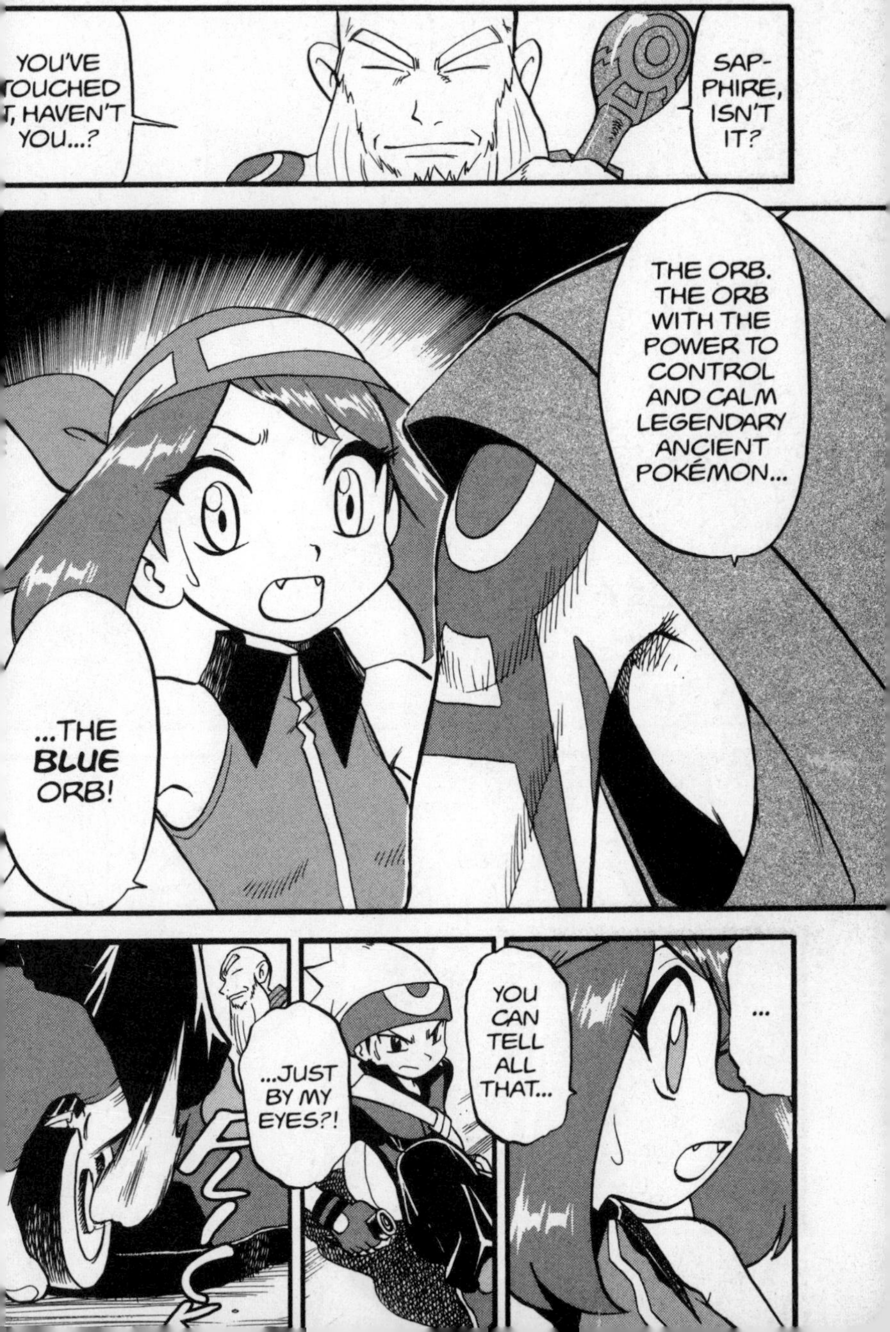
SAPPHIRE, ISN'T IT?
YOU'VE TOUCHED T, HAVEN'T YOU...?
THE ORB. THE ORB WITH THE POWER TO CONTROL AND CALM LEGENDARY ANCIENT POKÉMON...
...THE **BLUE** ORB!
...
YOU CAN TELL ALL THAT...
...JUST BY MY EYES?!

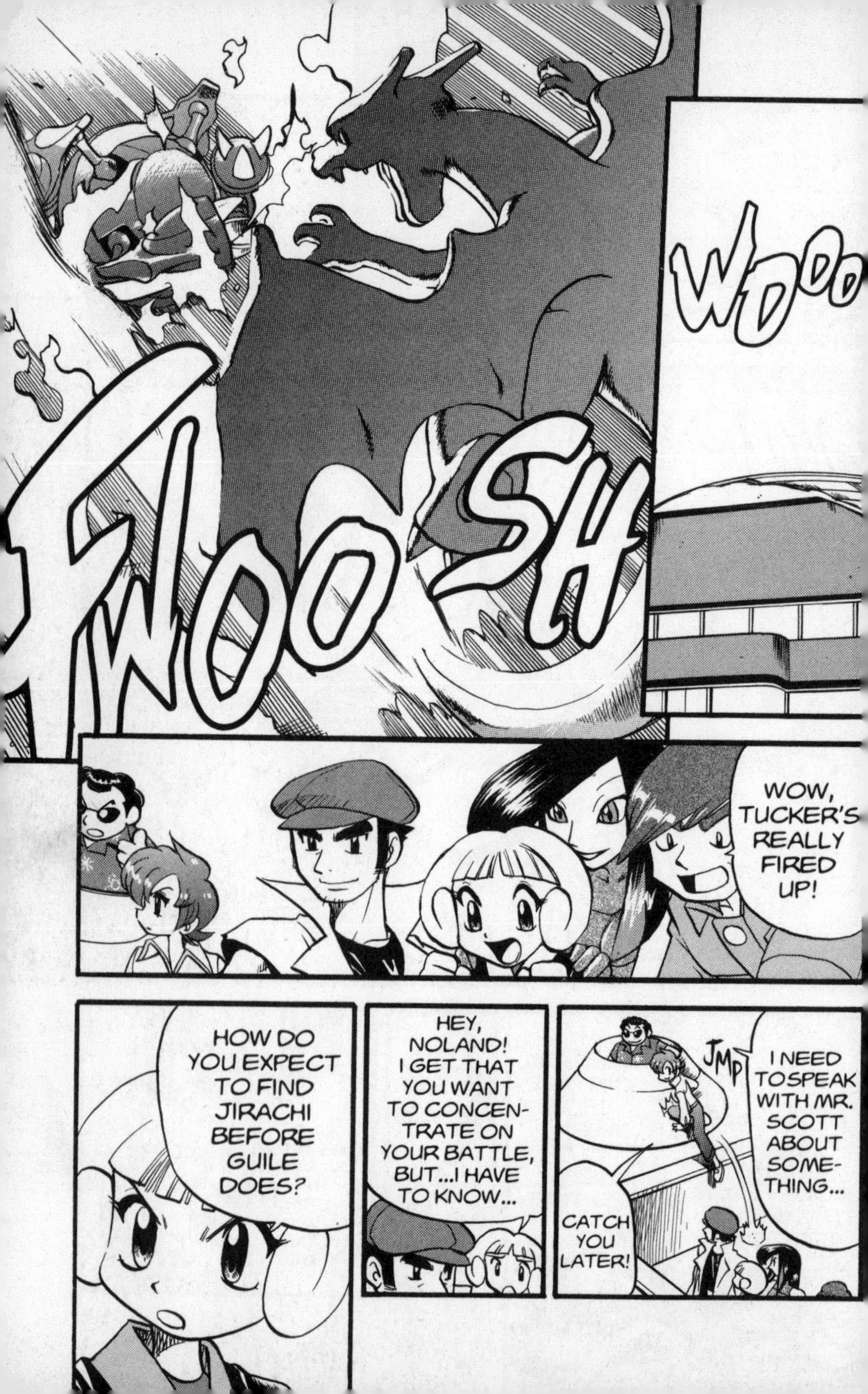
WOOO
WOOSH
WOW, TUCKER'S REALLY FIRED UP!
JMP
I NEED TO SPEAK WITH MR. SCOTT ABOUT SOME-THING...
CATCH YOU LATER!
HEY, NOLAND! I GET THAT YOU WANT TO CONCEN-TRATE ON YOUR BATTLE, BUT...I HAVE TO KNOW...
HOW DO YOU EXPECT TO FIND JIRACHI BEFORE GUILE DOES?

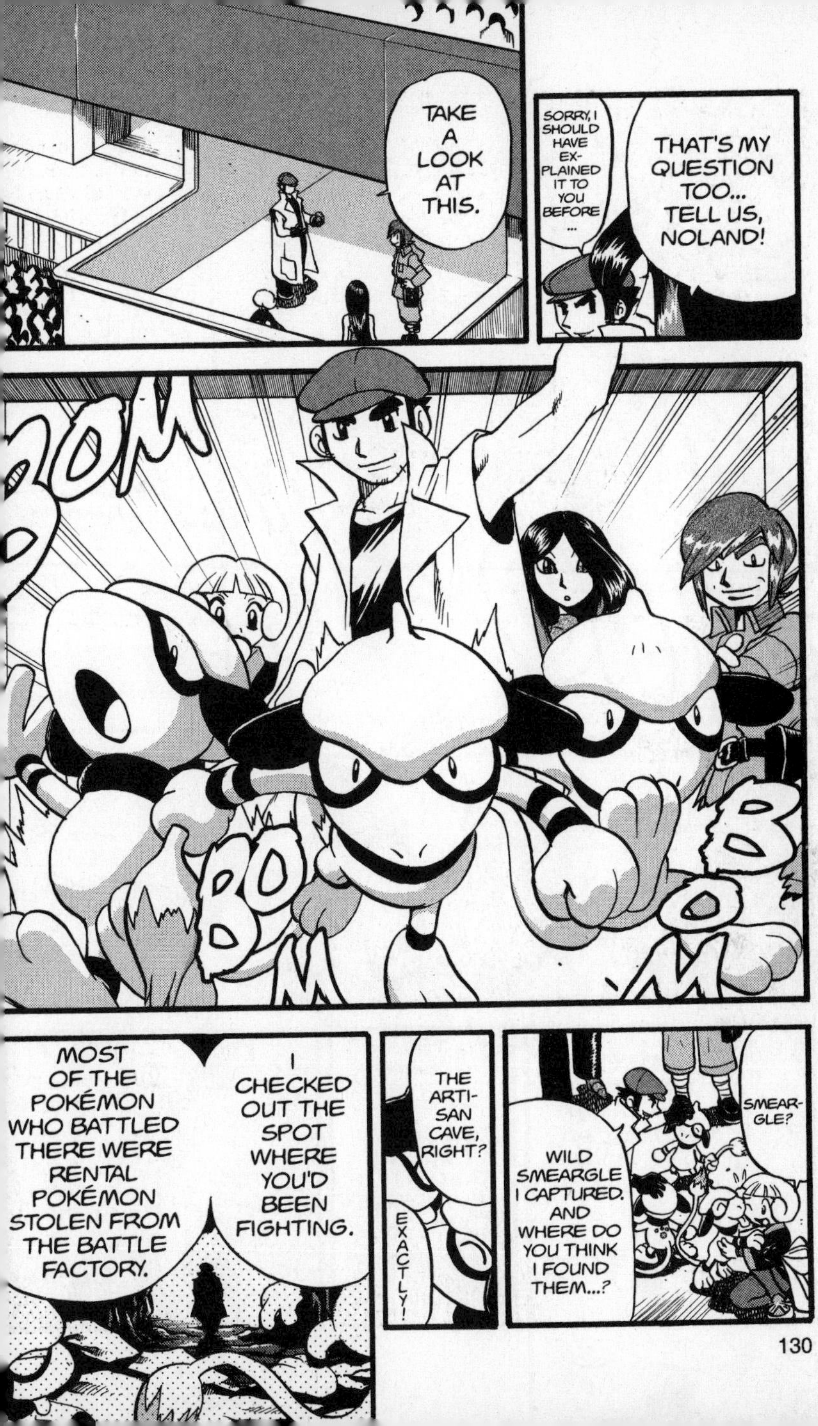
THAT'S MY QUESTION TOO... TELL US, NOLAND!
SORRY, I SHOULD HAVE EXPLAINED IT TO YOU BEFORE...
TAKE A LOOK AT THIS.
BOOM
BOOM
BOOM
BOOM
SMEARGLE?
WILD SMEARGLE I CAPTURED. AND WHERE DO YOU THINK I FOUND THEM...?
THE ARTISAN CAVE, RIGHT?
EXACTLY!
I CHECKED OUT THE SPOT WHERE YOU'D BEEN FIGHTING.
MOST OF THE POKÉMON WHO BATTLED THERE WERE RENTAL POKÉMON STOLEN FROM THE BATTLE FACTORY.

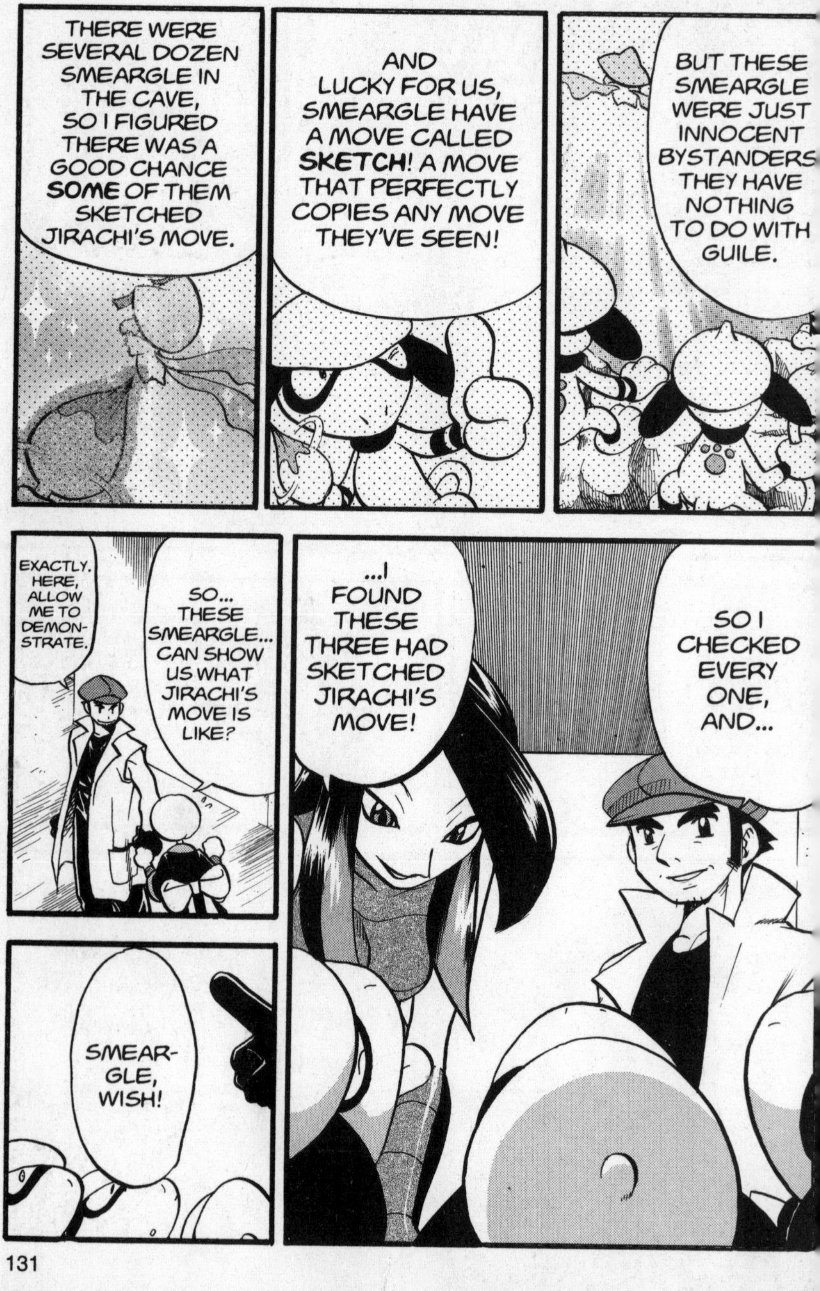

BUT THESE SMEARGLE WERE JUST INNOCENT BYSTANDERS. THEY HAVE NOTHING TO DO WITH GUILE.
AND LUCKY FOR US, SMEARGLE HAVE A MOVE CALLED **SKETCH**! A MOVE THAT PERFECTLY COPIES ANY MOVE THEY'VE SEEN!
THERE WERE SEVERAL DOZEN SMEARGLE IN THE CAVE, SO I FIGURED THERE WAS A GOOD CHANCE **SOME** OF THEM SKETCHED JIRACHI'S MOVE.
SO I CHECKED EVERY ONE, AND...
...I FOUND THESE THREE HAD SKETCHED JIRACHI'S MOVE!
SO... THESE SMEARGLE... CAN SHOW US WHAT JIRACHI'S MOVE IS LIKE?
EXACTLY. HERE, ALLOW ME TO DEMON-STRATE.
SMEAR-GLE, WISH!

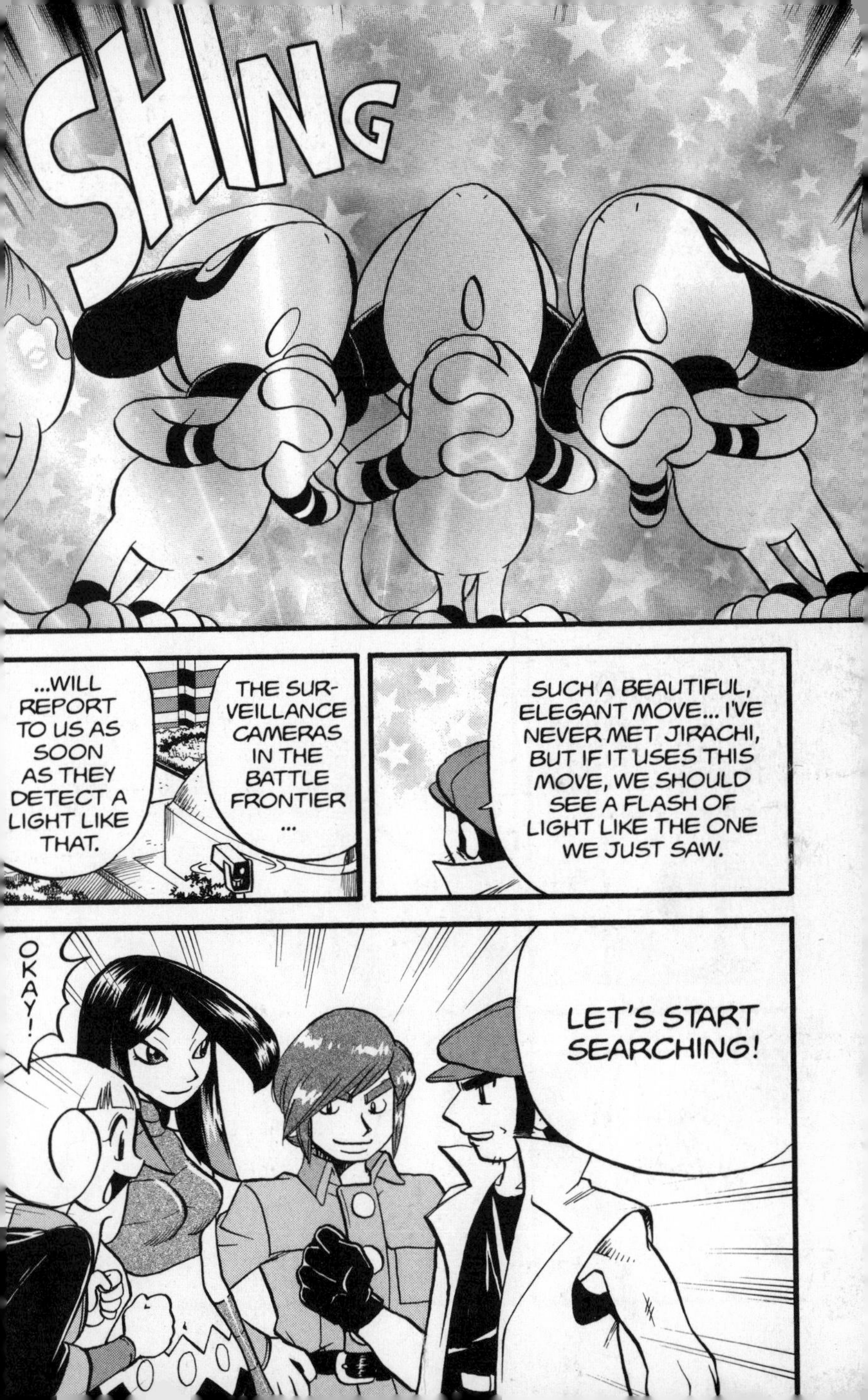
SHING
SUCH A BEAUTIFUL, ELEGANT MOVE... I'VE NEVER MET JIRACHI, BUT IF IT USES THIS MOVE, WE SHOULD SEE A FLASH OF LIGHT LIKE THE ONE WE JUST SAW.
THE SUR-VEILLANCE CAMERAS IN THE BATTLE FRONTIER ...
...WILL REPORT TO US AS SOON AS THEY DETECT A LIGHT LIKE THAT.
LET'S START SEARCHING!
OKAY!

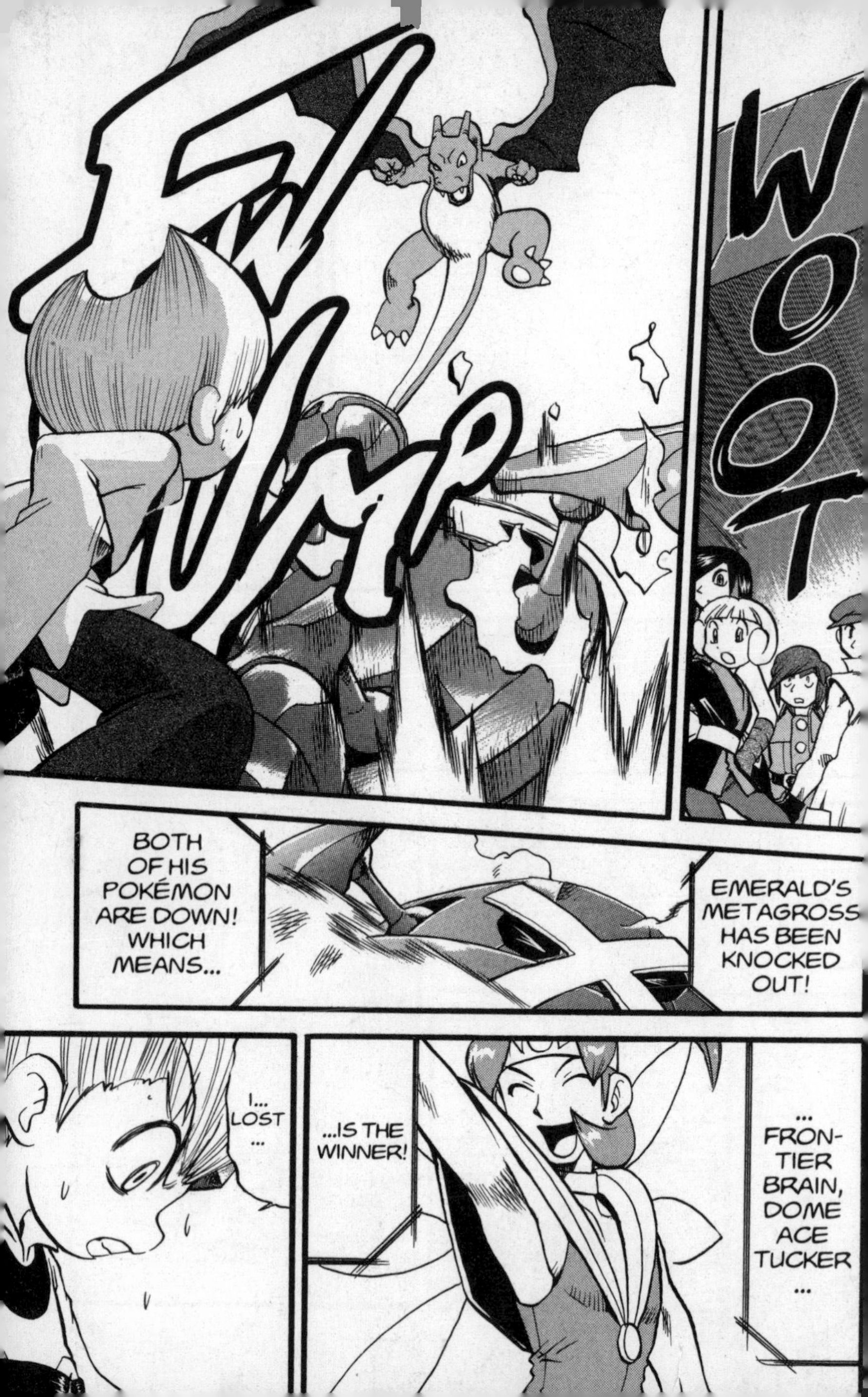
WOOT
FWUMP
EMERALD'S METAGROSS HAS BEEN KNOCKED OUT!
BOTH OF HIS POKÉMON ARE DOWN! WHICH MEANS...
... FRONTIER BRAIN, DOME ACE TUCKER ...
...IS THE WINNER!
I... LOST ...

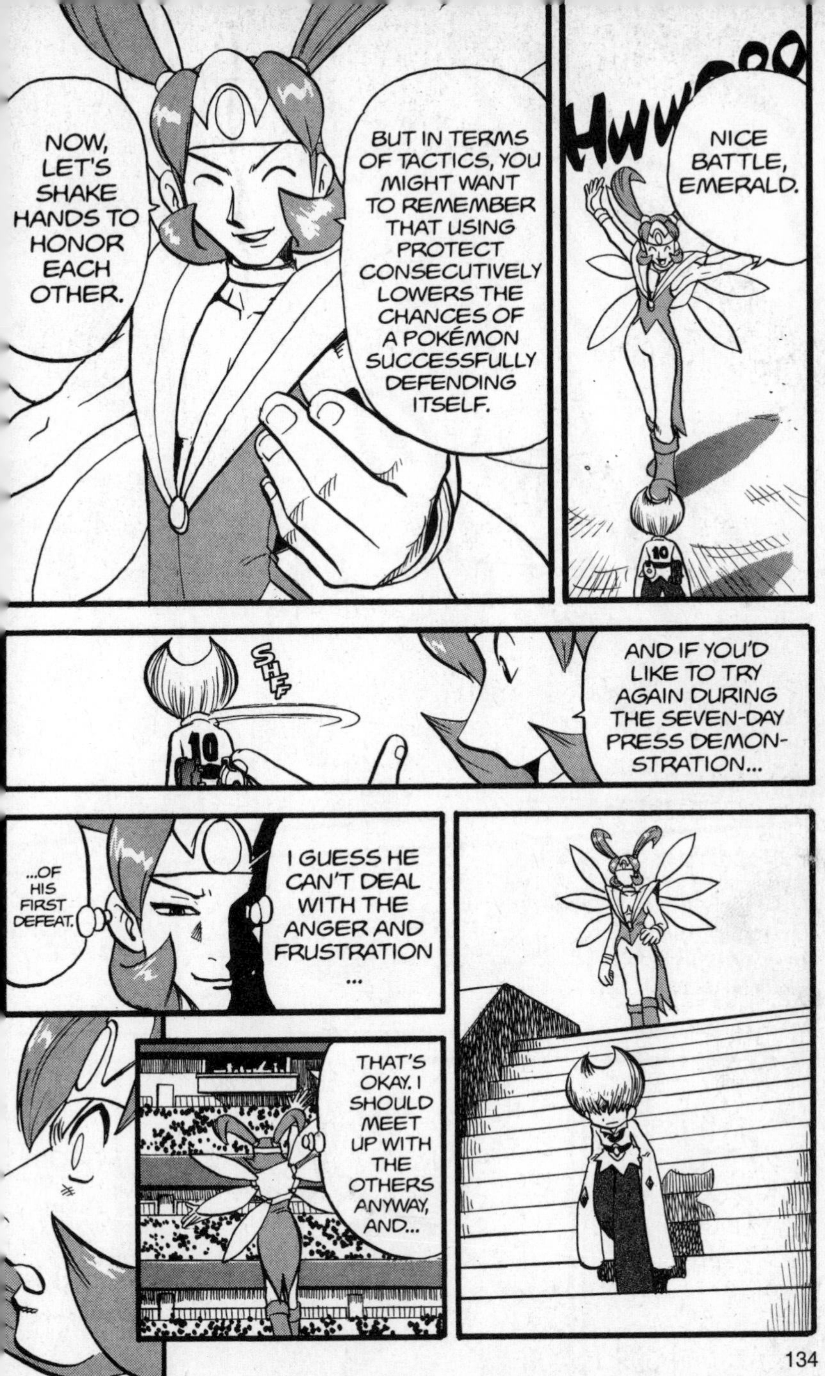
NICE BATTLE, EMERALD.
BUT IN TERMS OF TACTICS, YOU MIGHT WANT TO REMEMBER THAT USING PROTECT CONSECUTIVELY LOWERS THE CHANCES OF A POKÉMON SUCCESSFULLY DEFENDING ITSELF.
NOW, LET'S SHAKE HANDS TO HONOR EACH OTHER.
AND IF YOU'D LIKE TO TRY AGAIN DURING THE SEVEN-DAY PRESS DEMON-STRATION...
SHFF
I GUESS HE CAN'T DEAL WITH THE ANGER AND FRUSTRATION ...
...OF HIS FIRST DEFEAT.
THAT'S OKAY. I SHOULD MEET UP WITH THE OTHERS ANYWAY, AND...

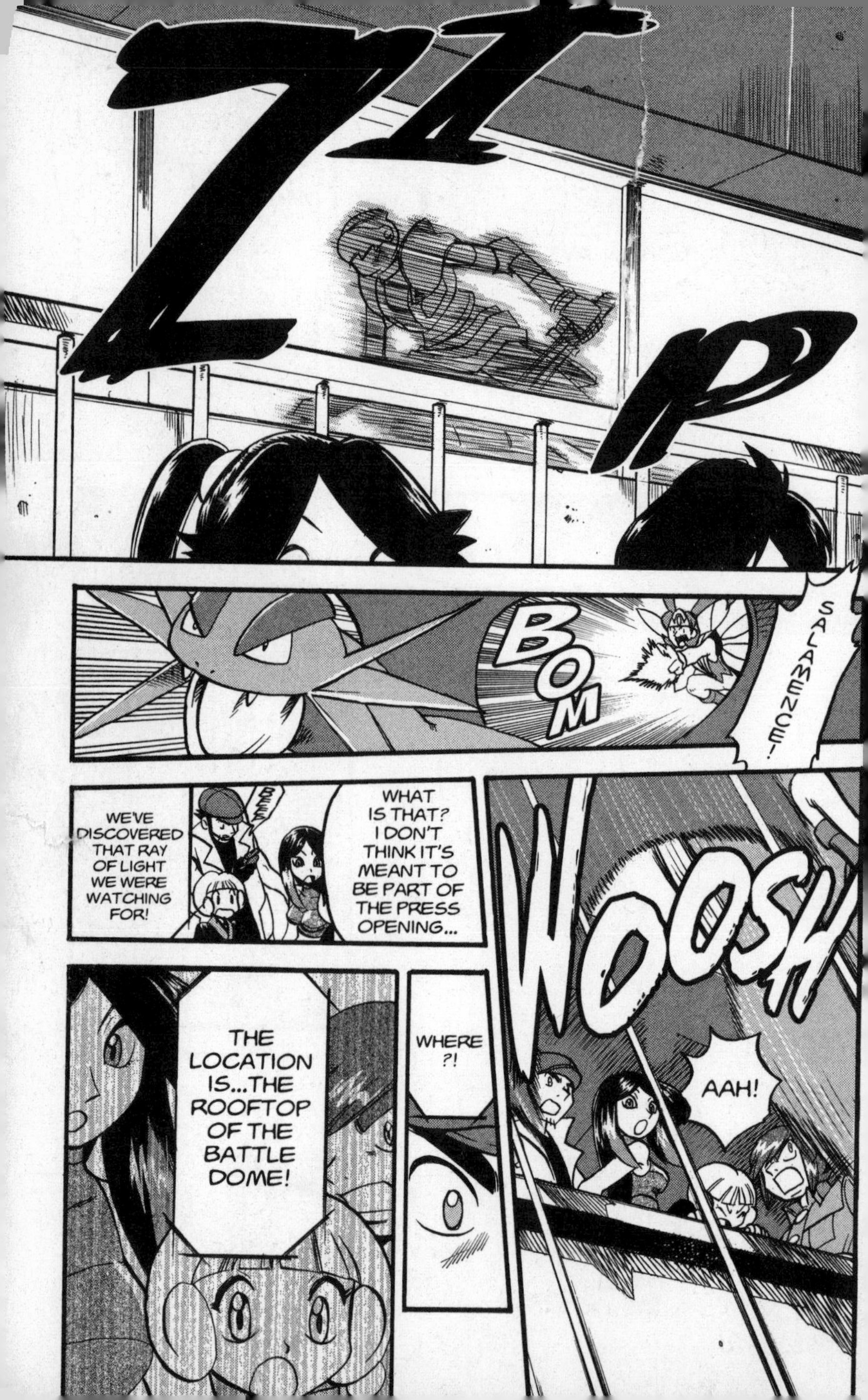
ZIP
SALAMENCE!
BOOM
WOOSH
AAH!
WHAT IS THAT? I DON'T THINK IT'S MEANT TO BE PART OF THE PRESS OPENING...
BEEEE
WE'VE DISCOVERED THAT RAY OF LIGHT WE WERE WATCHING FOR!
WHERE?!
THE LOCATION IS...THE ROOFTOP OF THE BATTLE DOME!

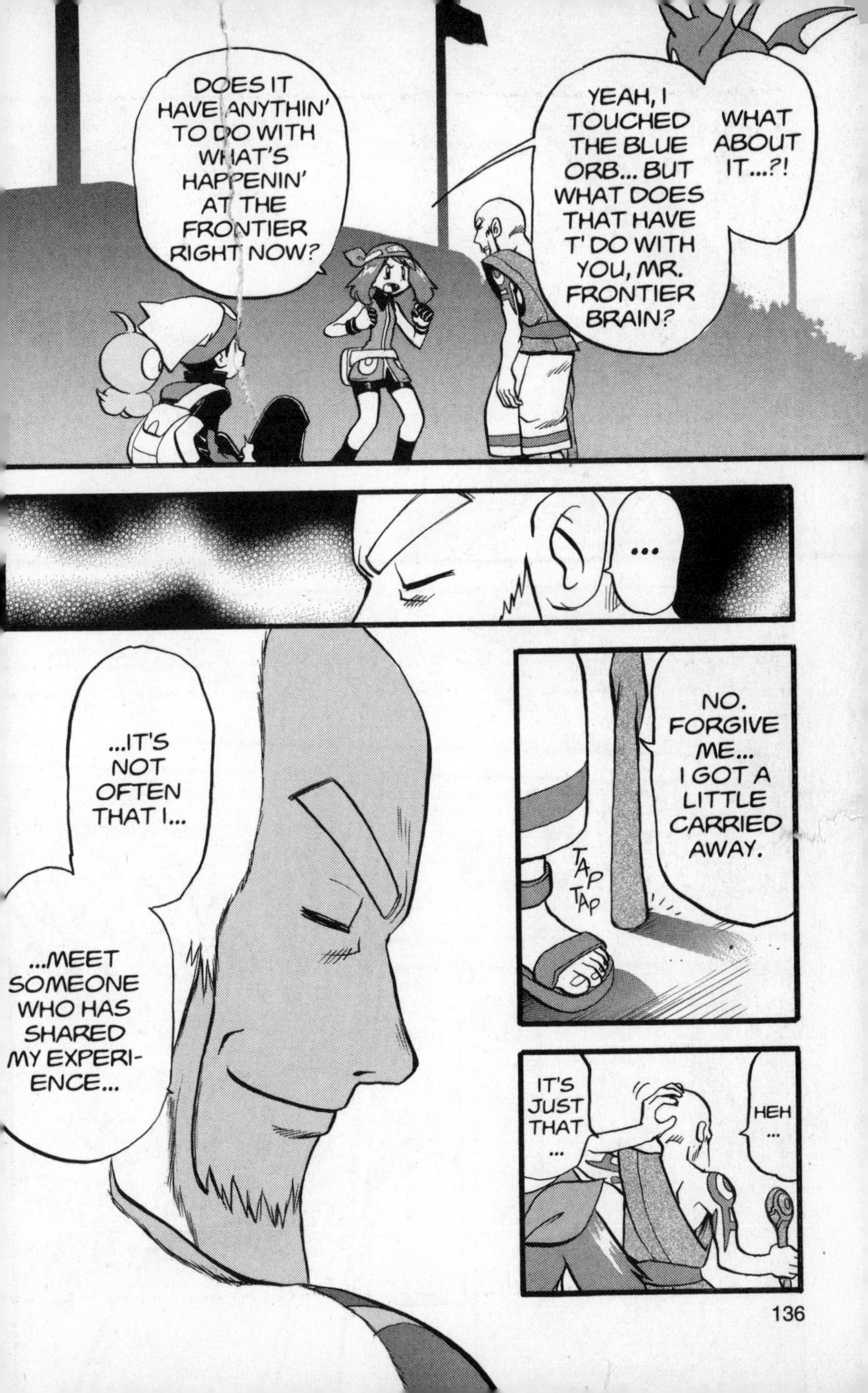
WHAT ABOUT IT...?!
YEAH, I TOUCHED THE BLUE ORB... BUT WHAT DOES THAT HAVE T' DO WITH YOU, MR. FRONTIER BRAIN?
DOES IT HAVE ANYTHIN' TO DO WITH WHAT'S HAPPENIN' AT THE FRONTIER RIGHT NOW?
...
NO. FORGIVE ME... I GOT A LITTLE CARRIED AWAY.
TAP TAP
HEH...
IT'S JUST THAT...
...IT'S NOT OFTEN THAT I...
...MEET SOMEONE WHO HAS SHARED MY EXPERI-ENCE...

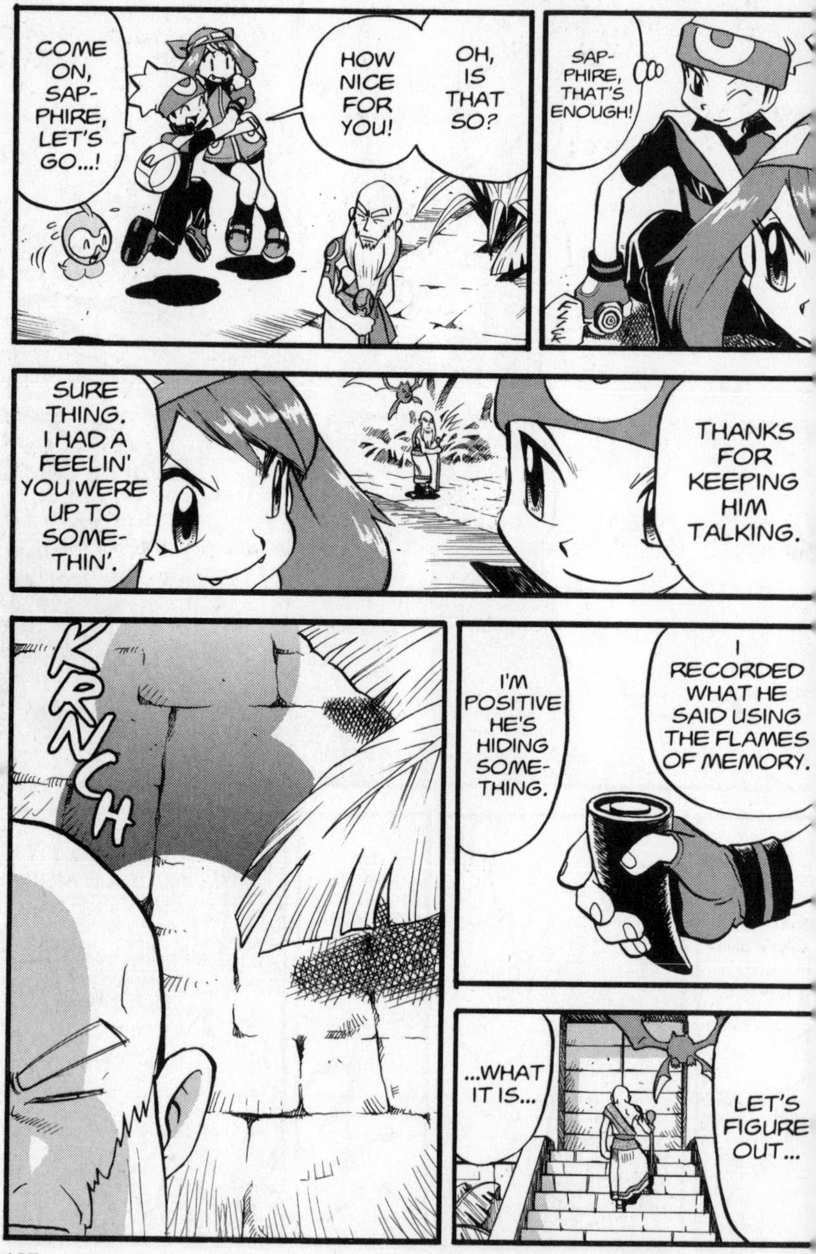
SAP-PHIRE, THAT'S ENOUGH!
OH, IS THAT SO?
HOW NICE FOR YOU!
COME ON, SAP-PHIRE, LET'S GO...!
THANKS FOR KEEPING HIM TALKING.
SURE THING. I HAD A FEELIN' YOU WERE UP TO SOME-THIN'.
I RECORDED WHAT HE SAID USING THE FLAMES OF MEMORY.
I'M POSITIVE HE'S HIDING SOME-THING.
LET'S FIGURE OUT...
...WHAT IT IS...
KRNCH

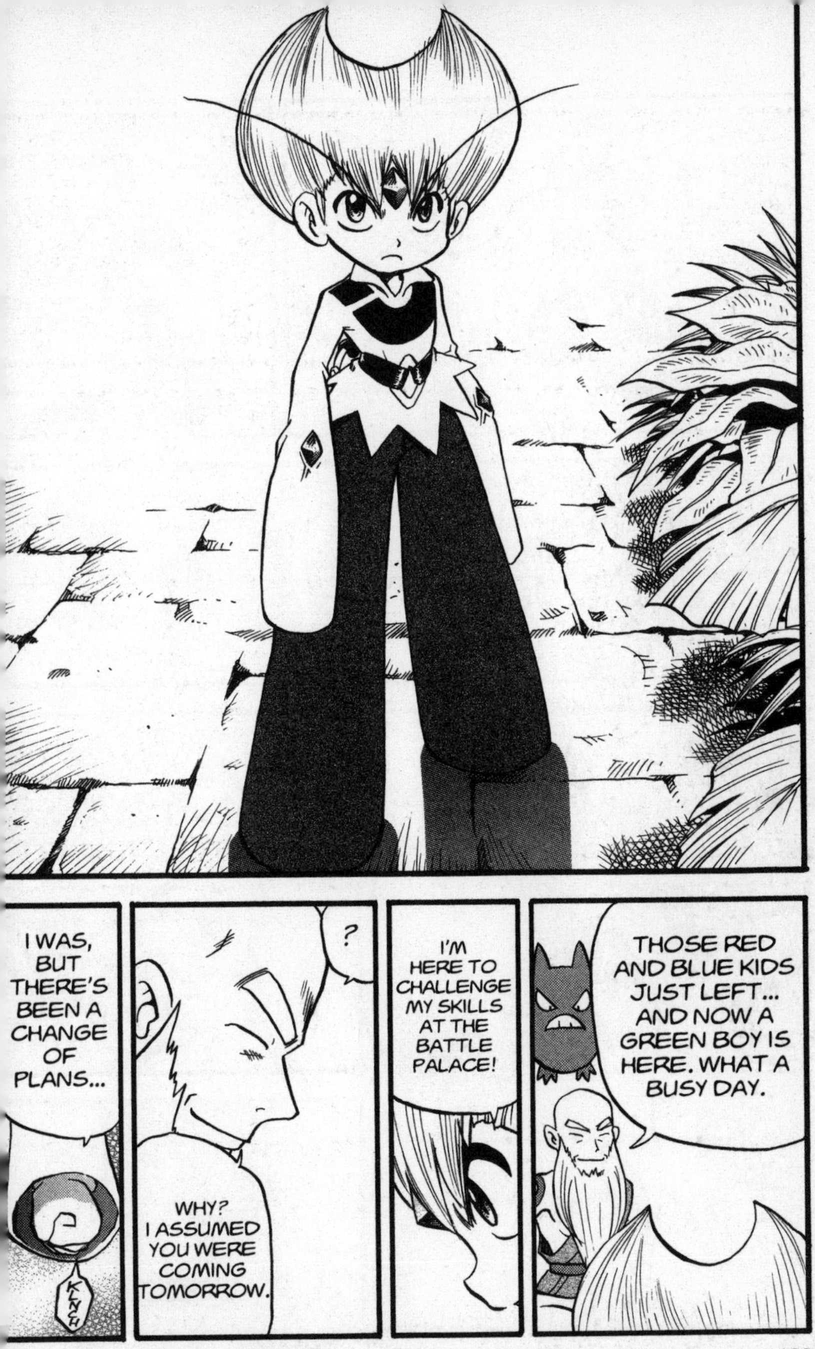

THOSE RED AND BLUE KIDS JUST LEFT... AND NOW A GREEN BOY IS HERE. WHAT A BUSY DAY.
I'M HERE TO CHALLENGE MY SKILLS AT THE BATTLE PALACE!
?
WHY? I ASSUMED YOU WERE COMING TOMORROW.
I WAS, BUT THERE'S BEEN A CHANGE OF PLANS...
KLNCH

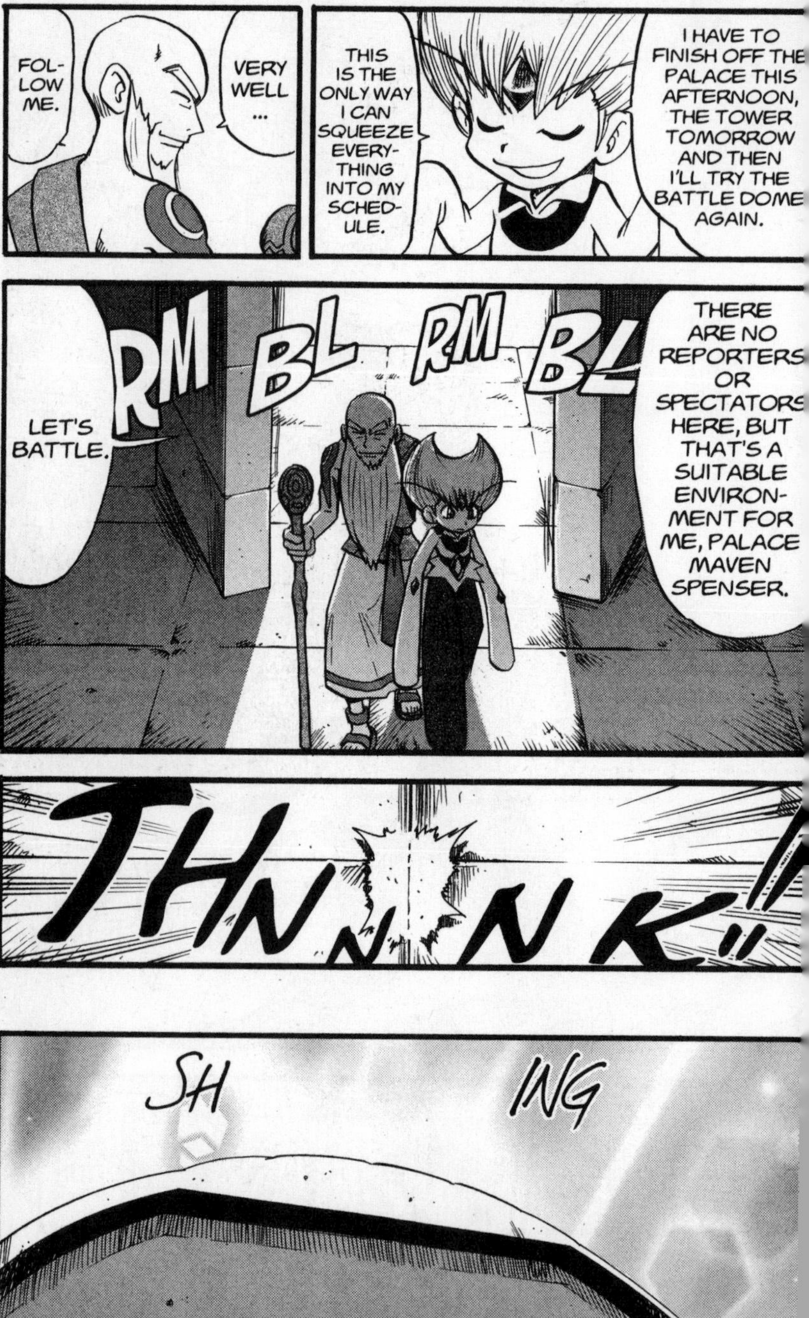

I HAVE TO FINISH OFF THE PALACE THIS AFTERNOON, THE TOWER TOMORROW AND THEN I'LL TRY THE BATTLE DOME AGAIN.
THIS IS THE ONLY WAY I CAN SQUEEZE EVERYTHING INTO MY SCHEDULE.
VERY WELL...
FOLLOW ME.
THERE ARE NO REPORTERS OR SPECTATORS HERE, BUT THAT'S A SUITABLE ENVIRONMENT FOR ME, PALACE MAVEN SPENSER.
RM BL RM BL
LET'S BATTLE.
THNNNK!!
SH ING

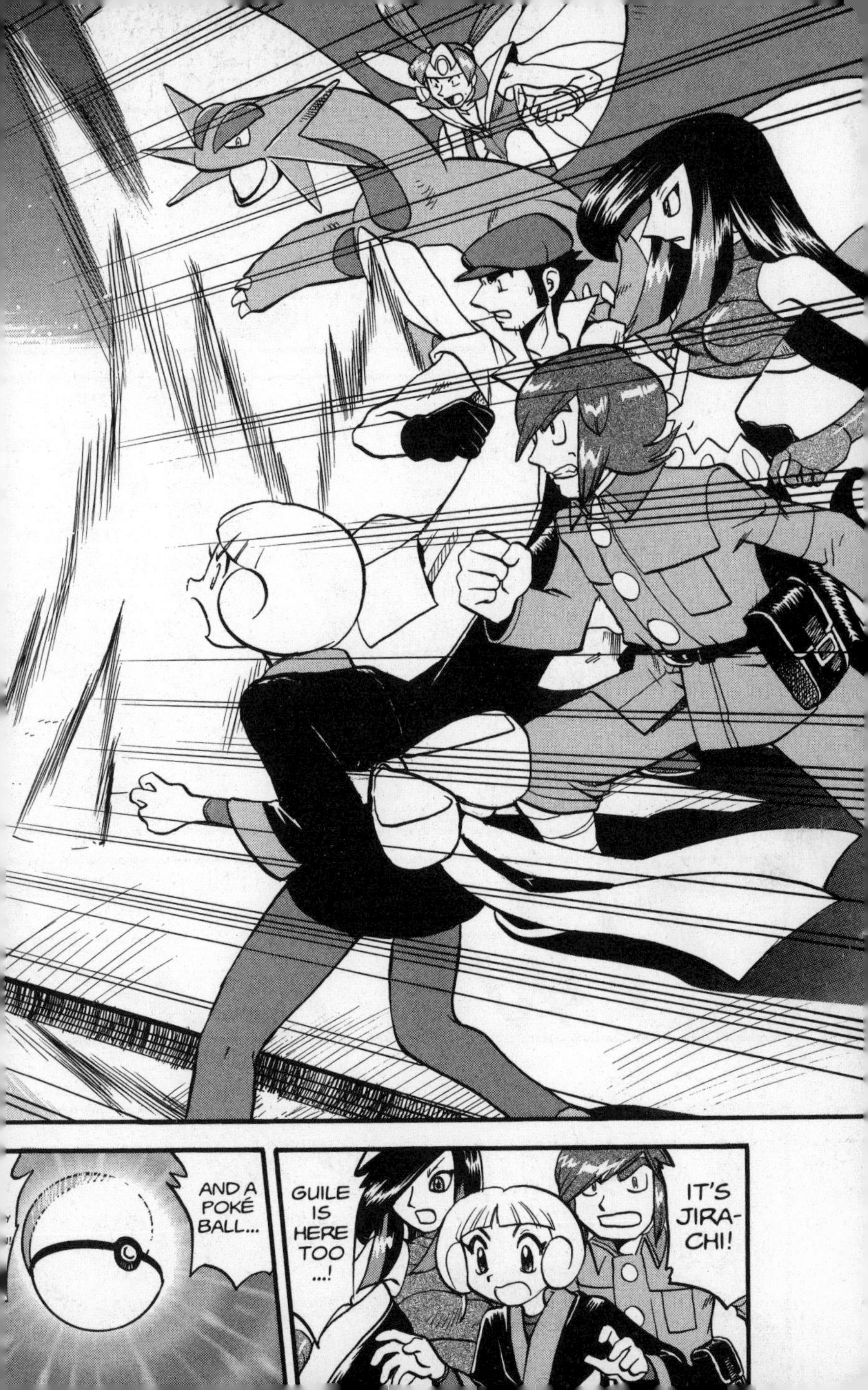
IT'S JIRA-CHI!
GUILE IS HERE TOO ...!
AND A POKÉ BALL...

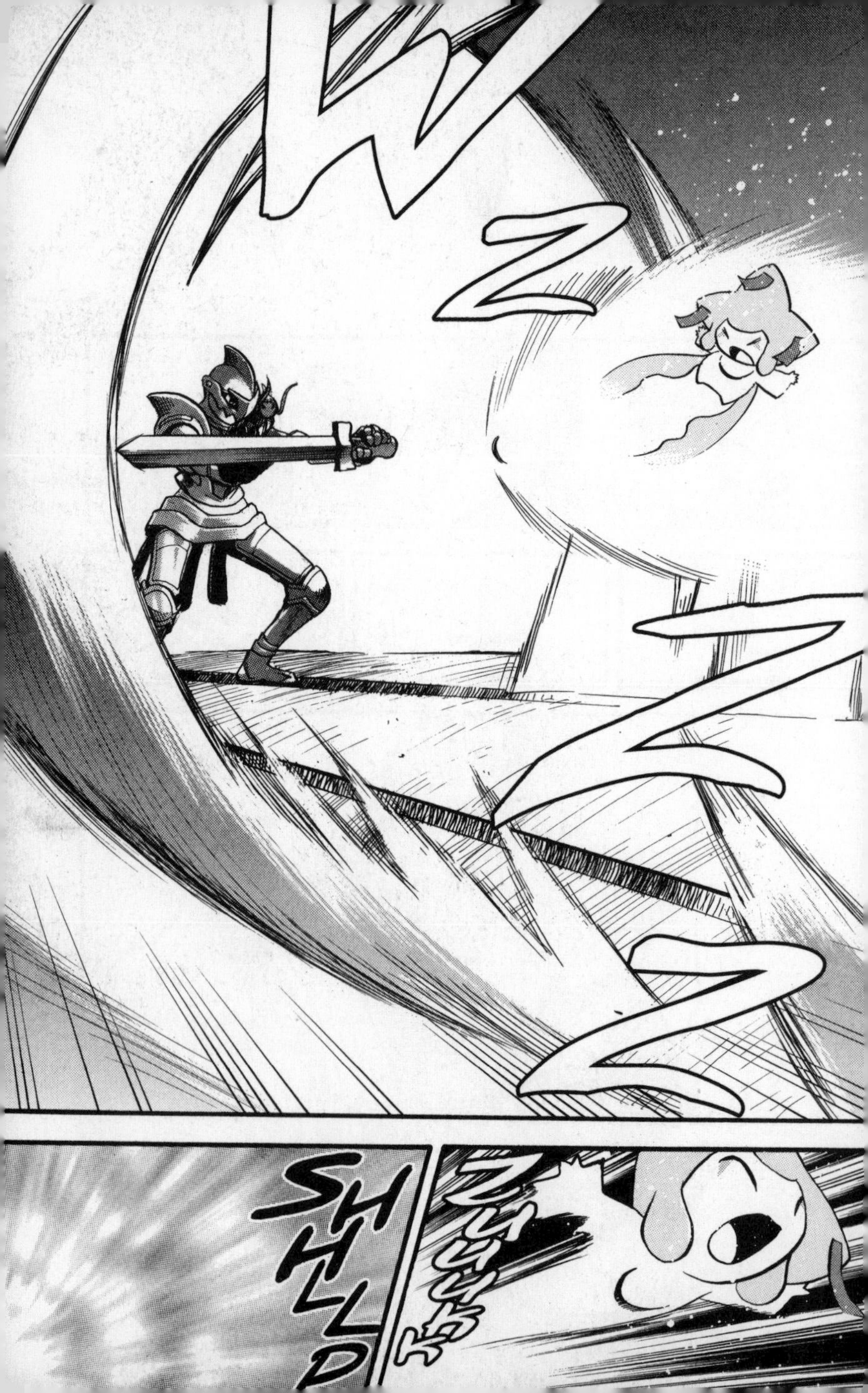
WZZZZ
ZUUUUK
SHHLLD

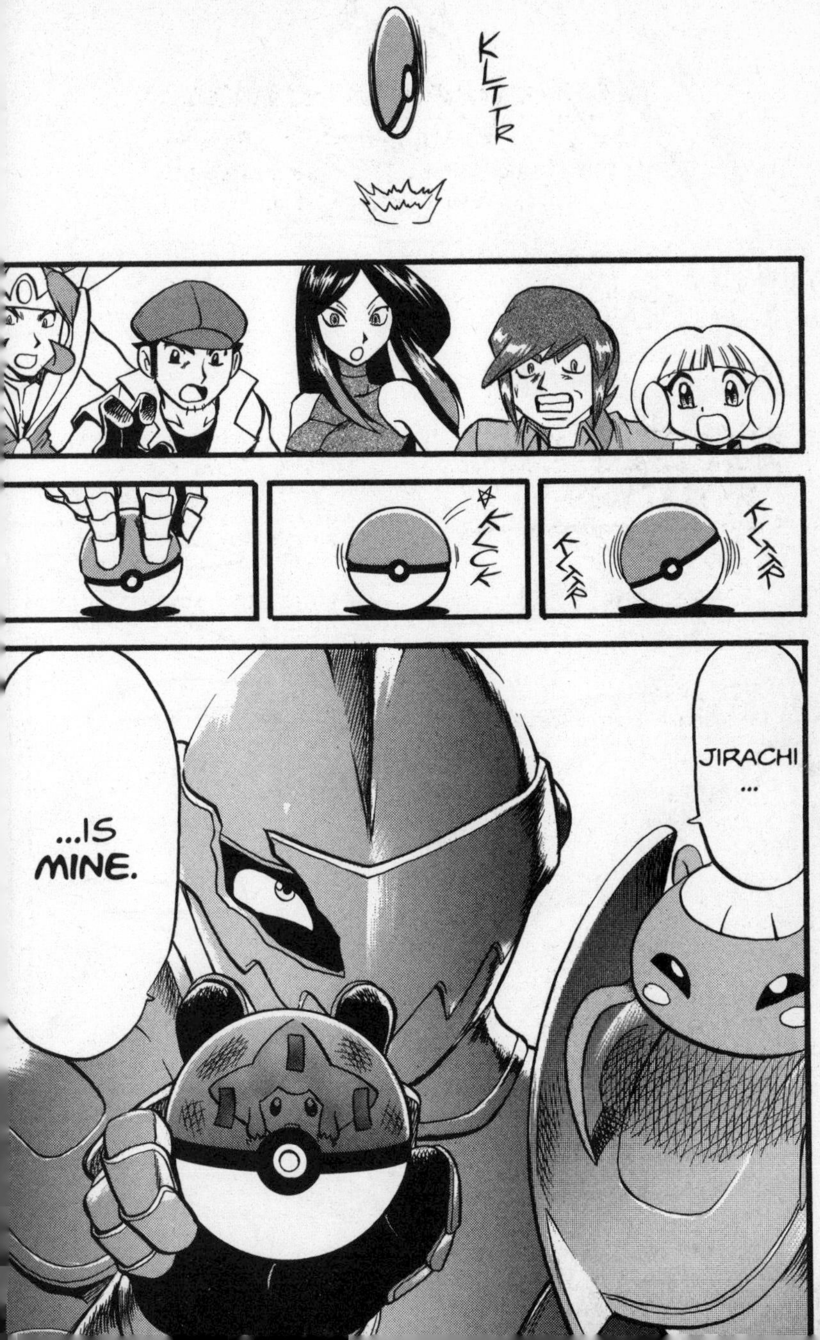
KLTTR
KLTTR
KLTTR
KLICK
JIRACHI ...
...IS MINE.

DEAR MEMBERS OF THE PRESS...

Thank you for visiting the Battle Frontier today. Permit me to continue explaining the rules of this facility...

OWNER: SCOTT

FACILITY RULES

BATTLE TOWER 2

① Single Battle
A one-on-one battle using three Pokémon. This is the only battle style Frontier Brain Anabel will take part in.

② Double Battle
A two-on-two battle using four Pokémon.

③ Multi Battle
A two-on-two battle using four Pokémon.

A two-on-two tag battle fought by teaming up with another contestant, such as a Pokémon Breeder, Kindler, Lass and others. The battle is fought by four Pokémon, two from the challenger and two from the tag partner.

■ THE TYPES OF BATTLE AT THE BATTLE TOWER ■

Apart from the three battle styles above, multiplayer battles will also be available after the official opening of the Battle Frontier. These will be Double Battles fought between Battle Towers from other regions.

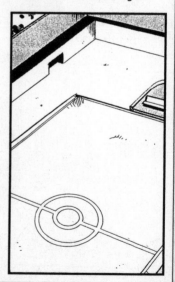

325

Standing in the Way with Starmie

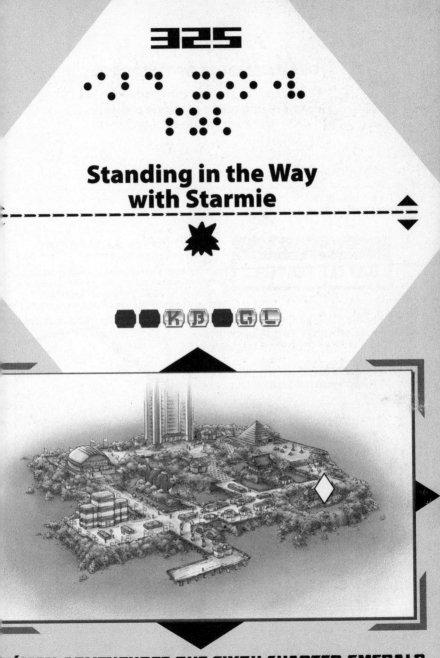

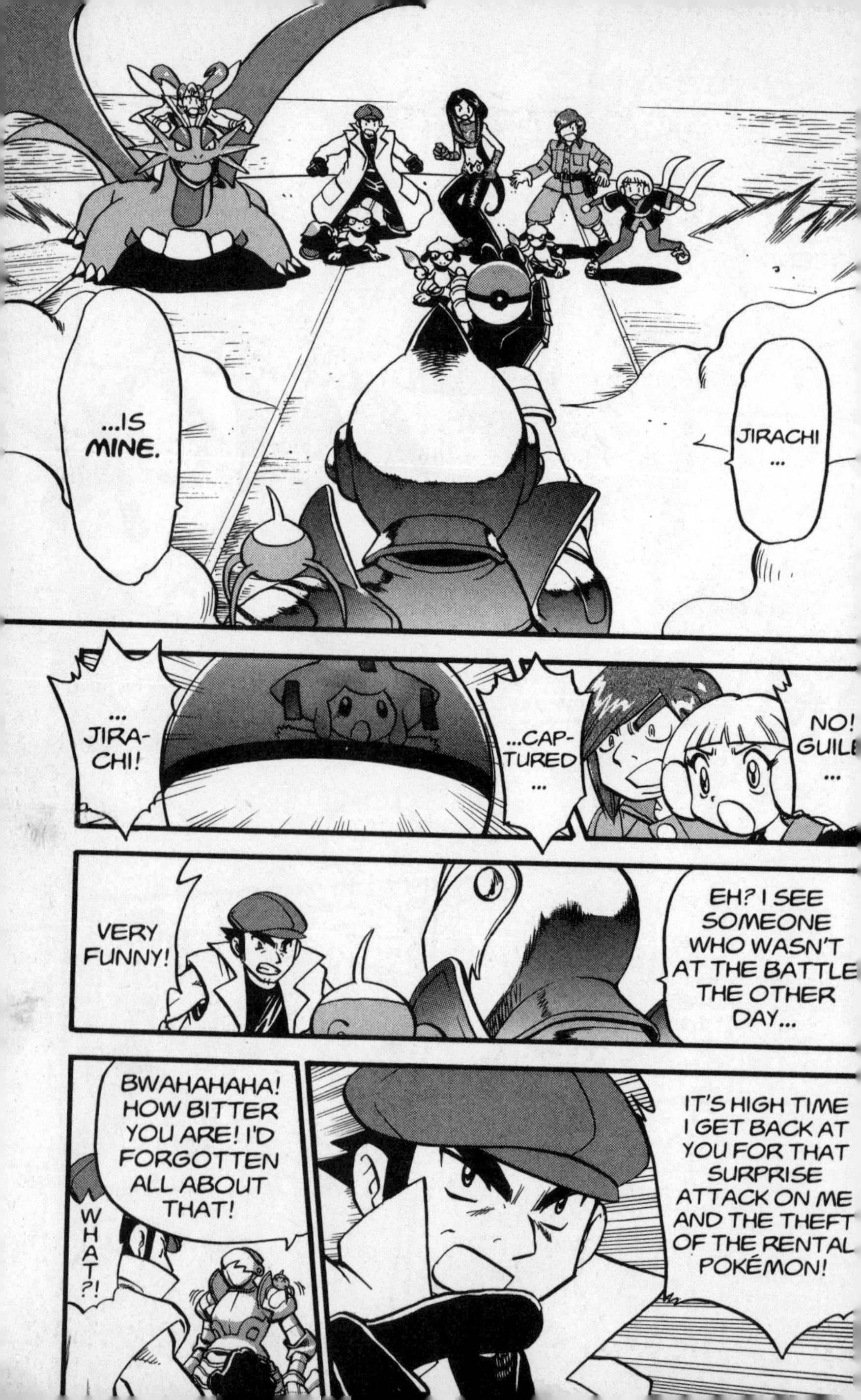
JIRACHI ...
...IS MINE.
NO! GUILE ...
...CAPTURED ...
... JIRACHI!
EH? I SEE SOMEONE WHO WASN'T AT THE BATTLE THE OTHER DAY...
VERY FUNNY!
IT'S HIGH TIME I GET BACK AT YOU FOR THAT SURPRISE ATTACK ON ME AND THE THEFT OF THE RENTAL POKÉMON!
BWAHAHAHA! HOW BITTER YOU ARE! I'D FORGOTTEN ALL ABOUT THAT!
WHAT?!

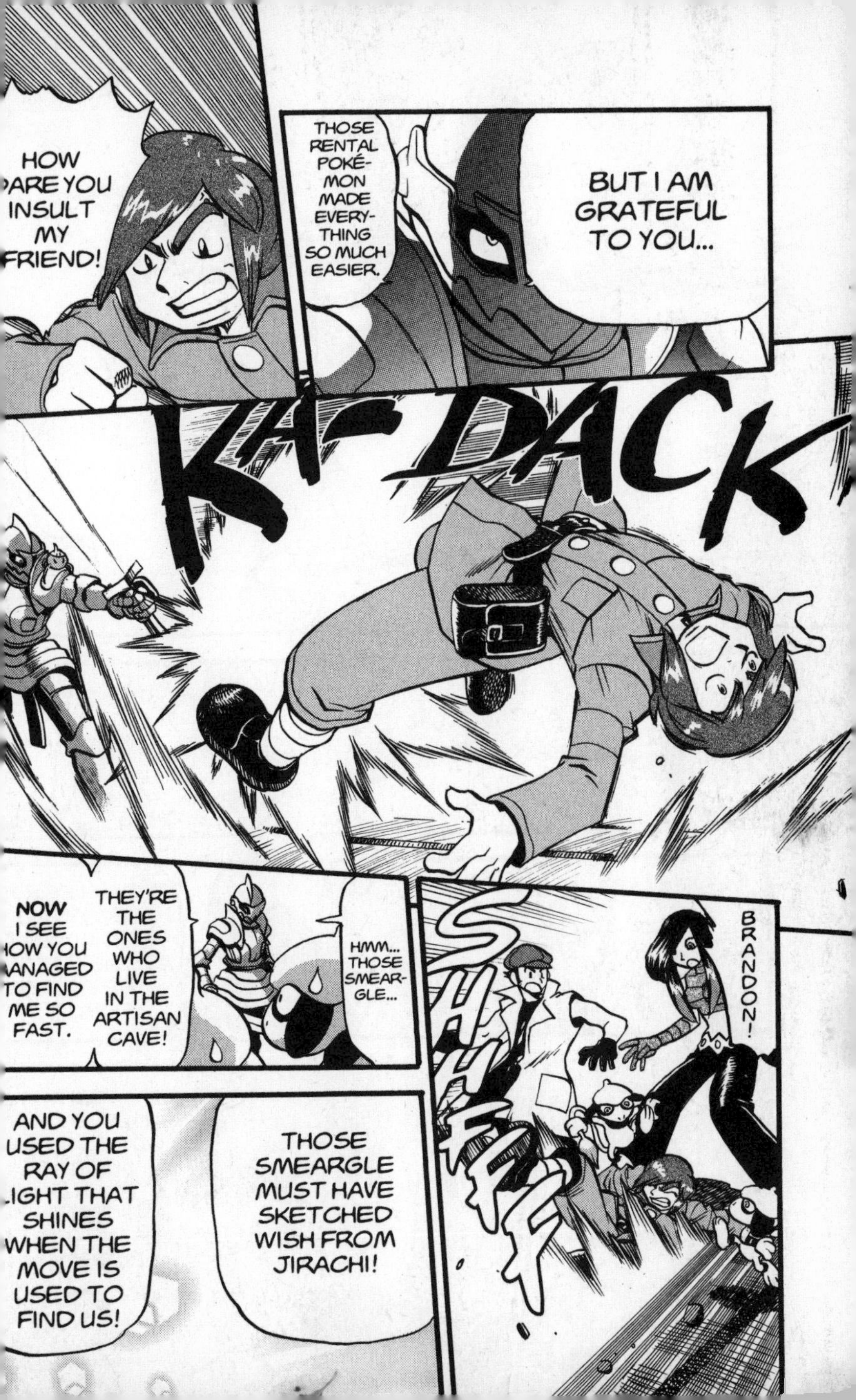
BUT I AM GRATEFUL TO YOU...
THOSE RENTAL POKÉ-MON MADE EVERY-THING SO MUCH EASIER.
HOW DARE YOU INSULT MY FRIEND!
KA-DACK
BRANDON!
HMM... THOSE SMEAR-GLE...
THEY'RE THE ONES WHO LIVE IN THE ARTISAN CAVE!
NOW I SEE HOW YOU MANAGED TO FIND ME SO FAST.
THOSE SMEARGLE MUST HAVE SKETCHED WISH FROM JIRACHI!
AND YOU USED THE RAY OF LIGHT THAT SHINES WHEN THE MOVE IS USED TO FIND US!

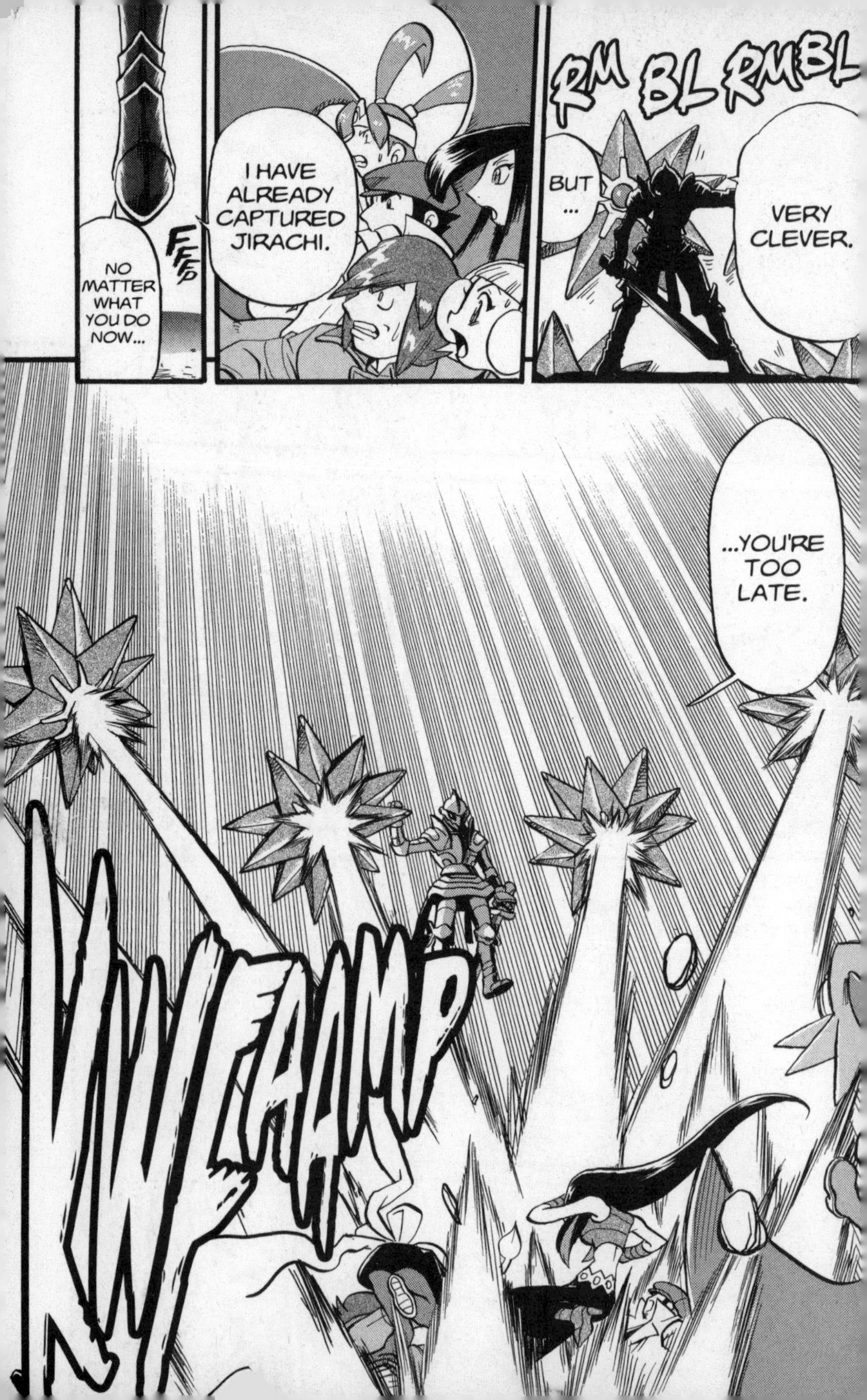
RM BL RMBL
VERY CLEVER.
BUT ...
I HAVE ALREADY CAPTURED JIRACHI.
FFFP
NO MATTER WHAT YOU DO NOW...
...YOU'RE TOO LATE.
WHAAMP

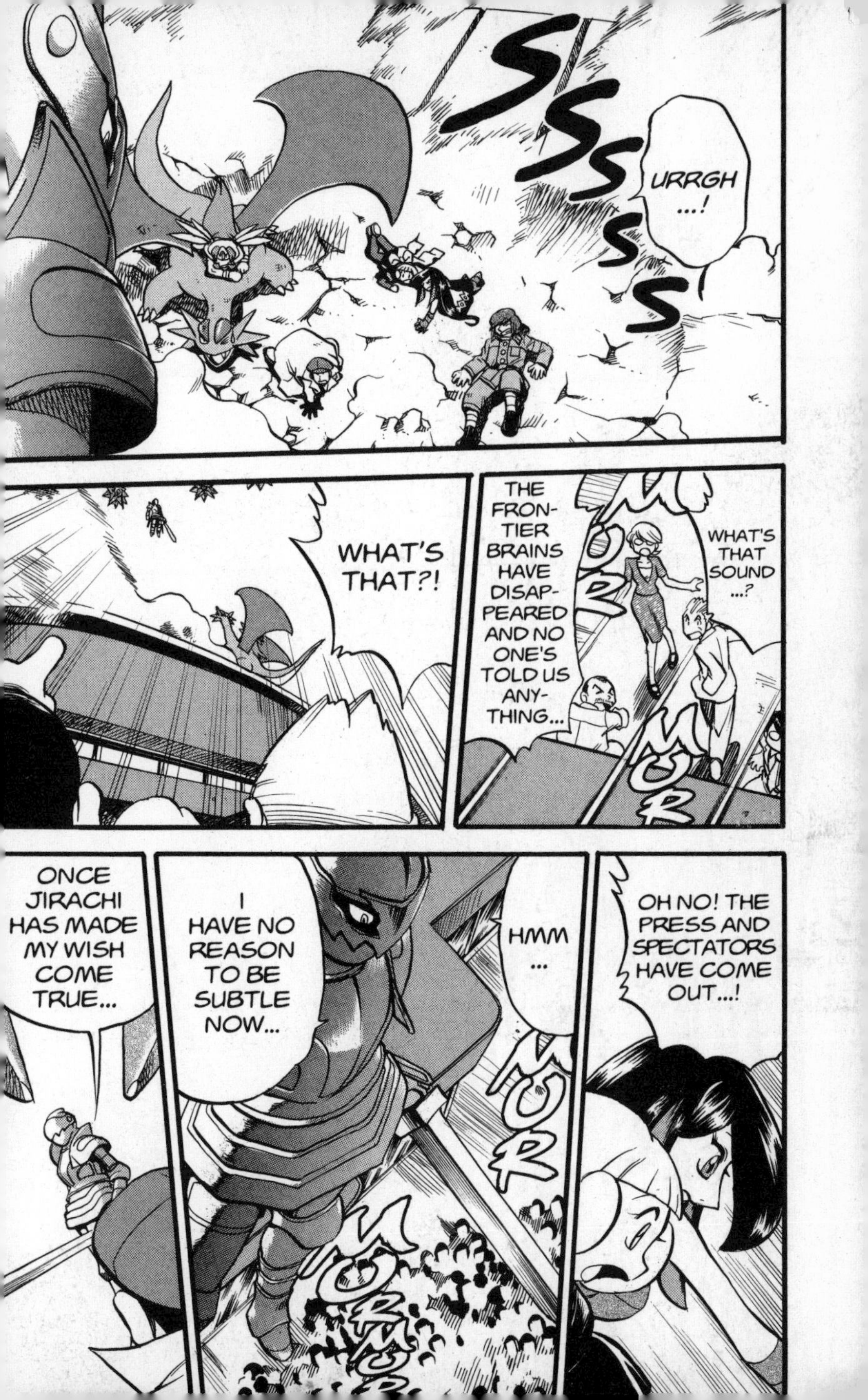
SSSSS
URRGH ...!
MURMUR
WHAT'S THAT SOUND ...?
THE FRONTIER BRAINS HAVE DISAPPEARED AND NO ONE'S TOLD US ANYTHING...
MURMUR
WHAT'S THAT?!
OH NO! THE PRESS AND SPECTATORS HAVE COME OUT...!
MURMUR
HMM ...
I HAVE NO REASON TO BE SUBTLE NOW...
MURMUR
ONCE JIRACHI HAS MADE MY WISH COME TRUE...

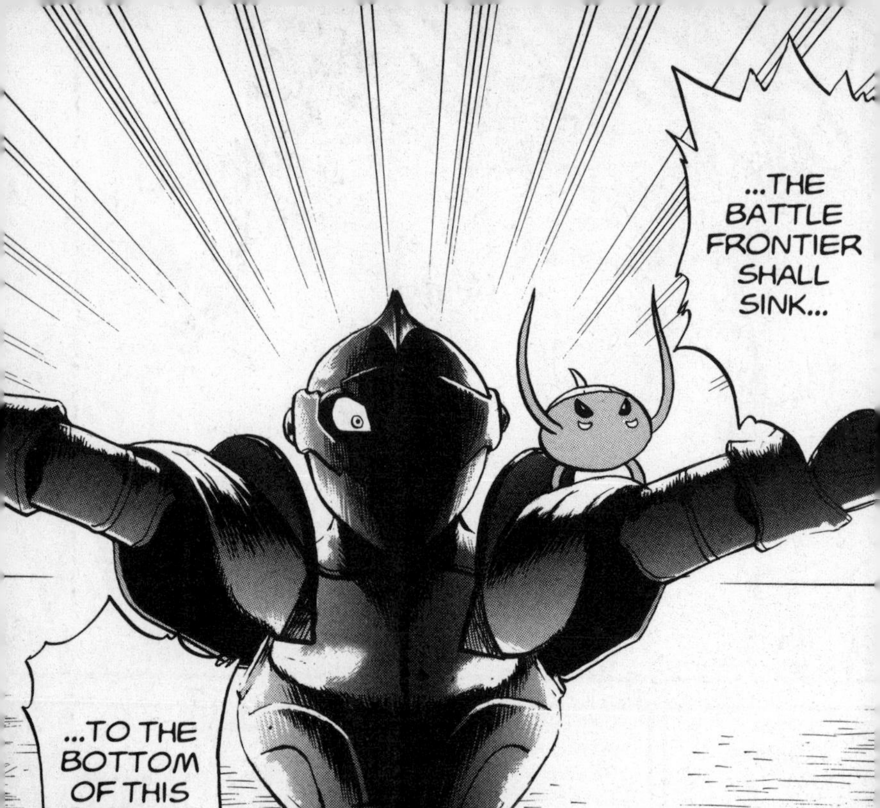
...THE BATTLE FRONTIER SHALL SINK...
...TO THE BOTTOM OF THIS MAGNIFI-CENT SEA!
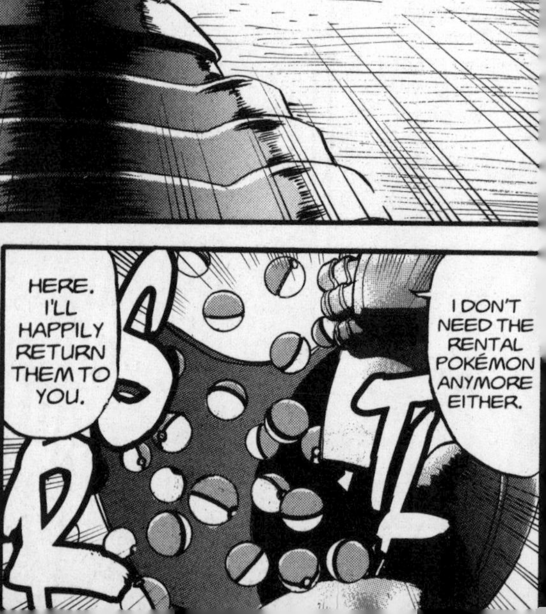
I DON'T NEED THE RENTAL POKÉMON ANYMORE EITHER.
HERE. I'LL HAPPILY RETURN THEM TO YOU.
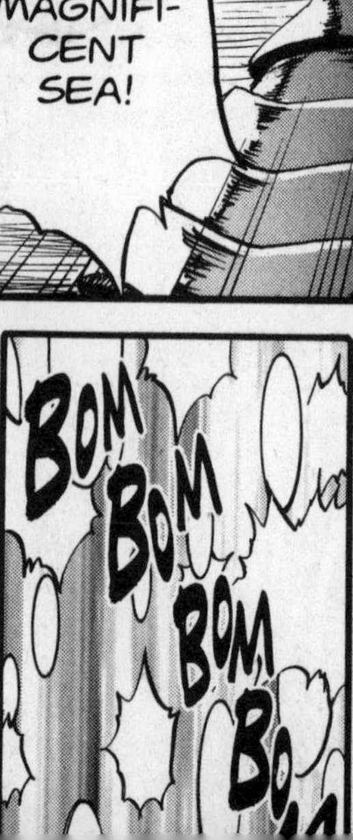
BOM
BOM
BOM,
BO

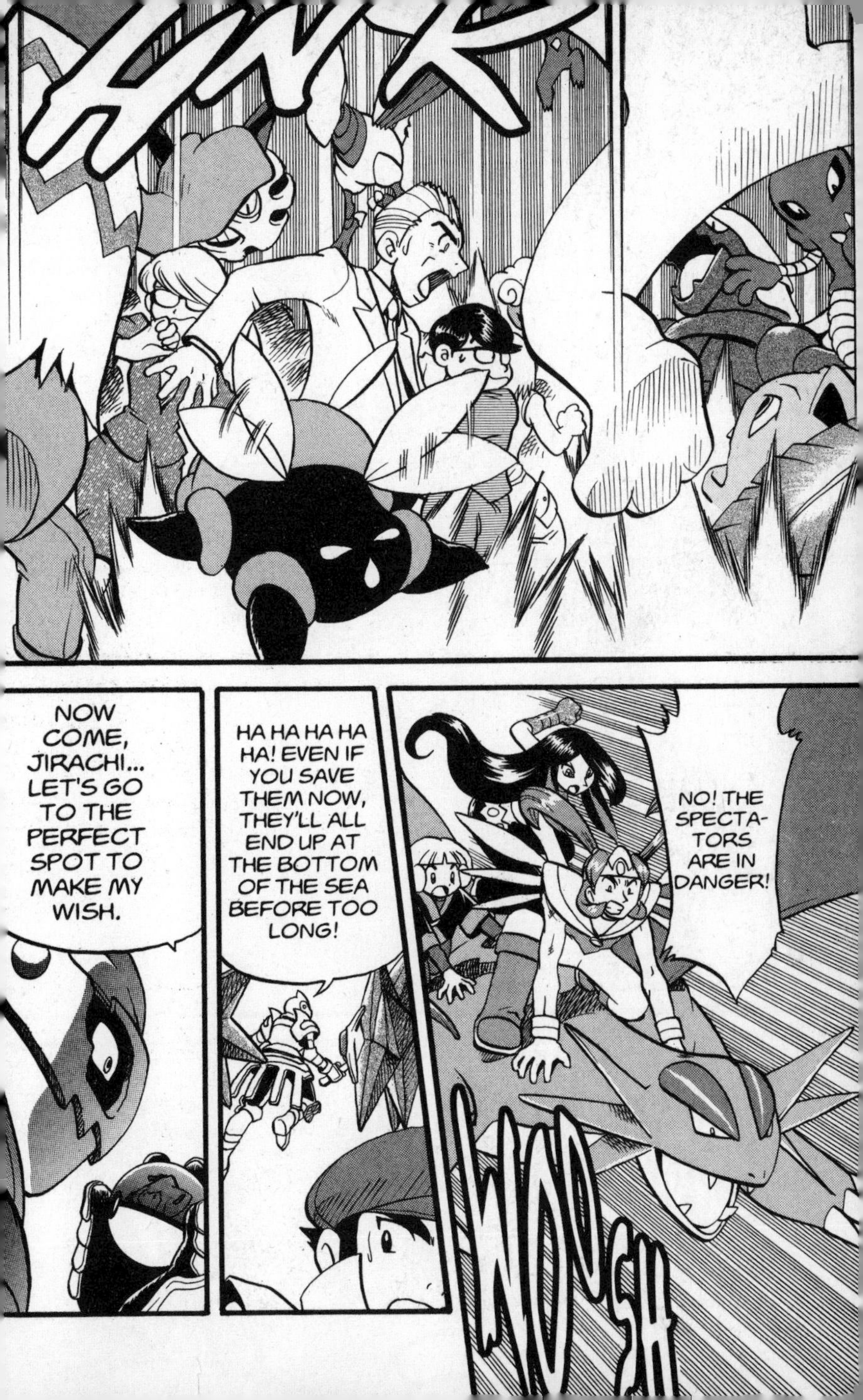
NO! THE SPECTATORS ARE IN DANGER!
HA HA HA HA HA! EVEN IF YOU SAVE THEM NOW, THEY'LL ALL END UP AT THE BOTTOM OF THE SEA BEFORE TOO LONG!
NOW COME, JIRACHI... LET'S GO TO THE PERFECT SPOT TO MAKE MY WISH.

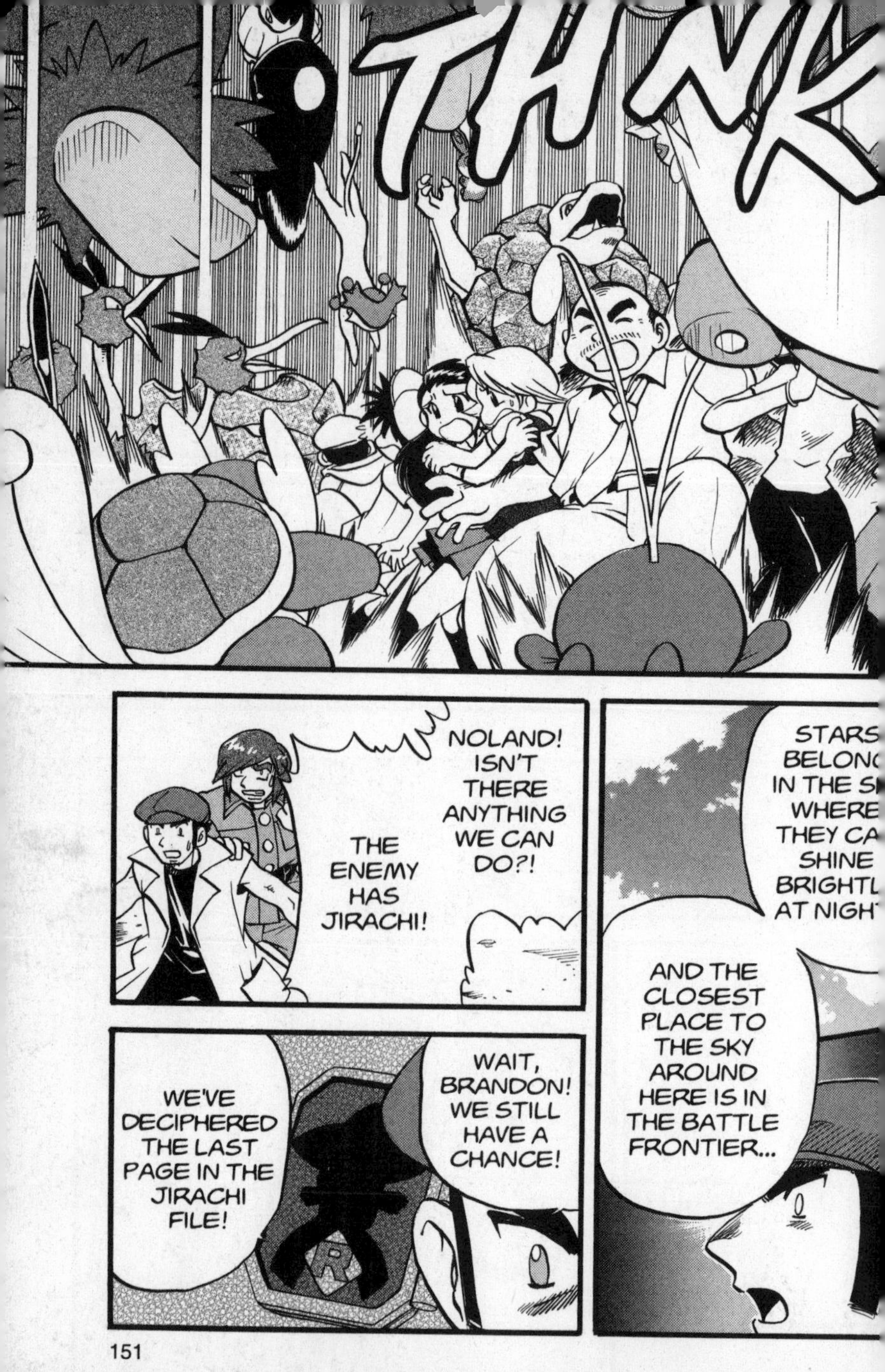
THNK
STARS BELON IN THE S WHERE THEY CA SHINE BRIGHTL AT NIGH
AND THE CLOSEST PLACE TO THE SKY AROUND HERE IS IN THE BATTLE FRONTIER...
NOLAND! ISN'T THERE ANYTHING WE CAN DO?!
THE ENEMY HAS JIRACHI!
WAIT, BRANDON! WE STILL HAVE A CHANCE!
WE'VE DECIPHERED THE LAST PAGE IN THE JIRACHI FILE!

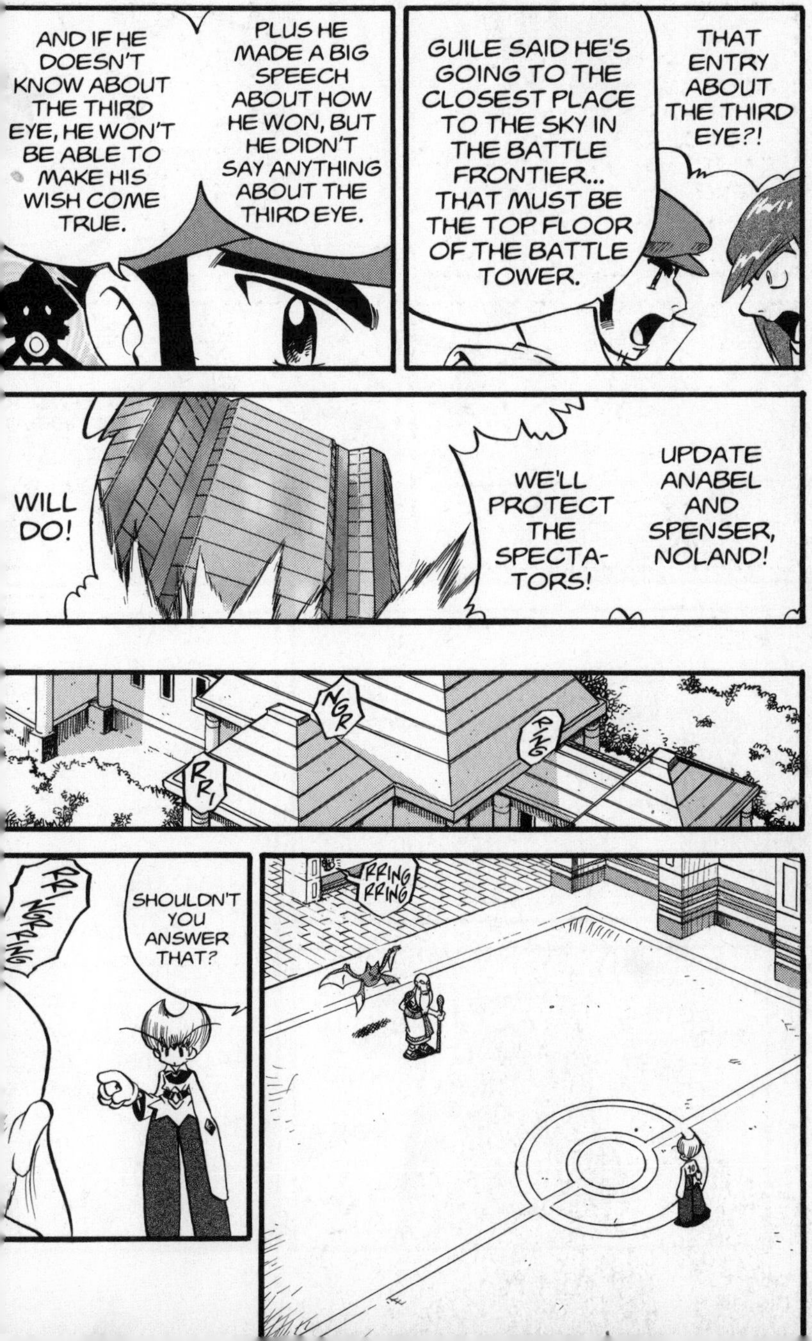
THAT ENTRY ABOUT THE THIRD EYE?!
GUILE SAID HE'S GOING TO THE CLOSEST PLACE TO THE SKY IN THE BATTLE FRONTIER... THAT MUST BE THE TOP FLOOR OF THE BATTLE TOWER.
PLUS HE MADE A BIG SPEECH ABOUT HOW HE WON, BUT HE DIDN'T SAY ANYTHING ABOUT THE THIRD EYE.
AND IF HE DOESN'T KNOW ABOUT THE THIRD EYE, HE WON'T BE ABLE TO MAKE HIS WISH COME TRUE.
UPDATE ANABEL AND SPENSER, NOLAND!
WE'LL PROTECT THE SPECTATORS!
WILL DO!
RING
NGR
RRI
RRING RRING
SHOULDN'T YOU ANSWER THAT?
RRI-NGRRING

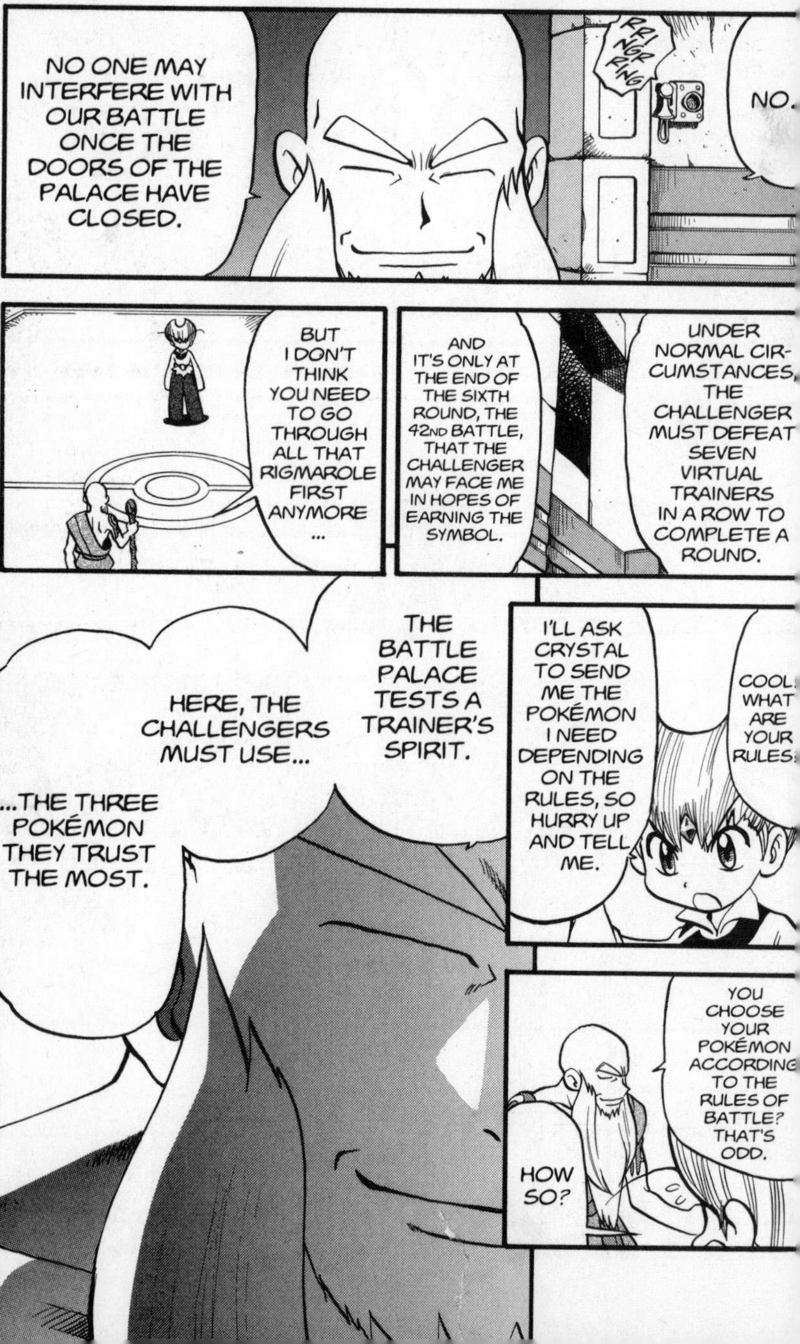
RRINGRRING
NO.
NO ONE MAY INTERFERE WITH OUR BATTLE ONCE THE DOORS OF THE PALACE HAVE CLOSED.
UNDER NORMAL CIR-CUMSTANCES, THE CHALLENGER MUST DEFEAT SEVEN VIRTUAL TRAINERS IN A ROW TO COMPLETE A ROUND.
AND IT'S ONLY AT THE END OF THE SIXTH ROUND, THE 42ND BATTLE, THAT THE CHALLENGER MAY FACE ME IN HOPES OF EARNING THE SYMBOL.
BUT I DON'T THINK YOU NEED TO GO THROUGH ALL THAT RIGMAROLE FIRST ANYMORE...
COOL! WHAT ARE YOUR RULES?
I'LL ASK CRYSTAL TO SEND ME THE POKÉMON I NEED DEPENDING ON THE RULES, SO HURRY UP AND TELL ME.
YOU CHOOSE YOUR POKÉMON ACCORDING TO THE RULES OF BATTLE? THAT'S ODD.
HOW SO?
THE BATTLE PALACE TESTS A TRAINER'S SPIRIT.
HERE, THE CHALLENGERS MUST USE...
...THE THREE POKÉMON THEY TRUST THE MOST.

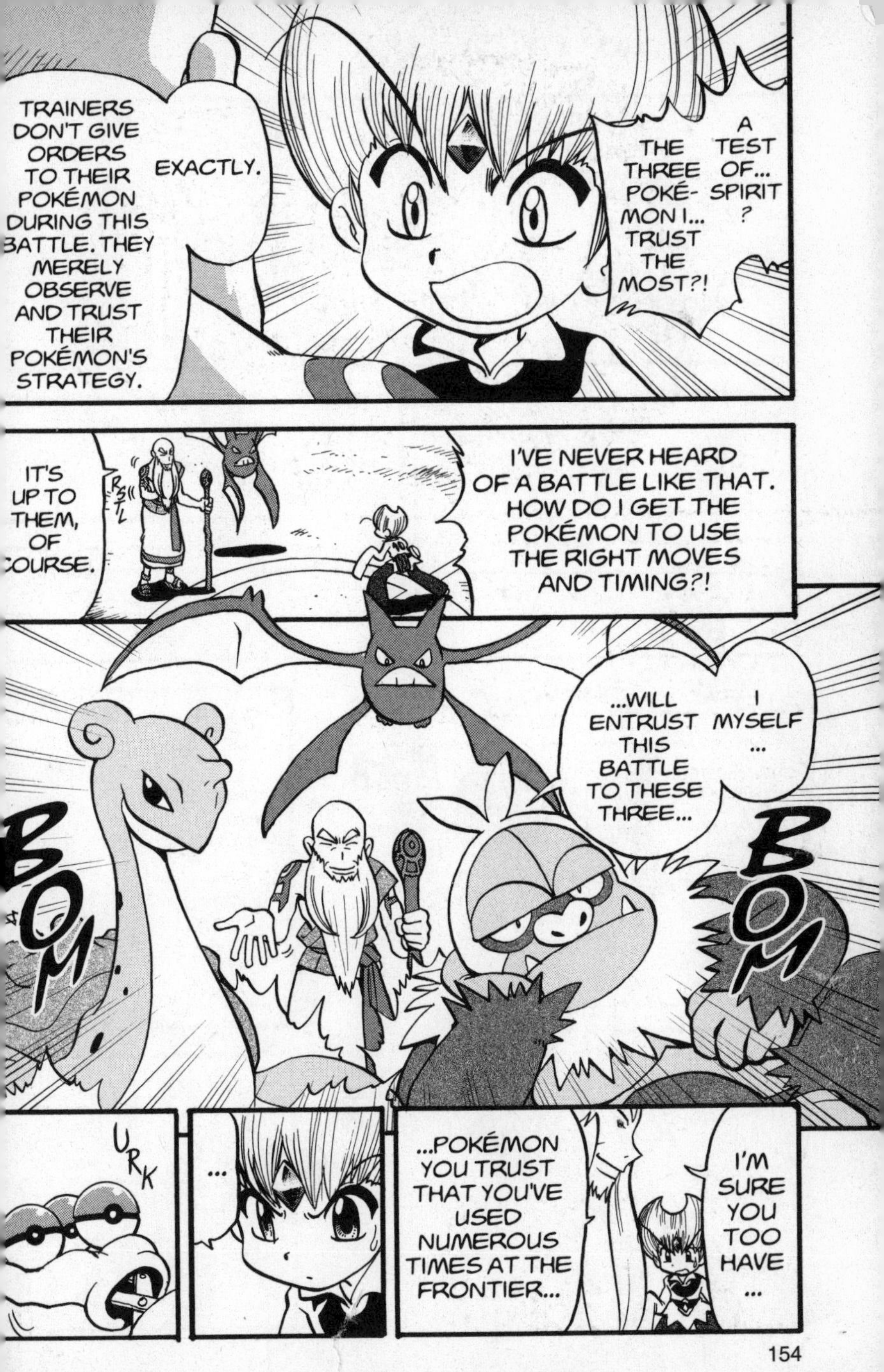
A TEST OF... SPIRIT?
THE THREE POKÉMON I... TRUST THE MOST?!
EXACTLY.
TRAINERS DON'T GIVE ORDERS TO THEIR POKÉMON DURING THIS BATTLE. THEY MERELY OBSERVE AND TRUST THEIR POKÉMON'S STRATEGY.
I'VE NEVER HEARD OF A BATTLE LIKE THAT. HOW DO I GET THE POKÉMON TO USE THE RIGHT MOVES AND TIMING?!
RSTL
IT'S UP TO THEM, OF COURSE.
I MYSELF...
...WILL ENTRUST THIS BATTLE TO THESE THREE...
BOOM
BOOM
I'M SURE YOU TOO HAVE...
...POKÉMON YOU TRUST THAT YOU'VE USED NUMEROUS TIMES AT THE FRONTIER...
...
URK

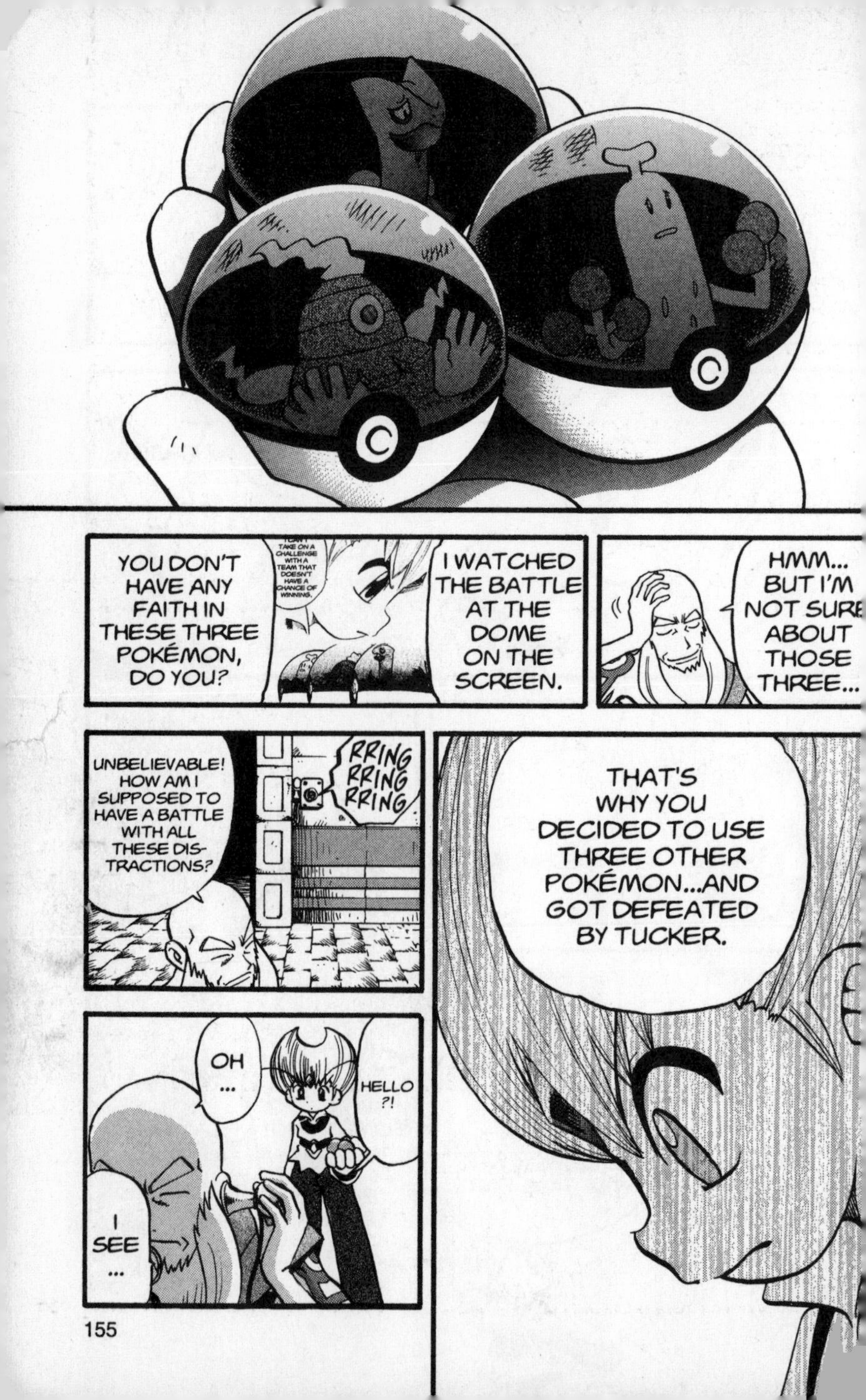
HMM... BUT I'M NOT SURE ABOUT THOSE THREE...
I WATCHED THE BATTLE AT THE DOME ON THE SCREEN.
YOU DON'T HAVE ANY FAITH IN THESE THREE POKÉMON, DO YOU?
I CAN'T TAKE ON A CHALLENGE WITH A TEAM THAT DOESN'T HAVE A CHANCE OF WINNING.
THAT'S WHY YOU DECIDED TO USE THREE OTHER POKÉMON...AND GOT DEFEATED BY TUCKER.
RRING RRING RRING
UNBELIEVABLE! HOW AM I SUPPOSED TO HAVE A BATTLE WITH ALL THESE DIS-TRACTIONS?
HELLO ?!
OH ...
I SEE ...

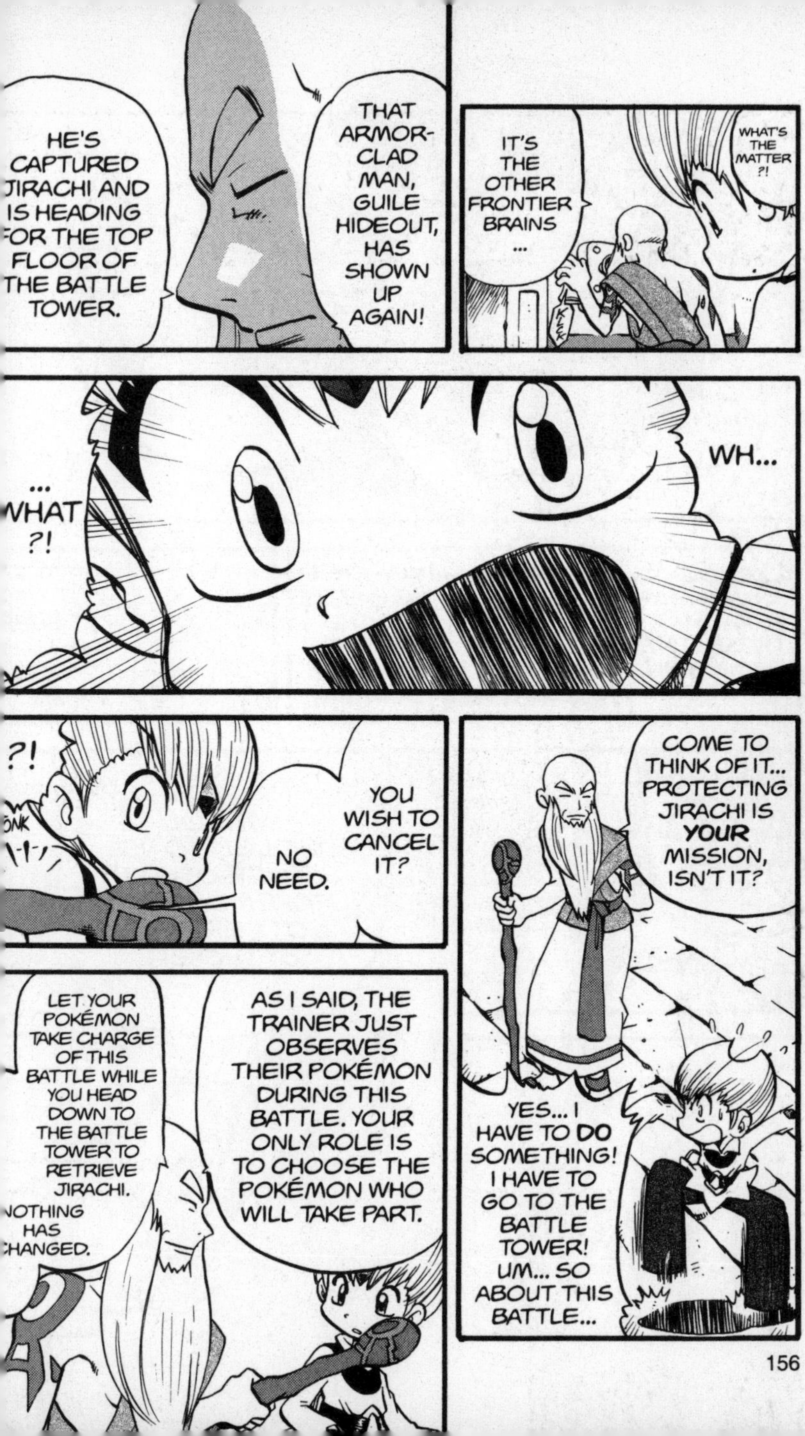
WHAT'S THE MATTER ?!
IT'S THE OTHER FRONTIER BRAINS ...
KLICK
THAT ARMOR-CLAD MAN, GUILE HIDEOUT, HAS SHOWN UP AGAIN!
HE'S CAPTURED JIRACHI AND IS HEADING FOR THE TOP FLOOR OF THE BATTLE TOWER.
WH...
... WHAT ?!
COME TO THINK OF IT... PROTECTING JIRACHI IS **YOUR** MISSION, ISN'T IT?
YES... I HAVE TO **DO** SOMETHING! I HAVE TO GO TO THE BATTLE TOWER! UM... SO ABOUT THIS BATTLE...
?!
YOU WISH TO CANCEL IT?
NO NEED.
AS I SAID, THE TRAINER JUST OBSERVES THEIR POKÉMON DURING THIS BATTLE. YOUR ONLY ROLE IS TO CHOOSE THE POKÉMON WHO WILL TAKE PART.
LET YOUR POKÉMON TAKE CHARGE OF THIS BATTLE WHILE YOU HEAD DOWN TO THE BATTLE TOWER TO RETRIEVE JIRACHI.
NOTHING HAS CHANGED.

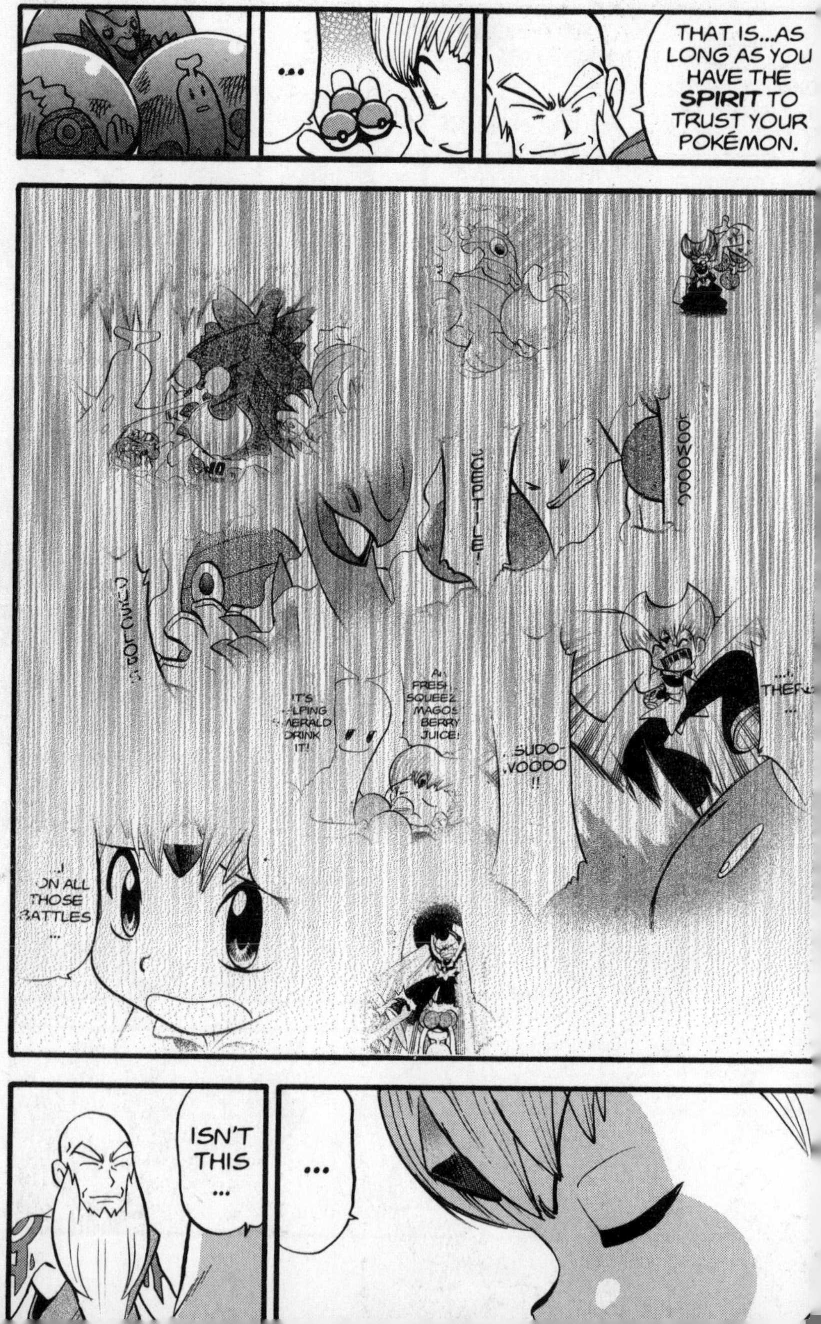
THAT IS...AS LONG AS YOU HAVE THE **SPIRIT** TO TRUST YOUR POKÉMON.
...
SCEPTILE!
SUDO-VOODO!!
FRESH SQUEEZ MAGOS BERRY JUICE!
IT'S LPING MERALD DRINK IT!
ON ALL THOSE BATTLES ...
...
ISN'T THIS ...

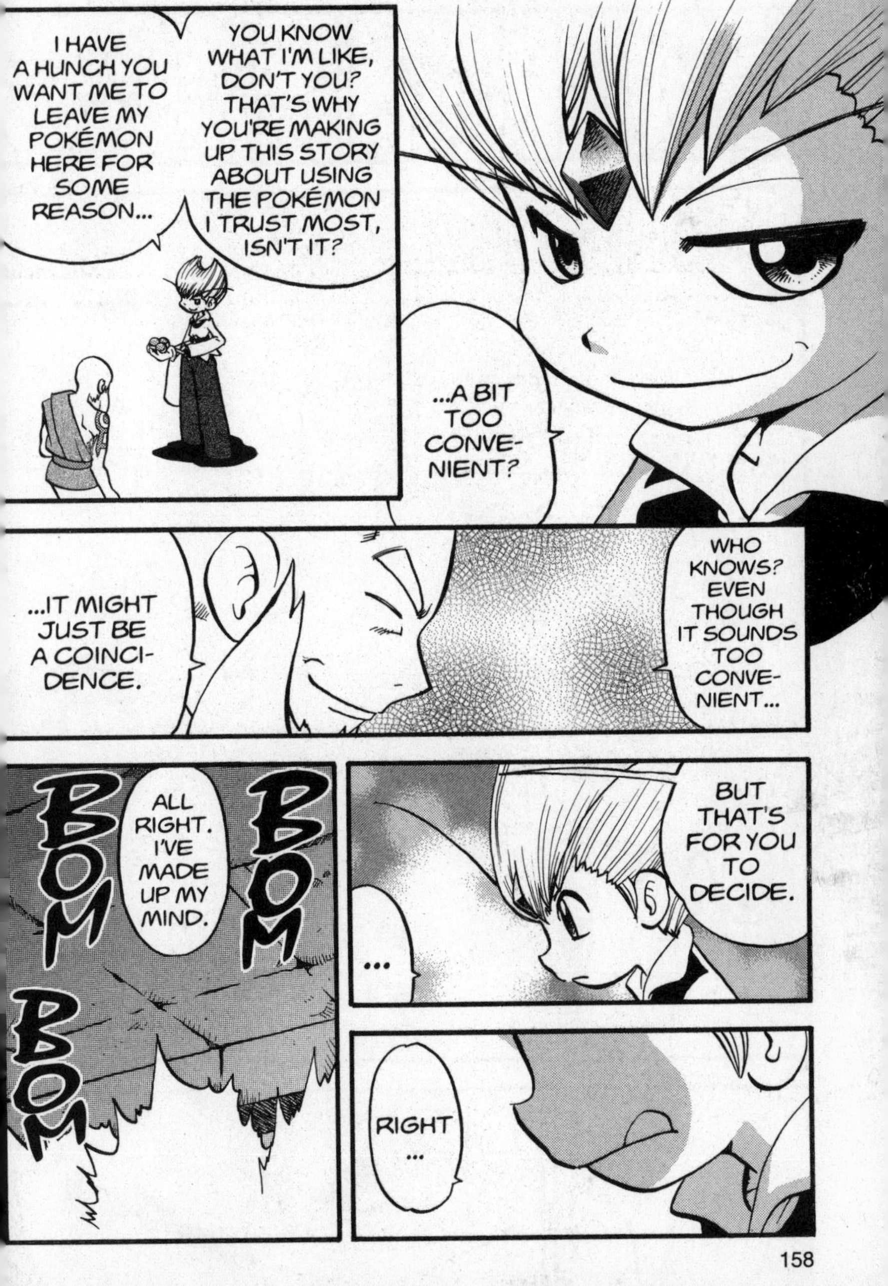
YOU KNOW WHAT I'M LIKE, DON'T YOU? THAT'S WHY YOU'RE MAKING UP THIS STORY ABOUT USING THE POKÉMON I TRUST MOST, ISN'T IT?
I HAVE A HUNCH YOU WANT ME TO LEAVE MY POKÉMON HERE FOR SOME REASON...
...A BIT TOO CONVENIENT?
WHO KNOWS? EVEN THOUGH IT SOUNDS TOO CONVENIENT...
...IT MIGHT JUST BE A COINCIDENCE.
BUT THAT'S FOR YOU TO DECIDE.
...
RIGHT ...
BOM
ALL RIGHT. I'VE MADE UP MY MIND.
BOM
BOM

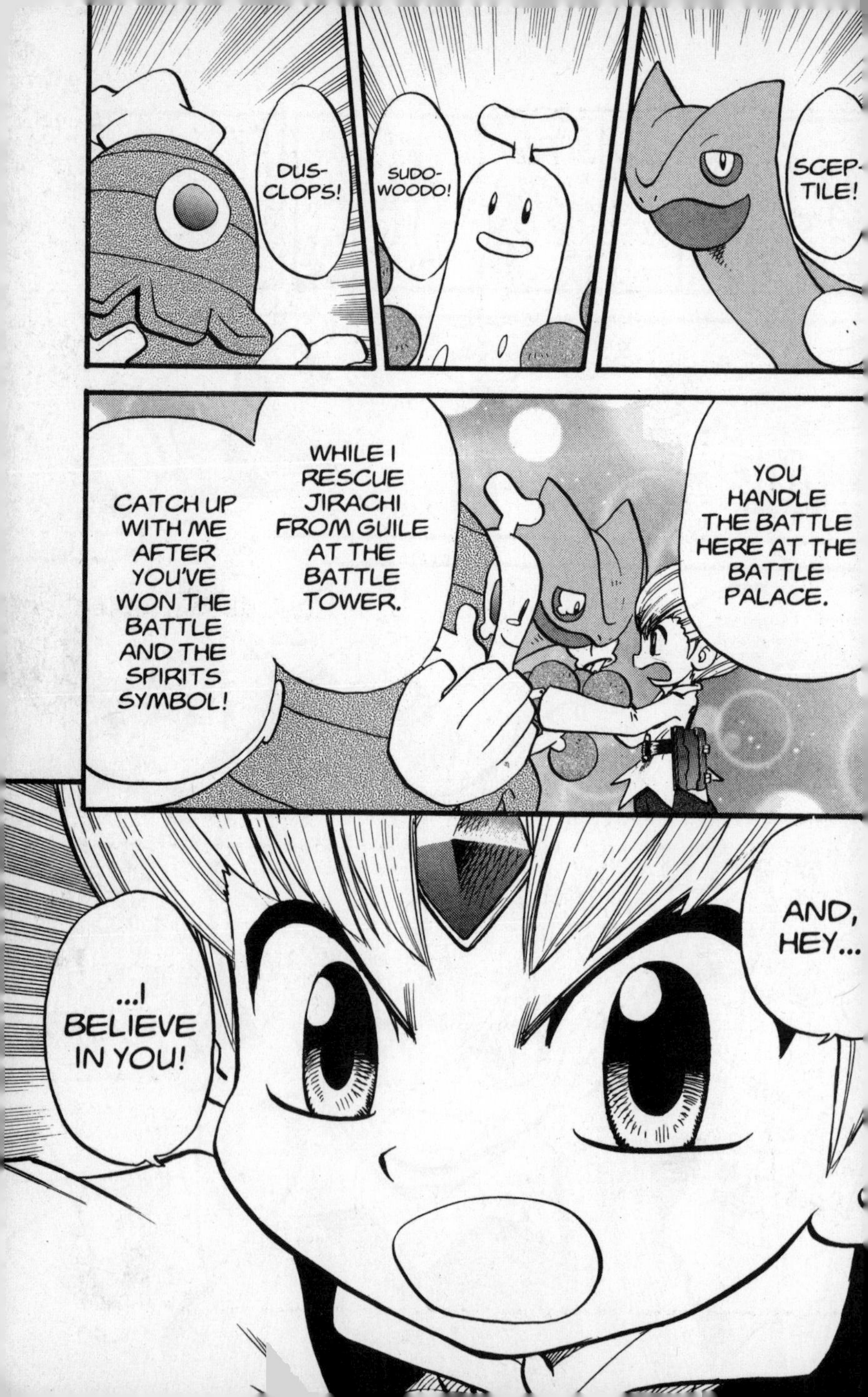
SCEP-TILE!
SUDO-WOODO!
DUS-CLOPS!
YOU HANDLE THE BATTLE HERE AT THE BATTLE PALACE.
WHILE I RESCUE JIRACHI FROM GUILE AT THE BATTLE TOWER.
CATCH UP WITH ME AFTER YOU'VE WON THE BATTLE AND THE SPIRITS SYMBOL!
AND, HEY...
...I BELIEVE IN YOU!

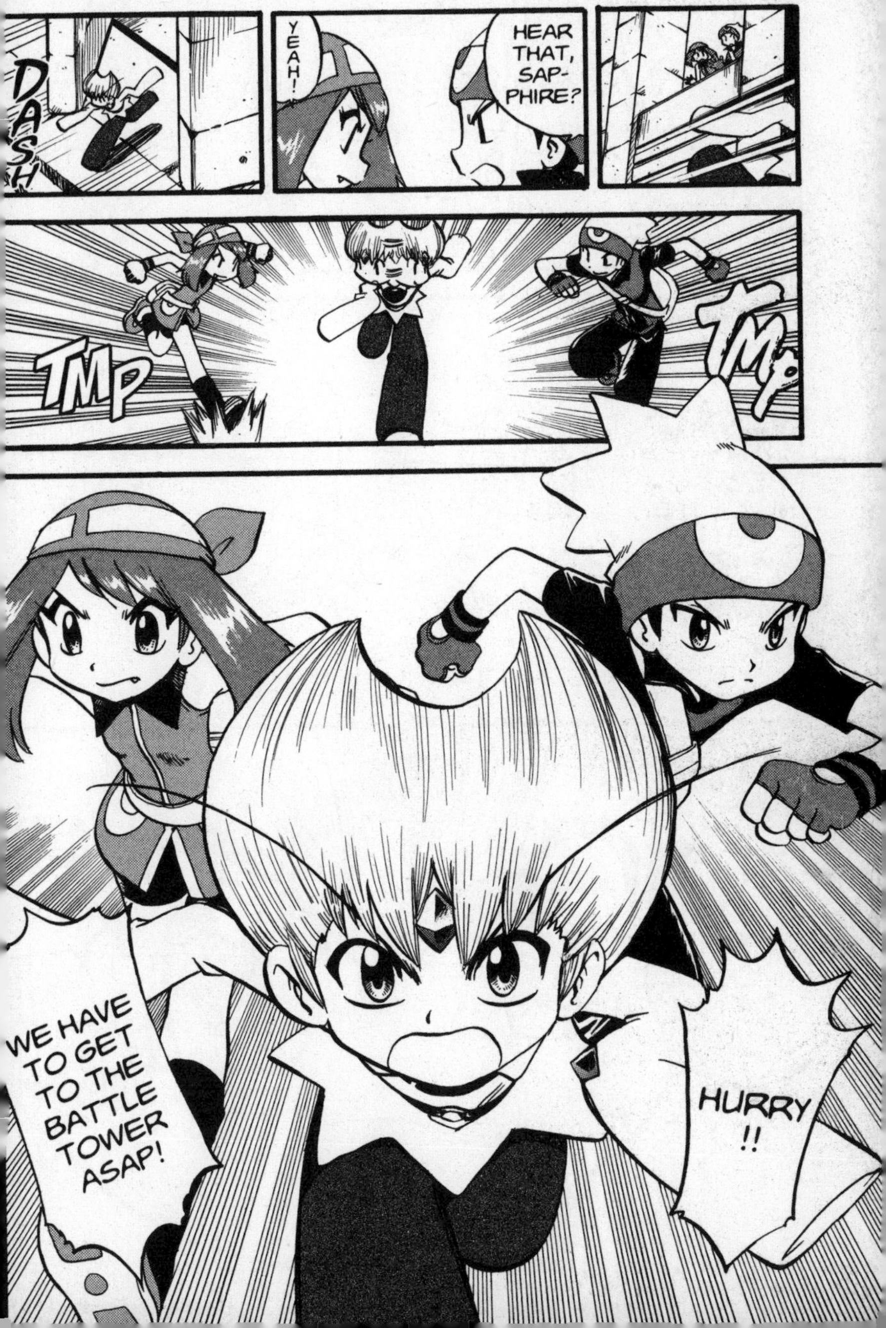
HEAR THAT, SAPPHIRE?
YEAH!!
DASH
TMP
TMP
HURRY!!
WE HAVE TO GET TO THE BATTLE TOWER ASAP!

DEAR MEMBERS OF THE PRESS...

Thank you for visiting the Battle Frontier today. Permit me to continue explaining the rules of this facility...

OWNER: SCOTT

BATTLE TOWER 3

■ **THE BATTLE SALON** ■

The Battle Salon is provided for Trainers who want to team up with a tag partner for Multi battles. You can find a compatible partner here to fight on your side.

■ **WINNING THE SHIELDS** ■

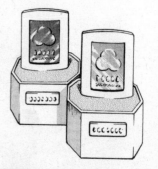

As with the other six facilities, the challenger receives a Symbol for defeating the Battle Tower Frontier Brain. At the Battle Tower, I, Scott, will personally award Trainers with a Silver Shield after fifty consecutive wins in Single battle and a Gold Shield after a hundred.

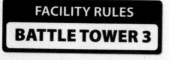

326

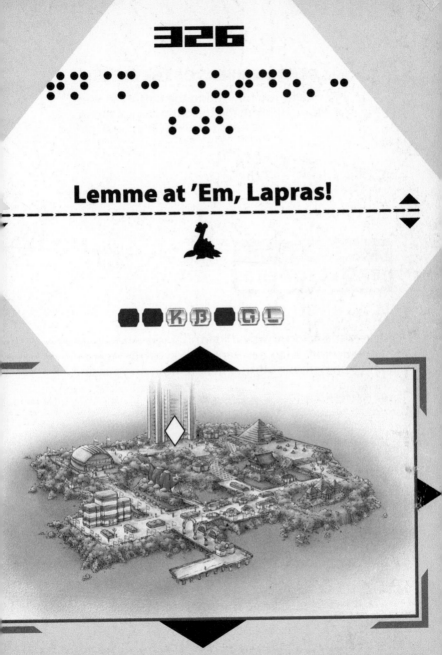

Lemme at 'Em, Lapras!

●●🄚🄱●🄖🄻

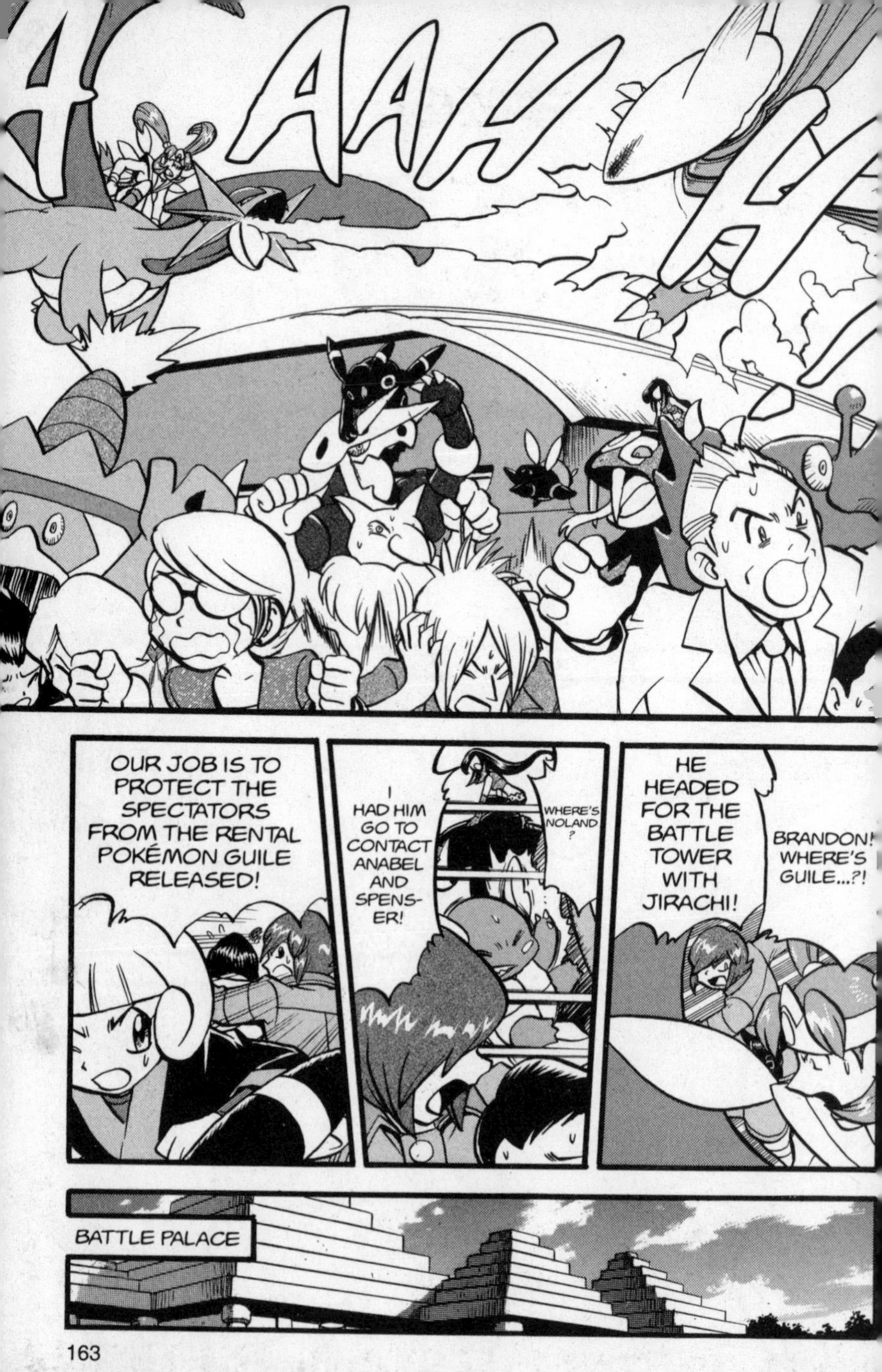

AAH
BRANDON! WHERE'S GUILE...?!
HE HEADED FOR THE BATTLE TOWER WITH JIRACHI!
WHERE'S NOLAND?
I HAD HIM GO TO CONTACT ANABEL AND SPENSER!
OUR JOB IS TO PROTECT THE SPECTATORS FROM THE RENTAL POKÉMON GUILE RELEASED!
BATTLE PALACE

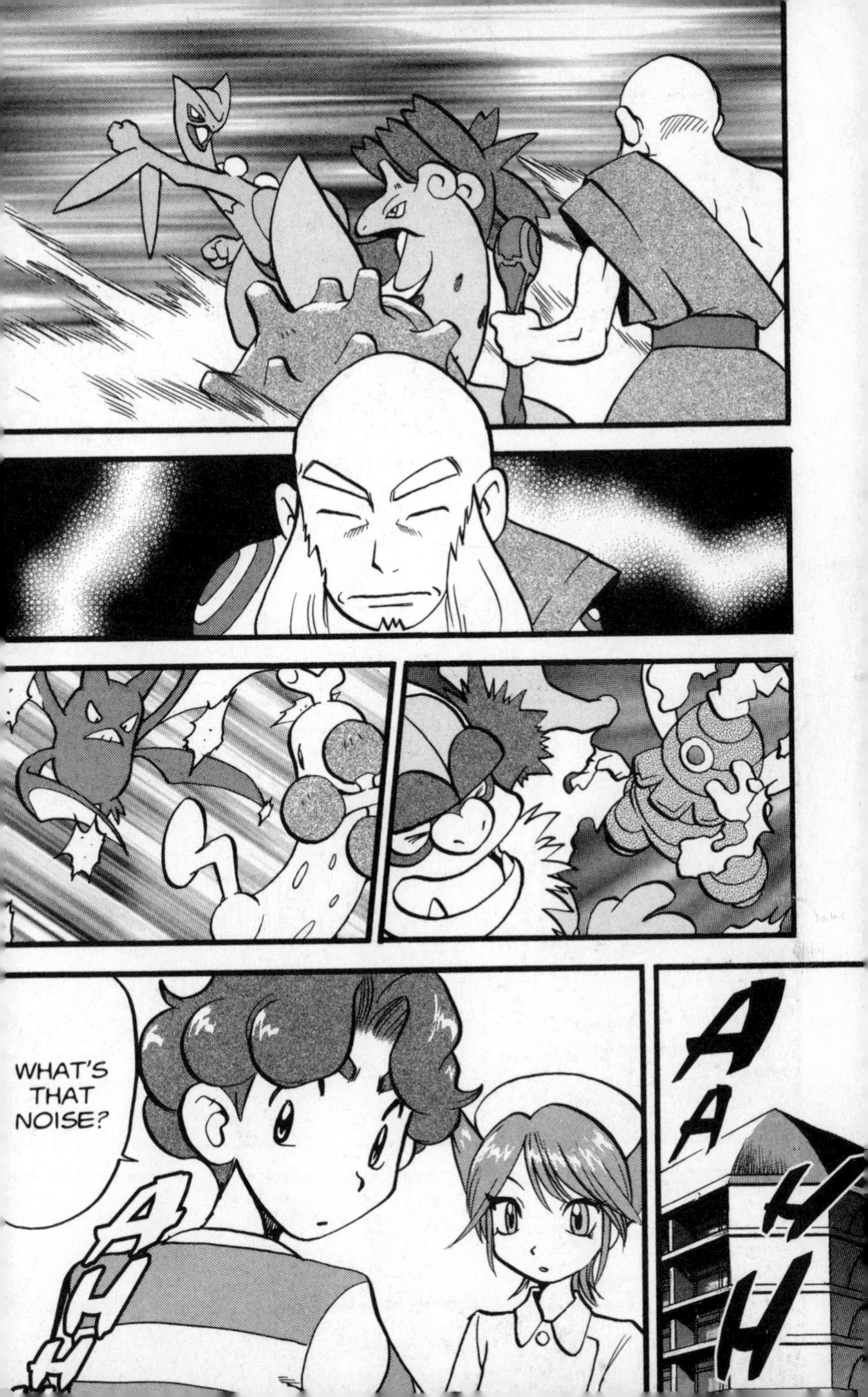

AAHH
WHAT'S THAT NOISE?
AHH

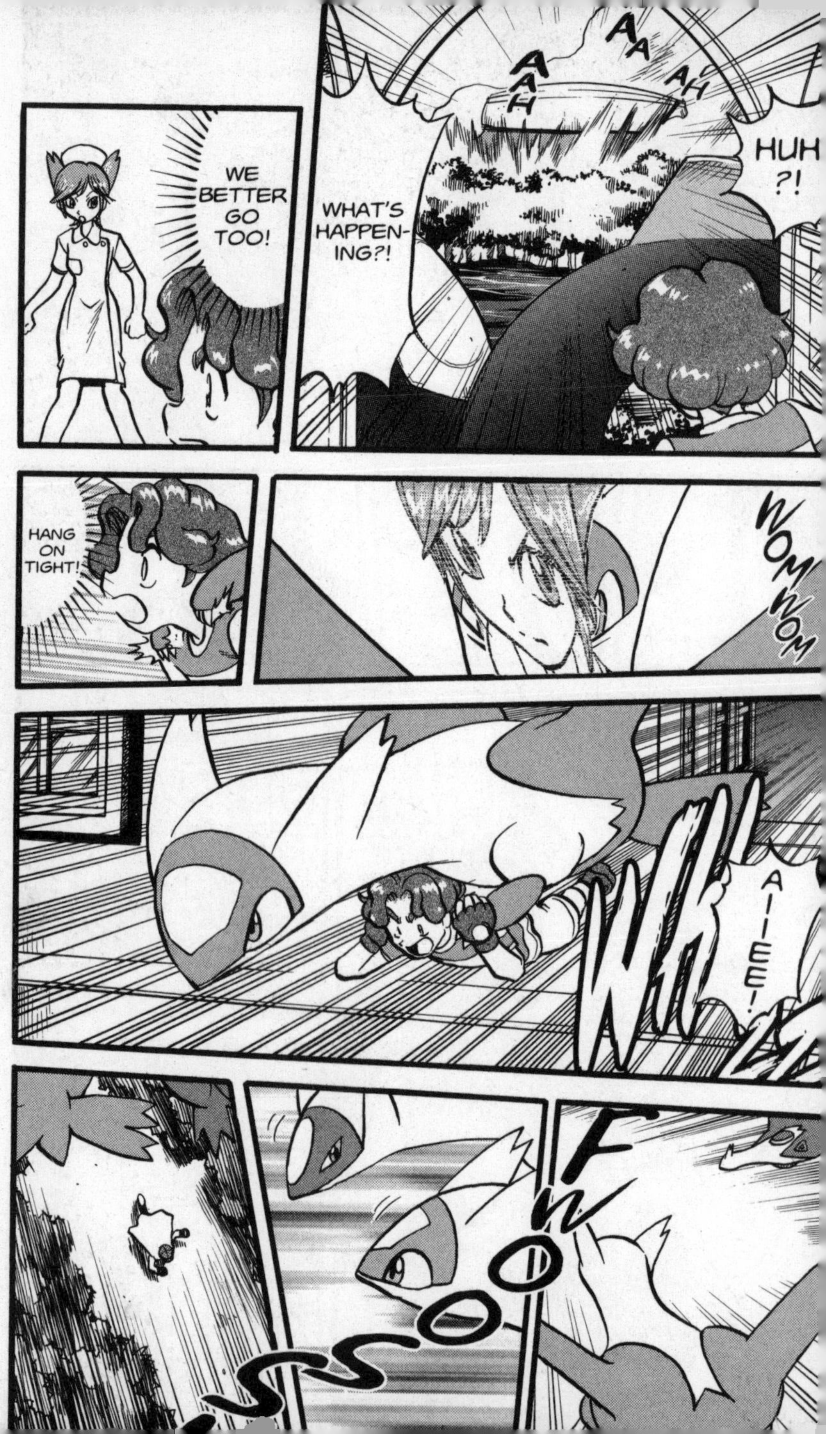
AAH
AAAH
HUH ?!
WHAT'S HAPPEN-ING?!
WE BETTER GO TOO!
WOM WOM
HANG ON TIGHT!
WHH
AIIEE!
FWOOO
SSS

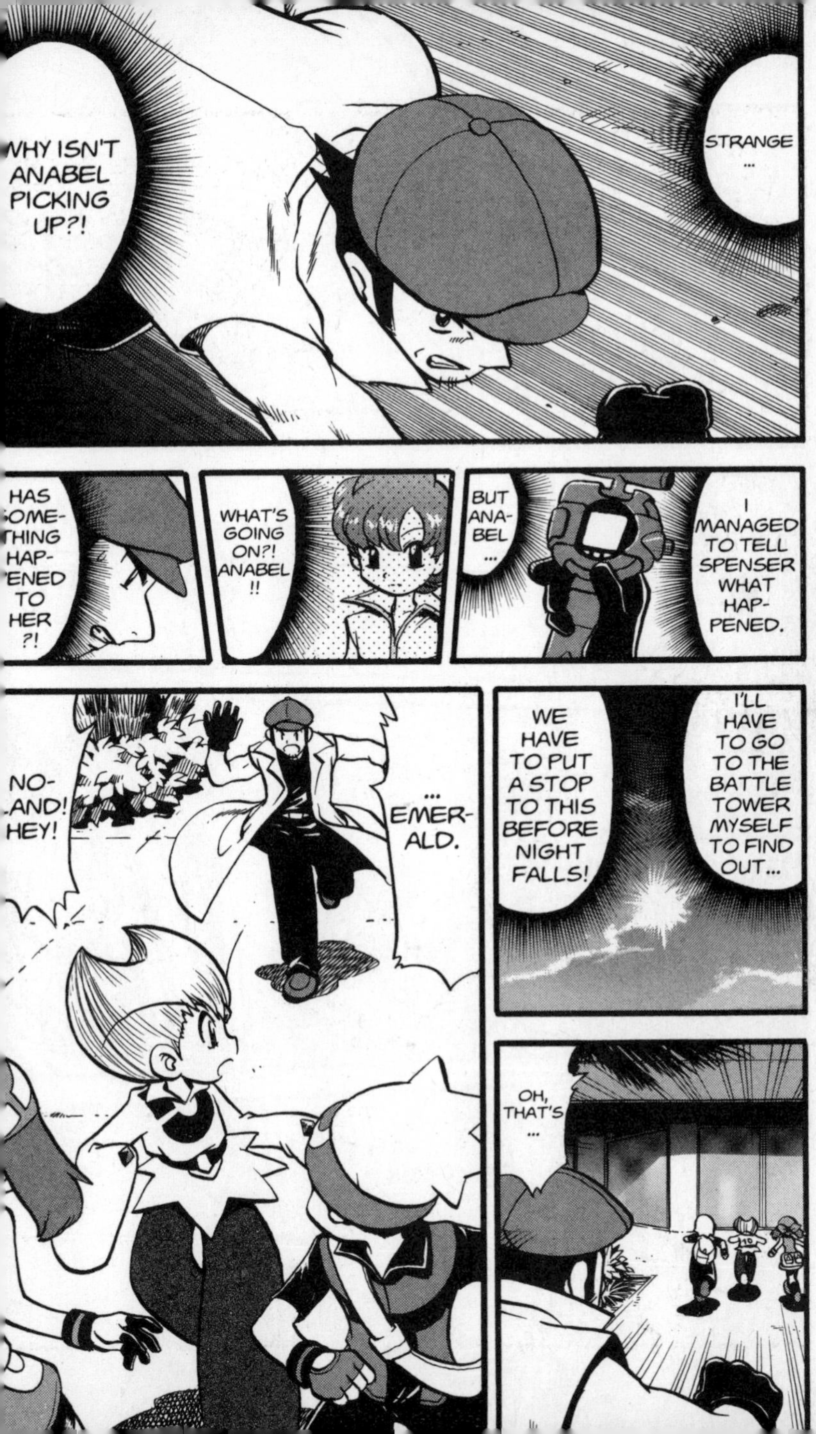
STRANGE...
WHY ISN'T ANABEL PICKING UP?!
I MANAGED TO TELL SPENSER WHAT HAP-PENED.
BUT ANA-BEL...
WHAT'S GOING ON?! ANABEL!!
HAS SOME-THING HAP-PENED TO HER?!
I'LL HAVE TO GO TO THE BATTLE TOWER MYSELF TO FIND OUT...
WE HAVE TO PUT A STOP TO THIS BEFORE NIGHT FALLS!
OH, THAT'S...
...EMER-ALD.
NO-LAND! HEY!

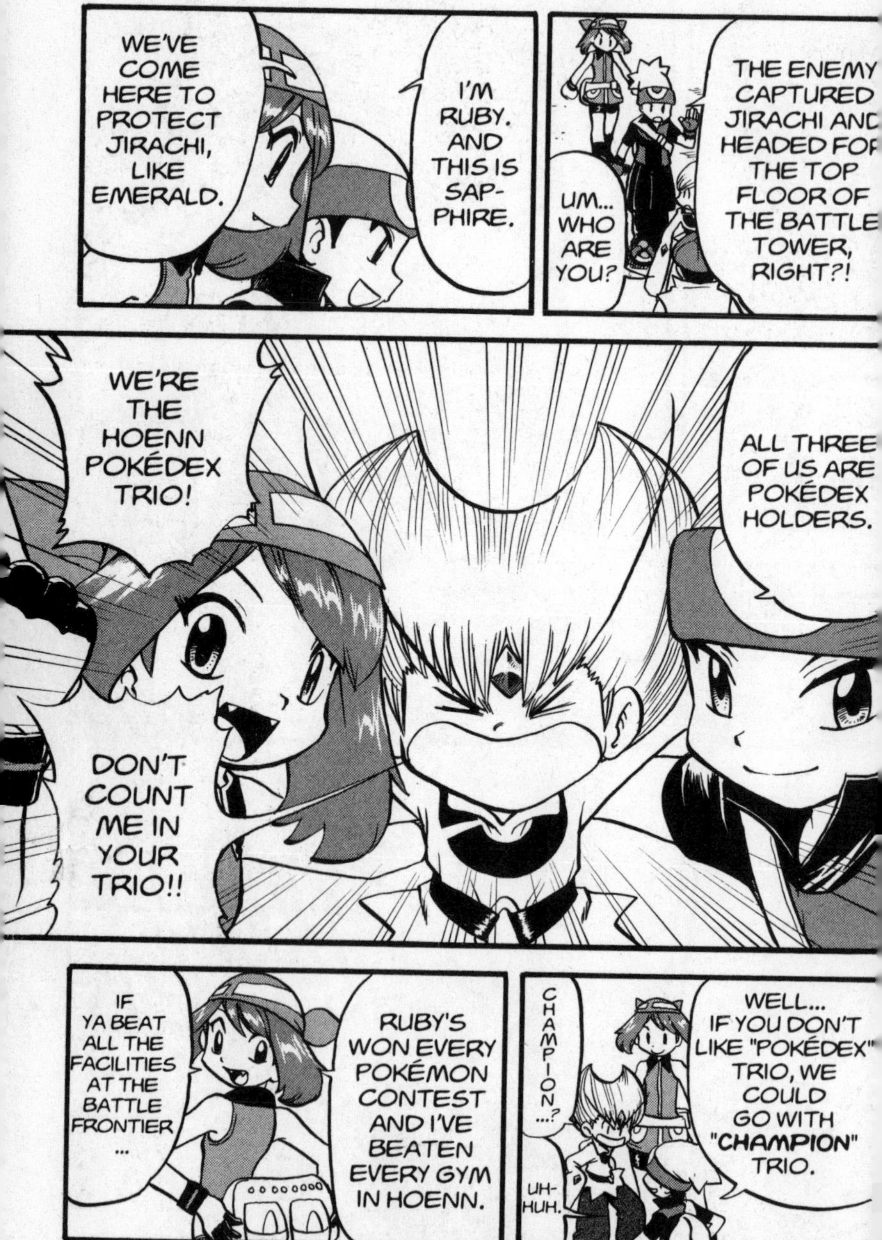
THE ENEMY CAPTURED JIRACHI AND HEADED FOR THE TOP FLOOR OF THE BATTLE TOWER, RIGHT?!
UM... WHO ARE YOU?
I'M RUBY. AND THIS IS SAPPHIRE.
WE'VE COME HERE TO PROTECT JIRACHI, LIKE EMERALD.
ALL THREE OF US ARE POKÉDEX HOLDERS.
WE'RE THE HOENN POKÉDEX TRIO!
DON'T COUNT ME IN YOUR TRIO!!
WELL... IF YOU DON'T LIKE "POKÉDEX" TRIO, WE COULD GO WITH "**CHAMPION**" TRIO.
CHAMPION...?
UH-HUH.
RUBY'S WON EVERY POKÉMON CONTEST AND I'VE BEATEN EVERY GYM IN HOENN.
IF YA BEAT ALL THE FACILITIES AT THE BATTLE FRONTIER...

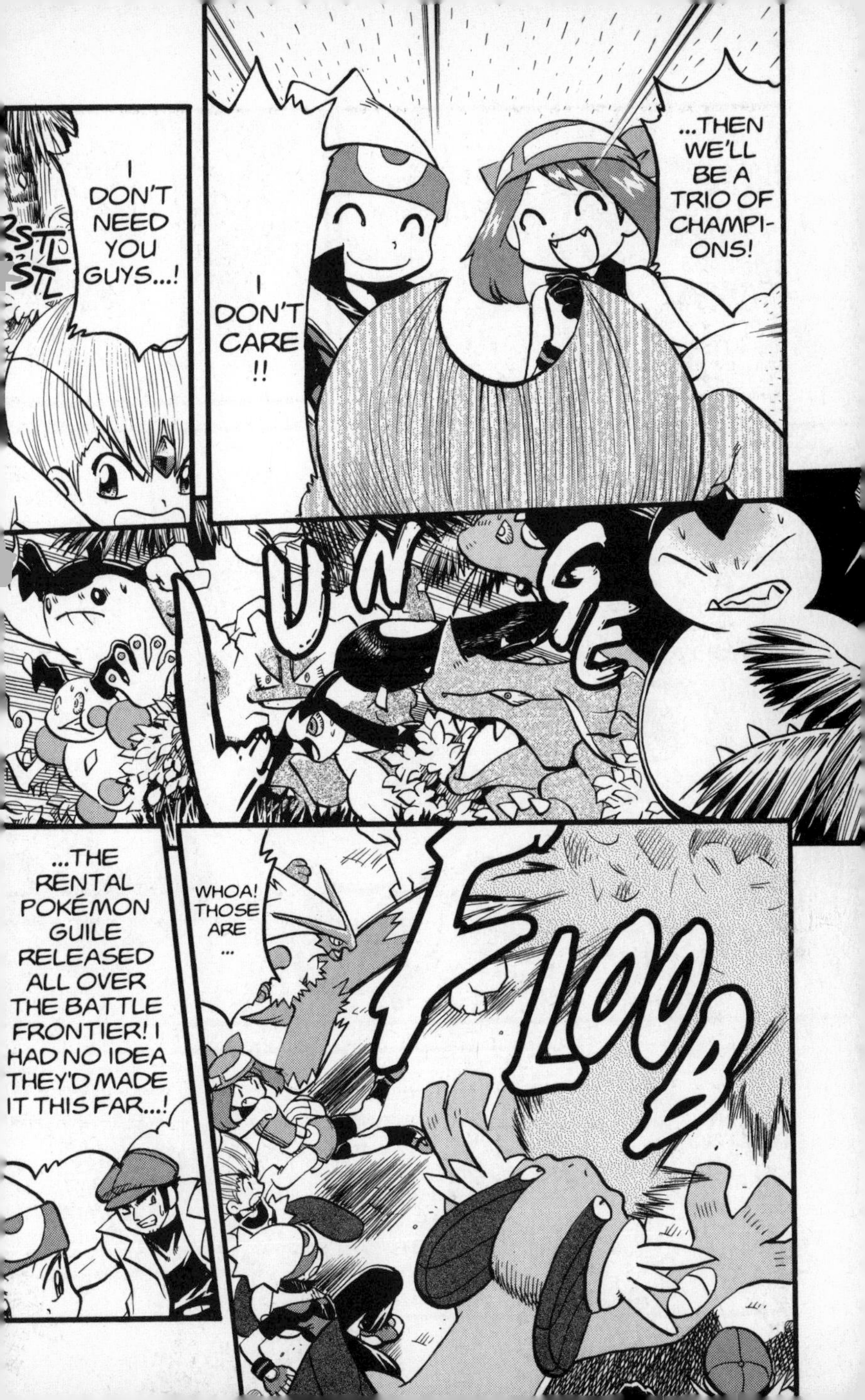
...THEN WE'LL BE A TRIO OF CHAMPIONS!
I DON'T CARE!!
RSTL
STL
I DON'T NEED YOU GUYS...!
UNGE
LOOB
WHOA! THOSE ARE ...
...THE RENTAL POKÉMON GUILE RELEASED ALL OVER THE BATTLE FRONTIER! I HAD NO IDEA THEY'D MADE IT THIS FAR...!

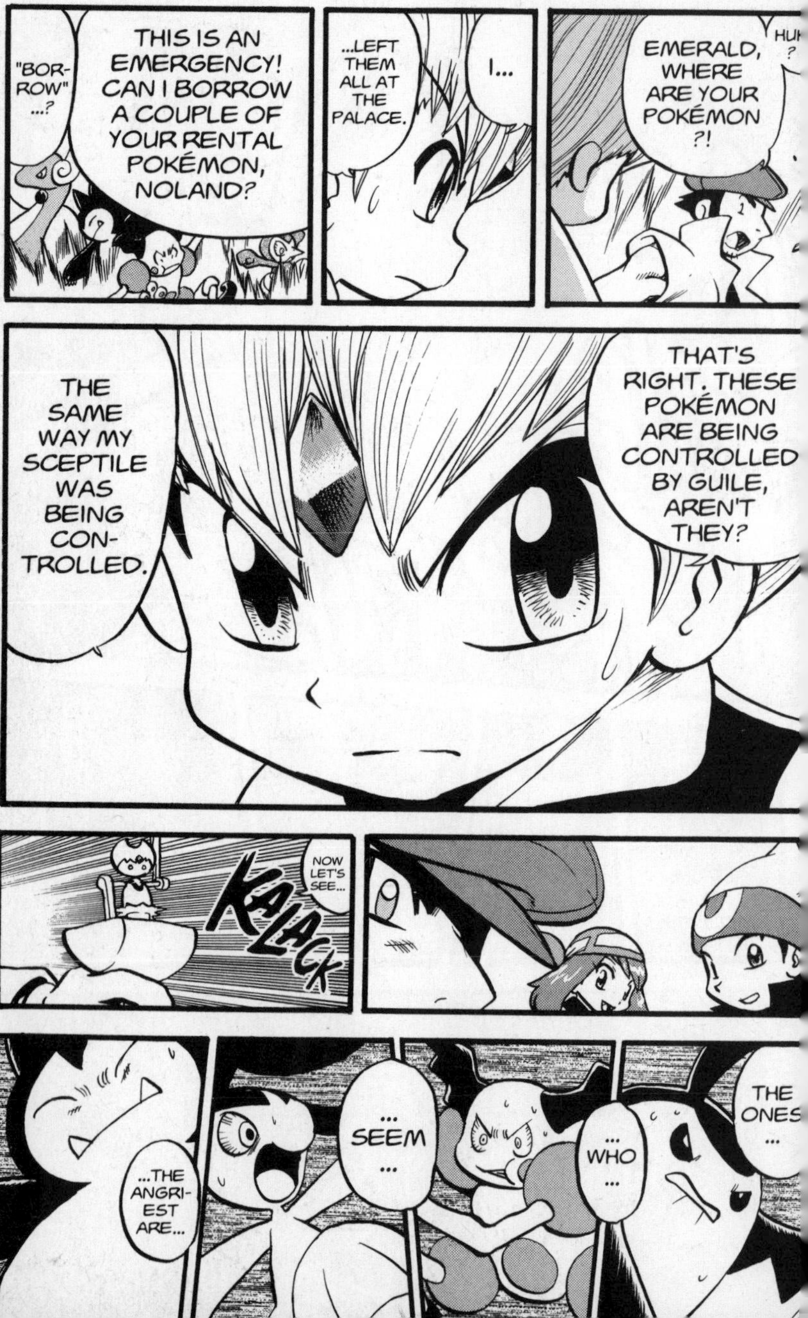
HU ?
EMERALD, WHERE ARE YOUR POKÉMON ?!
I...
...LEFT THEM ALL AT THE PALACE.
THIS IS AN EMERGENCY! CAN I BORROW A COUPLE OF YOUR RENTAL POKÉMON, NOLAND?
"BORROW" ...?
THAT'S RIGHT. THESE POKÉMON ARE BEING CONTROLLED BY GUILE, AREN'T THEY?
THE SAME WAY MY SCEPTILE WAS BEING CONTROLLED.
NOW LET'S SEE...
KALACK
THE ONES ...
... WHO ...
... SEEM ...
...THE ANGRIEST ARE...

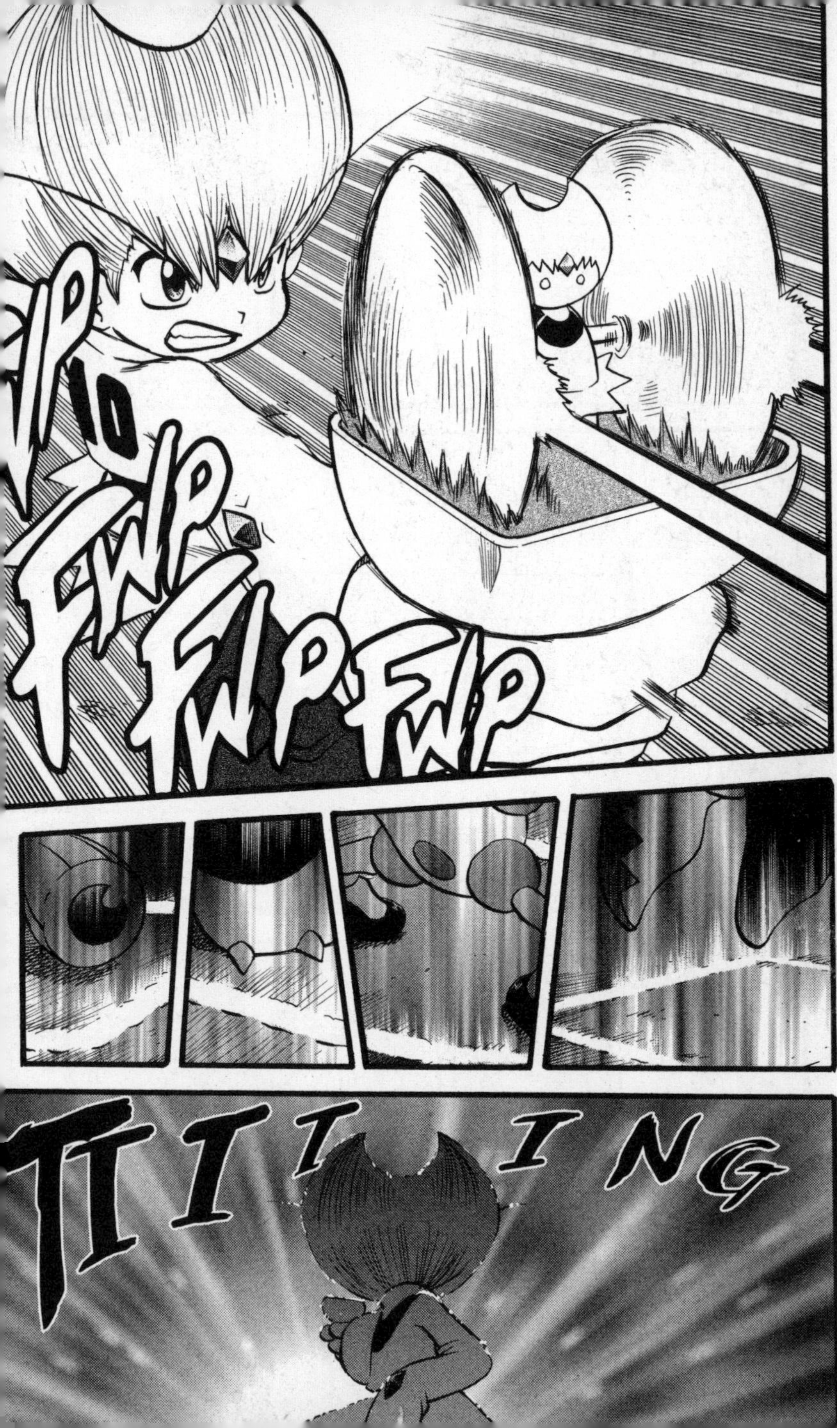
FWIP
FWIP
FWIP
TIIIING

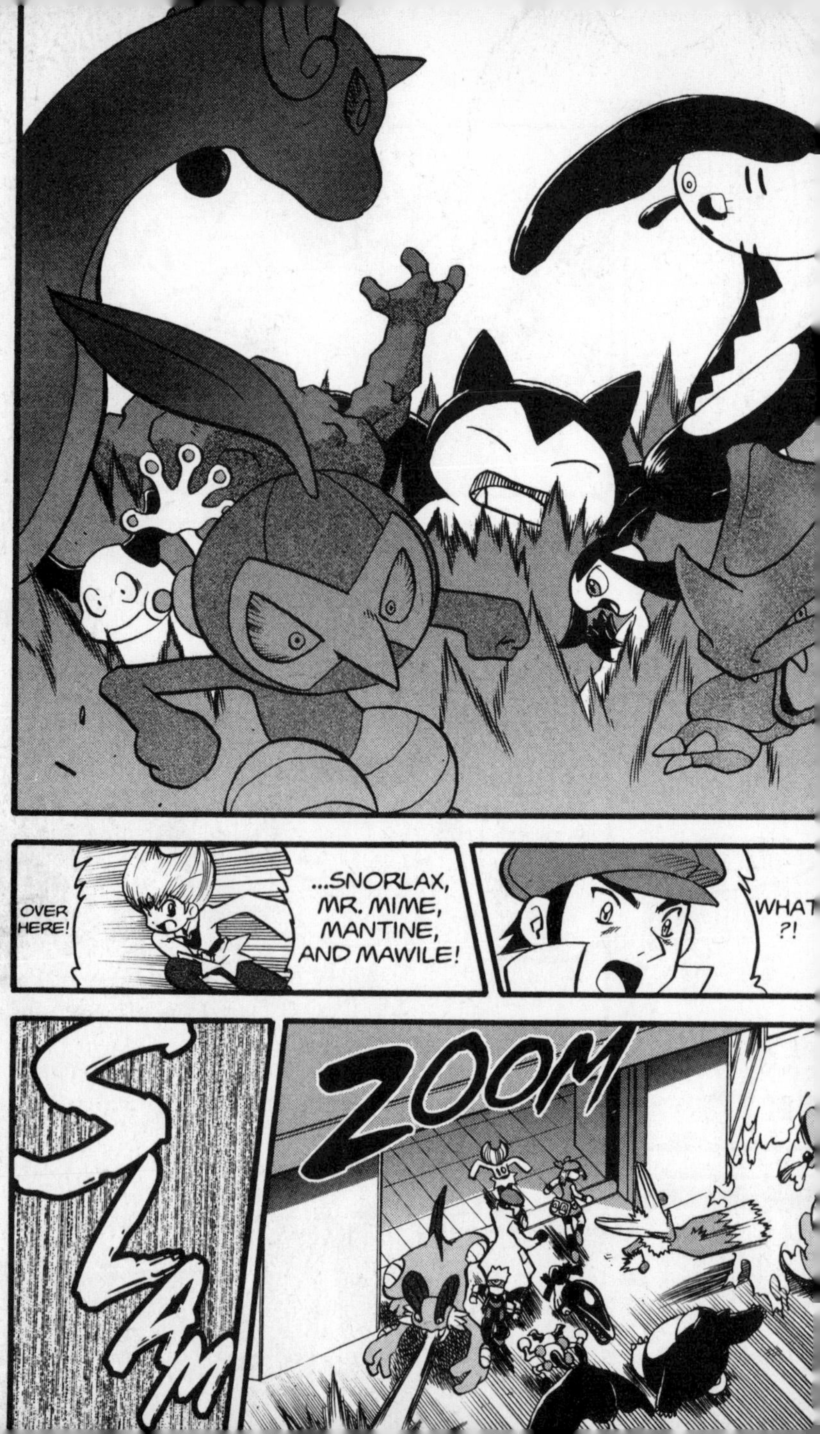
WHAT ?!
...SNORLAX, MR. MIME, MANTINE, AND MAWILE!
OVER HERE!
ZOOM
SLAM

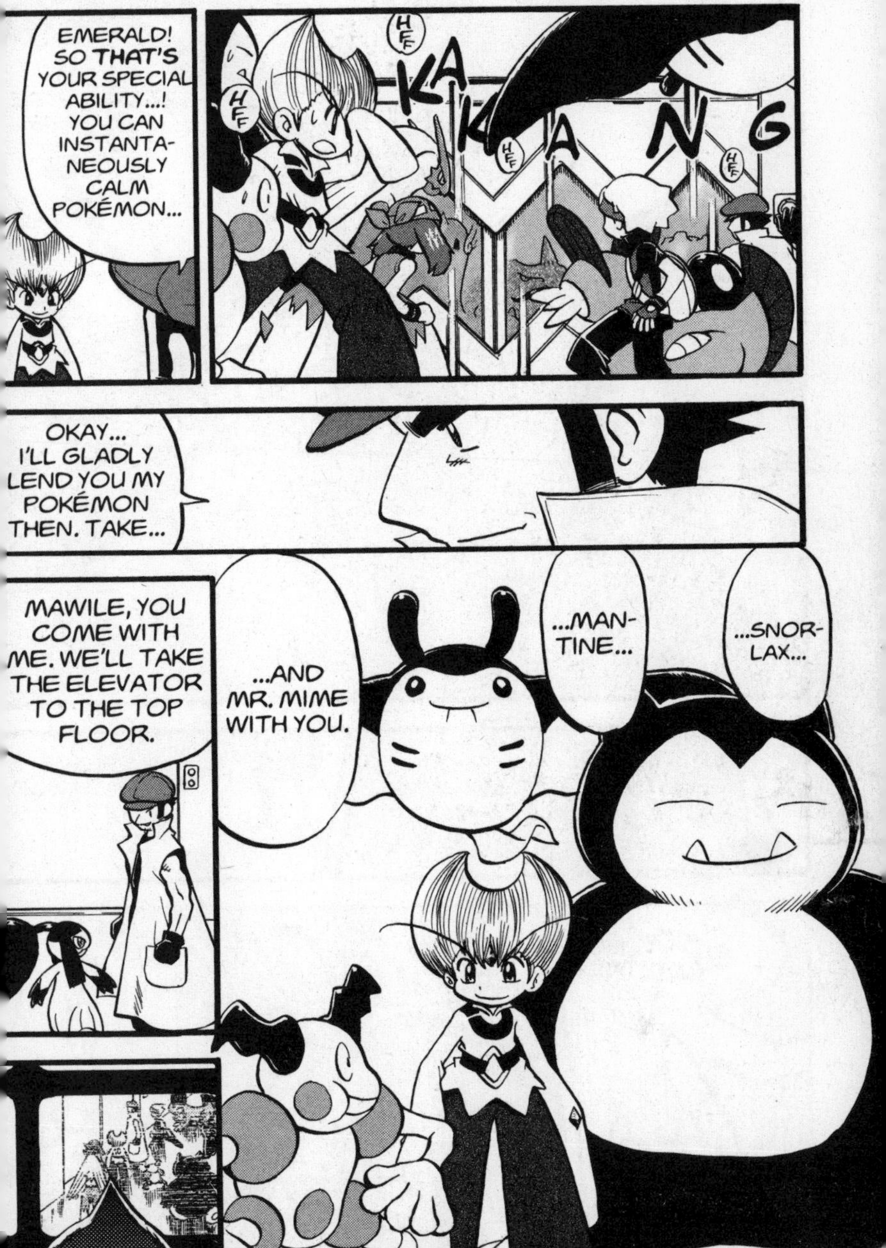
HEFF
HEFF
KA-KANG
HEFF
HEFF
EMERALD! SO THAT'S YOUR SPECIAL ABILITY...! YOU CAN INSTANTANEOUSLY CALM POKÉMON...
OKAY... I'LL GLADLY LEND YOU MY POKÉMON THEN. TAKE...
...SNORLAX...
...MANTINE...
...AND MR. MIME WITH YOU.
MAWILE, YOU COME WITH ME. WE'LL TAKE THE ELEVATOR TO THE TOP FLOOR.

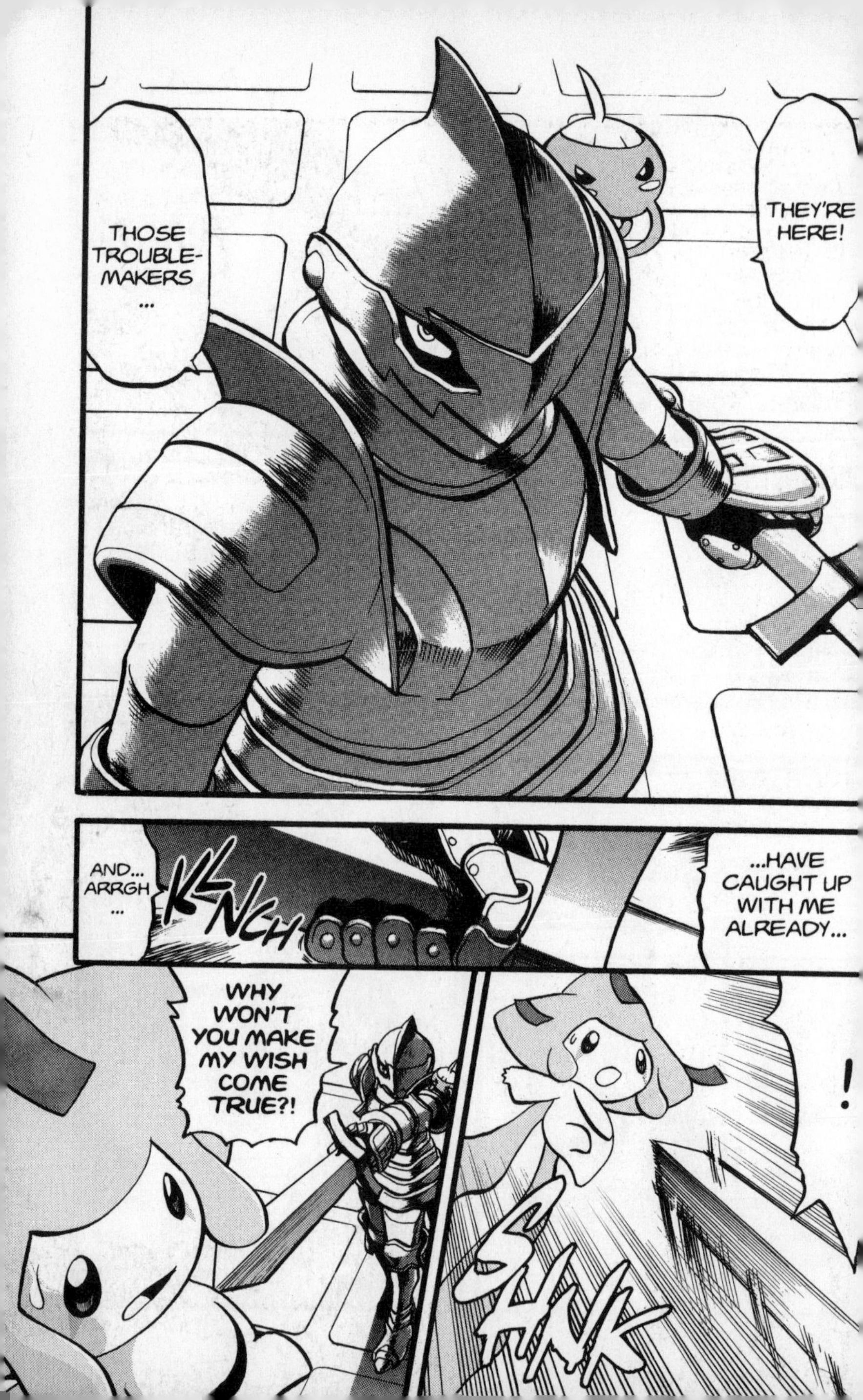
THEY'RE HERE!
THOSE TROUBLE-MAKERS ...
...HAVE CAUGHT UP WITH ME ALREADY...
KLNCH
AND... ARRGH ...
!
SHNK
WHY WON'T YOU MAKE MY WISH COME TRUE?!

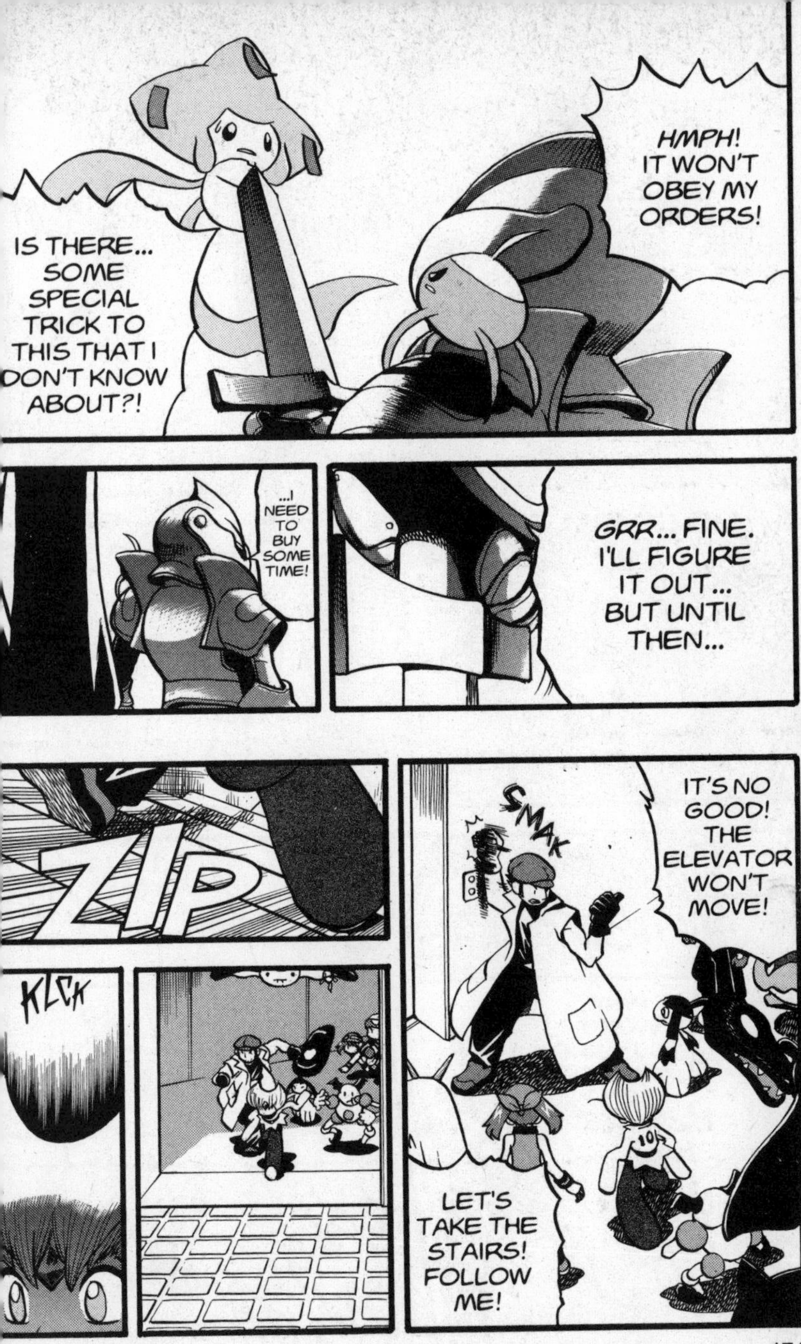
HMPH! IT WON'T OBEY MY ORDERS!
IS THERE... SOME SPECIAL TRICK TO THIS THAT I DON'T KNOW ABOUT?!
GRR... FINE. I'LL FIGURE IT OUT... BUT UNTIL THEN...
...I NEED TO BUY SOME TIME!
SMAK
IT'S NO GOOD! THE ELEVATOR WON'T MOVE!
LET'S TAKE THE STAIRS! FOLLOW ME!
ZIP
KLCK

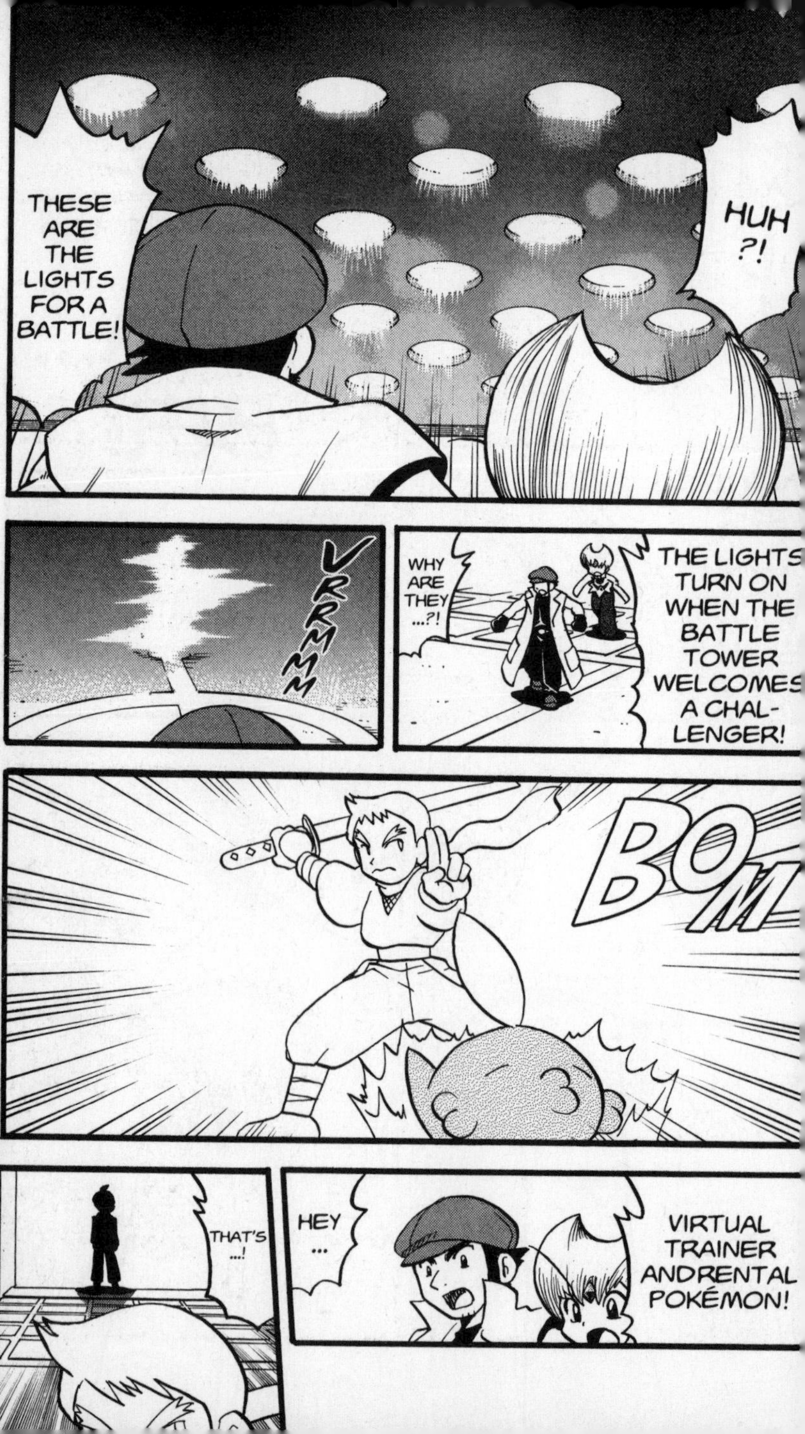
HUH ?!
THESE ARE THE LIGHTS FOR A BATTLE!
THE LIGHTS TURN ON WHEN THE BATTLE TOWER WELCOMES A CHAL-LENGER!
WHY ARE THEY ...?!
VRRMMMM
BOOM
VIRTUAL TRAINER AND RENTAL POKÉMON!
HEY ...
THAT'S ...!

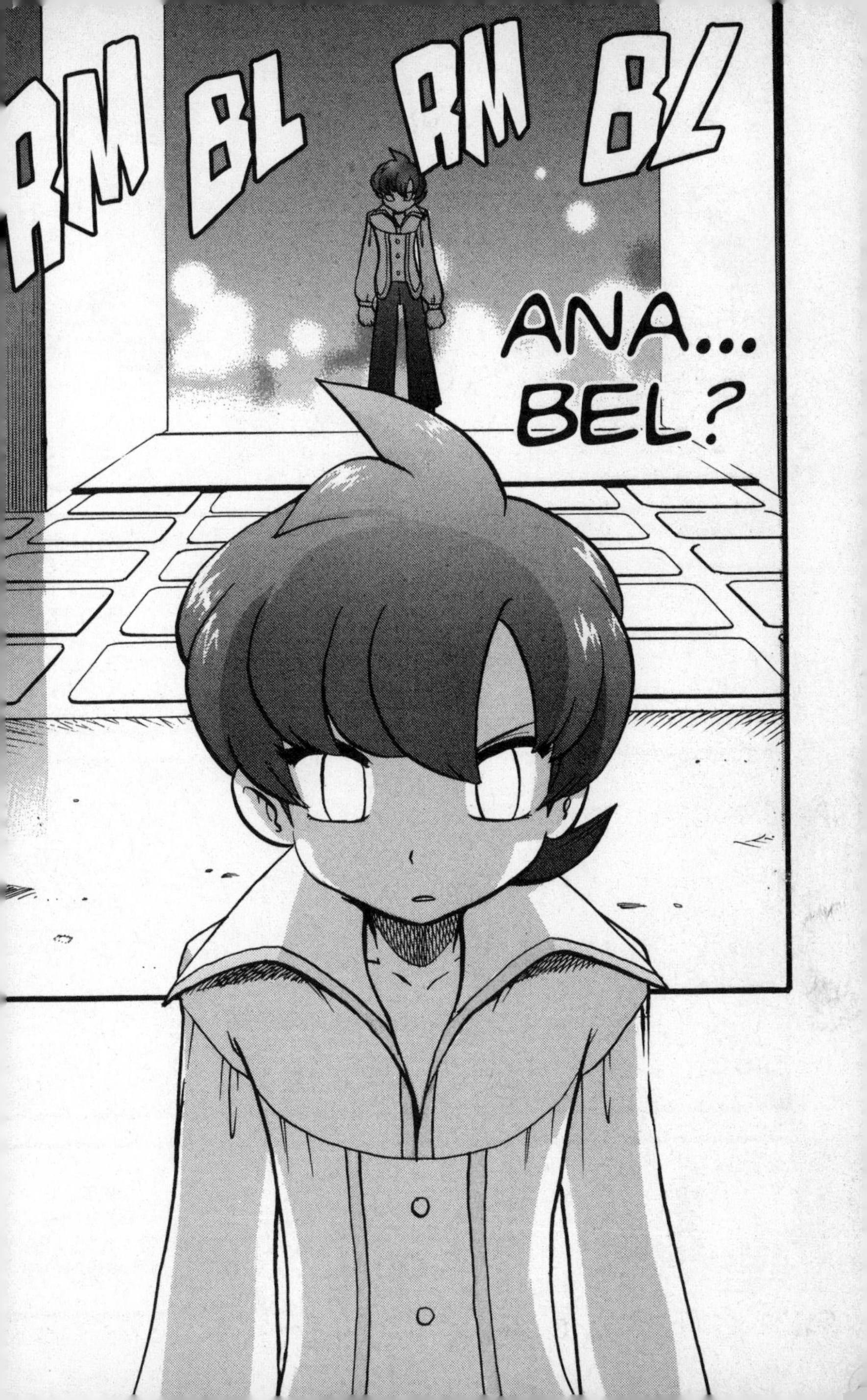
RM BL RM BL
ANA... BEL?

327

Facing Gulpin Is Hard to Swallow

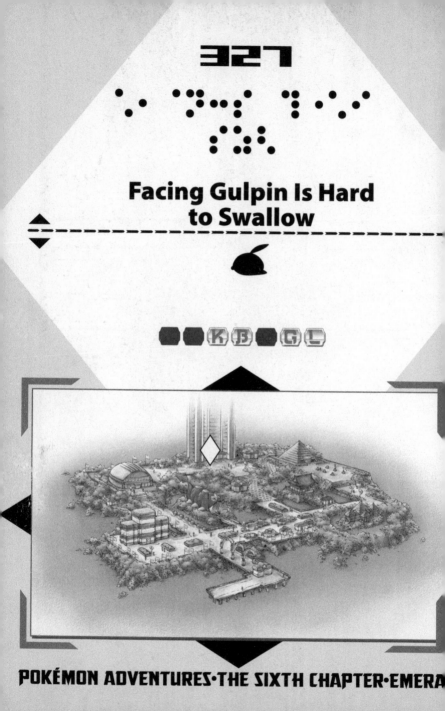

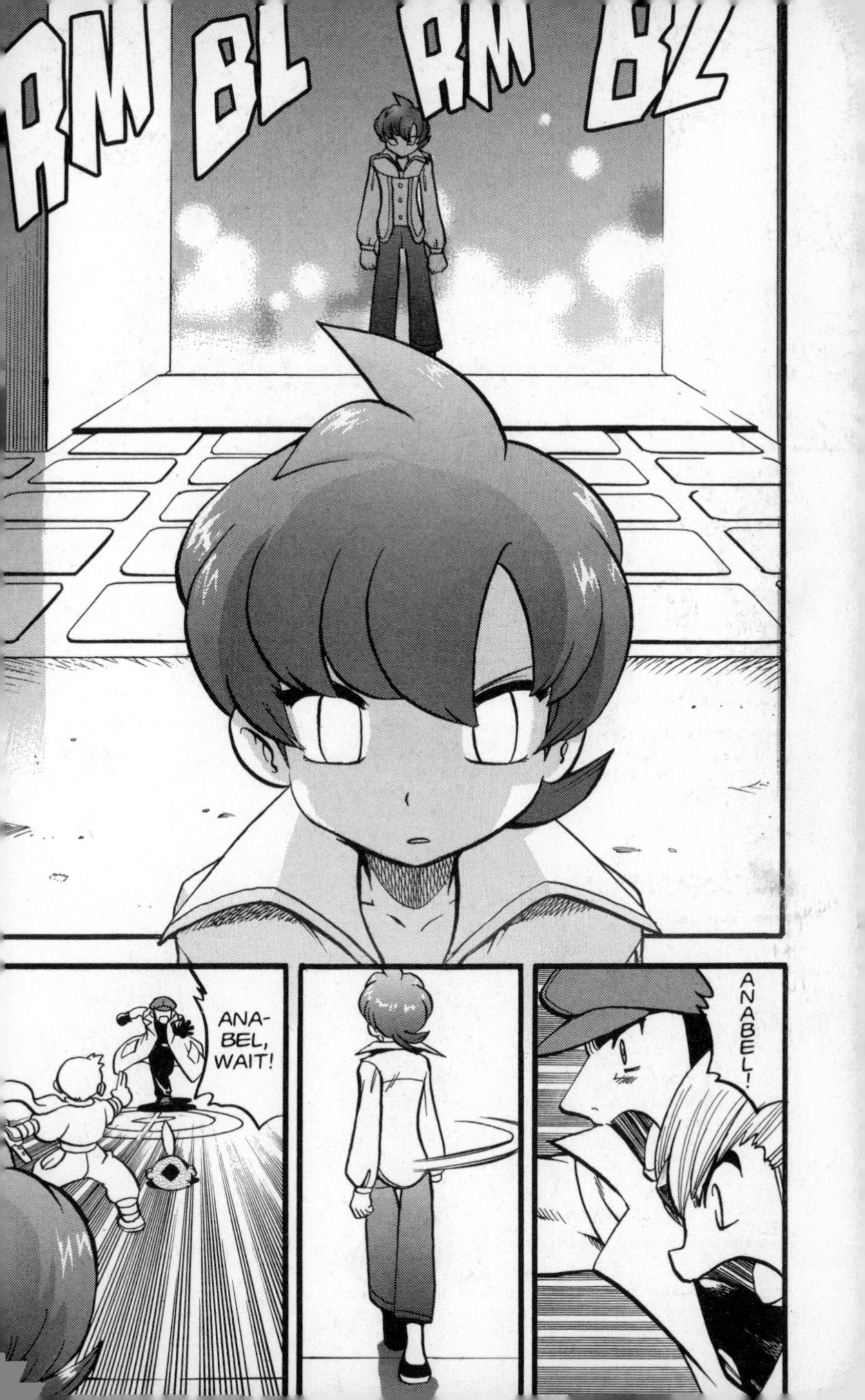
RMBL RMBL
ANABEL!
ANA-BEL, WAIT!

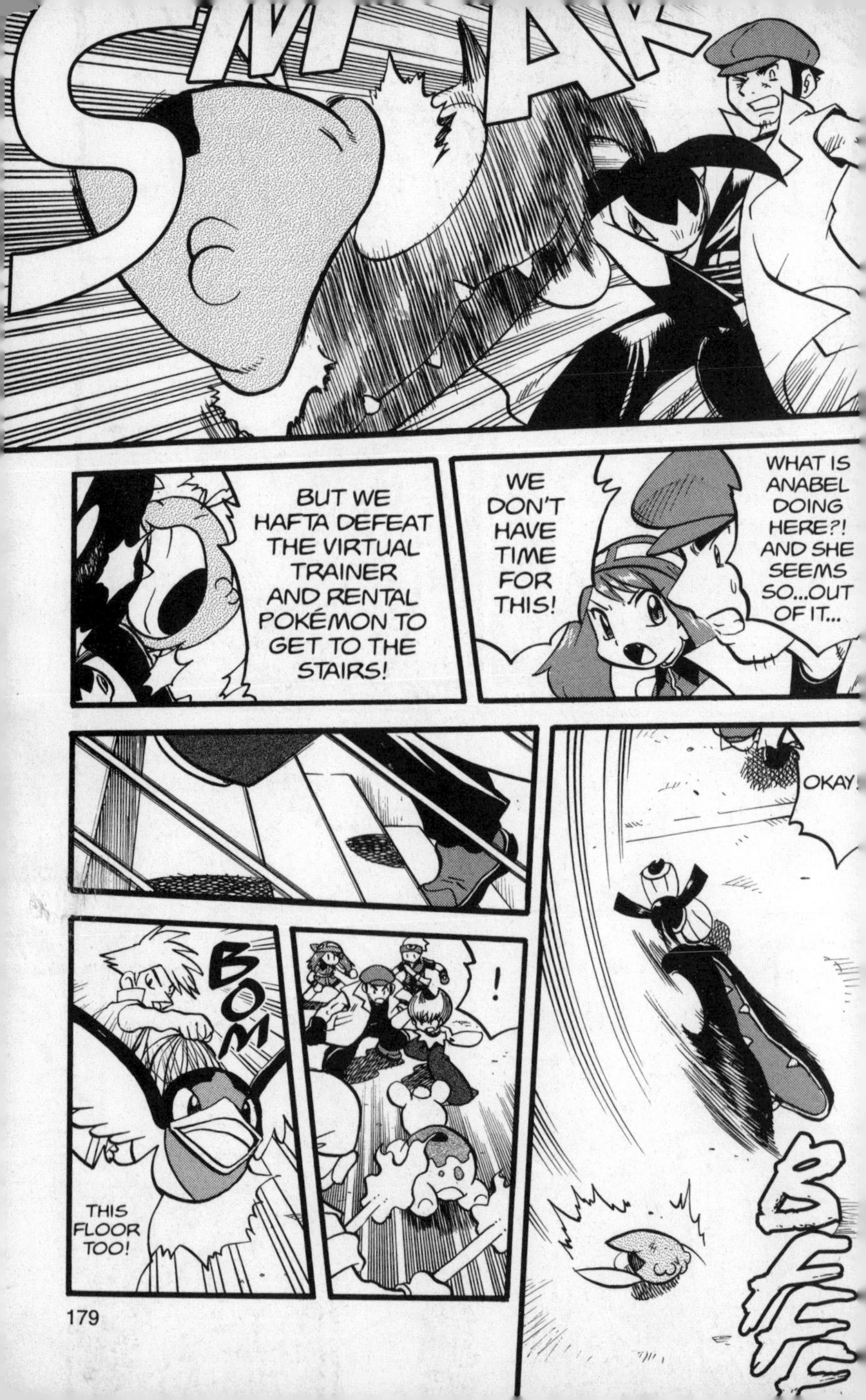
WHAT IS ANABEL DOING HERE?! AND SHE SEEMS SO...OUT OF IT...
WE DON'T HAVE TIME FOR THIS!
BUT WE HAFTA DEFEAT THE VIRTUAL TRAINER AND RENTAL POKÉMON TO GET TO THE STAIRS!
OKAY!
!
BOM
THIS FLOOR TOO!

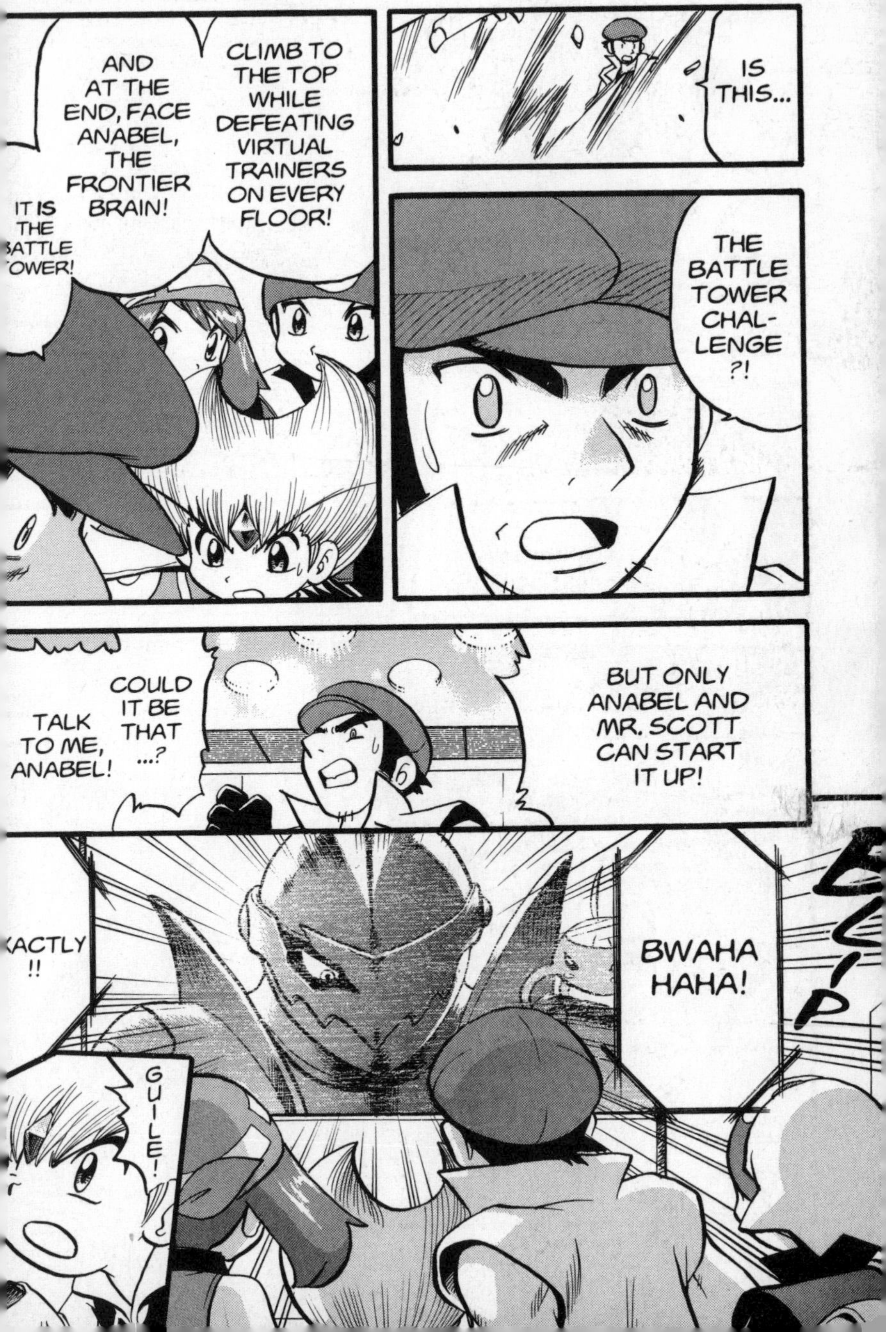
IS THIS...
THE BATTLE TOWER CHAL-LENGE?!
CLIMB TO THE TOP WHILE DEFEATING VIRTUAL TRAINERS ON EVERY FLOOR!
AND AT THE END, FACE ANABEL, THE FRONTIER BRAIN!
IT IS THE BATTLE TOWER!
BUT ONLY ANABEL AND MR. SCOTT CAN START IT UP!
COULD IT BE THAT ...?
TALK TO ME, ANABEL!
BLIP
BWAHA HAHA!
XACTLY!!
GUILE!

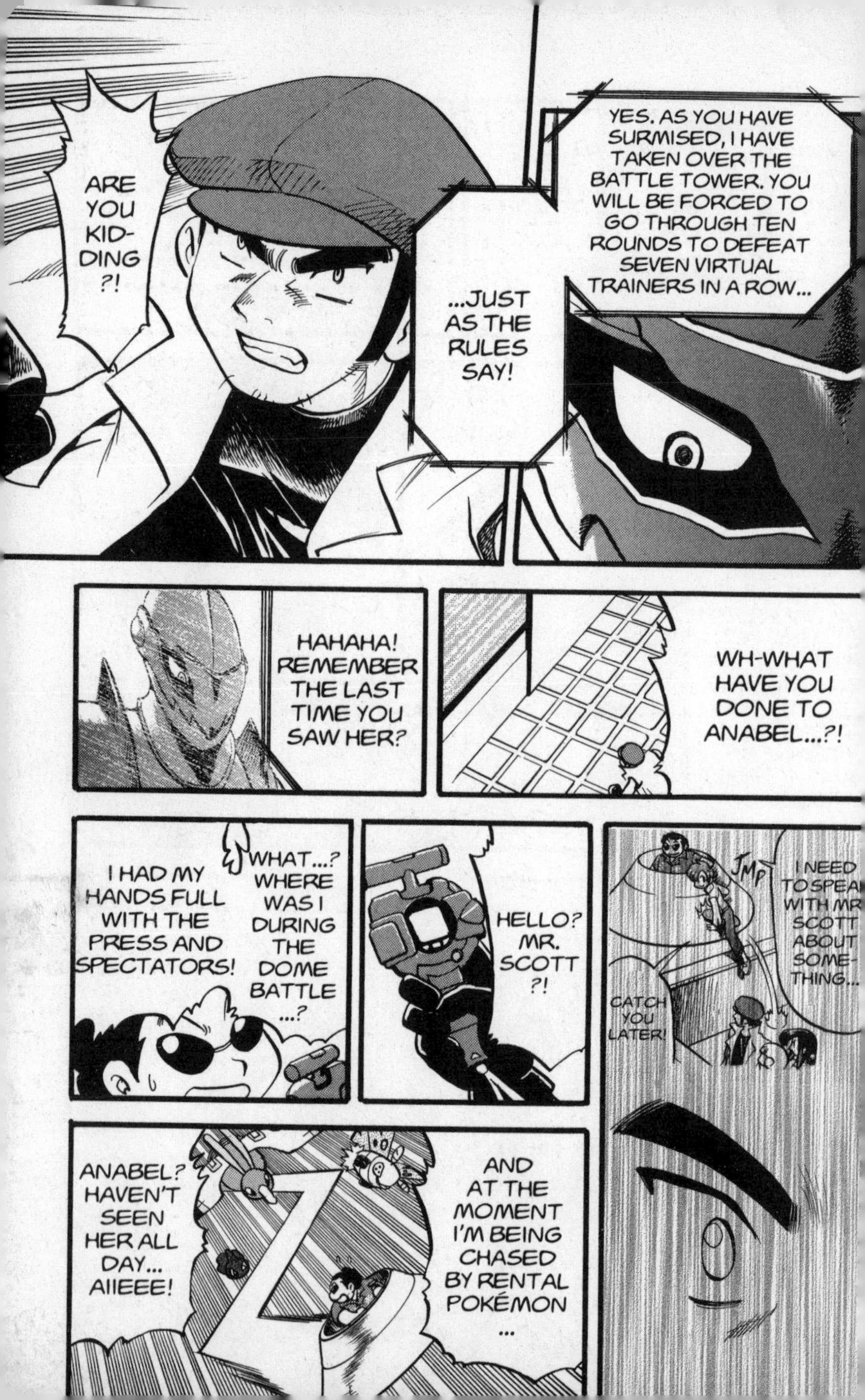
YES. AS YOU HAVE SURMISED, I HAVE TAKEN OVER THE BATTLE TOWER. YOU WILL BE FORCED TO GO THROUGH TEN ROUNDS TO DEFEAT SEVEN VIRTUAL TRAINERS IN A ROW...
...JUST AS THE RULES SAY!
ARE YOU KID-DING ?!
WH-WHAT HAVE YOU DONE TO ANABEL...?!
HAHAHA! REMEMBER THE LAST TIME YOU SAW HER?
I NEED TO SPEA WITH MR SCOTT ABOUT SOME-THING...
JMP
CATCH YOU LATER!
HELLO? MR. SCOTT ?!
WHAT...? WHERE WAS I DURING THE DOME BATTLE ...?
I HAD MY HANDS FULL WITH THE PRESS AND SPECTATORS!
AND AT THE MOMENT I'M BEING CHASED BY RENTAL POKÉMON ...
ANABEL? HAVEN'T SEEN HER ALL DAY... AIIEEE!

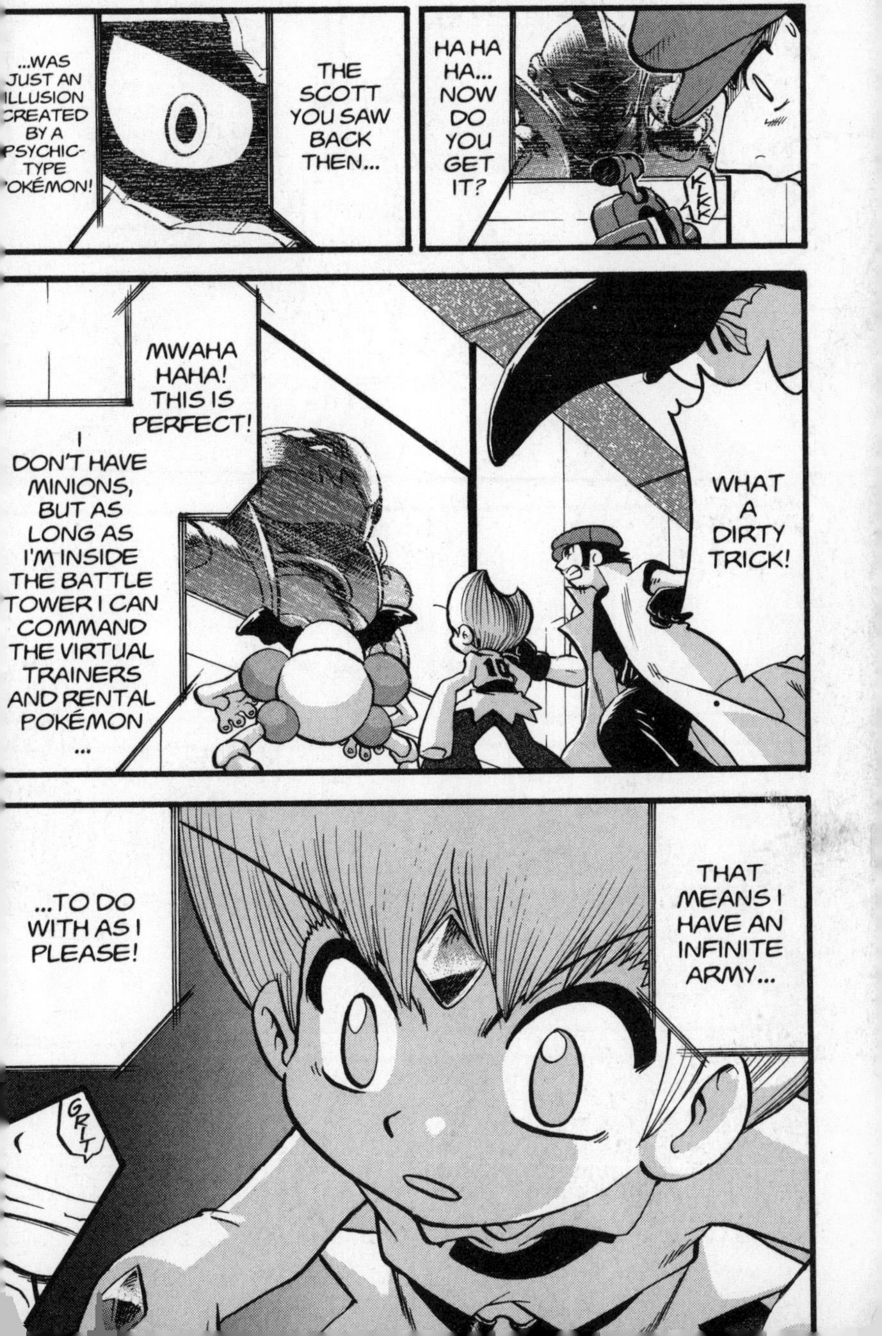
HA HA HA... NOW DO YOU GET IT?
KLKK
THE SCOTT YOU SAW BACK THEN...
...WAS JUST AN ILLUSION CREATED BY A PSYCHIC-TYPE POKÉMON!
WHAT A DIRTY TRICK!
MWAHA HAHA! THIS IS PERFECT!
I DON'T HAVE MINIONS, BUT AS LONG AS I'M INSIDE THE BATTLE TOWER I CAN COMMAND THE VIRTUAL TRAINERS AND RENTAL POKÉMON ...
THAT MEANS I HAVE AN INFINITE ARMY...
...TO DO WITH AS I PLEASE!
GRIT

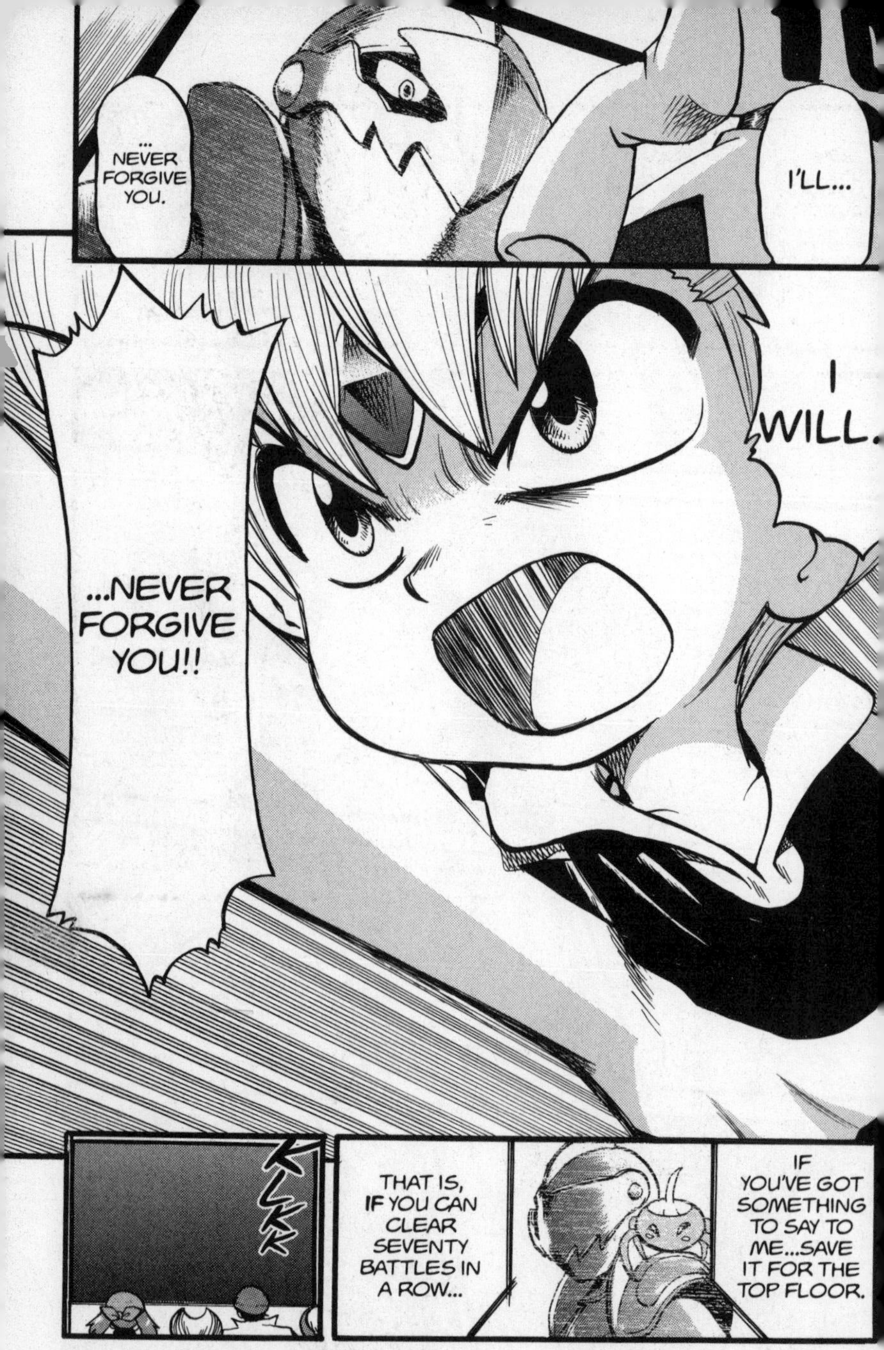
I'LL...
...NEVER FORGIVE YOU.
I WILL.
...NEVER FORGIVE YOU!!
IF YOU'VE GOT SOMETHING TO SAY TO ME...SAVE IT FOR THE TOP FLOOR.
THAT IS, IF YOU CAN CLEAR SEVENTY BATTLES IN A ROW...
KLIKK

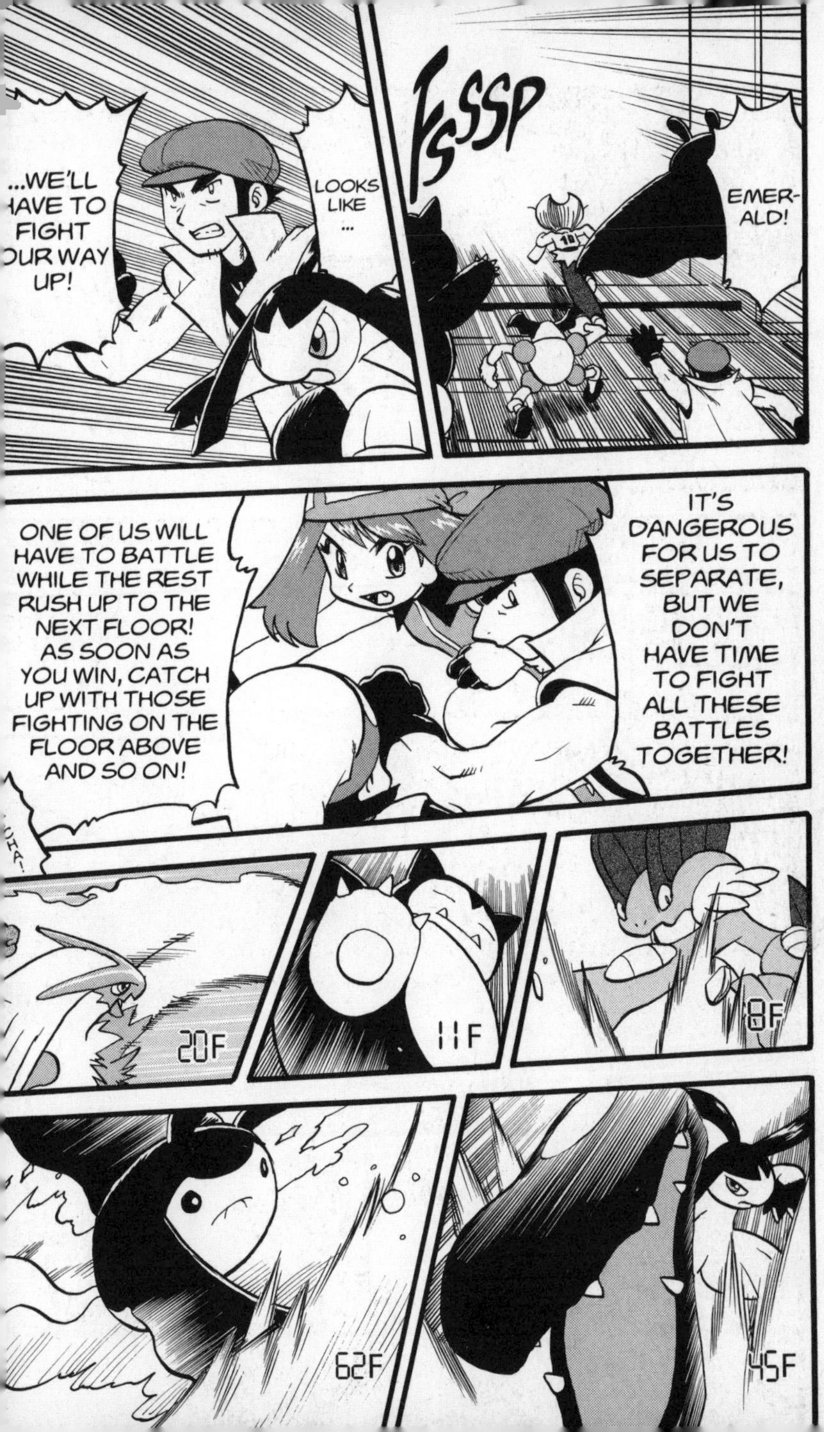
FSSSP
EMER-ALD!
LOOKS LIKE ...
...WE'LL HAVE TO FIGHT OUR WAY UP!
IT'S DANGEROUS FOR US TO SEPARATE, BUT WE DON'T HAVE TIME TO FIGHT ALL THESE BATTLES TOGETHER!
ONE OF US WILL HAVE TO BATTLE WHILE THE REST RUSH UP TO THE NEXT FLOOR! AS SOON AS YOU WIN, CATCH UP WITH THOSE FIGHTING ON THE FLOOR ABOVE AND SO ON!
CHA!
8F
11F
20F
45F
62F

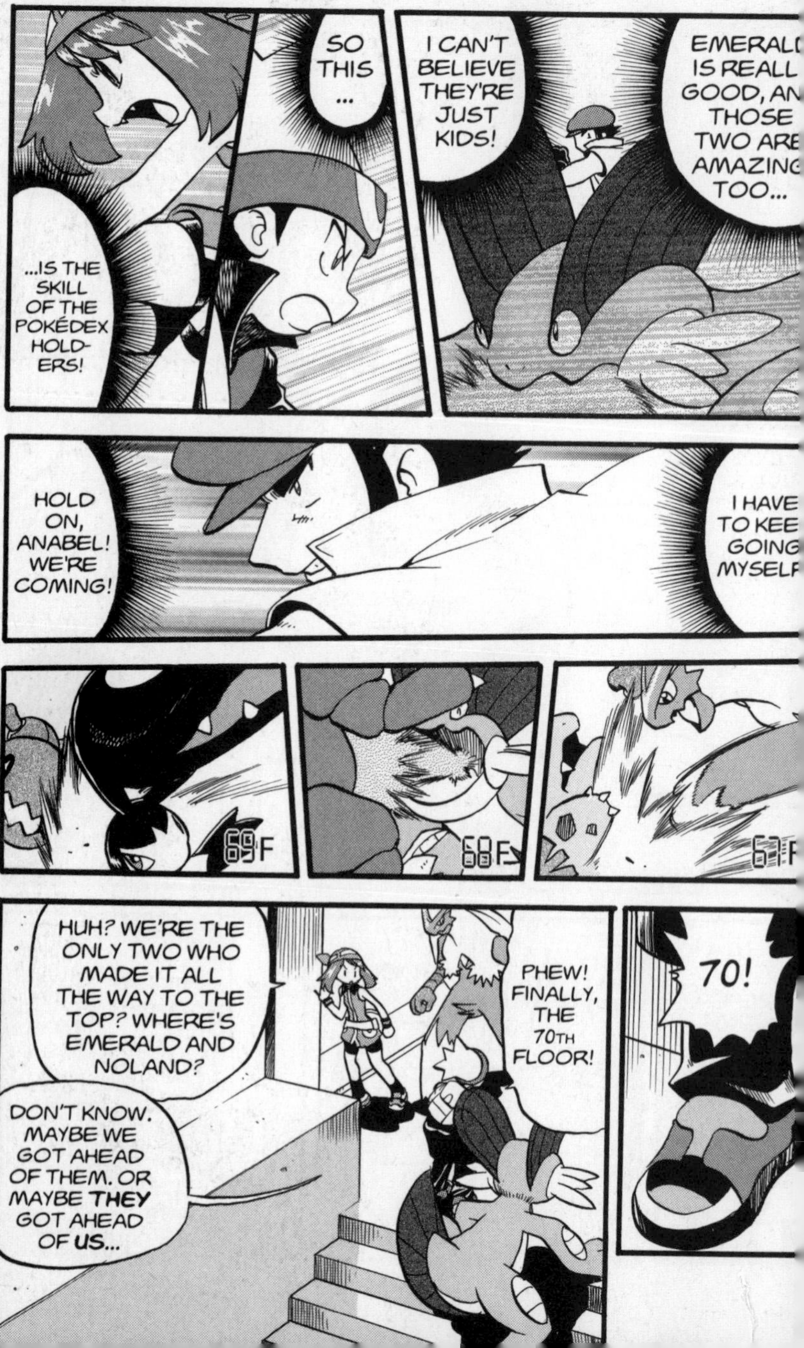
EMERAL IS REALL GOOD, AN THOSE TWO ARE AMAZING TOO...
I CAN'T BELIEVE THEY'RE JUST KIDS!
SO THIS ...
...IS THE SKILL OF THE POKÉDEX HOLD-ERS!
I HAVE TO KEE GOING MYSEL
HOLD ON, ANABEL! WE'RE COMING!
67F
68F
69F
70!
PHEW! FINALLY, THE 70TH FLOOR!
HUH? WE'RE THE ONLY TWO WHO MADE IT ALL THE WAY TO THE TOP? WHERE'S EMERALD AND NOLAND?
DON'T KNOW. MAYBE WE GOT AHEAD OF THEM. OR MAYBE THEY GOT AHEAD OF US...

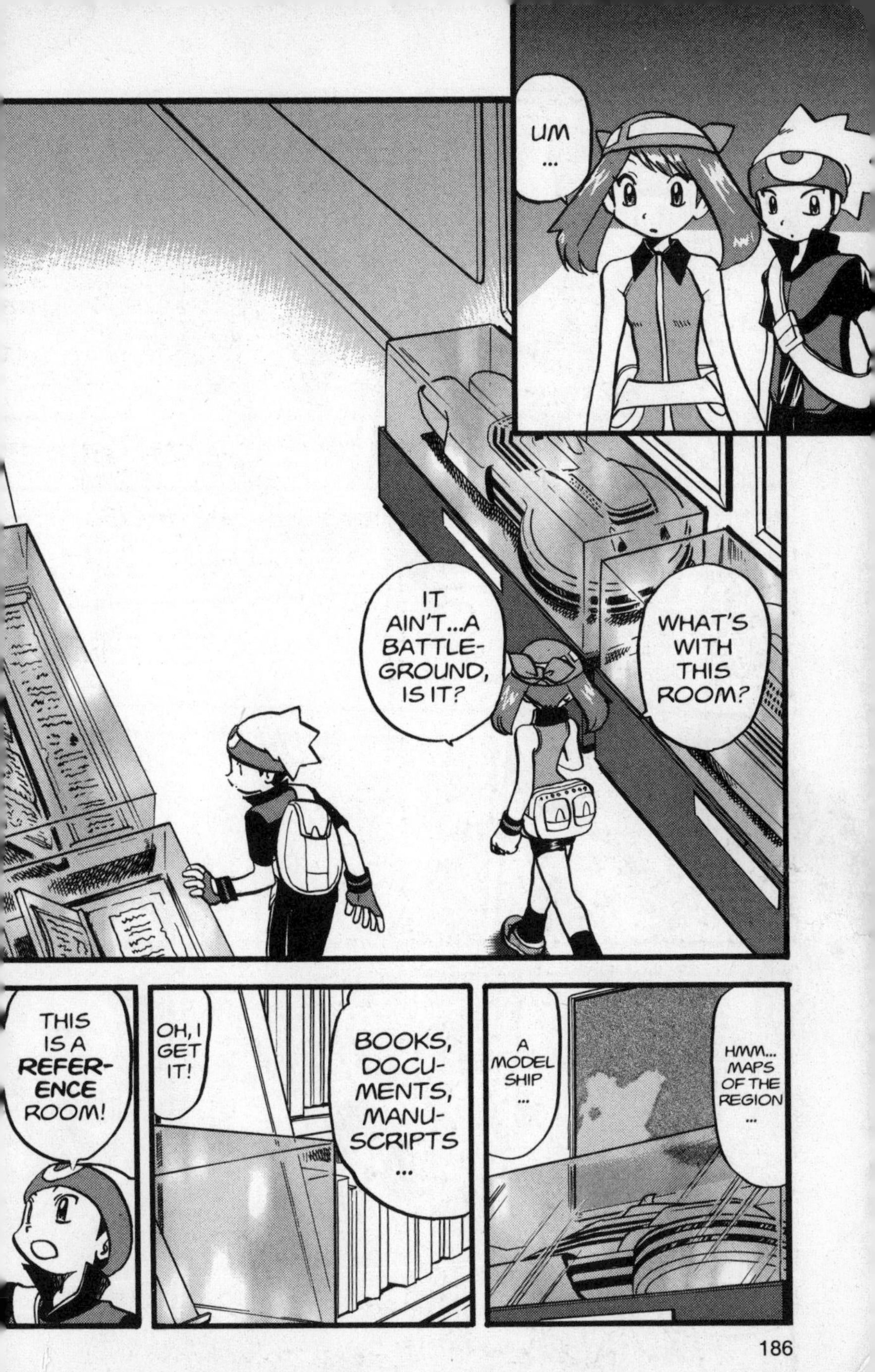
UM ...
WHAT'S WITH THIS ROOM?
IT AIN'T...A BATTLE-GROUND, IS IT?
HMM... MAPS OF THE REGION ...
A MODEL SHIP ...
BOOKS, DOCU-MENTS, MANU-SCRIPTS ...
OH, I GET IT!
THIS IS A **REFERENCE** ROOM!

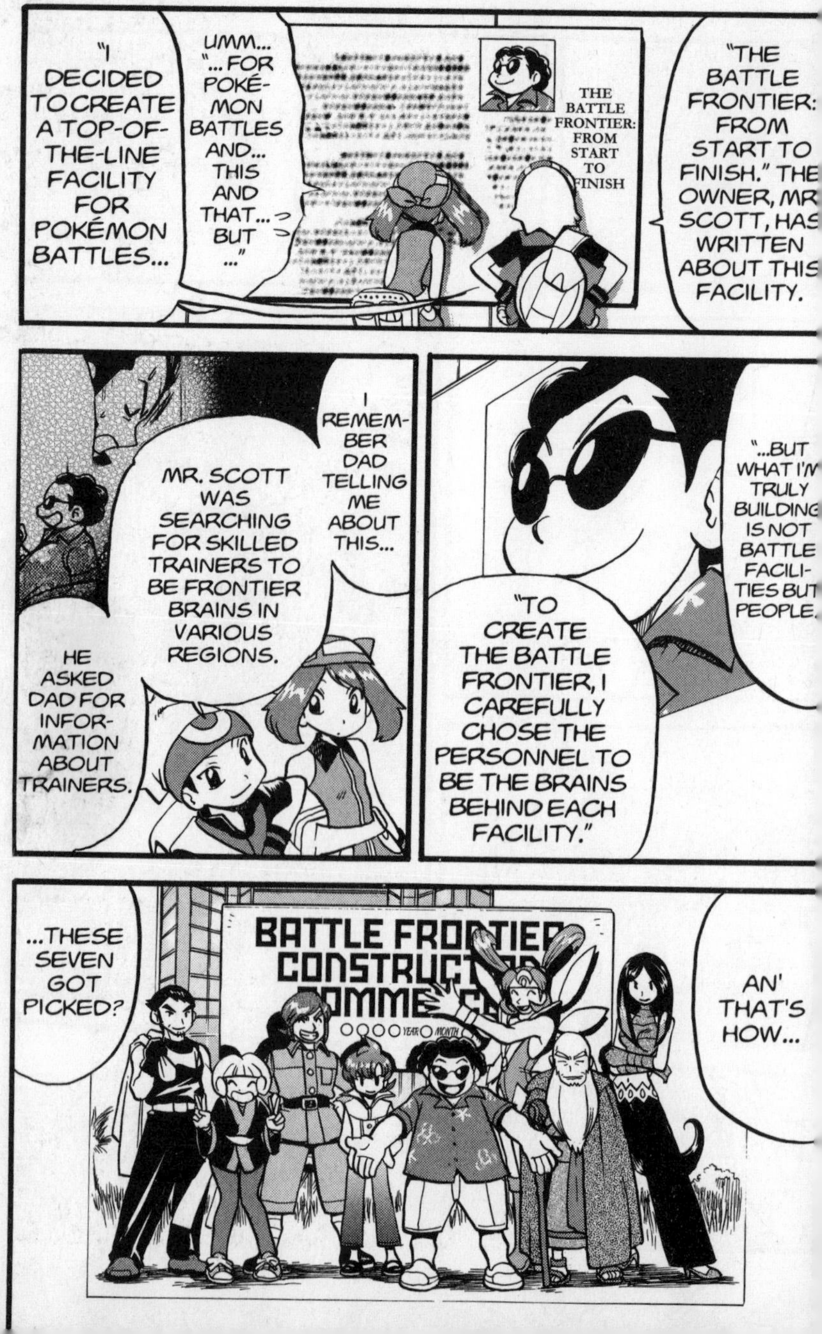
"THE BATTLE FRONTIER: FROM START TO FINISH." THE OWNER, MR SCOTT, HAS WRITTEN ABOUT THIS FACILITY.
THE BATTLE FRONTIER: FROM START TO FINISH
UMM... "...FOR POKÉMON BATTLES AND... THIS AND THAT... BUT ..."
"I DECIDED TO CREATE A TOP-OF-THE-LINE FACILITY FOR POKÉMON BATTLES...
"...BUT WHAT I'M TRULY BUILDING IS NOT BATTLE FACILITIES BUT PEOPLE.
"TO CREATE THE BATTLE FRONTIER, I CAREFULLY CHOSE THE PERSONNEL TO BE THE BRAINS BEHIND EACH FACILITY."
I REMEMBER DAD TELLING ME ABOUT THIS...
MR. SCOTT WAS SEARCHING FOR SKILLED TRAINERS TO BE FRONTIER BRAINS IN VARIOUS REGIONS.
HE ASKED DAD FOR INFORMATION ABOUT TRAINERS.
AN' THAT'S HOW...
...THESE SEVEN GOT PICKED?

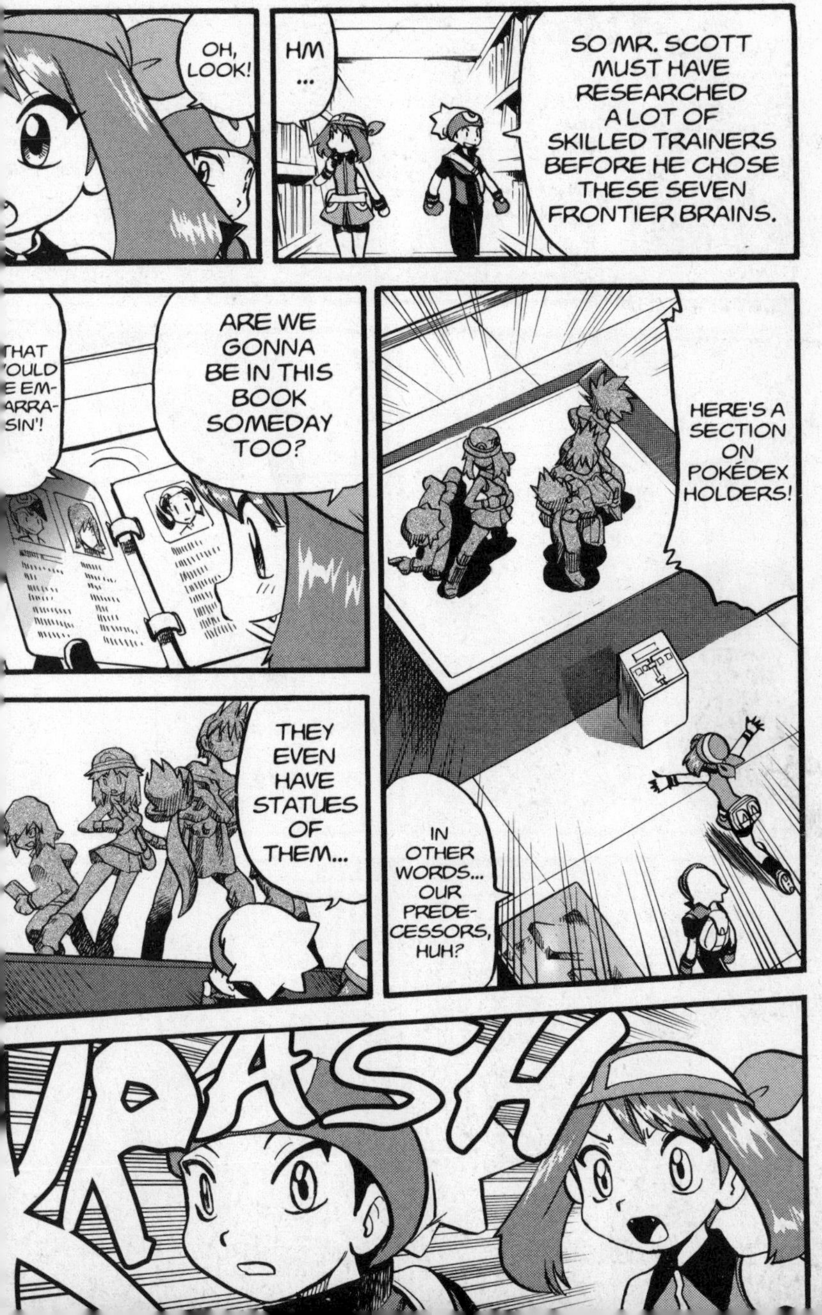
SO MR. SCOTT MUST HAVE RESEARCHED A LOT OF SKILLED TRAINERS BEFORE HE CHOSE THESE SEVEN FRONTIER BRAINS.
HM ...
OH, LOOK!
HERE'S A SECTION ON POKÉDEX HOLDERS!
IN OTHER WORDS... OUR PREDECESSORS, HUH?
ARE WE GONNA BE IN THIS BOOK SOMEDAY TOO?
THAT 'OULD E EM- ARRA- SIN'!
THEY EVEN HAVE STATUES OF THEM...
PASH

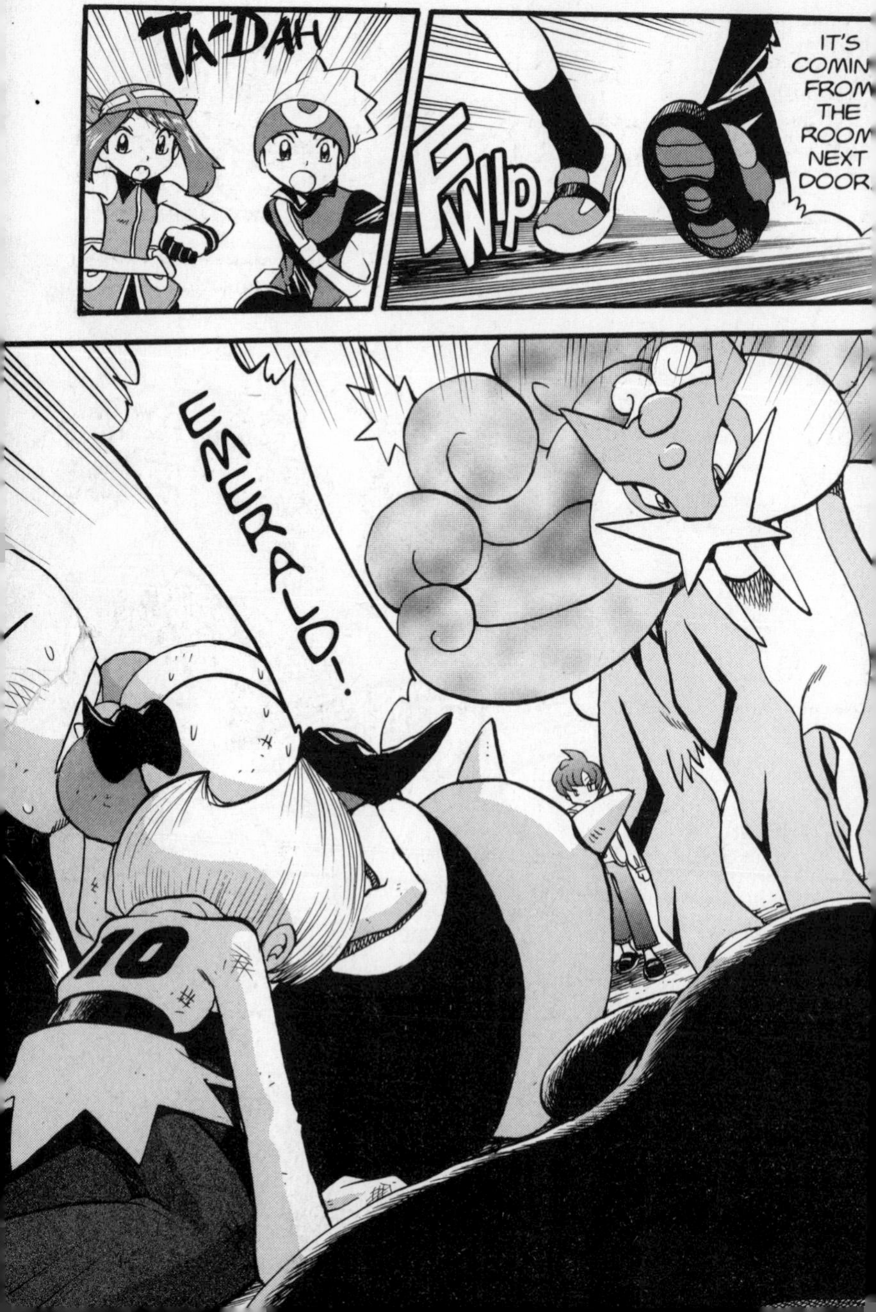
IT'S COMIN FROM THE ROOM NEXT DOOR.
FWIP
TA-DAH
EMERALD!

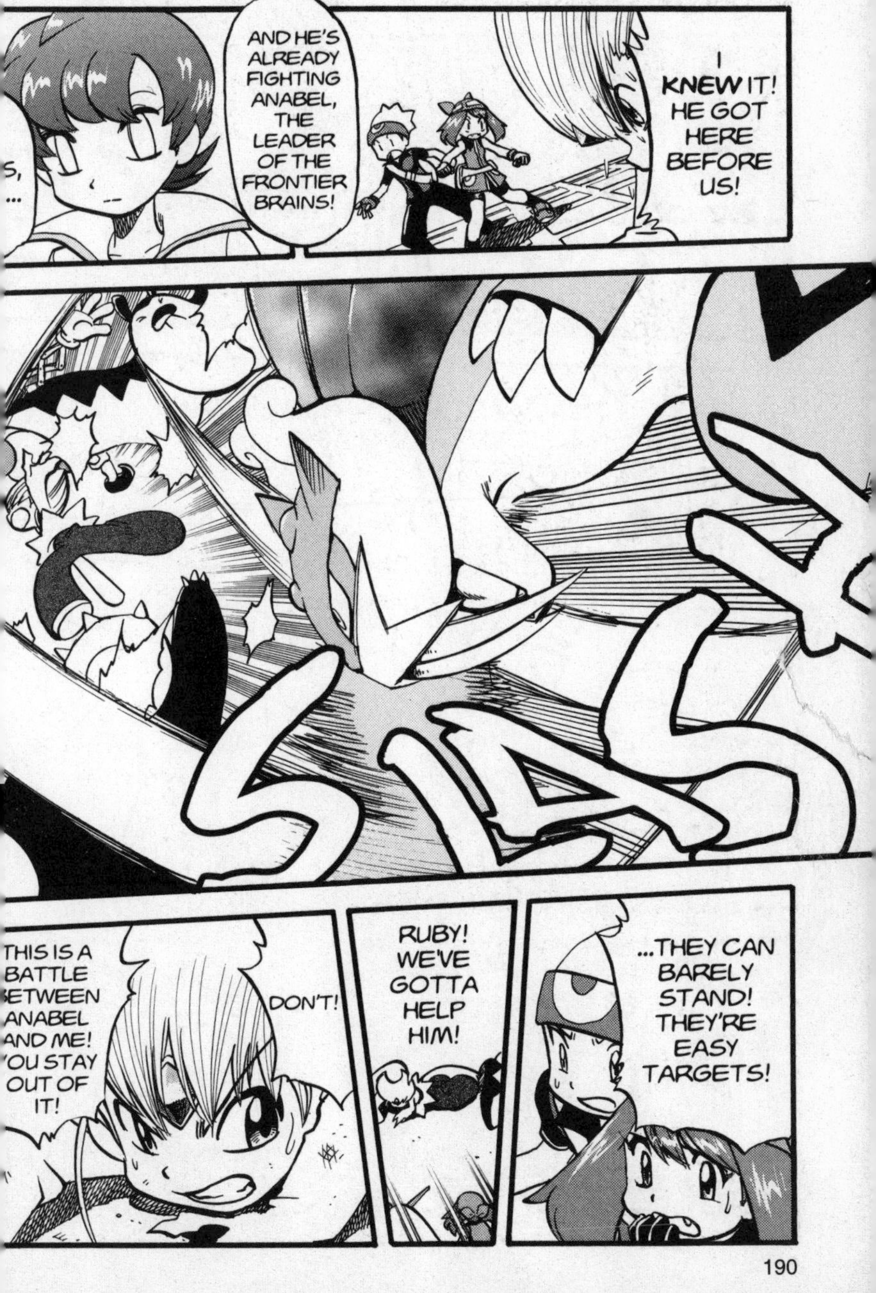
I KNEW IT! HE GOT HERE BEFORE US!
AND HE'S ALREADY FIGHTING ANABEL, THE LEADER OF THE FRONTIER BRAINS!
...THEY CAN BARELY STAND! THEY'RE EASY TARGETS!
RUBY! WE'VE GOTTA HELP HIM!
DON'T!
THIS IS A BATTLE BETWEEN ANABEL AND ME! YOU STAY OUT OF IT!

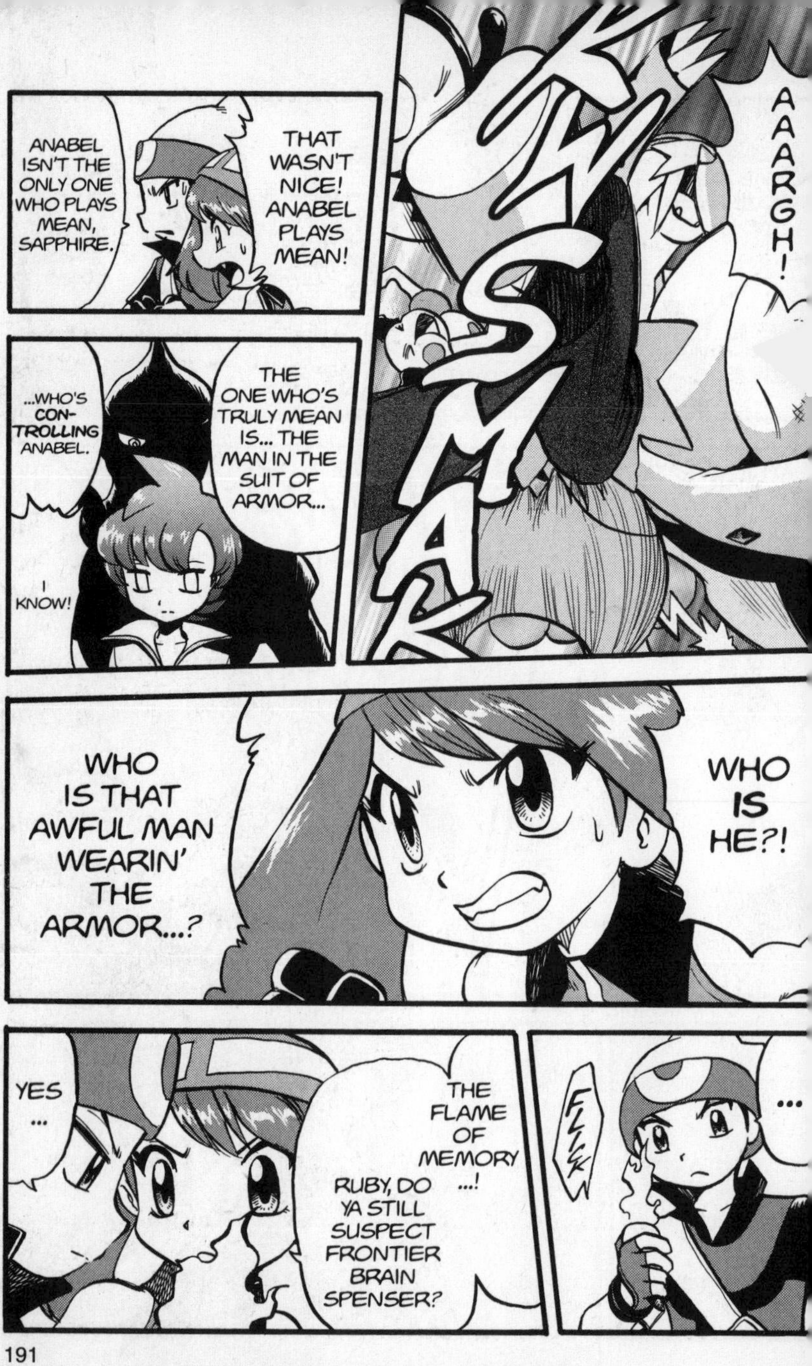
AAAARGH!
KWSMAK
THAT WASN'T NICE! ANABEL PLAYS MEAN!
ANABEL ISN'T THE ONLY ONE WHO PLAYS MEAN, SAPPHIRE.
THE ONE WHO'S TRULY MEAN IS... THE MAN IN THE SUIT OF ARMOR...
...WHO'S **CONTROLLING** ANABEL.
I KNOW!
WHO **IS** HE?!
WHO IS THAT AWFUL MAN WEARIN' THE ARMOR...?
...
FLICK
THE FLAME OF MEMORY...!
RUBY, DO YA STILL SUSPECT FRONTIER BRAIN SPENSER?
YES...

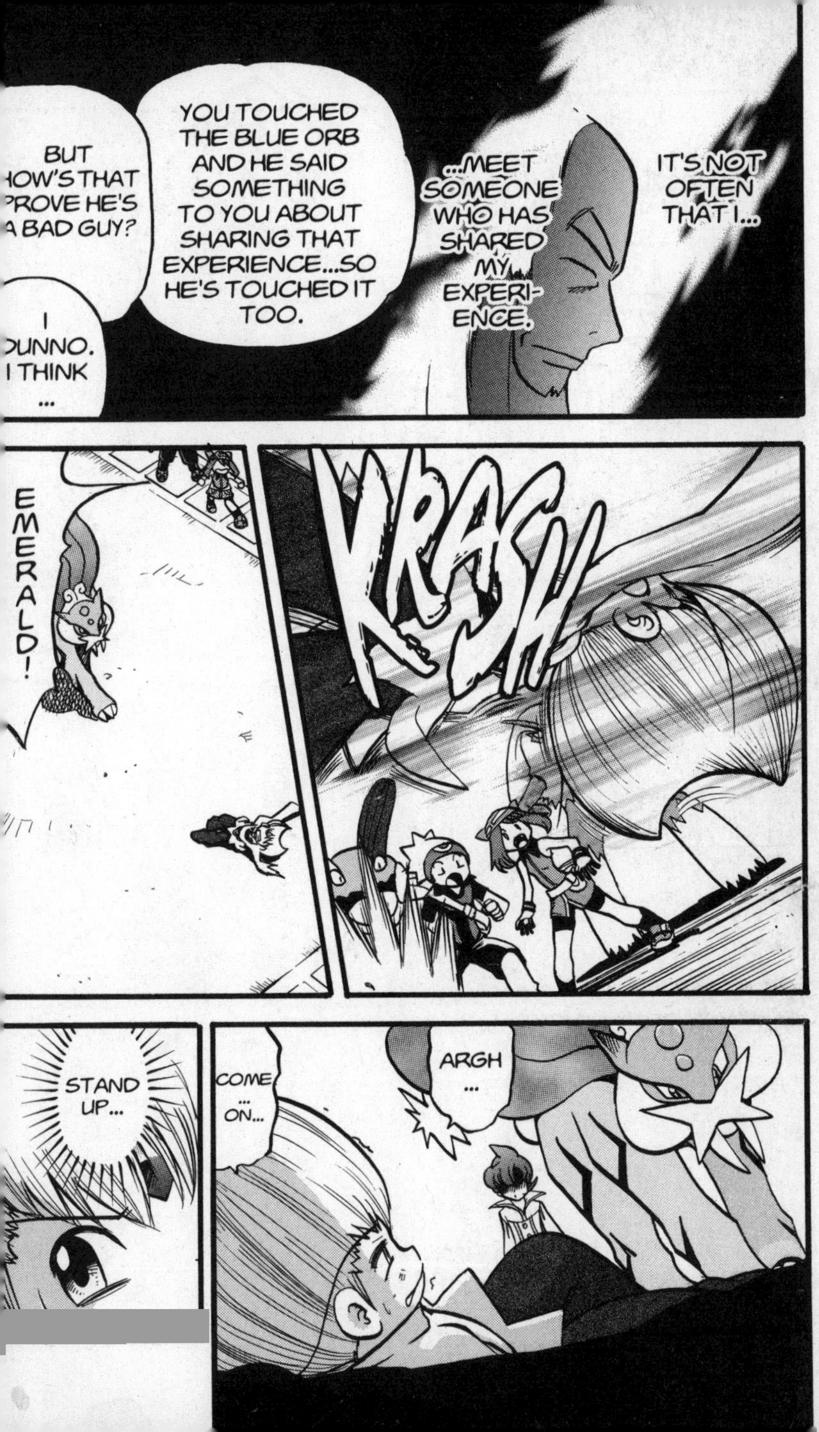
IT'S NOT OFTEN THAT I...
...MEET SOMEONE WHO HAS SHARED MY EXPERIENCE.
YOU TOUCHED THE BLUE ORB AND HE SAID SOMETHING TO YOU ABOUT SHARING THAT EXPERIENCE...SO HE'S TOUCHED IT TOO.
BUT HOW'S THAT PROVE HE'S A BAD GUY?
I DUNNO. I THINK ...
KRASH
EMERALD!
ARGH ...
COME ... ON...
STAND UP...

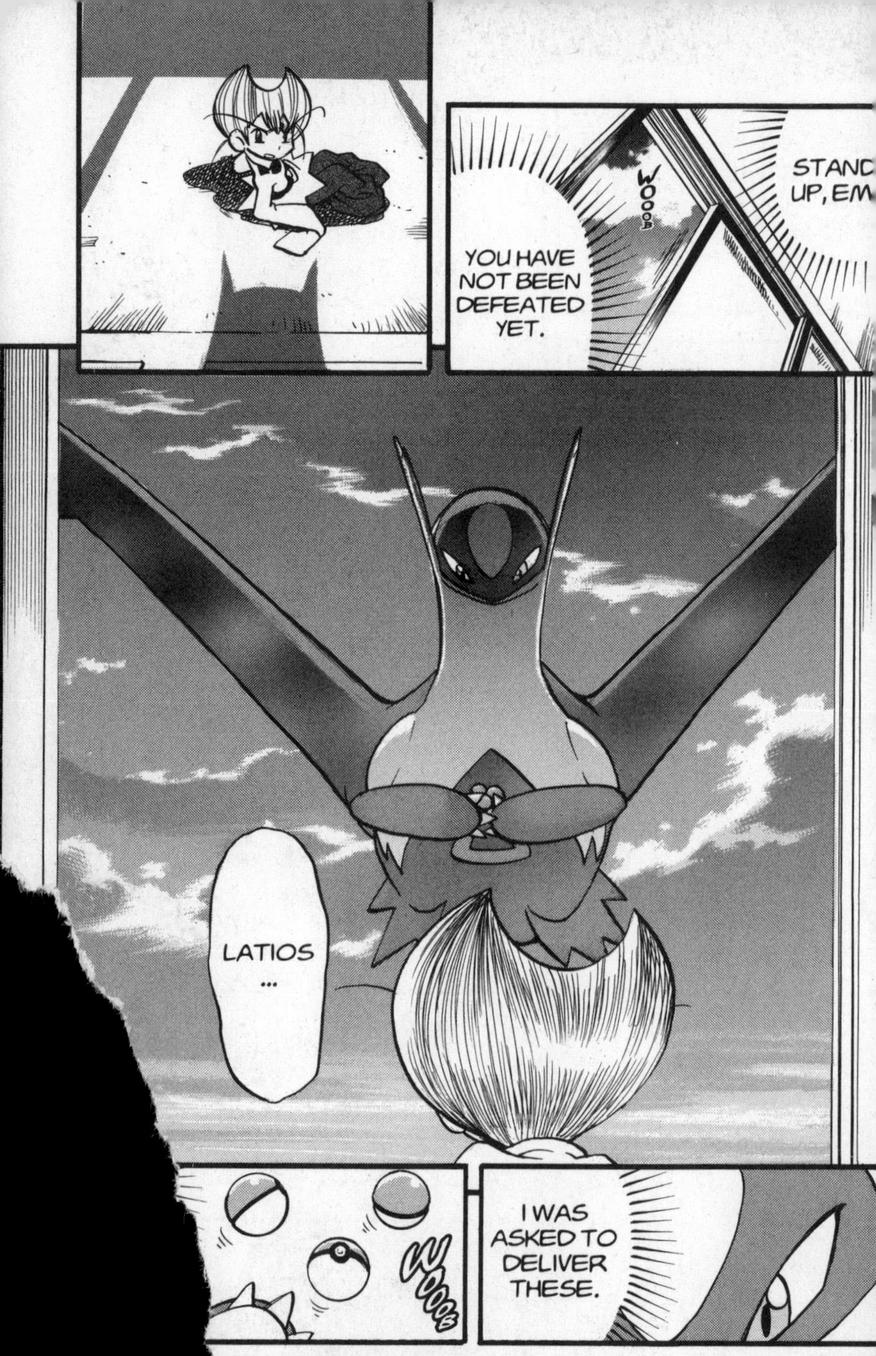
STAND UP, EM
WOOOB
YOU HAVE NOT BEEN DEFEATED YET.
LATIOS ...
I WAS ASKED TO DELIVER THESE.
WOOOB

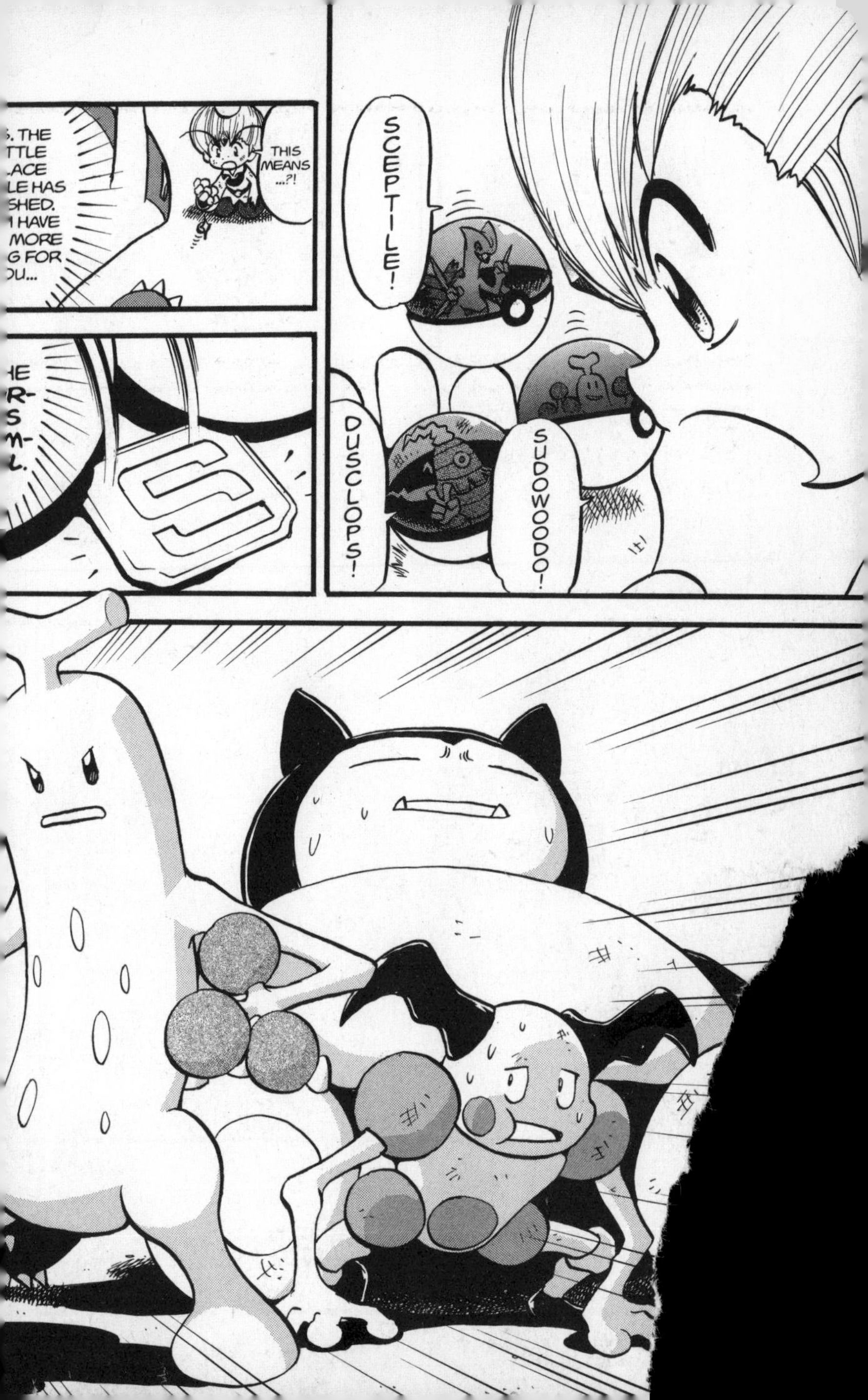
SCEPTILE!
SUDOWOODO!
DUSCLOPS!
THIS MEANS ...?!

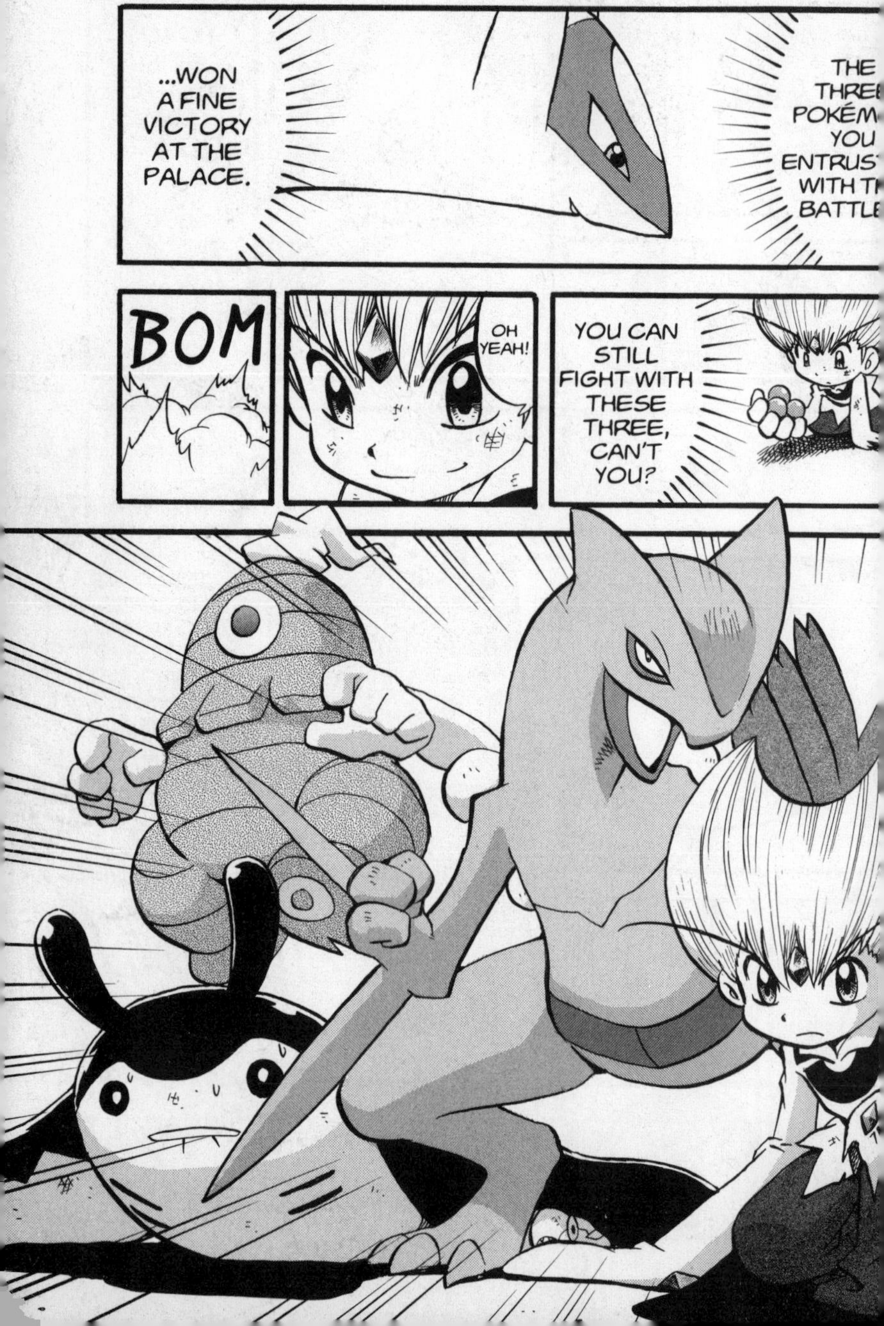
THE THREE POKÉM YOU ENTRUS WITH TH BATTLE
...WON A FINE VICTORY AT THE PALACE.
YOU CAN STILL FIGHT WITH THESE THREE, CAN'T YOU?
OH YEAH!
BOM

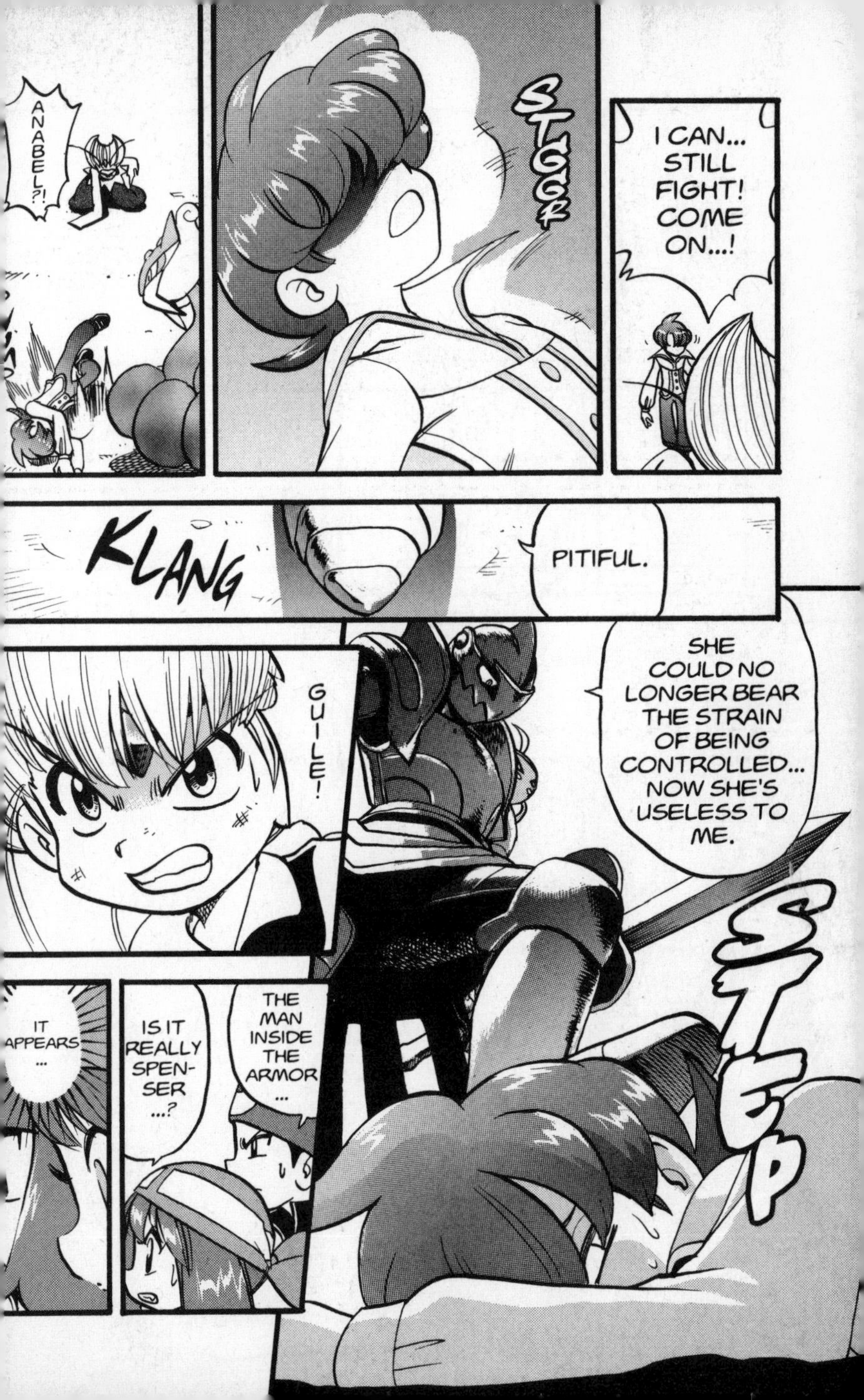

I CAN... STILL FIGHT! COME ON...!
STGGR
ANABEL?!
PITIFUL.
KLANG
SHE COULD NO LONGER BEAR THE STRAIN OF BEING CONTROLLED... NOW SHE'S USELESS TO ME.
STEP
GUILE!
THE MAN INSIDE THE ARMOR...
IS IT REALLY SPEN-SER...?
IT APPEARS...

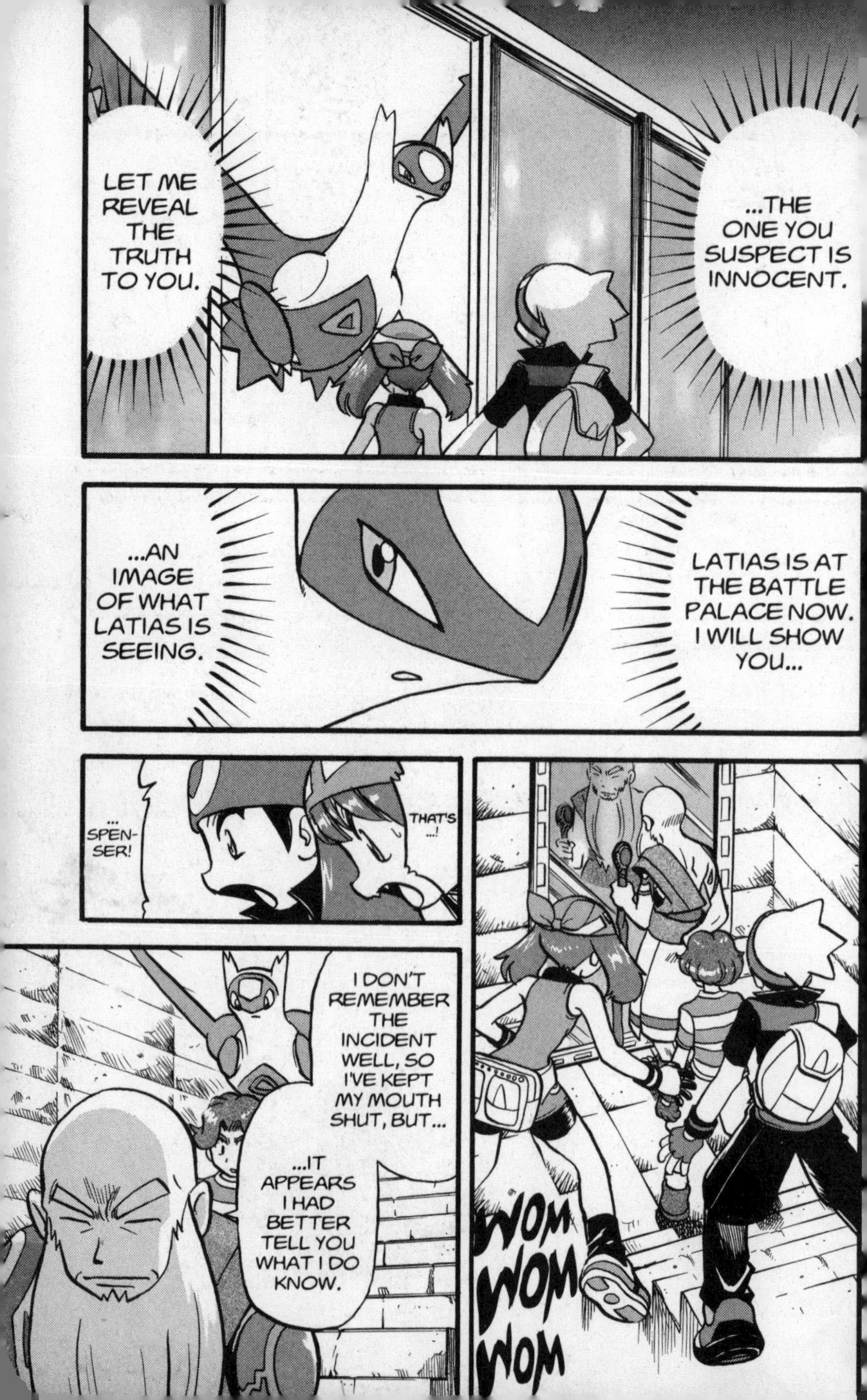
...THE ONE YOU SUSPECT IS INNOCENT.
LET ME REVEAL THE TRUTH TO YOU.
LATIAS IS AT THE BATTLE PALACE NOW. I WILL SHOW YOU...
...AN IMAGE OF WHAT LATIAS IS SEEING.
WOM WOM WOM
THAT'S ...!
... SPEN-SER!
I DON'T REMEMBER THE INCIDENT WELL, SO I'VE KEPT MY MOUTH SHUT, BUT...
...IT APPEARS I HAD BETTER TELL YOU WHAT I DO KNOW.

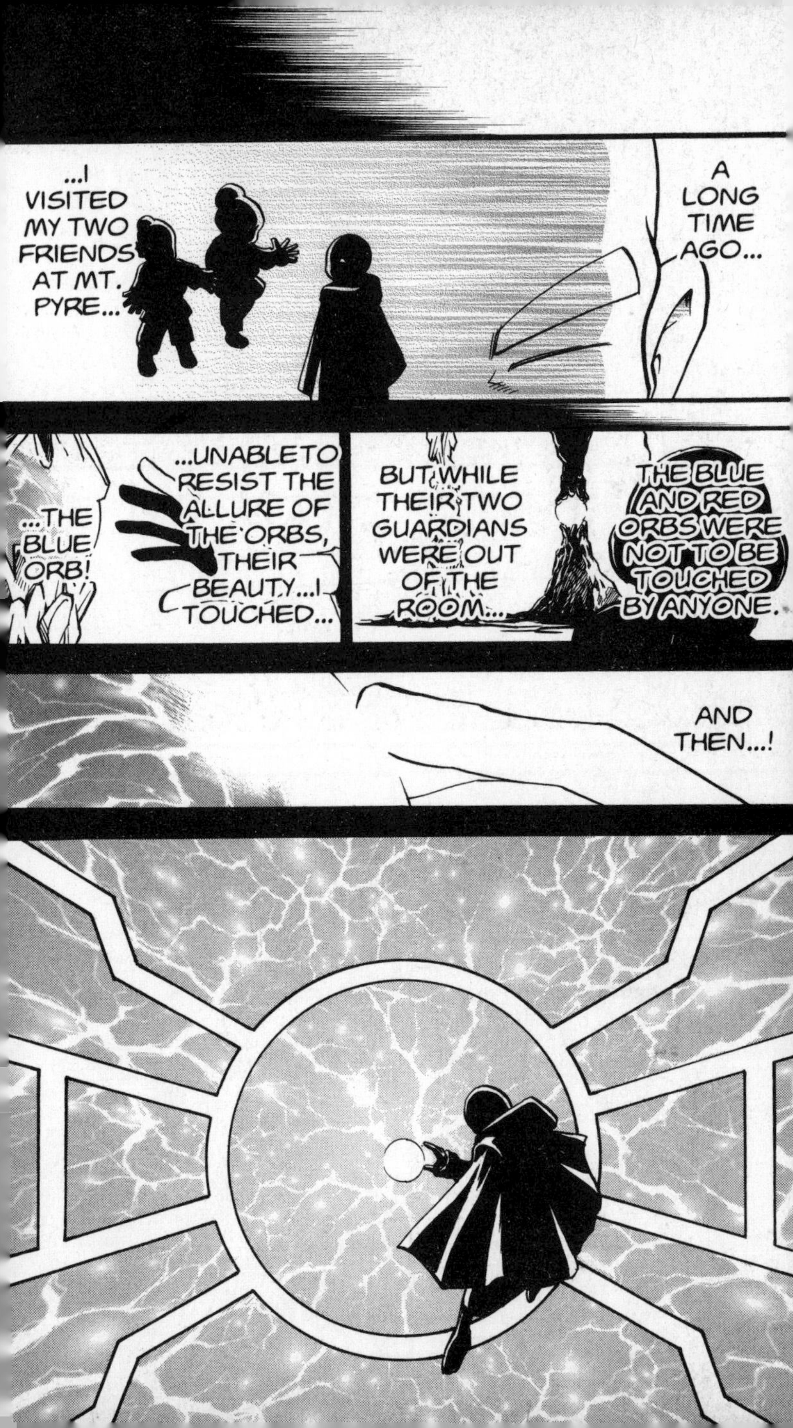
A LONG TIME AGO...
...I VISITED MY TWO FRIENDS AT MT. PYRE...
THE BLUE AND RED ORBS WERE NOT TO BE TOUCHED BY ANYONE.
BUT WHILE THEIR TWO GUARDIANS WERE OUT OF THE ROOM...
...UNABLE TO RESIST THE ALLURE OF THE ORBS, THEIR BEAUTY...I TOUCHED...
...THE BLUE ORB!
AND THEN...!

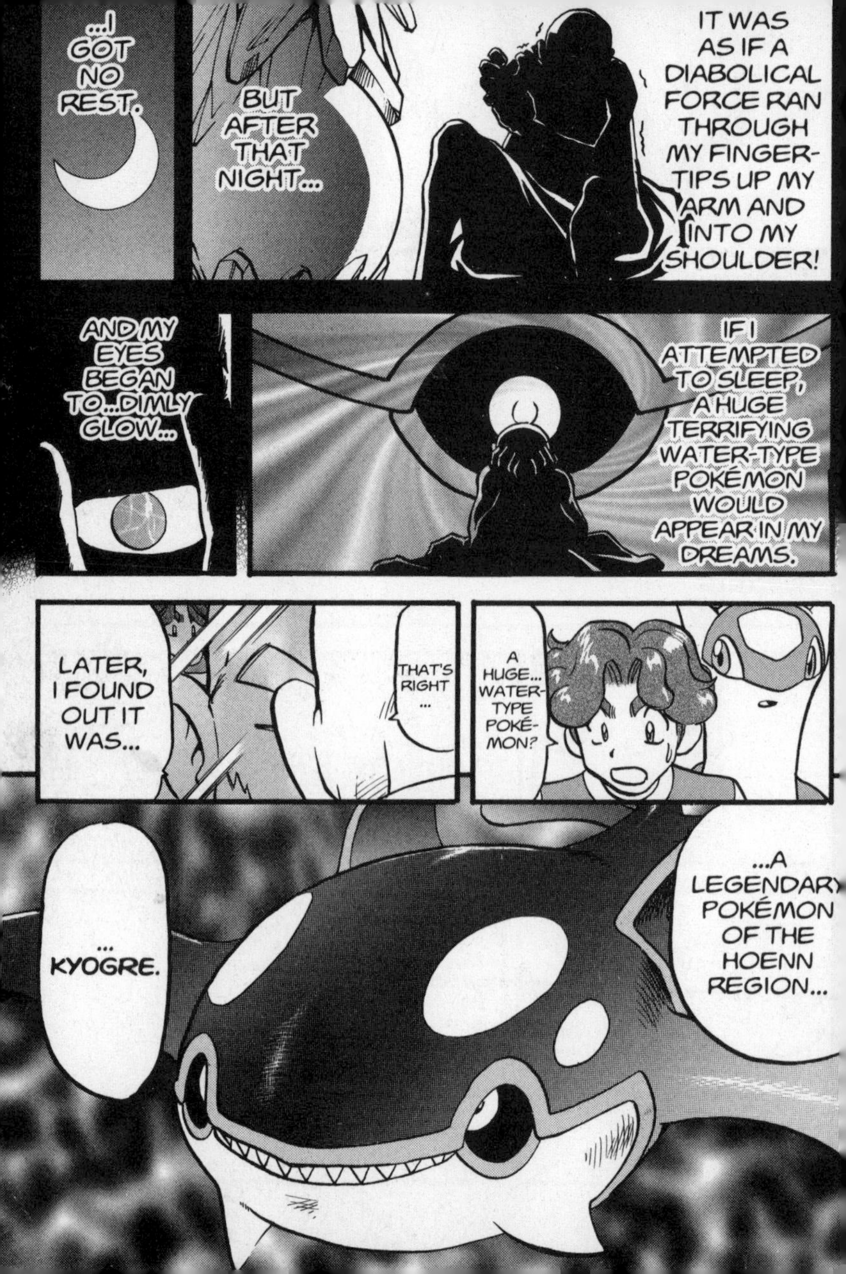
...I GOT NO REST.
BUT AFTER THAT NIGHT...
IT WAS AS IF A DIABOLICAL FORCE RAN THROUGH MY FINGER-TIPS UP MY ARM AND INTO MY SHOULDER!
AND MY EYES BEGAN TO...DIMLY GLOW...
IF I ATTEMPTED TO SLEEP, A HUGE TERRIFYING WATER-TYPE POKÉMON WOULD APPEAR IN MY DREAMS.
LATER, I FOUND OUT IT WAS...
THAT'S RIGHT ...
A HUGE... WATER-TYPE POKÉMON?
... KYOGRE.
...A LEGENDARY POKÉMON OF THE HOENN REGION...

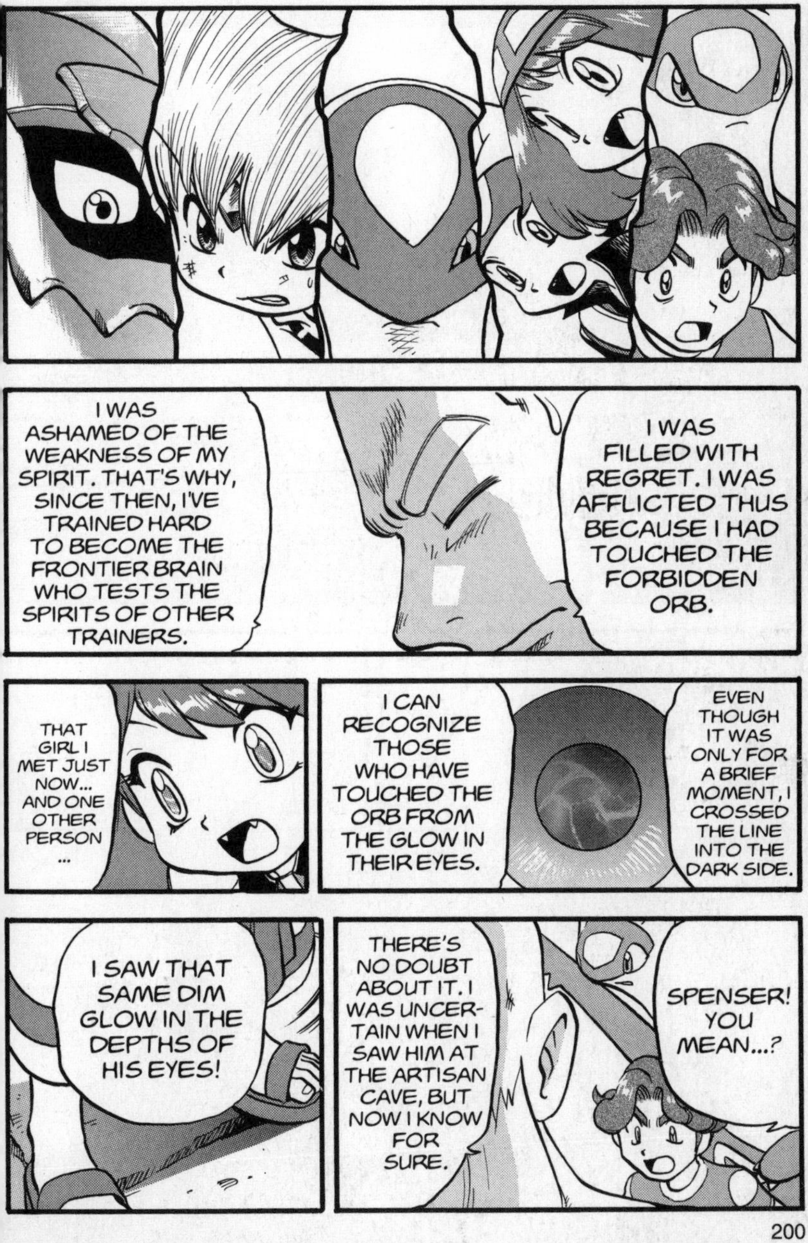
I WAS FILLED WITH REGRET. I WAS AFFLICTED THUS BECAUSE I HAD TOUCHED THE FORBIDDEN ORB.
I WAS ASHAMED OF THE WEAKNESS OF MY SPIRIT. THAT'S WHY, SINCE THEN, I'VE TRAINED HARD TO BECOME THE FRONTIER BRAIN WHO TESTS THE SPIRITS OF OTHER TRAINERS.
EVEN THOUGH IT WAS ONLY FOR A BRIEF MOMENT, I CROSSED THE LINE INTO THE DARK SIDE.
I CAN RECOGNIZE THOSE WHO HAVE TOUCHED THE ORB FROM THE GLOW IN THEIR EYES.
THAT GIRL I MET JUST NOW... AND ONE OTHER PERSON ...
SPENSER! YOU MEAN...?
THERE'S NO DOUBT ABOUT IT. I WAS UNCER-TAIN WHEN I SAW HIM AT THE ARTISAN CAVE, BUT NOW I KNOW FOR SURE.
I SAW THAT SAME DIM GLOW IN THE DEPTHS OF HIS EYES!

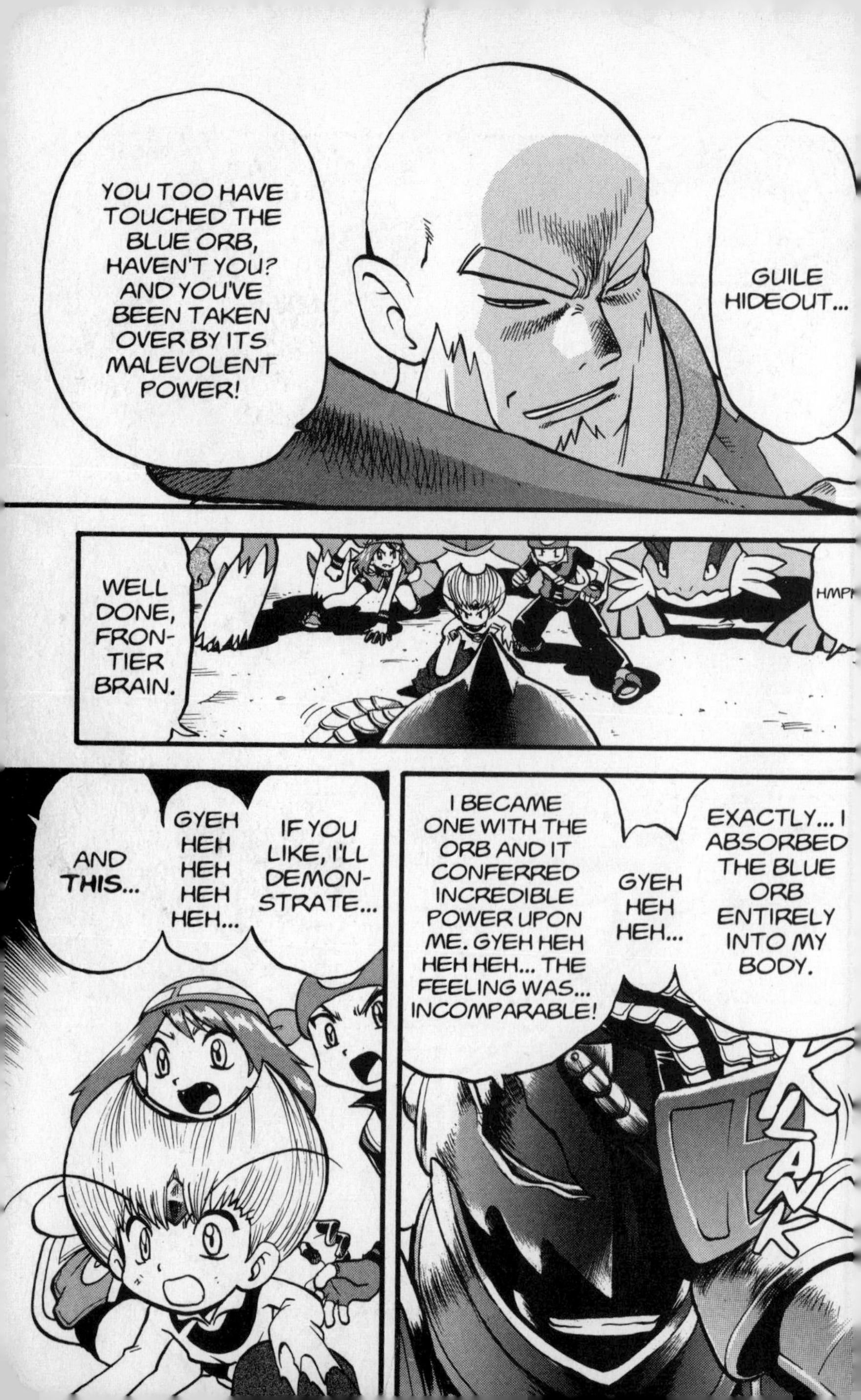
GUILE HIDEOUT...
YOU TOO HAVE TOUCHED THE BLUE ORB, HAVEN'T YOU? AND YOU'VE BEEN TAKEN OVER BY ITS MALEVOLENT POWER!
HMP
WELL DONE, FRON-TIER BRAIN.
EXACTLY... I ABSORBED THE BLUE ORB ENTIRELY INTO MY BODY.
GYEH HEH HEH...
I BECAME ONE WITH THE ORB AND IT CONFERRED INCREDIBLE POWER UPON ME. GYEH HEH HEH HEH... THE FEELING WAS... INCOMPARABLE!
KLANK
IF YOU LIKE, I'LL DEMON-STRATE...
GYEH HEH HEH HEH HEH...
AND THIS...

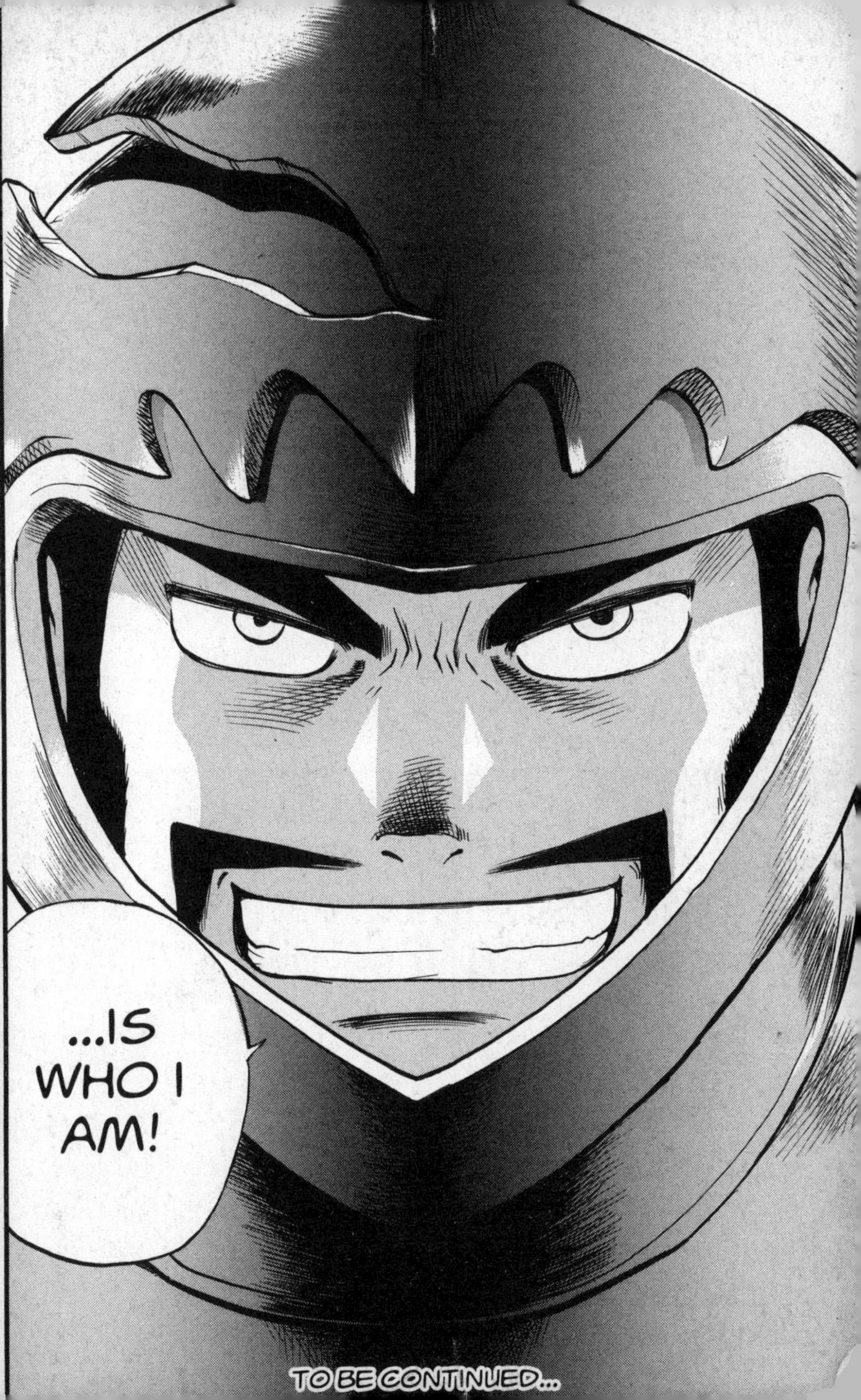
...IS WHO I AM!
TO BE CONTINUED...

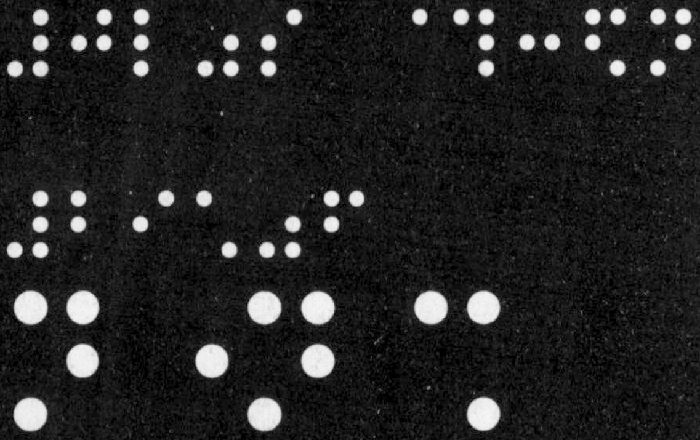

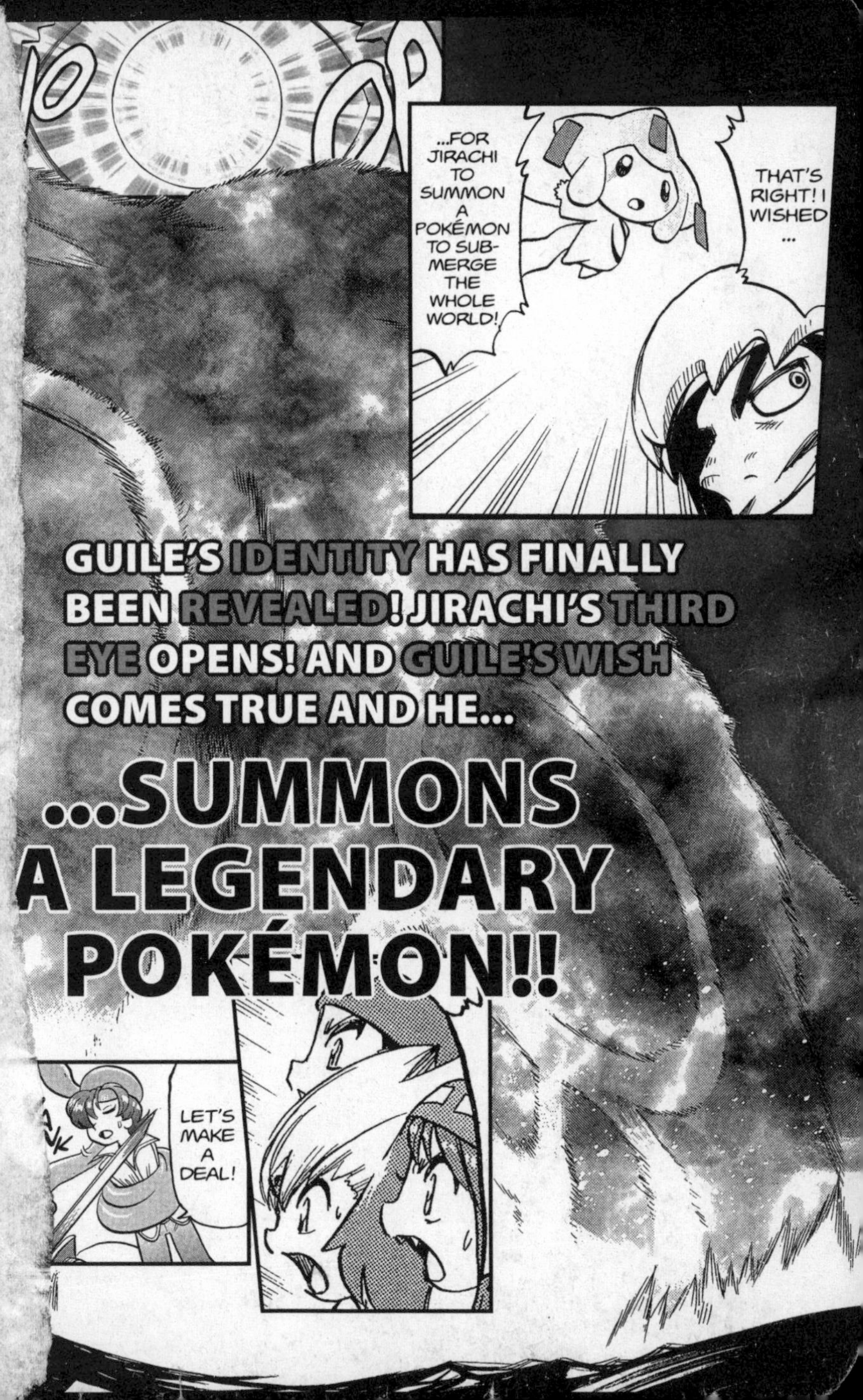
THAT'S RIGHT! I WISHED ...
...FOR JIRACHI TO SUMMON A POKÉMON TO SUBMERGE THE WHOLE WORLD!
GUILE'S IDENTITY HAS FINALLY BEEN REVEALED! JIRACHI'S THIRD EYE OPENS! AND GUILE'S WISH COMES TRUE AND HE...
...SUMMONS A LEGENDARY POKÉMON!!
LET'S MAKE A DEAL!

More Adventures Coming Soon...

Gold and Crystal are back! Professor Oak sends the two friends to help rescue Red, Yellow, Blue and Green—who have all been turned to stone! But first, the pair must fight a fearsome opponent that Archie, the former leader of Team Aqua, wished into existence using the powers of the Wish Pokémon Jirachi! If only our heroes had the power of the Ultimate Move...

Then, will Emerald ever acknowledge his love of Pokémon...?

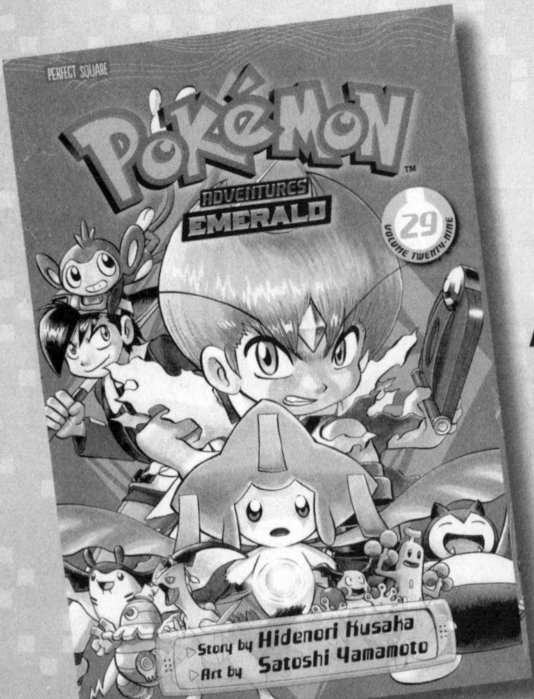
PERFECT SQUARE
POKéMON™
ADVENTURES
EMERALD
29
VOLUME TWENTY-NINE
Story by Hidenori Kusaka
Art by Satoshi Yamamoto

AVAILABL
JULY 2015

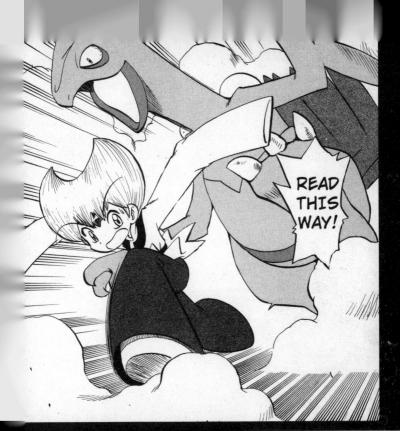

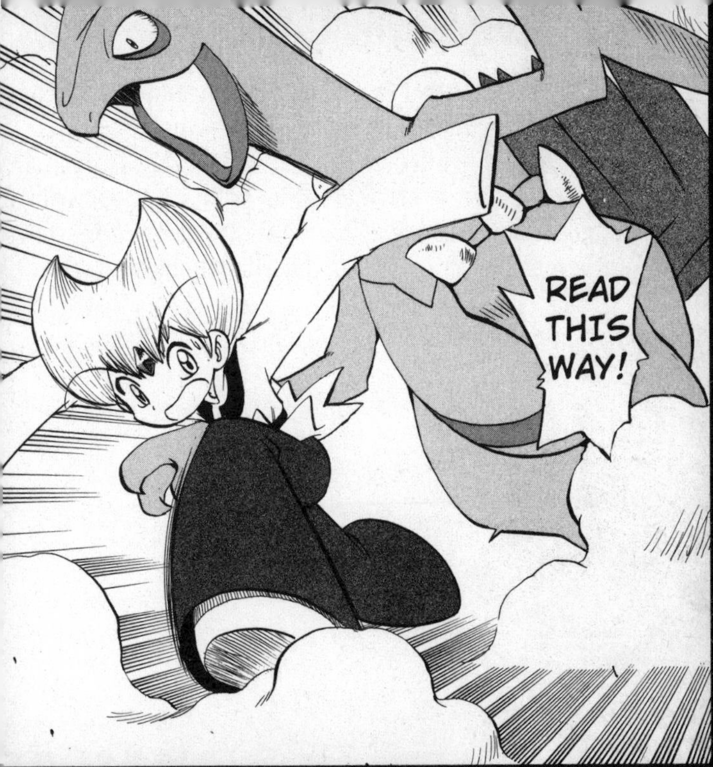
READ THIS WAY!

THIS IS THE END OF
HIS GRAPHIC NOVEL!

properly enjoy this VIZ Media phic novel, please turn it around l begin reading from right to left.

s book has been printed in the ginal Japanese format in order preserve the orientation of the ginal artwork.

ve fun with it!

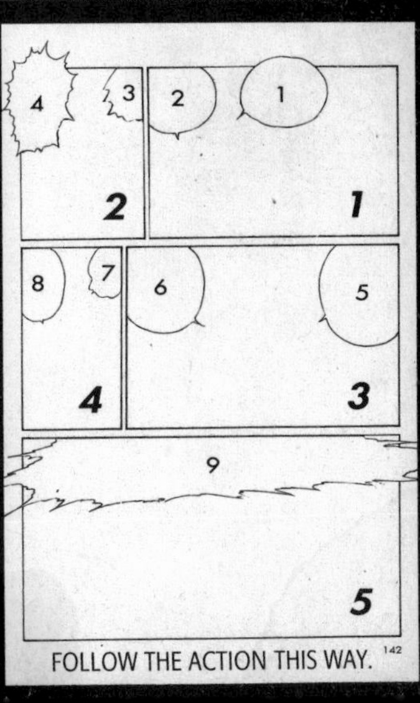
FOLLOW THE ACTION THIS WAY.

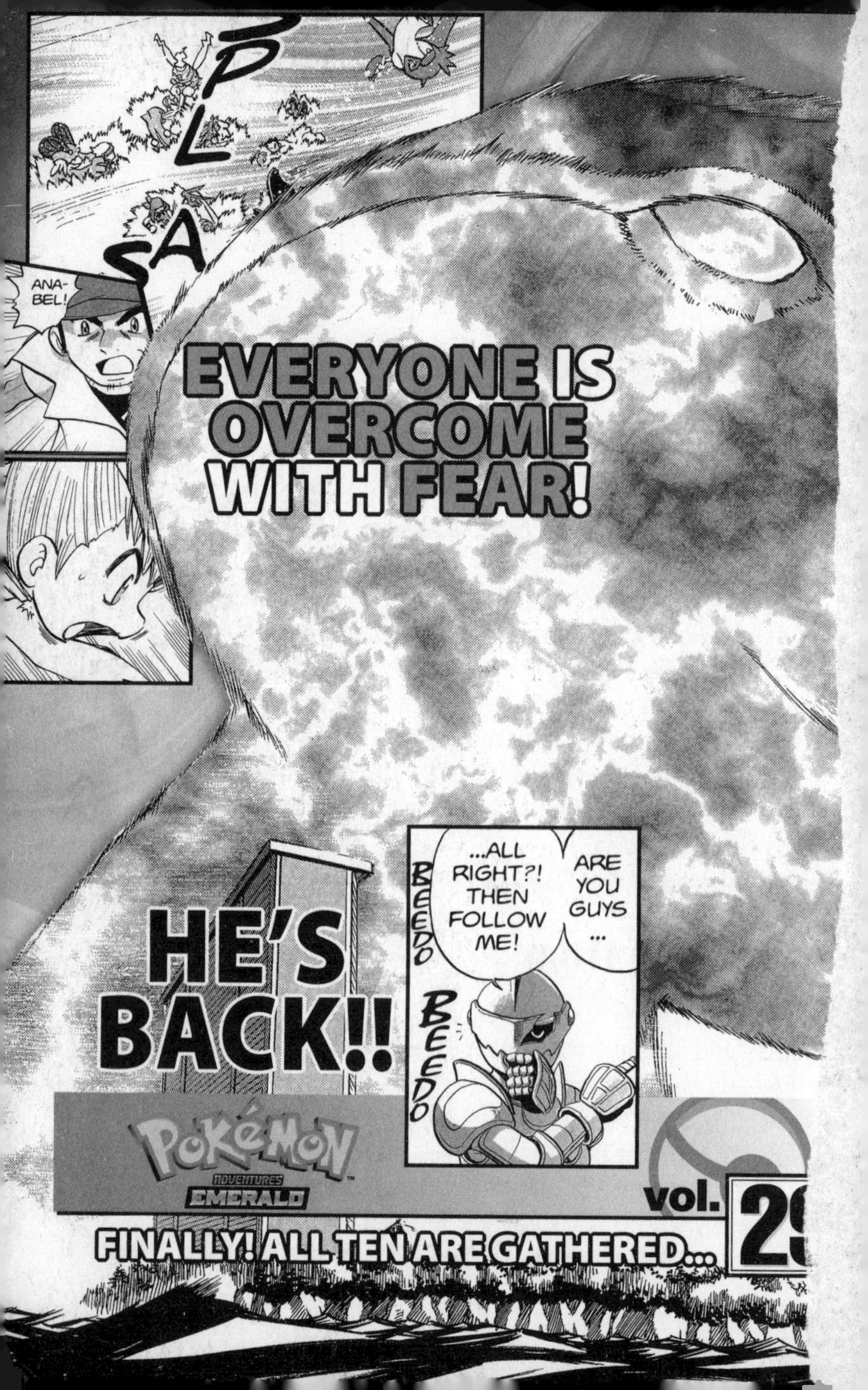
ANA-BEL!
EVERYONE IS OVERCOME WITH FEAR!
ARE YOU GUYS ...
...ALL RIGHT?! THEN FOLLOW ME!
BEEDO
BEEDO
HE'S BACK!!
POKéMON ADVENTURES EMERALD
vol. 29
FINALLY! ALL TEN ARE GATHERED...

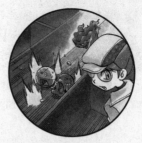

Message from
Hidenori Kusaka

The year 2007 has almost come to an end. I can hear the footsteps of 2008 coming around the corner.* I've also been hearing about new Pokémon projects, and I'm looking forward to them. Some of those projects might be connected to the *Pokémon Adventures: Diamond and Pearl* story arc that I'm currently working on... I often receive questions like, "Isn't it hard to have to suddenly change the entire direction of the story because of the new games and plots?" Don't worry about me! I believe manga is like a living creature—I'm just weird that way. And so I enjoy how it morphs into new things! *(laugh)*

*This volume was originally published in Japan at the end of 2007.

Message from
Satoshi Yamamoto

Ruby and Sapphire have finally joined Emerald! Emerald has been pushing the Frontier Brains around so much that it's fun to see someone boss him around for a change. Meanwhile, Emerald's battle against Guile and the race to capture Jirachi intensifies! Who is Guile anyway...?! Brace yourself for the heart-pounding excitement of this part of the Emerald story arc!